Rebound 1980

The Writings of Owen Wister

WHEN WEST WAS WEST

From a sketch by Frederic Remington

AUTHOR IN SEARCH OF MATERIAL, 1894

The Writings of Owen Wister

of The American Academy of Arts and Letters

*Membre Correspondant de la Société
des Gens de Lettres*

Honorary Fellow of the Royal Society of Literature

When West Was West

NEW YORK
The Macmillan Company
1928

PRINTED IN THE UNITED STATES OF AMERICA BY
R. R. DONNELLEY & SONS CO., AT THE LAKESIDE PRESS, CHICAGO

TO

CAROLINE LEWIS

UNSPARING CRITIC, UNFAILING FRIEND

. . . mihi parva rura et
Spiritum Graiae tenuem Camenae
Parca non mendax dedit, et malignum
Spernere vulgus.

PREFACE—*Two Debts*

NATURALLY, this book would not have its title, but for Mr. Rudyard Kipling. My second debt to him is a longer story.

Two letters from him directly concern one of these nine tales, all of which have been written since 1923, although several had been what is called "in my head" many years before I got them out of it.

At Fort Bowie, Arizona, in 1893, the Commanding Officer of that post told me how the length of a certain army chaplain's hair had proved a source of disturbance to a certain lively minded captain; how the lively minded captain took a captive Apache and carefully trained and rehearsed him; and how this training produced results which had been foreseen by neither the captain, nor the Apache, nor by anybody at the military post where the disaster occurred.

Early in 1895, Mr. Kipling and I dined with Roosevelt in Washington, and travelled north the next morning in the same Pullman. During the journey, we talked some "shop" in the smoking compartment, and among other striking incidents of the old frontier, I told this one about the Chaplain. Mr. Kipling urged that it be transmuted to

fiction. I said that it was too slight an anecdote as
it stood, and that I should have to wait until some
happy thought occurred which would give it more
substance.

"You must do it," he declared, "and when you
have done it, you must call it 'Absalom.'"

Presently, the first letter came from him:

                    "Naulakha
                    "Brattleboro
                    "Vermont
"Absalom"

                                    "June 17, '95
"Dear Wister—

"Here comes a notion to me . . . I've just come
across the wildest old book (1816. Trenton, N. J.)
called *A Star in the West* conclusively proving that
the Redskins generally are the lost tribes. I'll send
you the queer old thing if you think that anybody
at that post (some half crazed lieutenant) could
have picked it up . . . and bored the whole mess
with the truth of it. *At any rate this supplies a
motif* . . . . I'm as pleased as if I had thought it
all out myself . . . that tale is too good to be lost in
a smoker."

I replied, saying that it mustn't be the lieutenant
who found the book and bored everybody, it must
be the Chaplain.

To this he answered from England, that on his

return the old book should be sent, and continued:
". . . Of course that was precisely what the
chaplain did. He read the book aloud. He took it to
mess. He introduced it into his sermons . . ."

When Mr. Kipling returned to Brattleboro, he
sent the book—and then, 'Absalom' waited more
than thirty years!

'Strawberries' took vague shape one July day in
1911, among the dust and ashes of Fort Fetterman,
where I stood remembering its livelier days. As
some old friends re-appear in the tale, perhaps some
critic will discover it to be "scrapings and parings"
from *Lin McLean*.

The seventh tale in this volume waited thirty-five
years tò a month. In February, 1893, I grew familiar with many of the doings and most of the conven-
tions of a wide, wild farm and ranch community,
spotted with remote towns, and veined with infrequent railroads, in the central part of Texas. Out
of the experiences during that particular holiday,
Skip to My Loo was spun in February, 1928. It is
the latest of other spinnings from the same raw material. In February, 1893, I hadn't begun as yet to
hunt material deliberately, but in consequence of
Hank's Woman and *How Lin McLean Went East*,
which *Harper's* had already published, every second
or third person that I met, promptly said, "I'll tell
you a thing you ought to *write up*." It became a

familiar spectacle—me, passive in the clutches of a determined narrator; so that my companions used to poke each other's ribs, and say, "Look at Wister. So-and-so has got him now!" And I became a brilliant listener:—yet oftener than not, it wasn't what they told me, it was something else that drifted accidentally into sight or hearing, and which seemed worthless to them, but flashed on me as the true nugget in the tailings. They saw no "write up" in that doctor in the well with his burning fuse. That situation waited till 1924 to be spun from Texan raw material into the little drama I invented for it; while poor old *Em'ly* was spun into her web with the Virginian quite soon. I found a wife for him in Texas—not any actual school marm; but the type who taught in these frontier schools was apt to be a cut above the mothers of the children she instructed. I decided that when the time came, my southerner should wed a New England school marm. For the same reason, Edmund marries the school teacher in the tale *Where It Was*, to be found in another volume.

Does *Skip to My Loo* meet the technical specifications of the "short story"? That was the intention in this case. I detailed the raw material to a discreet and shocked friend, who said, "Don't try such a thing. It can't be told."—"But it belongs to the whole picture."—"Leave it out."

But that couldn't be. It was amusing to plan and

spin according to technical specifications, observing at the same time the only rule I never break:—

"Forget technical rules. Absorb, digest, perpend your subject; then try to interest your reader at the start, and sweat to keep him interested to the finish."

But what class of reader?

Well, news came in May, 1902, of a lady who had bought *The Virginian* in a train, and after reading thirty pages, threw the book out of the window. I had sweated in vain for her.

To-day, dated March 22, 1928, came this letter:

"———— Last year, in the ninth grade, I was forced to study your book, 'The Virginian,' and even though it was school work, I became very interested in it, as did all the other members of my class. You may consider this a very high compliment, for when a book, or, for that matter, anything, is taken up as school work, it usually loses a very large percentage of its color and interest for the pupil. There is one thing I should like to ask you; have you ever written another book of the same type as 'The Virginian'? I have been unable to secure any other ————"

Twenty-six years after publication. Long live sweating!

Never forget, though, that, according to Mr. H. L. Mencken, I am a wart.

OWEN WISTER.

Long House, Bryn Mawr, 1928.

TABLE OF CONTENTS

TABLE OF CONTENTS

WHEN WEST WAS WEST

Bad Medicine

CRESTED with eagle feathers, bronze and lean, festal in beaded buckskin, he leaned against a tree as he played his pipe: no common member of his tribe; a young chief among the Shoshones, by the haughty set of his head and the scorn of his nose. His face of war and hunting, antique as a Pharaoh's on a tomb, followed the turns of the music he was making, bowed and nodded over it, joined in its ups and downs—but always haughty, in spite of its animation. He was lost in his own performance just as far and deep as if he had been some artist with a white skin from foreign parts. The little boy was beautiful in buckskin too. Perhaps he was twelve. While an absent-minded hand rested on the player's leg, he held his great black eyes fixed upon the pipe as if he expected to see the sounds come out. They fluted forth like a

1

bird's, without stopping except for breath; trailing across the air irresponsibly like tendrils of a vine, rising in spirals, dropping through a series of quick loops—hardly a love song, more a youth song, just youth and all out-of-doors. The boy was lost in them as deep as the player.

Their wildness was nothing I could catch, as I sat in the halted stage and begged the driver to wait a moment. The notes gamboled and dodged beyond the grasp of my tame ears—all but one strain he came back to. This I had heard in many Wyoming Junes. While the world flushed slow to sunrise and grew golden as day enlarged, it sang skyward from the ground, the singer invisible in the sage-brush. Each time the pipe repeated it after prodigal excursions into the unknown, the child clapped his hands. Whatever other notes bubbled from the player's improvising fancy, he had stolen this from the meadow-lark when the wilderness was in flower with the prickly-pear, and the lady lark on her nest listened complacently. I had stolen it, too, in Wyoming Junes; got up early on purpose to get it right and set it down:

and sometimes

and sometimes other irregularities, both sharp and flat, as if the gentleman lark was bored for a moment, and his thoughts wandered to some sweet girl he had noticed on the other side of the creek. Can any bird observer match it as a specimen of original music made by a bird? Mozart never did better, but of course he did more.

They didn't hear the stage rattling up from Lander and the Agency; didn't move or change when it drew up to drop the mail at the post trader's store; did not notice me jump down from beside the driver; piper and audience remained as lost in the performance as when I had first caught sight of them, before I could hear the music.

I seized my kodak, stood forward by the horses, aimed it at the group, the boy saw me, came to life with a jerk, the chief's arm flung itself over his face, and both had vanished noiseless in their moccasins among the trees.

"I could have told you they'd do that," said the driver.

"But you didn't," said I.

"You'd have ought t've hid behind the stage." And he dragged the mail sacks into the store, while I talked.

The post trader's long, thin, unlighted cigar moved between his lips as he smiled indulgently. Then he removed it.

"I'd have said you had learned the ways of Indians by this time."

I pointed to some photographs exposed conspicuously for sale. They were always there for sale, whenever I came.

"Oh, well," said Mr. King. "Old Washakie's used to it; and there's a good picture of Sharp Nose. He's not afraid any more—though he wouldn't for quite a while after Washakie had given in. He was waiting to see if taking a person's likeness didn't steal away some part of his strength or spirit. He came to it finally. You never can tell. Sometimes a dollar will persuade them."

"I'll give five to get that picture. The man with the pipe might be a prince of some ancient empire. Is it his son? Who is he?"

I learned that Sun Road was the piper's name, the boy's, Little Chief Hare. Washakie was Sun Road's grandfather; they were heirs of royal blood, once mighty on the war path. Washakie had looked on with approval at Sun Road's adolescent endurance, when he danced gracefully at the Buffalo dance with an iron hook in his chest tied by a buckskin thong to a pole; or climbed subtly up steep rocks to kill a mountain sheep with one shot;—but Washakie had no inheritance to leave his descendants, except the inevitable extinction of his whole race.

"Then he'd be too proud to take five dollars?" said I.

"It wouldn't be pride that stopped him. They've got us white men beat on pride, but theirs takes other shapes. He might fall in with your wishes some day."

I had no intention of waiting for some day. I wished to get out of Fort Washakie and into the mountains as soon as horses and food and all necessaries were ready. Everything had been made ready by George Tews, Mr. King informed me; but my letter had come too late for George to secure an Indian as hunter. Tyghee, my hunter last year, had rheumatism, and the two others available were off hunting elk for their winter's meat. Sun Road had never hired as hunter, but Mr. King had sounded him, and thought he might agree to go with me, if I would let the child come too. He would go nowhere without the boy. The wife he had married at eighteen when she was fifteen, had died not long ago, and their other children had died; Sun Road was raising Little Chief Hare himself, would hardly let him out of his sight; I must take both, or do without—and Mr. King and George Tews could think of no other Indian on the Reservation likely to answer. I would like Sun Road: he was a pleasant Indian, and a good hunter.

"Does he speak any English?"

"None he can help. Quick as he got back from Carlisle, he chucked off the pants of civilization, and took to the tribal blanket like the rest of them. Those philanthropists back east imagine that five years of pants and spelling books will wipe out five thousand of mother nature. George Tews speaks Shoshone, you know, and Sun Road will speak English when he has to."

"Does he always dress up in his Sunday clothes? Tyghee wore plain overalls and shirt and hat like the rest of us."

"The Department Commander received the chiefs this morning before he left. Sun Road hasn't taken his feathers off because he knows they're becoming —for between you and me, he's a bit of a—" The post trader's eye glanced behind me—"onions you've enough of, I think, and George Tews says you prefer evaporated apricots to peaches."

The new presences behind us were the runaways, just inside the door, stolen back from their retreat as noiseless as they had gone. Both had their eyes on my kodak, which stood quite harmless on the counter, while Mr. King was inquiring in a voice unchanged whether I preferred the sweetened or the unsweetened brand of condensed milk. The runaways grew re-assured; they risked themselves away from the door; and as they advanced, Mr. King nodded casually to them, and continued his enumeration of my groceries. I saw Sun Road looking at himself in a mirror, and slightly adjusting the splendid knotted scarf at his throat.

"Don't forget I always take some rice along," I said to Mr. King. "And we smashed our lantern in Jackson's Hole, and I'll take some mixed pickles, and some marmalade, and I don't object to the boy, you can say, and you can say I'll promise not to use the camera on him, and of course you've got oat meal."

Sun Road was attending to his own beauty so completely in the looking glass, that I should have been sure he missed not only what we were saying, but everything not connected with his own gorgeous image; but the looking glass must have showed him Little Chief Hare, just about to touch the kodak with one venturesome, inquiring finger. With the same immediate swiftness that had saved him from the baleful eye of the machine, he had the boy safe away from it, and was reproving him in a low voice.

"George has the oat meal," said Mr. King; and

after a glance at Sun Road, "let me handle this matter while you're getting your bath. There's the ambulance. You made a bad beginning when you tried the snap-shot by way of introducing yourself. He was out there at my request, waiting to talk it over with you. But the fact that he came back to inspect you is a good sign. I'll report when you have had your bath."

The chance of losing Sun Road certainly had clinched my wish to take him. While the ambulance galloped me to the Hot Spring, I grew quite anxious that Mr. King would have good news after my bad beginning. In the little bathing cabin built for the post officers I threw off my stale clothes of travel, and got into the pool, a placid, glassy flat of turquoise, lonely in the sage-brush, veiled with steam, and sulphurous. From its deep middle now and then a huge, sluggish bubble rose and burst, like the breath of something down below. I never liked to be in it, it always looked as if it might do something uncanny; but it washed the body free of dust, it dissolved fatigue away, it softened the skin to satin.

Happy and clean and dry after the towel, I moved to the door where the ambulance waited as I put on fresh things and stared at the prospect. One way, long, far-off ridges, daubed with red, ended the view; the toy-like, distant Post lay on the plain the other way, and beyond it, the golden opens of the Continental Divide rose to the blue of its pines, and these to the bare white snow of its summit.

Blanketed Indians on their ponies moved across the view, and two of these were coming here—father and son. Son's legs didn't reach far on his pony's sides, and he bobbed as he rode beside the quiet form and the eagle crest of his father. Sun Road's right arm lifted now and then with a slow gesture, and slackened to its full length again as he touched his pony with his dangling quirt. I was all dressed by the time they stopped in front of me.

"How!" said Sun Road.

"How!" said I.

Did this descendant of wars and wildernesses know the centuries dividing us that his quietness mysteriously conveyed? With his drooping-headed, saturnine animal, he seemed to share some intimate lore of nature that I and all white men were shut out from. The black eyes of Little Chief Hare watched me as young, wild, furry things do that you meet in a wood suddenly, before they take flight.

"Mr. King say you go hunting."

"I go hunting."

"You want elk?"

"Elk, bear, mountain sheep, everything."

"George Tews go?"

"He goes."

"Maybe tomorrow?"

"Tomorrow."

Sun Road paused.

"We go," he announced then, with a motion of his hand toward the child.

Little Chief Hare understood the tone, if not the words, and his eyes gleamed.

"Tell him," I said, "he shall shoot with my gun, he shall fish with my rod and catch big trout in Wind River, in Gros Ventre, in Snake, in Buffalo Fork, in Yellowstone."

Did some change fleet over the Shoshone's face, and vanish before he spoke?

"You go Yellowstone?"

"Tell him," I pursued, "he shall see big hot water going up in sky, and big hot water in ground —bigger than that." And I pointed to the steaming turquoise of the pool.

Again Sun Road said nothing, immediately; presently——

"I don't know Yellowstone Park."

"I know Park. George knows. We shall not get lost."

In the silence which fell again, the trumpet notes of retreat sounded faint and tiny at the Post, and a bubble rose with a liquid gulp in the pool.

"This my boy, Little Chief Hare," said Sun Road.

The child shrank from the hand I offered him.

"He never go to school yet," said Sun Road, quickly. "Go pretty soon. Maybe one snow, maybe two snows."

The son watched the father speaking.

"He get big pretty soon. Learn book. Learn all same white man."

To make friends, I whistled:

and it affected father and son most happily. Sun Road responded with the first smile he had vouchsafed, and the beautiful white teeth of Little Chief Hare shone at me, his eyes sparkling with confidence. I put out my hand, and the child took it.

Sun Road nodded.

"Meadow-lark," said he.

"Yes," said I, also nodding, "meadow-lark." And I felt that our bargain was struck firmly.

This was all at the pool. Indian fashion, with no word or sign of leave-taking, Sun Road wheeled his pony and was gone with the bobbing little boy at his side. I slung my cast-off garments into the ambulance, locked the bathing hut, climbed up beside the trooper who drove, and the mules began their brisk gallop back to Fort Washakie. Off to our right in the sage-brush, father and son were likewise galloping, when the boy's pony must have put his foot in some hole, for he fell suddenly flat. The little rider could scarce have touched the ground before his father was off and had him, and the pony struggled up on his legs. Little Chief Hare climbed nimbly to the bare back of the animal, and away went Sun Road with the boy bobbing along by him as jauntily as ever.

"Plucky!" I commented to the trooper.

"Aw, what's the good in any of 'em! Living on good land the people ought to have."

So I abstained from additional comments; and was presently greeted by my military host at the porch of his quarters, where I supped, and drank, and smoked with him. He confirmed the good word that Mr. King had spoken of Sun Road; to see a young Indian mourn his wife so long and so sincerely—and one whom the eyes of the unwedded Shoshone maidens told plainly of their readiness to give him consolation—was not a common sight; nor was it common for young Shoshone fathers to attend to their sons so devotedly. I repeated the driver's remark; and we agreed that you could not better express the general American thought about Indians; and that, look at it any way you pleased, civilization was a tough proposition. Then I strolled

out of the parade ground to hear what more the
post trader might have to report on the subject of
my big game hunt.

Outside Mr. King's store, stood two Indian ponies
hitched to the long rail in front of the building, and
inside I found Mr. King, and with him, George
Tews, and Sun Road, and Little Chief Hare. By the
drop of their conversation, and the look of things,.
I felt discomfort of some sort to be in the air.
George, with his sombrero on the back of his head,
and his red scarf slightly to one side, leaned back
against a high desk, one elbow propping him, one
thumb hooked in his gun belt, his weight on one boot,
the other crossed over it. In his face perplexity was
plain. In Sun Road's face of the ancient ages I
could read nothing; he stood straight, his eagle
crest above all our heads, the beads on his shirt
winking a dot of light here and there, where the
rays from the lamp fell on them, and one of his
hands holding the hand of his boy. Mr. King was
twisting his long unlighted cigar between his meditative lips, while coats, shirts, dark overalls, bright
scarfs, the rough-dried pelts of bears, foxes, and
coyotes, and hides soft tanned, hung from hooks
in the dimness, and near by, the photographed faces
of Washakie and Sharp Nose stared at us with
haughty aloofness.

To these I pointed for the second time that day.

"Is that still the difficulty?"

Mr. King took the cigar in his fingers. "No. I satisfied his objections to your kodak. Must you go to the Park?"

Then I knew that I had obscurely known it at the turquoise pool, in the pauses and the very few words which had followed instantly upon my uttering the word Yellowstone: that stream was one in which I had promised Little Chief Hare he should catch trout. Sun Road had said that he did not know the Park, and I had assured him that I knew it, to which he had responded with silence, and after silence a change of subject. It all grew rapidly clear to me; when he came to the pool he meant to go with me, when he left the pool he meant not to go, and had told his change of mind to Mr. King. Yet, last year, Tyghee had gone readily all through the Park with me, unwincing and indifferent to the geysers and the smells and the rumblings, which had terrorized all red men until the white man came and confronted the infernal powers without harm.

Crestfallen, and disgusted at the prospect of failure in my hunting, I addressed Mr. King:

"What's the use of Carlisle, what's the use of spelling books, what's the use of the Lord's Prayer?"

But Mr. King just rolled the cigar in his fingers, and smiled. I turned to Sun Road.

"You tell me yes, you go. You tell Mr. King no, you not go. What is this?"

"Plenty Indian take you hunting," said Sun Road.

"Who?"

"Tyghee knows that country."

George Tews said something in Shoshone.

"Paul La Rose knows that country," Sun Road answered in English.

That country, that country, that country, I thought impatiently. Why doesn't he come out with it? Is he ashamed to acknowledge what's really the matter? Didn't he know about Tyghee's rheumatism, and that Paul La Rose and Dick Washakie were away getting their winter's meat? Of course he knew it. But I would go to the Park.

"Tyghee," I said, "went with me to that country last year."

"Tyghee is sick now," responded Sun Road. Did he mean to convey by this that the devils in the Yellowstone had punished Tyghee for his temerity? I returned to the charge.

"Sun Road, you told me yes, you would go."

"I promise Colonel Saunderson break good pony for his little girl."

"I will speak to Colonel Saunderson."

"My son going to school pretty soon. Must raise him good. Camp no good for little boy."

"In camp I will give the little boy better food and better blankets than you give him. Did you not say to me at the Hot Spring, 'we go,' and did I not promise my rod and my gun for Little Chief Hare to shoot and fish?"

"My father," said Sun Road, "is an old man. Cannot cut hay field. Must stay to cut it."

And with this he walked out with Little Chief Hare; and there among the hides and pelts stood we three white men.

"We'll go without him," declared George Tews, always happy and hopeful.

"But Tyghee," I exclaimed to Mr. King, "wasn't afraid of the Park!"

"It's like the photographs," said the post trader, "they have to be educated to it. In Jim Bridger's time, all the Indians warned him to keep away from the land of holes that let the devils come up on earth."

"Let's you and me go alone," repeated George Tews. "We can make out."

"And who will guard camp when we're both off in the woods? Suppose we give up the Park."

"I don't think that would change Sun Road now," said Mr. King. "But he failed to sell his horses this year, and he's very poor."

"Then tell him I'll pay him double. I've come two thousand miles for a holiday."

The post trader meditated. "Leave it to me. Our

best chance is through the Indian agent. You and George get your packs ready to pull out about ten tomorrow morning."

We were up early to do this: the first packing of an outfit is a long matter. The horses were caught, the cinches tightened, the sacks evened, the ropes thrown, the diamond hitches tied, while the sun rose high, and we wondered what the agent could do. Whatever it was, he did it; at last the two appeared in the distance, coming across the sage-brush from among the teepees, the father lifting his arm from time to time to let the quirt drop lightly on his pony, the son bobbing by his side, and a meek pack animal behind them, led by a rope. No feathers to-day; plain overalls and flannel shirt, like everybody —but anybody would have looked at Sun Road for all that; and perhaps he knew it.

"How," said he.

"How," said I; and this was all the explanation that ever passed between us.

More passed between Mr. King and me; and he approved my sudden thought of paying half the bribing salary on the spot. Some words in Shoshone from Mr. King helped Sun Road to understand the significance of the check I put in the Indian's hand; and to see it translated into good large bills out of the post trader's safe, completed his grasp of the fact that the sum was at once placed to his credit on the books. He gave me no thanks; thanks come no more than "Good-bye" into the Indian's convention; he stood looking about at the various wares for sale.

"Having come to it," said Mr. King, aside, "he'll stand by it. They set more value than white men upon their given word."

Sun Road touched a jar of candy. "How much?"

A pound of it was weighed out and given to Little Chief Hare, who took it without thanks, but with obvious interest. More words in Shoshone caused Sun Road to take a little ready cash along; he had been leaving himself penniless, and there was candy to be purchased in the Park.

That day we made Bull Lake early, but camped there lest we overdrive the packs at the start. We pitched no tent, and needed no fire but the little one for cooking, for it was warm, and so remained after the long summer's dusk had ceased to filter its violet into the canyons of the Divide, and night hawks were dipping and speeding through the silent air. George and I sat together near the small glow of the cook fire, and heard the night hawks and the quiet gurgle of the outlet from Bull Lake as it flowed by us down into Wind River. The lake lay above us half a mile perhaps, concealed among foot-hills, and a few yards from us in its direction, Sun Road sat apart. He had given his word; was he not going to give his company?

"What do you know about the strange sounds in

the lake?" I asked George; "I've never heard them."

"I only know what they claim," said he, with a motion of his hand toward Sun Road.

"Could you get him to say?"

Tews relighted his pipe. "Sun Road," said he in English, "you know about Bull Lake."

"I know what?" The Indian did not turn his head.

George looked at me and shrugged his shoulders. "Some folks say," he suggested, "that big fish make noise there." This unlikely theory was held by some.

"I never catch any," said Sun Road. "Maybe some fish can talk."

"Some say it is big wind, somewhere back in the mountains," persisted George; "big wind in rocks down canyons, far off."

He stopped; but Sun Road merely sat still.

As a last try, George repeated the legend that was here when the white men came, ingeniously hinting doubt of it. "Well, I'd sooner believe it was fish than buffalo down deep in that water. Some folks say one time—heap snows come and go since that time—Indians chase buffalo away off beyond Crow Heart Butte, chase cows, calves, bulls, in that flat country so they run across Wind River among hills here so quick that Indian horses can't keep very close. They follow trail over hills up and down till it take them high, and they find no more trail, no more buffalo; big lake away below, straight down steep top to water. Then they know buffalo see water too late. Big buffalo that lead the herd see water, but they can't stop, because cows and calves behind not see water, so big ones get pushed over, and they fall in water deep down, and cows and calves go after them all same big cattle stampede. They never come out again. Can't get on top of water any more. Can't see daylight any more. Big bull buffalo deep down they mourn for daylight sometimes, and that noise in lake come from them. But I know buffalo can swim," finished George insinuatingly, "and I'd sooner think some big fish make that noise." And with this he stopped; and still Sun Road sat smoking.

"Don't you think big wind blow in canyon sometimes maybe make noise?" suggested George, after waiting again.

"I know nothing about that. I go after my horse," said Sun Road; and we watched him and his boy merge with the dusk, as they went up along the stream.

If they returned before we rolled into our blankets, we neither saw nor heard them.

"Will he talk more," I said to George, "if he grows more used to us?"

George doubted it.

I pursued my drowsy thoughts.

"After all," I said presently, "I 'touch wood.' "

"But you do it in joke."

"Well . . . yet I do it . . . in case, I suppose."

"Do you suppose every man alive has his private 'in case'?"

"Hasn't the whole race always feared something hostile somewhere, that it had to placate?"

"Haven't there been some bluffers?"

"Bluffers . . . yes. Probably bluffers . . . if you knew."

"Have you ever wanted to kill somebody?" asked George, after a little.

"Why, yes. More than once."

"I have seen Sun Road do it. I was along with a party of them after winter meat up North Fork. He'd warned one of the party to be more careful about pointing his gun around when he was handling it in camp. One day the gun went off into Sun Road's leg. Sun Road up and put a bullet through his heart."

"What then?"

"Nothing. That was all right with the Indians."

"I wonder what he believes about Bull Lake. Money changed his ideas about geysers."

"You will find that he has brought his ideas along with him."

By the time my eyes opened in the morning, there

stood Sun Road by the stream, gorgeous with paint; his long black hair had been washed and bound anew, and it shone beneath the broad rim of his hat.

"What's that for?" I asked George, after breakfast.

We were breaking camp, throwing on the packs together. Sun Road lifted no finger in this. Having got his own horses ready, he merely waited, it was not his business.

"He has been making medicine," said George.

"What for?"

"I never know. He may have gone to Bull Lake."

"Did you hear him get up?"

"I never hear him."

"Do you think he says his prayers in the morning?"

"Oftener than we do."

In single file, over the sage-brush hills we went, Sun Road in the lead, with Little Chief Hare getting experience in pack animals and their wandering ways. Sun Road would not stoop to this; his part was to lead on the trail, and find game in the mountains; but his eye was on his boy, constantly; I could hear him at times drop words that I knew were words of instruction.

Without adventure, we crossed Meadow Creek, and Dinwiddie, and saw Crow Heart Butte fall behind us, and the streaming, clouded current of

Wind River grow clearer between its banks, as we
followed it up toward the enclosing hills; and camp
after camp, although we were a friendly party of
four, we remained two parties of two: Sun Road
and Little Chief Hare sat together on the other side
of the fire from George and me each night, while
each day they were together in the lead, with the
four pack horses filing along the trail between us.
It was at one nooning by the river, when whiffs
from the scented pines had begun to float down and
mingle with the wide-spread smell of the sage-
brush, that I thought I would let the outfit go on to
camp, and stay behind to fish: for as we had drawn
nearer to the mountain forests and their odors, we
had come to where the trout were plentiful in the
clear water of Wind River. And through George I
invited Little Chief Hare to come along and have
a try with my rod, as I had promised. It was easy
to see that Sun Road objected; and while they were
talking, I whistled:

and the charm worked. My knowledge of that native
strain made enough tie between us for the father to
smile, and the little boy to clap his hands eagerly.
Consent was given, Little Chief Hare was entrusted

to me; and on that, a second piece of happy strategy flashed upon me. I had been taking pictures with my kodak as we went through the country, and as I had invariably turned its back and mine ostentatiously upon Sun Road, with equal ostentation I now handed the distrusted machine to George for him to put it in the packs. The move could not have been lost upon Sun Road, and it probably increased his faith in me.

Presently the child and I were left by the river, watching the outfit leave us; and as the last of it went out of sight round a bend, I looked at the wild bluffs of the river, the flowing water, the steadfast mountains—and my hand was touched softly. There was the child, reminding me of my rod and the trout, his black eyes expectant. Again he was like a thing from the woods, which had made up its timid and curious mind gradually to come up and see what you were holding out for it to eat.

I jointed my rod, attached the reel, ran the line through the rings, and Little Chief Hare laughed at the reel's clicking. He watched my choice of fly, his eye followed my casting, and a little excited sound came from his lips when a trout whipped up, and soon was flopping in the grass. He was as good as gold. Very strange and new it was to feel his shyness change to confidence while neither could say a word which was intelligible to the other. He settled, when I allowed him to take my rod, into a gravity like his father's, and his concentration upon how it was to be done right, brought him rewards which must have made his stoic heart beat far beyond the demonstrations he made. When it was time to stop fishing and find camp by supper, the fecund hour had come, the trout were jumping and striking distractingly in each new pool we tried, as we moved slowly up stream; yet Little Chief Hare stopped like a clock when I pointed to his proud string of fish, and to the western sky, and he understood that we must go: no remonstrance, no sulking, just obedience on the stroke.

As we rode through the after-light of sunset, which crimsoned the heights of the Divide, but left us in shadow, down along Wind River to meet us came Sun Road; and at the sight of his father, the boy held up his fish and rushed to meet him. In Sun Road's nod to me and his few words, there was obvious commendation. What the two said together on the rest of the way to camp, I couldn't do more than imagine: Little Chief Hare talked in a stream, broken now and then, briefly, by his father's deep voice.

"I think he explained minutely," said I to George that night, "how he caught every particular trout."

"Before I had camp fixed," said George, "Sun

Road began to look down the river. I told him you couldn't miss the trail. Then he watched the sun; next, he started to find you."

Comradeship between the red and white members of our party grew more apparent after this trout fishing; and it was during the next forenoon that I saw that some of the same things could make both races laugh. Near the cabin of two young men, who had been seldom seen willing to do a stroke of work for themselves or any one, we passed them seated at the corner of their field of very weak hay, resting after having cut a small part of it, which might possibly have cost them an hour's effort.

"Don't injure your health," said George.

"Maybe hay all cut before snow come," I heard Sun Road say to them.

And not far beyond, when we passed a dry dead horse, all ribs, I spurred up to the Indian and said: "He eat that hay."

Sun Road took this joke like any white man; and at our next camp, as we sat at supper, he unexpectedly remarked: "That horse eat Brigham and Carson's hay," and laughed again. Presently he was off to see his horses, and we heard him singing. This did not cease after he returned. He began a new song, and Little Chief Hare sat by him to listen.

George Tews knew it, and gave me a version of it—a ballad of war, of the victory of the Shoshones over the Blackfeet on Warm Springs Cave, above our camp. The Blackfeet had raided the Shoshones, and killed men, and taken women and children. Feigning they had no more warriors, the Shoshones enticed the enemy back, and sprang upon them among the hills, and slaughtered them quickly. The last few took refuge in the cave. Did a Shoshone fear what a Blackfoot dared to do? The Shoshones followed into the cave. When all the enemy there were dead, the Shoshones surprised the camp of the enemy and recovered their stolen families and took horses and captives to their own people. Blackfeet fear what a Shoshone does not, a Shoshone only fears to be afraid.

It was a border ballad in essence; change the names, and versify it fitly, and who would know it from Percy's Reliques?

"Ask him," I said, "what that means about following into the cave."

But George explained it: at some time or other, the cave had been an active geyser; geysers were "bad medicine." Well, the cave had not proved bad medicine for the Shoshones. True; but very bad for the Blackfeet. Well, but Tyghee and others were beginning to see through this superstition; better for Sun Road to do likewise; better to begin dropping some of those ideas that he had brought along.

There was a sign next morning that one idea

might possibly be dropped: while George was posing for a picture of him throwing the diamond hitch, Sun Road, instead of holding aloof from all such operations as "bad medicine," came up and watched intently. I was careful to go on with my business without taking any notice of him.

On the other hand, we had a sign that another idea had not been dropped. I had decided to see the cave, at which Sun Road had said nothing and manifested nothing; but at the point where we must turn from the trail and ford Wind River, he drew rein.

"What way now?" he asked George.

George pointed across the stream and up the foot-hills.

"My son wait here with packs," said Sun Road. So the horses were eased of their loads and Little Chief Hare left in charge of them.

"At least he will venture there himself," I said to George.

"You show trail," said Sun Road to George; and George took the lead, with the Indian last.

"Does that mean he doesn't know the way?" I said to George; "or what?"

George shook his head, and we proceeded in silence up the hills, crossing once or twice on our way a few yards of hollow sounding stone.

The place was the very spot to surprise and hem

in an enemy; near it, a few could show themselves, while many lay concealed until it was too late; and a great silent view across Wind River and away to the sharp peak of the Ram's Horn where Horse Creek headed, subdued the heart with its mystery. As we dismounted on the bare steep hill, I made George pose again for me with his horse; and again Sun Road drew close to watch the operation. If wild old legends could assume a visible shape, no better scene could be chosen for it. Not far below the ridge where we stood, and not far above the tops of pines that grew thick to the bottom of a narrow cleft, and thick upon its further side, lay ambushed the cave which had been a geyser once, but had long since roared and steamed its strength away. We left our horses, and climbed down to the arena where the boiling spouts had played. Their flow had left its brittle sediment descending among the sombrous pines like a white scar, and we stood contemplating this deserted caldron of nature. A pool lay there, not large, filling the extinct crater, and out of it oozed a slender trickle down the hill. A hood of rock threw the water into partial shadow; and where the shadow was, the stony funnel of the crater loomed, not deep to the eye; it soon narrowed and curved out of sight. A little below the surface of the water, in a crevice, were lodged some white fragments of encrusted stone.

I touched the water and found it hardly tepid; but close behind us, almost hid by rank grass that dangled from above, was another vent, from which a faint steam issued, a favorable hot house. An arm's length inside, however, the steam became so hot that I pulled out my exploring hand with a jerk, and put it in the pool, and washed off the sticky mud. As I trailed my hands through the water, the subterranean spark of life, that held on here, sent a bubble and a sluggish current welling up from the unseen depths of the crater, similar to the turquoise spring at Washakie; and this set the fragments in the crevice to a light motion. The wobbling of one piece revealed it to be what was left of a human jaw. This brought the ballad and the legend to close quarters, and I lifted it out and remarked:

"Bad medicine for Blackfeet," and I handed it to George, but I watched Sun Road, for Sun Road's eye was fixed upon it.

George said nothing while he turned the encrusted relic one way and another in his hand.

And then Sun Road said:

"Heap bad medicine for Blackfeet."

Was it a beginning? Had an idea been dropped?

"Give," said Sun Road, taking the bone from George. Whether it was the effect of the air, or of too much handling, the bone broke in two, and fell, and Sun Road kicked the pieces back into the pool.

I stooped rapidly to recover one.

"Maybe Little Chief Hare like?" I suggested.

"No; no;" his father instantly forbade me, with great emphasis.

And so our visit to the scene of the old fight ended. We climbed up from the cave, and were presently riding back to Wind River. Had an idea been dropped? The feet of our horses struck hollow sounds again, as we went over the volcanic artery which lay underground; and soon after, the cheerful sight of our pack animals grazing, with Little Chief Hare waving his hat, came into view below us. I felt as if I had passed out of the sinister and brooding spell of that bare hill, where its legend seemed still to lurk. George and I had been rather quiet in the presence of that cave of slaughter. Suppose Sun Road's demeanor had been bravado to show us that a Shoshone only feared to be afraid —would not even this be working on the ideas that he had brought along, might he not be subjecting those ideas to some dawning criticism? He was already almost as curious as he was suspicious about kodaks. Bad Medicine! What a good word!

Very singular was the line which Sun Road drew between himself and Little Chief Hare. He had stepped in to stop any chance of the boy's going with us to the cave; he would not hear of the jawbone being presented to his son as a trophy; he would not expose him to the malignity of the unknown; and yet, he wished him to go to Carlisle, to be made like the white man.

This double state of mind showed itself sharply one early morning after we had got down into Jackson's Hole. In the days before the dam at the outlet of Jackson's Lake, long marshes spread above its inlet, where wild geese spent the night. Thither, just after the dawn, I stole away from camp on foot, to see if I could get one. As I prowled along the cut bank of Snake, I heard a low singing that I was not meant to hear. Sun Road was secretly up and out, down by the water's edge, engaged in some rite with Little Chief Hare. I came upon them unaware, before I could draw back; Sun Road bent over the stream, his paints around him, his hair unbound; and I receded quickly, not to see more, and not to disturb them. Perhaps it was me they heard, or it may have been the wild geese; these wild birds, warned no doubt by some sentinel, rose from the marshes a good two hundred yards off, and the singing ceased instantly. I returned to camp, whistling the song of the meadow-lark; and father and son appeared not long after. I had seen the brilliant paint on several other mornings when Sun Road came in from attending to his horses. So it was not only Bull Lake. Was he making medicine for hunting? Sometimes, probably. But always?

Our party of four had become congenial in the
great solitudes. For a long while, ever since Warm
Springs Creek, we had ceased to be two parties. By
day, when I went trout fishing, Little Chief Hare
came with me, shy no longer. In excitement over
some particularly strapping fish, he would burst out
talking and then burst out laughing when he remembered I couldn't understand a word. We taught
each other a few words; and thus by Wind River,
and Brooks Lake, and Black Rock, and Buffalo
Fork, we grew companionable. And so it was,
though less so, when I hunted with Little Chief
Hare's father. And the two no longer sat apart
when the camp fire was blazing; we all watched it
together each night in the great solitudes.

It was at the Thumb of the Yellowstone Lake that
we first felt the shock of other voices. Two stage-
loads of tourists arrived while we sat at our camp
lunch in the open, by the shore; and at the sight
of us, a strident chorus of ecstasy was lifted, and
cameras were pointed at our Indians. Sun Road
flung a blanket over Little Chief Hare, and I requested that we be let alone. Some of the tourists
were not pleased; but their hour for departure came
duly, and we were left in peace.

Through the afternoon, Sun Road began gradually to investigate the paint pots heaving up con-
tinuously their viscous discharges. He watched intently the cook of the lunch station catch a trout

in the cold lake, and drop it into the boiling water in a cone that rose above the surface a few yards from where he stood. While among the steaming paint pots, he never let go the hand of Little Chief Hare, held him particularly tight in the vicinity of a piece of the volcanic crust which I told him was dangerous, according to the signs posted around its borders; but the exploit of the cook made him relax his caution at length. He allowed Little Chief Hare to catch several trout and boil them, and did the same himself.

He showed some reluctance to go near the most alarming sight that I know in the Park, the mud geyser; and next morning he walked into our camp with all the signs of having celebrated one of his shy, secret rites. Had he been, in his own more elaborate way, touching wood?

To keep safe from kodaks, he no longer rode in the lead, he made himself inconspicuous among the pack horses, while George Tews took his place. The figure of George in his cowboy dress evoked sufficient excitement and admiration when stages drove by, and I imagine that his likeness may be seen today in many American homes. I could see Sun Road contemplating these wholesale operations in photography with a face that revealed nothing.

At the canyon, out on Inspiration Point, I noticed a young lady watching Sun Road more than she

watched the view. She was lovely. Her looks and
her dress suggested a type much superior to the
common, loud-voiced tourist. Was he aware of her?
As he stood far out at the end of the point gazing
at the falls, and the majestic world of crag and
tawny citadel and saffron minaret into which their
waters descended, he took off his hat. Was it a sign
of reverence to the Powers who had made this sub-
lime scene? Without the sombrero, the nobility of
his head was far more striking.

She spoke low, with the voice of gentlefolk: "How
handsome, how superb! He is a part of all this.
How I should like to see him in Indian dress! I
shouldn't think of taking his picture without his
permission, and I would never find the courage to
ask him."

Presently she and her companion, an older lady,
went away together.

Sun Road had not moved. He began playing his
pipe there, all to himself. He turned toward me and
sounded the song of the meadow-lark, and nodded.
Little Chief Hare begged for the pipe, and tried it.
But his fingers had not yet the cunning of his
father's.

After we left the canyon, we left the tourists, we
took what was then a mere trail by Tower Creek.
But the morning after we reached the Mammoth
Springs, where there was a crowd most of the day,

12447

Sun Road appeared in all his glory, except the crest of eagle feathers, which he had probably left at Washakie. In his barbaric and royal splendor he walked into the hotel among the travelers, and at a counter where souvenirs, and odds and ends of the West, were sold, he bought some little figures of soldiers and cowboys and ponies, carved in wood and painted; Little Chief Hare was to see these presents when they got home to Washakie. And here was the young lady of Inspiration Point.

With the older lady, she was making some purchases at the counter; and in her surprise at seeing Sun Road almost at her side, and clothed with the very magnificence that she had wished to see, she made an impulsive gesture. She held out to him several photographs of Indians that she had chosen. I saw him look at them gravely, and then at her as any man looks at a beautiful woman. It was plain that she asked him if there was not some likeness of himself, and was disappointed at his answer.

While I was at a table attending to the mail forwarded here to me, both ladies came up, introduced themselves, expressed their enthusiasm for the canyon, spoke of great scenery in Europe, and of their admiration for the appearance of Sun Road. He was the first Indian they had ever seen, and they were eager to hear all that I could tell them about him. During this he joined us. For the first moments

they were less at their ease than he—he was used
to talking with the ladies at Fort Washakie. In re-
plying to their questions, his sentences were not
long, but his English was more fluent than any he
had chosen to speak in camp. Presently the younger
lady produced her photographs.

"Do you know any of these?" she asked him.

"Yes. That is Sharp Nose. He is an Arapahoe.
That is Washakie. He is my grandfather."

"And why is there no picture of his grandson?"

Sun Road looked down; he looked at Little Chief
Hare who was half hiding behind him; last, he
looked at me. It was quite a long, strange silence.
The younger lady must have come to feel something
oppressive, or obscure in it, for she now spoke with
a certain embarrassment:

"Has no one wished for a likeness of you?"

"Do you wish it?"

"Oh, might I? May I?"

He paused again, this time looking intently at
her.

"I like you to do what you wish."

"But—" began the elder lady, and stopped, with
her eyes a little startled.

"It's a high compliment," I put in, smiling. "He
has never been willing before."

"Oh . . . but then . . . but I shouldn't. . . ."

"I like you to do what you wish."

"It—it will only be very small. Not like these you buy."

"You will give one to me?"

"Oh, yes. And one of your little boy?"

"No. Not my boy."

We went where the light favored, and Sun Road placed himself as he was asked.

"You keep Little Chief Hare," he said suddenly and quickly to me.

Then he stiffened, straight, facing the instrument, controlled from head to foot. At the click of the machine I saw his taut muscles respond as if a galvanic current had struck them.

"You will send me one?" he said again.

I think the elder lady was relieved when we separated.

When they departed in the stage for the train, Sun Road was at hand, and ceremoniously took his leave of them, while many watched it. He was not unaware of this.

After that final breaking down of his opposition at the Mammoth Springs, he ceased to hide himself from the general curiosity; nor was it long—not two days—before the notice he attracted began to give him pleasure, and to be courted. He did not betray any sign that he knew they were staring, or heard what they said; he merely resumed the lead of our outfit, sitting his horse with august grace, no longer in dusty and wrinkled overalls, but haughty and wild in his native dress.

After the dripping, gouty excrescences of the Mammoth Springs, we ascended into natural meadows and dull pines along the route of the stages; and I saw that Sun Road had ceased to avoid the cameras. Meeting them at almost every mile since the Thumb, and seeing George suffer himself to be taken so constantly, had diminished the Indian's opposition to them until it had wholly given way under the charm of the young lady. That was the end of it, and the beginning of something else. Before we had reached the Norris Basin, the sight of each approaching party no longer aroused aversion, but expectancy, in Sun Road: always in the lead, he seemed to sit a little more erect, to become a little more a prince of the wilderness; and it was now his likeness, not George's, that travelers carried away upon their films.

For the sake of the fishing, we camped two nights near the Norris Basin, at some distance from the volcanic sights where tourists clustered, yet not beyond the sounds made by the steam. These were not new to Sun Road's ears, but they were more numerous and frequent than heretofore. When dusk fell, and the stages had departed with their loads, and all human movement was gone, the sounds seemed to gain volume in the great overhanging quiet, and to draw closer; one might imagine them stealing upon our camp under cover of the darkness. In the morning and all the next day, Sun Road was slightly restless; and when night came and the ominous noises rose again, I wondered if he was anxious to be further from the presence of unseen powers.

"He is not scared of geysers," said George, "he is feeling lonesome away from the limelight."

In any case, Sun Road was plainly more at ease when we were riding on again along the public route, where admiration waited for him. He said nothing—he was daily receding into his taciturnity of the first days—but one saw him on the watch for fresh tributes. The rites which he performed secretly away from camp in the early dawn—were they to placate offended deities, or to render his person more resplendent in the sight of men and women? What hurt could his ancient gods do him for braving their forbidden haunts that was comparable to this steady lowering of the man and his once true dignity to the level of a show at a circus? He liked their stares, their exclamations, and to be near when they plied us with questions about him. He vouchsafed them but few words; to allow them his likeness was enough condescension. He dramatized himself with unerring instinct—and the kodaks were an influence more malevolent than any cave with a white jaw-bone. In truth, they had drained out of him a portion of himself, something that he had been was gone, as if he had lost his spiritual virginity.

His new appetite must have been glutted at the next important show place. He was encircled here by enthusiastic travelers, turning their lenses upon him like the evil eye of civilization, piercing to his weak spot. They persuaded him to dismount. We watched it apart, sitting in our saddles, while the noon blazed fiercely down upon the white, glaring bareness of the volcanic formation, where steam spouted, and excited figures swarmed; petticoats, knickerbockers, sun shades, moving, mingling, chattering; and in their midst, the silent Indian chief, posing, displaying himself. They forgot the natural prodigies they were there to see, they lost the eruption of the geyser which gave the place its name. Its outburst of scattered spray and violent steam startled Little Chief Hare, who cowered by my side watching it, and keeping close to me until the display died down.

And yet, something of the untainted Sun Road persisted. Did he divine my mortification at this degrading change in him? What did he think of my never once making a move to take his picture? Was this why he ceased to sit with us by the fire at night, and went back to his old place beyond it, and

resumed completely his original reserve, and called
Little Chief Hare away from between George and
me to the other side of the fire? I don't know—I
can never know—but something of the ancient Sun
Road persisted. Below the upper geyser Basin—the
great one where the Inn stands today—we met the
official photographer, and halted to have our whole
outfit taken by him. The Indian spoke a sharp word
to his son, and Little Chief obediently moved out of
range. His father would not expose him to the eye
of civilization. It consumed some little time. Three
plates were used, and these were all that the man
had with him. He showed us some of his pictures,
and their size made an instant appeal to Sun Road.
Sun Road had made an instant appeal to the man.
He wanted that figure alone, without the rest of us,
for his collection on sale. His plates were gone. He
had plenty at the wooden and canvas building which
then served as a hotel.

"I wait here," said Sun Road royally. "You go
get them." And he extended an arm in the direction.

The man hesitated, looking up the Firehole River,
and then at the Indian, and last at the sun.

"I would do anything he wants," said he, "to
catch him just as he is. But by the time I got back,
it would be too dark."

"I think we'll have to be getting along," said I.

"You'll be here tomorrow?"

"No. We pull out early on the Sheridan trail."

"I'll try it today. I'll be ready up there." He hastened to pack his things, and drove off in advance of us.

The sun went low and lower as we followed the road up the Firehole River. When we reached the Castle geyser, a languid stream breathed from its crater, last sign of a recent eruption. None of the important cones and vents were active, except the incessant Saw-mill over the river, spitting its petulant vapors and paltry spurts of water that trickled over the formation and down the bank; other disturbance was at a lull, and the naked crust of the whole area lay white up to the black edges of the pines. The glare and the heat were long gone. Above us, on the ridge of the Continental Divide near by to our eastward, the top of one tall pine glowed like a golden spark, and as I watched it, darkened in the encroaching shadow, and I was aware of the swiftly cooling twilight.

A few stray, cautious figures lingered singly among the volcanic sights across the Firehole, keeping themselves well within the indicated limits of safe walking. Somewhat apart from them, stood the photographer with his camera mounted.

"Well," I called to him, "we're too late."

"No hurry," he replied. "We've forty minutes

before Old Faithful starts up again. I'm going to try a flash-light with the geyser in the background."

"Aren't you rather far from it?"

"That's what I want—just an appropriate background for your Indian chief. Let him come over here when he's ready."

Sun Road heard all that, and understood enough of it to make himself ready as soon as we had found a camping place somewhat beyond the primitive hotel, where the trail entered the trees near the water. There, while George and I were throwing off the packs, Sun Road prepared himself for the professional photograph. I had supposed his war crest had been left at Washakie. Its eagle feathers were on his head when I turned and saw him among his possessions, out of which something fell. This he quickly gathered up and concealed in a fold of his blankets, as Little Chief Hare stood watching his father.

"Let's go along and see it," said George. "The horses can wait."

"I can see it just as well from here," I answered; and I began to unroll my bedding.

When next I looked up, the three were across the little bridge down the Firehole below our camp. George, holding Little Chief Hare's hand, followed Sun Road, whose appearance at once drew the few

stray figures from their belated sight seeing. These
slowly and curiously gathered and followed toward
where the man with his camera stood waiting. The
twilight had deepened, and with it, as always, the
silence seemed to deepen; against the silence, the
sounds of Old Faithful on the verge of its next
eruption grew more turbulent, and the ascend-
ing clouds of steam swirled white in the cold air.
Within a minute, the pent-up water would burst out
and Old Faithful leap to its full stature; and the
photographer was busy to be on time for his background. He had placed Sun Road where he wished
him to stand. The Indian intently listened and
obeyed his directions, while the man looked through
his camera, giving orders and making adjustments.
He hung his cloth in front of the instrument and
drew the slide from the first plate, standing ready.
Tall and motionless before him, Sun Road waited,
absorbed, rigid; a figure, even in this dusk, wholly
different from the city-bred shapes which had lined
themselves to look on from behind.

I saw the column of Old Faithful shoot up, and a
blinding flare follow like a stroke of lightning. Like
lightning, it left me for a moment sightless; the
whole scene vanished in an obscurity through which
the roar of the geyser resounded. Then I began to
see again. The figure of Sun Road was no longer
there. The camera stood where it had been. I looked

at that, and at Old Faithful, now at the climax of
its fury. Then I grew aware of a confusion beyond
the camera, and shouts were raised, and I saw the
man running from his camera, and I began to run.
When I had got over the bridge and again to the
level of the formation, I saw a group shouting more
desperately, and wildly waving arms. Next, beyond
this, I discovered the figure of Sun Road as I came
among them. Then I began to shout. The Indian
heeded neither voices nor gestures. With his head
thrown back as if in defiance, his eyes were fixed
upon the geyser; and nothing else in the world ex-
isted for him. As he watched this portent, for which
he had been so utterly unprepared, and whose arrival from the depths below had apparently been
attended by lightning from above, if he was aware
of us at all, it is likely that he thought our terror
was on our own account, and not for him. He stood
on the hollow crust from which visitors were warned
away. The column of water sank to half height, because its force was spent; but Sun Road must have
taken this as a threat of some kind, as if the shaft
was about to step down from its pedestal, and come
in search of him; for he made an abrupt and backward start. At this, a rending crack went across the
crust where he had sprung, and the whole surface
gave way. The tall figure sank with it, stretching

his arms to Little Chief Hare, and clouds of steam burst from the cavern into which he had gone, and everything was hidden from our sight. George by my side fastened both his arms around the child, who struggled to follow his father.

When I could notice anything, I saw that we were standing alone. The others had withdrawn, the dusk was deeper, Old Faithful was silent, the steam from the opened cavity had dissipated, allowing ledges and recesses to be seen dimly below the water, upon whose heaving surface floated a scarf and some small objects. These must have been the toys which Sun Road had purchased for Little Chief Hare.

George lifted the boy, whose arms clung round his neck as he leaned his head down and wailed. We kept him in our tent between us that night, we feared to trust him outside; and we found that he wanted to come. We were not his people, but we were something he knew, and we had his confidence. He was asleep long before we were; but later, when I waked up, I heard him crying quietly in the dark. I put my hand out, and he took it, and went to sleep again, holding it. By the next night we were far from that fatal place on the trail to Fort Washakie.

I had lost the heart to hunt; George shot us one deer for meat; but Little Chief Hare went about with me, and at times my attempts to make him understand me would bring a faint smile. The last picture of him in camp that stays with me was at Bull Lake crossing. He was seated on a pile of blankets, seriously attempting to play on his father's pipe, making trials at the phrase of the meadow-lark.

Captain Quid

I T is always something to have a reputation, even
a bad one: to live and die without anybody's noticing it—think of it! Owing to one great gift,
sweet Verbena Frankish escaped this lot.

During her maidenhood, which she passed in
Caesar Borgia, Kansas, the town of her birth, she
sat and listened when neighbors called upon her
mother. At the age of fourteen, when boys began to
call upon her, she sat and listened. They continued
to call, and Verbena continued to listen, and the
boys of Caesar Borgia never got tired of this listening, and found it enough. Some even abjured cigarets; Verbena knew that tobacco was part of Sa-
tan's apparatus. There was a misty helplessness
about her hair, and a clinging appeal in her eyes,
and the boys called, and called. At parties, one arm
after another would encircle her waist, while she
danced dreamily, and always listened.

By the time that Verbena was almost seventeen,
her aunts and the Baptist minister, and persons of
that sort were saying:

"We should all pray that Verbena finds a strong,
brave husband to shelter her."

And men of forty were saying:

"What's come to Kansas manhood that some young buck hasn't claimed that peach for his own?"

And certain mothers were saying:

"If that girl was mine, I'd teach her."

But Verbena's mother always said:

"I have never felt a moment's anxiety about the future of my child."

While such things were being said in Caesar Borgia, Kansas, at Lime Rock, Connecticut, a red-headed boy of seven had been thrashed by his father for painting the cat sky-blue; thrashed at eight for bringing his little brother into intimate relations with a cigar; thrashed between whiles for dropping on the bull's back from a tree, for experiments with gun-powder home-made upon his grandfather's flint-lock, and for other continuous miscellanies. But his father died when the boy was eleven; and though his mother's pleading could make him cry because he adored her, it couldn't always make him remember his sincere promises to be good. He raged through his 'teens in bare feet, or in moccasins, shot hawks, slept in the woods, was expelled from his first school for locking the teacher in the wood closet, and from his second for accidentally hitting a preacher in the eye with a chew of tobacco. It led him to perfect his aim. At seventeen, he knew more of whisky than was desirable, had gone further with women than usual, declined to enter Yale, and was caught by his uncle, the Senator, trying to enlist in the army. The Senator reminded his mother that ever since the Revolution, there had been red-headed Monks who turned out well, if you only gave them time; you could see their portraits in both of the State Capitals; James might get killed, but would never deserve hanging; and he got the boy appointed to the Military Academy, from which his mother was not alone in fearing that he would be speedily ejected.

But at West Point, a man abruptly waked in James Monk. Even his dress became careful. His misdeeds were passed over for the sake of the promise in him, and he graduated with credit, being assigned to the cavalry, and ordered to report for duty at Fort Klamath, Oregon. By the end of the war in the lava beds, James was entirely a man, known to have in him the makings of a star Indian fighter. By the time he was twenty-five in years, he was thirty in responsibility, with no leaning toward wedlock.

"If ever Jim does it," said voices at Walla Walla, his next military post, "she'll never forget she's got a husband."

"And he'll seldom remember he's got a wife," said others.

"He'll do it perhaps," still others said, "when polygamy is made legal."

James did it in five weeks. He was on a scout south of the Umatilla reservation when she arrived for a visit to cousins in Walla Walla. Till that day, not an officer had ever heard of her. Then all heard of her immediately, and declared Verbena Frankish to be the best girl the post had ever entertained: the prettiest, and sweetest, dearest little girl.

"She knows how to keep still, too," Mrs. Wade remarked.

It does take a woman . . . !

And Verbena listened: listened to them all, sat with them all, walked with them all: and Walla Walla was a large post. Each day you might discern her blond hair from afar, shining beside some manly shape in uniform whose turn it was.

"I'm Tuesday," said a young captain to a first lieutenant.

"I used to be Thursday," muttered the other.

"Cheer up, old man. Never say die."

Then James Monk rode in from the Umatilla scout. In one week they were engaged, in four he went east on leave to Caesar Borgia, whither she had returned, and where they were married.

"My child," said Verbena's mother when the ceremony was completed, "has never given me one moment's anxiety.'' She lifted her hands to the shoulders of James Monk, and he turned scarlet under the long, affectionate look she gave him. Then, before everybody, and to his horrible embarrassment, she kissed him, saying: ''I know Verbena is in safe hands.'' After that, he couldn't recall, even obscurely, how he got on, or how he got off.

The watchers at Walla Walla welcomed and discussed the honeymooners, wondering how soon the fair little dainty bride, tripping so snugly by the side of her pirate-looking groom, would discover that verily she was in overwhelmingly safe hands.

''Which is the better half in this case, Mr. Wade?'' asked Mrs. Wade.

And that first lieutenant answered: ''Julia, there aren't going to be any halves. Poor little thing!''

''Well, Mr. Wade, I wonder.''

It certainly does take a woman . . . !

So the blond Verbena and her James, each from an early age having escaped the destiny of existing unnoticed, didn't stop now. Guessing was brisk, even before their first baby; by the time their last arrived, they had put the weather out of business as a topic.

It wasn't her wrongs or his infidelities—there were none; James's morals after marriage withstood every strain; he was quite old-fashioned; and it wasn't that James took to drink. Even in his first year out of the Military Academy, before ever he had laid eyes on Verbena, in the long, idle, dangerous lull which had followed upon the whirl and the stress of the lava beds, he had felt the lure and the joys of whisky creeping upon him. Nothing to do, nothing ever to do, and the wilderness, and remoteness, and a tempestuous, ambitious young soldier, and a bottle right in the room, and more where it came from! But at Klamath were two majors, not related by blood, but twins through alcohol: watery voices, loose jowls, necks rolling over their collars, legs that waddled, reddened eyes that oozed. James took note of it. He was heading for that. One night he locked himself in his quarters, stood up, muttered, "The last one, so help me God!" made a thorough job of it,—and knocked off as rigidly as if he had been a prohibitionist. By self-discipline he mastered the great art of moderation in time, and could trust himself.

And now he had laid eyes on Verbena, and she was his, and he was hers, and Walla Walla found that the interest of watching this young couple did not wane. They were to be seen together daily, taking the air slowly along the parade ground; slowly, because he was absurdly careful about Verbena.

"She keeps her yellow head pretty close to his shoulder," said Lieutenant Wade.

"Why, look at his pipe!" said Mrs. Wade.

"What for?"

"Mr. Wade, when did you ever see him smoke?"

"Come to think of it, I never did. Funny to take it up so late."

Mrs. Wade pondered. "She must have made him."

"Yes, he looks hen-pecked."

"You needn't laugh, Mr. Wade. He shaved off that sorrel-colored down on his lip weeks ago."

"Because he looks better without it."

"That's what she made him think. And now she's told him a pipe's manly."

"Lord, Julia, how I'd hate to have thoughts like yours!"

Verbena's pride in her soldier's standing was visible to all Walla Walla; but none in Walla Walla could see what lay behind the pipe. It disappeared. Well, why not, if he didn't like it? Then why was he so irritable? Next, it was in his mouth again, and his temper like sunshine, and everybody guessing and happy. She had said to somebody he had a hacking cough. Oh, was that it? Hadn't she said his hand was unsteady, and he wouldn't be able to keep his lead at target practice? Somebody had heard she had declared nicotine was a deadly drug and the law should forbid it. The trouble was, nobody had heard James cough, nobody had seen his hand shake, and not a soul could quote a word spoken by Verbena directly. But how much better fun this made it!

"It's perfectly simple," said one lady. "She hates the smell."

"I think it's her uncle," said another. "The one that dropped dead from a tobacco heart, running for a train."

"She did have an uncle," said a third. "But death was self-inflicted, I'm pretty sure."

"It's Kansas," said a captain. "Kansas knows you're in danger of hell, if you enjoy something it doesn't happen to."

The fun didn't die down at once, when James with his wife and his troop was transferred to Fort Custer, in Montana.

"I'll miss him less than I'd have expected," said Lieutenant Wade. "I loved Jim Monk the bachelor, Jim Monk the husband is somebody I simply don't know."

"She's jealous," said his wife.

"No such luck. He's crazy about her."

"It's his pipe, Mr. Wade."

"Jealous of his pipe? My God, Julia!"

"I don't say she knows it."

"All right. Have it any way you please. But I'll ask you to explain him."

"Haven't you done it, Mr. Wade?"

* * *

"I have never seen her look more lovely."

This was Mrs. Hipple, wife of Colonel Hipple, the post commander at Custer. The other Walla Walla troops had gone to Yuma. That was army life then. You saw some people every day for a year, and often longer, and nobody else. Then you never saw them at all; they would be a thousand miles away; then suddenly you would be seeing them every day again. So now at Custer, James and Verbena had a perfectly fresh set of spy-glasses turned upon them.

"Lovely," said the Colonel. "Yes, indeed."

"Horace, did you hear when it was expected?"

"What's expected?"

"Mercy, Horace, their baby!"

"Baby? Why they were only married last month."

"I know they act so. But it was in October. Mary Wade wrote me all about it."

"October. Well, they've been prompt."

"Mary said he used to be quite wild."

"Can't believe it."

"Well, Mary would know, Horace. And he's wild about her now. And she's looking lovelier every day. I think I'll just go around to the O'Neils and find out when it's expected."

Some offspring arrive more punctually than some trains. This one did. But Indians were less regular.

Upon a day when Verbena's event was close at hand
and she and James had never wanted more to be
with each other and to sit together and wait, a glum
James rode out of the post northward at the head
of his troop. The Piegans were rumored to be preparing for a raid on their neighbors the Crows.
There was no help for it; the trouble must be headed
off and white settlers protected in their lives and
property.

Before the soldiers returned the event was suc-
cessfully over, and Verbena quite beyond the chance
of danger. Moreover, Mrs. Frankish, Verbena's
mother, had come from Caesar Borgia well in advance. Mrs. Frankish thought highly of her son-in-
law.

"It's an ideal union," she said to Colonel and
Mrs. Hipple on the great day that made her a
grandmother. "He weighs eight pounds and a half.
He's to be James Junior."

"That's right," said the Colonel. "And now that
collection of pipes will have to take third place in
the affections of James Senior."

"Pipes?" Mrs. Frankish looked vague.

"Why, all those corn-cobs and clays and brier-
woods and meerschaums and German students and
everything."

"Oh, yes! Oh, yes!" said Mrs. Frankish hur-
riedly. "To be sure. Aren't they perfectly lovely!"

Presently she took her leave.

"Horace," said the Colonel's wife after some thinking," did you notice her? She has never seen those pipes. Their existence was news to her."

"Well, it mightn't interest her."

"It interested her very much. Horace, Verbena has locked them up. And that throws a light on something in Mary Wade's letter that I couldn't understand."

After that visit to Colonel and Mrs. Hipple, Mrs. Frankish was very wary. She waited to welcome James home from his triumphant handling of the Piegans, whom he quieted by firmness and sincerity, not a shot being fired; then she had to hasten back to Caesar Borgia. All that Lucretia Hipple could be sure of was that two days before James and his men rode into the post, every pipe was to be found on the rack. Lucretia took care to call in and ask to see the baby have his bath, so she saw the rack too.

"It didn't look to me as if they were in quite the same position," she said to Horace. "That carved German one used to be in the lower right-hand corner. But he'll just suppose his mother-in-law dusted them."

"I hope he doesn't spoil that pretty girl," said Horace, thoughtfully.

Then James's troop was transferred to Fort Bayard, in New Mexico. Both infantry and cavalry were stationed at Bayard, and between these two branches of the service the heartiest intimacy did not invariably obtain. But the topic of James and Verbena drew them into relations of the most harmonious confidence.

"I consider it an ideal union," asserted Mrs. Dexter (cavalry).

"Now something's coming!" said Major Dexter.

His lady contemplated him for a moment over the billowy Atlantic of her bosom.

"I consider it an ideal union," she slowly repeated. "And I will never admit she is losing her looks."

"Better not," advised the Major. "She isn't."

"How much younger is she?" asked a second lieutenant's wife (infantry).

"Four years older, my dear," answered Mrs. Dexter. "You'll know these things when you've been longer in the army."

The second lieutenant's wife did not speak again at once.

"Well, I wish James Monk would let me kiss her little nose just once," said Major Dexter.

"You have picked out the very thing that keeps her from being a real beauty," said his wife, sharply.

"Just as lief take her ear."

"Harry Dexter, if you're trying to make this conversation vulgar——"

"Not for worlds, Maria. Trying to elevate it."

"Well, it's plain she makes him happy," said Mrs. Parminter. She hadn't spoken before.

"Wasn't there something about his smoking?" This was the second lieutenant's wife, venturing once more.

Mrs. Dexter gave her a look of clemency this time. She had hoped somebody would ask this. It was better drama.

"Until that first baby," she stated, "he had always refused to get rid of his collection of pipes."

"Oh, then you were there!" cried a fourth lady.

Mrs. Dexter ignored this. "It was the mother who stepped in."

"His?"

"Hers. And who'd have thought it to look at her!"

"The mother?"

"Her. You'd have said she was sixteen. Dear me! I must get ready to go to Silver City."

"How can we bear it?" protested the fourth lady.

"Well, I can spare a minute. It was Mrs. Hipple who wrote me from Custer that her mother had stepped in. Mrs. Wade saw them at Walla Walla, and she told Mrs. Hipple it began there."

"Maria, do you know you're not helping me to be quite clear as to what began there?"

"Harry, if you've not learned by this time that I am always very careful about what I am willing to repeat, even in strict confidence like this, you're never going to learn at all. Of course he still smokes cigars; not many, but I'm told they're of the best. But who knows when she will draw the line at cigars? After that Christmas pipe at Custer you can expect anything."

Mrs. Dexter sat back, and her broad Atlantic rose and fell serenely. You could have heard a pin drop.

"After the baby was born, Mrs. Frankish—that's her mother—went back to the family home in Caesar Borgia, Kansas—the family home, where the uncle committed suicide with prussic acid in the parlor and Verbena saw him do it. Of course with an uncle like that in the family a queer niece is no surprise. Her mother always tried to counteract it. Verbena's very smart. You never hear her tell him not to smoke. So when their baby was expected and her mother had come from Caesar Borgia and he was off hunting——"

"The father? And their first?" It was the fourth lady. She couldn't help it.

Mrs. Dexter took no offense at the interruption; it was a tribute to her narrative powers. "Yes, he was off hunting Indians. He was ordered to go. The mother——"

"The baby's mother?"

"No, hers—it hadn't come. Her mother was almost glad to have him out of the house at that time, for he was so needlessly anxious and concerned that he would have been in the way and Mrs. Frankish had plenty of experience and ran the house, and after all it's her mother a daughter wants then. But she had no trouble. She was young and her bones gave. Yes. Eight pounds and a half that first one weighed. I've never heard the weight of the second one.

"But the mother had stepped in already. She found his pipes all hidden away when he had gone after the Indians. She was used to him smoking and whistling all day, in and out of the house, so she saw how it was in a flash. Verbena never said a word to him in her hearing, but a woman can always guess right. She wasn't going to have trouble between those two, if she could stop it. It's not known what advice she gave Verbena, but when he came back he never knew she had meddled with his pipes!"

Here Mrs. Dexter stopped.

"How does she make him?" wondered the fourth lady.

"I believe I have already stated," Mrs. Dexter replied, "that she takes good care to keep those domestic scenes behind the curtain."

"Did you say something about a Christmas present?" asked Mrs. Parminter.

"It had happened before it came. When that poor man returned to his home, and his young wife, and the boy who was going to bear his name . . . well her mother ought never to have let him go into the room the first time and see her alone. But who would have intruded upon them at such a moment, and how was she to know that Verbena would be so smart?"

Mrs. Dexter looked at the clock, and once again you could have heard a pin drop.

"I've hardly time to tell the rest," she said. "But there's not much. I know not a word of this will go out of this room. At Christmas Mrs. Frankish sent him a beautiful pipe from Caesar Borgia. He didn't let her know. Just thanked her. But there was something in the way he wrote, and she got an idea. Of course she found out. And the next Christmas she sent him a box of cigars. But to look at that harmless appealing thing, with her baby eyes—who would have thought it! Now remember. Not a word!"

It was evident now that Mrs. Dexter had finished.

"Maria," said her husband most incautiously, "you haven't said what did happen."

It was a triumph for Mrs. Dexter. She rose in a stately manner. "I must go and get ready for Silver

City," she answered. "Since Harry seems to be the only person present who hasn't listened to me, perhaps one of you ladies will tell him over again."

"Well, I must run along, I'm late already," said Mrs. Parminter. And she hurried away to tell it all to everybody.

The fourth lady and the second lieutenant's wife looked at each other.

"How old is your son Albert?" one of them asked Major Dexter.

"Twenty-five."

"Can you remember when he was born?"

"Perfectly."

"Can you remember your first sight of him and his mother?"

Harry Dexter dropped his eyes.

"Then think," the lady advised him. "Think back. If, at that time, your wife had asked you to make some sacrifice—think it out."

They left him with this; they deemed it enough. He stood in the room alone, thinking it out.

"Well I'll be damned!" he said at last.

Other details were confided to other audiences in other posts. At Lowell Barracks, hard by Tucson, they knew a part of the Custer incident which Mrs. Dexter had quite missed. Mrs. Frankish had told Mrs. Hipple that when James came back from his Indian excursion he had passed the pipe rack on his way to his wife, replaced the common pipe he had with him among the Piegans, taken his pet meerschaum, and with this in his hand had entered the sacred chamber where his wedded love and his first offspring were waiting to receive him. Mrs. Hipple said that the young father had knelt a long while by the bedside. Well, of course, there it was!

Fort Riley had another version: it had happened after the baptism of James Junior. Long before the child came, she had banished his indulgence from the house, and he confined it to the club and to his rides or walks about the post. Then she had told him that she considered a pipe in public ungentlemanly, so he used to sit in the Indian agent's private room up the river. Lowell Barracks had been told that James for a year had been allowed no smoking. When he came there from Bayard for a shooting contest, a snare was set for him—Mrs. Day invited him to supper and bought the best cigars to be had. He came, but before she could lead him astray he pulled out a cigar of his own and asked permission to light it. It gave the veteran lady quite a shock. If James from first to last ever knew how they talked, they never knew he knew it.

"And what are we to believe now?" asked Mrs. Day of Mrs. Slocum when he had gone back to Fort Bayard. Mrs. Slocum was another veteran.

"I never noticed him with a cigar till this evening," observed Captain Slocum, "if that'll help you."

"Perhaps that's it," Mrs. Day mused. "She's got him down to that. Or perhaps it's when he feels safe."

"Do you suppose he ever thinks he made a mistake?" said Mrs. Slocum. "Sometimes he doesn't look a day over twenty-five."

"Not a day!" assented her friend. "Especially when he laughs. I wonder how long she'll be able to hold him?"

"Do they have children still?" Mrs. Slocum asked.

"Quite regularly, I'm told," said Captain Slocum.

"Can he actually be afraid of her?" Mrs. Day inquired.

"Don't you believe he's afraid of her!" asserted Slocum. "Any hard fighter will pay a good deal for peace."

"Yes; but he usually draws the line somewhere," Mrs. Slocum remarked.

"One place he draws it," said Captain Slocum, "is at the children. I saw it."

The ladies' eyes instantly converged upon him.

"It was at McKinney. His two biggest kids were just about big enough to toddle round and fall down now and then. They'd begged him to let 'em ride his horse, and he was walking beside the horse and holding Charlie in the saddle. Charlie had the reins, shouting, and James Junior was yelling that it was his turn, when out comes Verbena from the house and tells him it's dangerous and to take Charlie right down. Jim just turns his head a little and looks at her and says, 'That's my business, dear.' She went back into the house. His kids were always crazy about him at McKinney. He took 'em camping at Cloud's Peak.''

"Can't somebody tell her how imprudent she is?" croaked Mrs. Slocum.

"Her mother has tried and tried," said Mrs. Day. "But what can you do with an obstinate will?"

"Well, ladies," said the Captain, "strong will or not, they're lovers to this day."

The thought of it made each of the women breathe a pensive sigh.

Not many months later, James and Verbena were stationed at Fort Bowie, Arizona. Little was near there but cactus, mountains and hostile Apaches. It was between massacres, with nothing doing. One night a young officer at the club, while they were playing cards, came out rather strongly. Glasses of whisky were beside all the players but James. Talk had dwelt so far upon the recent burning of the Butterfield stage and the massacre of its passengers in Apache Pass, when the aroma of James's cigar changed the subject.

"How much do those cost, Captain?" said Jack Whetstone. Whetstone was Monk's young second lieutenant, only two years out of the Military Academy, but already most companionable to his Captain.

"Oh, these don't come high. I'll take one card."

Monk extended his case to Whetstone who accepted with alacrity one of the admirable cigars.

"I'm glad they don't come high," said Whetstone, "for I'd like to order some and cease being a dead beat."

"Give you a box next lot I get from San Francisco."

Possibly the whisky may have helped Jack to make his next remark.

"Captain, with your taste for Havana products, in your place I'd never have dared to go on increasing our population."

The players heard themselves draw in their breath. They sat motionless. They saw the hand of James Monk quiver as it held the cards he seemed to scrutinize. Whetstone as soon as his words escaped him would sooner have bitten his tongue off than speak them. He had been a little spoiled and privileged. Successes across the bridge in Juarez had spread romance about him among the ladies at

Fort Bliss while he had been stationed there. Dismay at what he had said held him dumb. The silence seemed endless before James Monk looked up from his cards, and rested his eye upon Whetstone.

"This is a gentleman's club," said he, very quietly. "I said I'd take one card."

They played the game out. Not much ease returned to it, it broke up early. After a general, impersonal good-night, Monk walked out, leaving an awkward group, who began to laugh. But Whetstone did not laugh. He stood alone by the table for a moment; then he rushed out, and caught up with his Captain, striding along in the dark.

"Captain, that was unspeakable. I apologize. I'll apologize before them all."

A short pause followed. Monk had stopped.

"Accepted, Jack. It's enough. Better swear off the whisky if you can't trust your tongue. Come and take pot-luck with us tomorrow. Good-night."

And Jack was left alone, vainly trying to say thank you, with the tears starting to his eyes.

Next day, he met a major who had been in the card game, a jolly, bluff, coarse, sensible major.

"Well, Mr. Whetstone, you're alive."

Jack remained serious.

"Ever seen Captain Monk let go when he's mad?"

Jack shook his head.

"You got off cheap. Well . . . well . . . poor fellow . . . she's got him in her pocket. In her pocket, sir. Godo'mitey! Why . . . why . . . she'll have him down to Star Plug before she's through. They think she's through. Godo'mitey!"

Rolling blood-shot eyes, the major went on without waiting for any response.

But Jack would have made none.

The Monk family with Whetstone, their invited guest, were seated at dinner, James at one end of his table, Verbena opposite. On one side of her strapped in his high chair, with his napkin under his chin, was little Albert who had come at Fort Hall; on her other side, little George strapped in another high chair with his napkin under his chin. George had come at Laredo. Nellie had come at Assinaboine, Charlie at Wingate, Gertrude at the Presidio. Nellie and Gertrude sat along in the middle opposite each other; Jack, the guest, next Gertrude, but on each side their father the chairs of Charlie and James Junior were still vacant although the soup had been served.

"Give them another call," said Captain Monk; and while Gertrude ran out to the back door, where her voice could be heard calling in the direction of one of the post wood-sheds, the rest of the family went on with the soup.

"I can see them just as well as ever," declared Gertrude, coming back, "but they won't move."

Verbena now undertook the job, and for her they moved at once, reluctantly filling the chairs on each side of their father.

"Don't you like your soup?" he inquired.

"I hate it," said Charlie.

"Oh, Charles," his mother said, "when there's many a starving boy in Caesar Borgia would be thankful for that nice hot soup!"

"Don't make 'em eat it, dear," remonstrated James. "They shall have two helps of beef to make up. What made you so late, boys?"

"Oh, nothing," said Charlie.

"We were just playing," James Junior lucidly amplified. He had lately gone into long trousers.

Jack Whetstone was silent. He knew. He had seen them as he came to pot-luck. But he was their friend and hoped for the best.

"If you expect to grow up and catch Indians," said their father, "you'll have to step livelier."

"There will be no more Indians, then, Captain," said Verbena, smiling. "Eat your beef, Charlie."

Charlie in obedience lifted a fork very slowly toward his mouth. Half-way there it faltered, and then abruptly crashed down upon his plate.

"Charlie!" cried his mother. "What's the matter? James, do look at him!"

James was already looking, but before he could speak a horrible strange sound from his first born on the other side diverted his eye. James Junior sat with face set and a heaving of his immature frame. Both parents now started up in alarm at the green faces of their young, but in that moment the whole ghastly incident rushed to its culmination. The entrance of no hostile Apaches could have more upset what had been so lately a peaceful domestic scene. Plates tobogganed to the floor; Nellie and Gertrude got down and ran screaming from the room; while little Albert and little George, unable to fall from their high chairs because of the straps, sat with their napkins still under their chins, bawling with mouths wide open and eyes tight shut.

Pot-luck was served somewhat later in the kitchen while the dining-room windows were lifted to admit as much air as possible; but only three assembled to finish the meal, and the guest left as soon as was polite.

The limp young smokers lay upstairs in their beds sleeping it off.

Two or three days later the peculiarly excellent aroma of the cigar that Jack Whetstone was smoking caught Major Brewster's attention.

"So he's given you another of those?"

Whetstone nodded.

On still a later day the Major stopped the Lieutenant at the stables.

"How many more has he given you?"

Jack stood silent, smiling, and he blew out a ring of smoke.

"Godo'mitey!" cried the Major, "She's made him part with the lot."

Jack never told what he knew. The pale Verbena's one unguarded word to her James at pot-luck in the kitchen was locked in his loyal breast: "To think of their learning it at their age and in this house!" The words escaped her. "Well, dear, there's no place like home." The gallant James had tried to carry it off. Jack stood proof indeed, even to the probing of the ladies, but guessing had never been easier: Nellie and Gertrude hadn't lost a second.

Ten minutes after the event the whole post had known what Charlie and James Junior had done, and could foretell what the consequences to their father would be. Why hadn't he locked his cigars up? They wondered that Captain Monk "with his experience," as they put it, should consider the cigarets, to which he presently had recourse, as even a forlorn hope. She certainly would never stand cigarets, even his allowance of three a day!

I have forgotten to mention the youngest member of the Monk family, younger than little George, who had come at Laredo; little Christine was coming in June; it was January now. Mrs. Brewster knew it was going to be a girl this time;

somehow she just knew it, she declared. She was to be godmother and she chose the name: Christine. Verbena loved it. James loved whatever Verbena loved.

"Anything that pleases her," he said to Mrs. Brewster. "Christine, Mary Anne, Bridget, Pensacola—anything she wants."

"You're always so perfect!" exclaimed the lady.

"Better get some boys' names ready too. Gustavus, Napoleon—how're they for starters?"

"Oh, Captain Monk, darling Verbena and I are that sure, this time!"

"All right. Boy, girl, anything that pleases Verbena."

"Major," said his wife that evening, "do you know I sometimes wonder if Captain Monk is—not that I've ever heard him say a thing—but I do wonder if he—every now and then——"

"Is tired of it?" completed the Major.

"Oh, Major, I'd never say that!"

"So you want me to say it. What?"

"He's still on his three cigarets," said the lady. "I shouldn't wonder if she kept them shut up safe from the children. Nobody knows what she said to him."

"Has anybody known what she's ever said to him?" cried the Major. "She's never once been caught at it."

June tenth: that was Dr. Stoff's date for Christine. In April one day, the cigarets disappeared.

"Well, I suppose she's happy now at last," said the Major. "It's taken her about fifteen years."

"I can't think," said his wife, "I simply don't see how darling Verbena did it."

"I always told you she would."

"Have you any idea, Mr. Whetstone?" He was paying a call and the lady appealed to him.

"No, indeed, Mrs. Brewster." Jack would never discuss this subject. But before April was over Verbena stunned them all by lifting the veil herself. It may be that she felt secure, that her final victory after her long campaign, so well conducted, so persistent and indomitable, had given her a belief that she could do anything; or her delicate condition may have affected her judgment for the nonce. At any rate, a court-martial at Bowie had brought officers from both Bayard and Grant and these visitors were being entertained one evening by James. He had provided refreshments of various simple sorts for them, and although he had abstained from drinking with them, he had lighted a cigar for the first time since the pot-luck incident because it was the first time since then that any group of strangers had visited the post and sat in his company.

All was going naturally when the door opened

and Verbena appeared. The gentlemen rose and she greeted them most sweetly; a soft pathos in her voice was noticed and admired. She was charmingly clad in white and folds of it fell about her in a way at once appropriate and concealing. Then her glance fell upon James who had no thought of hiding his act. With a lift of her pretty brows she went to him, and taking his cigar from between his fingers in the sweetest and most attractive manner, she spoke caressingly:

"Ah, naughty!"

Then for a brief second she placed the cigar between her own lips and drew one puff. They all said afterwards that she looked bewitching.

"It would harm me less than him."

This was her good-night to them, and she left them with a smile, shaking a playful finger at James.

Before breakfast next day Mrs. Stoff was round to see Mrs. Brewster who was just starting to see her.

"The Doctor waked me up to tell me," Mrs. Stoff began at once.

"The Major waked me up too."

"The Doctor says he didn't turn a hair."

"The Major says not a man in the army could have behaved better. He didn't light another one; he just said that the joke was on him, and they just said that they wished their wives took care of them like that and then they drank her health, and the cards got going, and I guess it was two o'clock when the Major sat on my bed and told me. But I do wish Verbena wouldn't.''

''He turned red though.''

The sight of Jack Whetstone rapidly coming along from his quarters distracted the two ladies. They called out to him with one voice. But he merely lifted his hat and sped onward. Nobody needed to tell him what they were doing, and he ground his teeth.

''Hags!'' he said to himself. ''Buzzards! Damned if ever I marry!''

In this hot, youthful, unjust state he entered the private room of Captain Monk wondering what could be the matter that the Captain's striker had brought him so early a message. The sound of people at breakfast came through the door; and while Jack stood waiting he scowled gloomily at the rack for pipes, so orderly, so interesting, so deserted. Absorbed in his mood, he did not hear the quiet entrance of his superior officer; gave a slight start at being spoken to and turned quickly away from the rack. The Captain appeared not to be aware of the rack.

''Have you heard the news?''

Monk was cool and natural and good natured; but serious too.

"N-no," stuttered Whetstone, with a wild fancy that it must have to do with last night.

"They've got the Butterfield stage again. Over near Wilcox."

"Oh," said the boy, with relief, and there was some surprise in Monk's glance at him.

"A clean sweep," he said with a touch of severity.

"That's bad." The boy took it in now.

"Sit down a minute," said Monk.

The boy sat, his eyes intent on his Captain.

"This has got to stop," pursued Monk slowly, and brooding over it as he went on. "We've been sent here to do it. If we don't do it, what good are we? Nobody escaped this time. Four passengers inside. Must have been just about daylight, as usual. I expect it'll be some of Cochise's band. They should have let the cavalry finish the old fox up that time they caught him and had him sure. But they put him in a Sibley tent and he cut a hole in it . . . Well, that old nanny goat of a Secretary of War is not going to have the chance to hinder me. I'll stop it somehow, or I'll——"

Captain Monk did not say what he would do if he failed, and the young soldier waited.

"Stage was burned to ashes, as usual. They must have shot the horses first. The state of the bodies— but I don't want to make you sick. One woman, too. I want to get a look at the place. You'll go with me. Put on your oldest shirt and things—it's rough country. I'll fix it up with the K. O. E Troop is hunting them now, ordered out from Fort Grant. Fifty men on horseback in broad daylight, riding around and around. So likely to make the Indians come right in and surrender! The nanny goat has telegraphed that all arrests must be peaceful. Indians mustn't have any cause for dissatisfaction. Pity he didn't tell us never to disturb them on Sundays. Well, you scatter now and get ready.'' And the Captain went to the Colonel.

''Work it out yourself,'' said the Colonel. ''We'll call it a roving detail. Report to me when you're ready. Oh, by the way: are you expecting Mrs. Frankish?''

''Not just yet, Colonel.''

''But you are expecting her?''

''About June the first.''

The Colonel smiled slightly at the prospective father. ''Can't you head her off?''

James Monk looked a little surprised.

''I mean,'' said the Colonel, ''the Indians. Of course, if you expect to have them thoroughly discouraged by then——''

''I can't be sure, Colonel. The sooner the better, of course. Nothing would stop my mother-in-law.''

''I see. I see.'' The Colonel's tone was dubious.

James was not quite certain that his commanding officer did see. ''I'd hate to lose her visit,'' he now

said frankly, "as much as she'd hate to lose it herself. She has always been welcome, she always will
be, and it's a pleasure and a comfort to have her."

"I see! I see!" repeated the Colonel, but this
time very heartily. "Allow me to congratulate you.
I have sometimes met men whose feelings for their
wife's mother were—were—er——"

"Yes," said James Monk succinctly.

"But," the Colonel hurried on, "about her journey across the San Simon and up into these hills.
I don't like that. Let me know in time and I'll send
the ambulance with an escort to meet her in Lordsburg—that is, unless you've got the Indians discouraged by then. Now, Captain Monk, I count on
you. You understand the fix we're in just as well
as I do. Some mean skunk who calls himself a hardy
settler and a great-souled pioneer plays the Indian
some stinking trick. Next, the justly outraged Indian, like the simple savage that he is, scalps, mu-
tilates, and otherwise annoys, not only the great-
souled pioneer with his wife, his maid, his ox, his
ass, and everything that is his, but also any other
white people he can catch. That puts him in wrong.

"Then the surviving population of the territory
clamor for justice and military protection. Then we
try to give it to 'em. Then all the women in Boston
with their sisters the clergymen denounce our brutalized American army. Then the Secretary of War

runs to the President, and the President, mindful
of a second term, tells the Secretary to allow none
but peaceful arrests. Then the Indians do it some
more. And then the surviving population denounces
the pampered inefficiency of our American army.
So we get it in the neck on both sides—east and west
—and there you are.''

Some hours after this conversation two objects
which were neither vegetable nor mineral, though
quiet as the earth, sat behind a gray rock. Cactus
was to the right of them, cactus to the left of them,
and sand was beneath them. The Chiricahua Mountains blazed bleakly around and above them, and
the flat blaze of the San Simon valley, which was
ten miles away and didn't look two, sent up its heat
to the sky whence the heat had come. If you were
unused to the sight, you might have taken the two
objects for Indians, and you would have been
wrong: anybody living in that country would have
known them for white men, and with field-glasses
might have discerned the yellow stripes on one pair
of visible legs. These belonged to James Monk; Jack
Whetstone sat beside him and the shirts and faces
of both were brown with dust. A large rip slanted
across Jack's trousers where a cactus had laid them
open; for it was a rough country, and they had
climbed about in it, up and down.

Monk once more lifted his glasses to his eyes, and for a long while studied various distant places through them. Then he handed them to Whetstone and spoke.

"Get to know it well," he said. "Learn it by heart."

In a little while Whetstone said, "I think I've got it all now."

"Look at it again, and follow me. The road comes from Stein's Pass over there across the valley and up into this draw. That's the stage road. The railroad is surveyed round the north end of these hills."

"I can see the road away across the valley."

"Right. Now when the draw narrows, you see that turn among the rocks. That's the kind of place they would choose. They'd lie fifty yards back, each side. Now go back further—back to the big cactus. There's big cactus back a hundred yards each side. See? That's about where we'd take our position."

"I see," said Whetstone.

"The stage would get to that narrow turn, and shots would drop the horses. Then the Indians would show, and then—well, we'd get into the game then."

"You mean, we'd spring up above and have 'em surrounded?"

"That's the idea. Trouble is, this isn't the only good place through here for an ambush. We've got to study several others."

"How can we know which one they'll choose?"

"That's going to bother me. There's a sergeant I could borrow from B Troop who has his ways of finding things out in this country, but he's sick in the hospital with rheumatism. Come along. We've a lot of work to do yet."

The dusty figures rose, and climbed back to where they had their horses tied. On the way little quail ran and then clustered among the thin weeds.

"Shoot!" said Monk. "It's a good chance," and he got his shotgun from the saddle.

They went to it and bagged enough for their purpose; the birds were not wild.

"Look out!" Monk suddenly warned; and near a bird he was stooping to pick up Jack saw a rattlesnake which he killed at once.

He dangled it. "Small one."

"Yes. Wouldn't be able to pierce your boot; but nasty in your finger or your face."

"How nasty?"

"Couldn't say. Wouldn't care to find out by experiment. Don't bother to keep that rattle, you'll find plenty of bigger ones."

"I thought your kids might like it."

"I guess they will, thank you. Now come along.

And tie the quail very conspicuously. And put up your shotgun and keep your rifle ready."

More dusty still, they returned in the afternoon, as to their lives safe and sound, but in Jack's trousers the rent had developed to such an extent that he thought he had better get off at the stable and slink to his quarters by a back way.

"No such thing," said Monk.

"But, Captain! Look!"

"Let 'em see it. With the birds it makes a first rate blind— Why, Toney, good day to you!" This was addressed to a dark slim girl riding a gray donkey down a trail into the post. A red fillet bound her black Indian hair.

Toney sat on her burro and showed her beautiful teeth. She smiled kindly on the officers. She was driving another burro whose load of wood was quite as big as the patient little gray donkey.

"You lucky day," said she. "You kill heap quail."

"You got heap wood, Toney. Who you sell him?"

"Sell him Missis Colonel. Yas, you got heap quail."

"Hope more tomorrow."

"You more tomorrow? No get tired quail! Very good, very nice eat, yas."

Once again Toney smiled sweetly on the two, and proceeded toward the house of the commanding officer with what might have been mistaken for a walking wood-pile.

Monk's eye followed her, and he laughed. "Well, if she guesses what we're at, our white ladies won't and that's more important."

"Toney wouldn't tell?"

"Not she."

"But she's a full-blooded Apache."

"She's had white friends and she's the white man's friend. Her father's a scout and she's been to Carlisle. But she has learned English by the best method known and she can speak it much better than you heard her—when she chooses."

The quail were bestowed where they would do the most good; congratulations followed and good wishes for the morrow. No blind could have been more successful with the white ladies who in the next two or three days were already beginning again to think about Verbena and James. James, meanwhile, rode daily into the desert. He studied the rocks, crawled into the nooks, riveted each detail in his brain. He jotted notes where he sat or stood, he shot quail for the benefit of all observers. Sometimes he went an hour without a word to the devoted Jack, proud and dusty and mute beside him. On these excursions Jack grew slowly into knowledge of his Captain, until one day their final step of intimacy was taken at a jump.

"Now here's the first thing," began James Monk.

Again the two were sitting down among the stones above the road in the unchanging blaze of the Arizona noon. The twin knobbed hilltops so melodiously named Dos Cabezas in that Spain-haunted southern land rose to their left, and still further to their left, westward, the pass opened out upon the gaping waste of the Sulphur Springs valley.

"Can it get hotter than this?" asked Whetstone.

"Wait till you feel July. This is only May ninth. Now first, before we go over the whole performance point by point, let's stage it. Scene, Chiricahua Mountains, somewhere in Apache Pass. Time, probably just before or soon after sunrise. It'll not be so hot, Jack. It's the only cool hour in the twenty-four. The patrol of the road we're keeping now will have been withdrawn two days before—time for the Indians to get wind of it and plan another shy at the Butterfield stage—if they'll only be so accommodating as to do it. And I sort of think they will. We can't time 'em to the minute, and if I can help it I'll not trust to our getting to the spot in one march. The day the patrol's withdrawn, you and I will be ready at any news to leave the post with our detail. We'll travel by night and hide in the scrub trees on the top by day, well off any trail. They'll come by one of their trails, or they'll come by the road from Dragoon Summit. We've got all trails marked on our maps. Enter the stage, bound for Tucson and dressed for the part. Enter Indians. Enter soldiers of pampered and brutalized U. S. cavalry. Alarms and excursions. See?'' Monk, absorbed over his scheme, looked at the mountains.

''But you never say where you think it's going to happen,'' said Whetstone.

''Well, that's merely because I prefer knowing to guessing. If that sergeant hadn't rheumatism— but he has. It's the Indians who will choose the place, and I've got to find out their choice. And that's where I plan you're to come in.''

Jack stared.

Monk's meditative eyes still contemplated the general distance. ''What's your opinion of Toney?''

Jack stared more. ''Toney? Who sells the wood?''

''You can't have helped noticing her, surely?''

''I've seen her coming and going with those burros. What d'you mean, noticing?''

The Captain turned astonished eyes on his Lieutenant. ''She's exceptionally attractive.''

The Lieutenant's eyes ventured to twinkle at his Captain. ''Of course I noticed that she smiled at you.''

Monk remained serious. ''I'm a married man.''

"Would a full-blooded Apache appreciate that?"

"You're not twenty-five yet. She'd appreciate that more. Suppose her smile had been really for you?"

Bewilderment grew in the Lieutenant's face, and he was silent, waiting.

"They're women, Jack, they're women. She's a girl, you're a man, and you're both human. Follow that smile up."

"I——" Jack began and stopped, leaving his mouth open.

"You think I've dragged in topic number one. But it belongs here. I think you can find out through Toney. Her eyes, her hair—take a look at her next time! She has helped two civilians. One of 'em's DeLong over at the store at Dos Cabezas. She has been useful to him—very useful. Saved his life twice. Warned him of raids."

"Toney hears things?" Jack asked precipitately.

"Toney hears anything she goes after."

"But, Captain! I——"

"She's not white, I know. What of it? When I was your age—but look at her." Monk paused, not satisfied with his Lieutenant's expression. "I'm talking seriously, Jack. Follow it up. It's our best chance. I must know for sure, if I can. These horrible murders have got to stop. Consider it your duty to follow it up."

"'Captain''—a flush mantled up to the rim of Jack's hair—''I think I'll have to—I guess I don't mind telling you—I know you'll never mention it——''

It was now the Captain who stared at his Lieutenant. And as he stared, a confessing smile flickered upon the face of that youth.

"Do you mean to say," began Monk, "do you ——'' He rose up straight—''You little rascal! Oh, you damned little rascal!''

Jack, reassured, brought it out with a voice that trembled on the edge of mirth. "Captain, I'd followed up that smile before we ever started our reconnaissances.''

"You *had?*''

"Quite a while.''

"And I sat here," mused the Captain, "never thought of your Mexican experiences—I'm an idiot —I sat arguing and persuading——'' his words failed, and his emotions abruptly expressed themselves in a long and accurately aimed squirt of tobacco juice.

At that dumfounding sight, Jack's respect and restraint still held against the cloudburst of discovery that frothed in him. Words disjointed went rocking through his thoughts, while his Captain stood closely looking at him. Pipe . . . renounced . . . cigars . . . were they . . . but then cigarets

. . . and now . . . but, no, it couldn't be . . . that beautiful aim . . . an old hand . . . oh, my lord. . . . And the boy, silent but limp, fell backwards and cried "Ouch!" loudly as he touched the hillside.

Monk sprang to him. "Snake?"

Jack sat up ruefully. "Cactus." And then respect and restraint struggled faintly again. His Captain had them all fooled—Verbena, everybody. To think of Verbena filled the boy with savage delight. While James Monk was carefully picking the porcupine lances of the cactus out of his back, respect dissolved in confiding affection.

"Captain, you've stunned me."

"I guess I've about got 'em all out of your shirt," said Monk. "Take it off and let's have a look at your back."

Whetstone removed the garment.

"Here are some more," Monk said. "Mustn't give 'em a chance to work under the skin. Bad. Well, young fellow, the stunning is mutual."

"Captain, if you want to know about Toney, I'll tell you."

"I don't want to know. That's a fellow's own business."

"I think I'd like to tell you."

"That's all right then. Go ahead."

Jack finished when the last cactus spine had been

extracted and he was putting on his shirt. "So you see, Captain, the foundation for your plan is laid."

"You've been very close. Keep so. Don't let the ladies begin to regret you're not any steadier than you were at El Paso."

"Oh, I've learned my lesson."

Monk, without concealment, brought his tobacco out and cut a fresh piece from it.

Jack whipped out a cigar and held it to him.

Monk shook his head.

"It's one of your own, you know," said Jack. "Won't you?"

"I prefer this, thank you." And the two got on their horses.

"Captain, when did you start?"

"Start chewing, you mean? Oh, back home. I started everything pretty early. But nothing ever got me. Since then I've always chewed; right along."

Still dumfounded Jack rode by his side, whispering, "To think of it, to think of it, to think of it."

Captain Monk stared at Arizona.

"It's a nasty habit," he resumed thoughtfully as they rode along the hill. "So when I took to courting, I took up my smoking again, like a gentleman. That is, I meant to."

"I see," said Jack in a low voice, and not looking at him.

"But when I've been on serious duty," pursued his Captain, "I've always found myself going back to my little old plug. You can learn to chew—invisibly—in the house, and so you get to doing it out-of-doors as well. Sometimes in a tough Indian situation I've found myself chewing a lot. It's a comfort. It helps. A woman is not likely to understand a thing like that."

"No," said Jack in a voice still lower.

And then they rode on silently, while Arizona slowly softened, and violent shadows began to stretch eastward; and so they returned to the post; and when young Jack went to bed that night, he would cheerfully have died for his Captain.

May was not quite over when the Colonel sent his compliments one evening to Captain Monk, and would the Captain be so obliging as to call on a little matter of business about sending an ambulance to Lordsburg? The Captain went over.

"Have a cigar?" began the thoughtless Colonel. "Oh, I forgot. Well, well, yes. Here we are, and June's coming."

"Three days more," said Monk.

"Hot," said the Colonel. "Awful hot. Well. Now, then. Your mother-in-law."

"She wants to come early the first week, Colonel."

"And you didn't wish to head her off. And our

friends the Indians haven't been discouraged yet.''

''I think it had better wait till after Mrs. Frankish has arrived. She's with friends at Bayard.''

''Tell me your point.''

''Just this, Colonel. I think that the longer we patrol the road, the quicker the action we're likely to get.''

''You may overdo that. What if they tire of hovering about here and go off somewhere else to pillage where they're less watched?''

''I'll risk it, Colonel. What I'm counting on is their impatience. They've acquired the habit of considering the Butterfield stage their particular prey. Keep 'em away from it, keep 'em waiting till they're worked up over it, and then withdraw your patrol. They'll be more in the mood to think you feel safe than that you're up to something.''

''You've completed your study of the country?''

''The day after I made my last report to you. Those Indians will sneak in from the south—or else from Dragoon Summit. They may feel bold.''

''Well, Captain, I'd not care to be one of the passengers in that stage.''

''That's all fixed, Colonel. Warning's to reach them, and they'll have the choice of waiting over at Lordsburg, or coming on and taking the risk.''

''And how is the stage driver going to like it?''

"Very much better than usual, Colonel. Jake Varris will be the man. When I put it up to him, he said that if they didn't get him first he'd be ready to get some of them."

"Look here. Why not make your passengers wait over at Lordsburg and fill the stage with soldiers?"

"I'd thought of it, Colonel. I'm afraid of it. Hard to manage quietly enough."

"You seem fairly confident of the place they'll choose."

"Whetstone and I have felt that way more and more as we have studied the situation."

"How is that boy turning out?"

"He's going to make a first-class cavalry officer."

"There was talk of some foolishness—across the bridge—Juarez—that sort of thing. So he's steady now?"

"I'll be more than satisfied if my own boys grow up like him."

"Well, well, that's good! Let me know when to send the ambulance for Mrs. Frankish."

"Why, Colonel, that's very kind, but the road will still be patroled."

"Send it all the same, Captain. Your wife will feel more comfortable. We must save her every strain we can just now."

"Thank you, Colonel, she will appreciate that as much as I do."

So, Mrs. Frankish, thoroughly protected from the enemy, rattled into Fort Bowie on the third afternoon of the new month, and Verbena was saved all strain. Her mother brought the latest news from Caesar Borgia and the army gossip fresh from Bayard. She was made welcome by the ladies of the post; they congratulated her upon the health, the beauty, and the number of her grandchildren.

"Yes, I'm well trained!" she declared. "Why, I've learned how to spoil the children without Verbena catching me at it! But it has been an ideal union from the first, and I've always said so. James simply adores her, and I've yet to see a happier wife."

"Or a happier husband," said Mrs. Brewster.

"Doesn't he look young!" exclaimed his mother-in-law with bright quickness. "You'd never in the world take him for forty. Well, that's what love does! We all think Christine is just the sweetest name."

And then, one day Mrs. Frankish ceased her excursions and sat indoors with her daughter; Dr. Stoff had thought it would be prudent for Verbena to keep rather quiet. There was whispering in the post that afternoon. Captain Monk and Lieutenant Whetstone had gone after quail again. Such a good influence for Mr. Whetstone! So fortunate! He was now known to be a strictly well behaved young man; what a pity nobody had a daughter old enough for him! Marriage was just what he needed, and he would make such a good husband! His hair grew so nicely over his ears, and had you ever noticed his eyelashes? Would it do to ask Mrs. Frankish or Verbena if they really were shooting quail? Or could it be something about the stage? Had the patrol really been drawn from the road? Perhaps it was going to be put back.

The Colonel had seemed quite surprised at the suggestion that there was more in the quail shooting than appeared. In fact, he didn't believe it. Captain Monk had been busy making maps of the region, and was often away from morning till night with Lieutenant Whetstone. Why was this particular day chosen to make comments on their absence? No one had an answer for that, and yet none seemed quite satisfied. Mrs. Brewster couldn't bear it alone for another minute. She went to see Mrs. Stoff.

"The Major is out," said she. "And he wouldn't say any more than the Colonel."

"Then you feel just the same as I do!" exclaimed Mrs. Stoff.

The ladies sat a moment in silence, with rumor restless in their brains.

Then Mrs. Brewster rose. "I intend to ask Verbena. She must know if there's anything."

Mrs. Stoff rose also. "I'll go with you."

"Would you, dear? Just in these days? You see, I've always been so particularly close to her."

"It's no more than my duty," said Mrs. Stoff, "after the message she sent me this morning by Dr. Stoff, hoping her friends wouldn't forget her, now she had to keep so quiet."

"Oh, well, you know best," said Mrs. Brewster; and they acted upon it at once, and were soon sitting solicitously with Verbena, to show her that she was not being forgotten.

Presently Mrs. Brewster came right out with it. "I thought I saw the Captain and Mr. Whetstone."

"So early!" said Mrs. Frankish in surprise. "Why it's only four o'clock."

"Perhaps it wasn't, but I thought that the Captain would be here. It must be half an hour ago."

"It couldn't have been," said Verbena, "or he surely would have been in to see me. He has been getting home about seven, and I tell him not to hurry or worry."

"Do you suppose they will put back the soldiers to guard the road?" asked Mrs. Stoff.

Mrs. Frankish appealed to Verbena. "Has James said anything about it to you?"

"Not since he told me the patrol was to be withdrawn," Verbena answered. "Why should they put them back?"

"Well, that's it. Nobody seems to know."

Verbena shook her head. "James would have told me."

"But perhaps it's a military secret," said her mother, cheerfully.

Verbena shook her head again. "He would have told me."

"Well, dearie, your father didn't always tell me everything. And I didn't expect him to."

"James is different, mother."

"So you have always assumed!" said Mrs. Frankish, still more cheerfully. "But I've yet to discover it."

Verbena colored. "It is not," she said, "that I ever interfere with James, or that I ever would. I do not have to expect him to tell me his plans; he simply does."

"Well, we mustn't stay too long," said Mrs. Brewster, getting up.

"Yes, we mustn't tire you," added Mrs. Stoff, following her example.

They were about to go out of the door when it opened violently and through it burst Nellie and Gertrude. In the hands of each was something creased and bright which they held up to the company. It appeared to be tin foil. On their heels followed Charlie and James Junior.

"We know what it is!" screamed the little girls out of breath.

"Shut up. You shut up!" said James Junior, grabbing the tin foil out of Nellie's hand.

But Gertrude waved hers beyond her brother's reach. "It goes round tobacco!" she shrieked.

"Chew tobacco," shrieked Nellie.

"Shut up, shut up!" repeated James Junior.

"The kind they sell at the canteen!" added Gertrude, still at the top of her lungs.

"And it's daddy's!" asserted Nellie in a deafening voice.

Verbena had gone very white.

"Give it to me," she said.

It was thrust at her with excitement.

"Isn't it daddy's?" persisted Nellie.

"Where did you get it?" asked Verbena of James Junior; but the boy stood sullen and silent.

"We got it in the shed where father oils his guns. And you know we did!" said Gertrude; and she glared at her brother triumphantly.

"And we said it was daddy's and they said it wasn't," said Nellie. "You know you did," she added harshly to Charlie. "And you tried to take it from us. Mother, isn't it daddy's?"

Verbena sat quite still holding the tin foil more and more tightly.

"Run along, children," said Mrs. Frankish, "mother's tired."

"Well, we'll just go along now," said Mrs. Brewster.

"And we'll be in to see you tomorrow," said Mrs. Stoff. "Good-by."

"Good-by," said Mrs. Frankish. "Do come in tomorrow."

The children went out of the door, Nellie and Gertrude dancing in front, happy in having proved themselves perfectly right about everything, Charlie and James Junior dumb with rage at their sisters, all the more because it had begun to dawn upon their male minds that they had somehow mismanaged in a crisis: they should not have contradicted the girls. As for Mrs. Stoff and Mrs. Brewster, these visitors had brought away from the Monk household, information of a sort so far superior to their expectations that they utterly forgot all about patrols and Captain Monk and Lieutenant Whetstone who were at that very moment proceeding cautiously together through the dry, stunted, thorny woods high up in the Chiricahua mountains while the pale Verbena sat with her mother.

"Did you know about this?" she presently asked.

"Gracious, no!" said Mrs. Frankish.

"Did you ever suspect?"

"Verbena, have you taken leave of your senses? I'm just as surprised as you are. Only, I don't wonder he had to do something."

"Do you think the boys knew?"

"Of course, they didn't, not beforehand. You're getting worse and worse, Verbena. Of course decent boys would want to shield their father."

"He has deceived me," said Verbena.

"That doesn't surprise me at all," observed her mother.

"He has never deceived me before."

"Well, dearie, that's no fault of yours, I must say. There've been times when I've hoped he would."

Not very much later, Dr. Stoff was summoned in haste. Evidently Verbena's experiences of the afternoon had accelerated the advent of little Christine who appeared before midnight in the shape of two bouncing boys.

With thoughts far other than those of paternity, and in happy ignorance of tin foil and that his domestic strategy after all these years had slipped a cog, James Monk moved stealthily beneath the night-watching stars. He was intent upon the military strategy which had rendered his absorbed mind so incautious in that shed where he oiled his guns.

Close beside him among the trees rode Jack Whetstone, and their men were near at hand. Their men had joined them after dark at a place appointed, having left the post ostensibly bound for Stein's Pass. Perhaps so much care was not needed, but it was taken by Captain Monk. They were still several hours' march from where they were going, and yet they seldom spoke; when they did, it was with voices lowered by the suspense of their errand. While yet in the screen of the woods, the Captain stopped and dismounted. Thence to the goal they must be infantry, and from here the horses were led back to wait in the heart of the forest.

"Your guess as to the place was right all along," said Jack, "once you were willing to make it."

"I wasn't willing to rely on it, though."

"What would you have done if Toney had named some other point?"

"Don't ask questions I can't answer."

"Then here's one you can if you will. Did the Colonel say anything about arrests?"

"He employed the customary formula."

"What? None but peaceful?" Jack swore a muffled oath.

"There'll be no arrests."

"That's pretty nervy of you."

"Well, not so very. I thought the Colonel winked. I know I did."

The plateau where the trees grew thick began to fall away, and the growth became more sparse. With this change, their voices dropped still lower when they spoke at all, although much ground was yet to be covered, and they had more than enough night left in which to cover it. The gap of the pass could be discerned below them, and beyond it the unfeatured dimness where the valley lay. The light from the clear stars disclosed no small objects; but in it the large lines of the mountains loomed in differing depths of shadow, and from their slanted slides rose now and then the shape of an outstanding cactus or of some lone rock. Arizona's towering space was cool and mute. The quiet feet of the men as they descended once or twice dislodged some pebble that rolled for a moment with a tiny sound.

After an hour more of silent, supple climbing downward and along over the half-seen hill, some of them halted. Their Captain's cautiously pointed hand showed them where they were to lie in hiding here. They disappeared, stooping and crawling in silence. Those that lay near together could smell each other's sweat.

With Captain Monk the rest moved out of their hearing further downward, crossed the stage road quickly, climbed up and back among the rocks and mounds for a while, dispersed and lay low, hidden from those opposite and from themselves. Their grip was on their guns; they were to wait for one word from their Captain. He kept his Lieutenant with him in a bare space which they had often marked for their own. Cactus grew thick around this little clear spot of ground and small stones and thin weeds covered it. By looking between two bristling clumps of Yucca, you got in daylight a slit of view out of the gap and over the flat to Dragoon Summit; but you must not lift your head as much as six inches and your body must lie close against the earth. The sweat dried in the backs of the wet shirts, the damp chests and bellies of the men began to grow cold.

"This waiting is the longest part," whispered Jack.

He saw Monk's head nod. He saw, above Stein's Pass, a change come in the sky; but he was not sure of this, and he watched it until he had no doubt. Another hue was flowing in among the stars. It flowed, filling and spreading, and he watched it so hard that his whole thought was there. A color was coming into it, something not yet pink; and underneath this the shadowed world was all at once deep purple. Liquid depths submerged in darkness rose from it point after point amid the changing tides of light, purple, and purple again, and again purple with pools of blue beginning, and next some wide shadows of saffron and amber, and suddenly he noticed that all the stars were gone and a great lake of rose had flooded the east.

And then his Captain's elbow touched him lightly, but it was like a stroke of ice or fire. Monk's head was turned from him looking between the Yucca clumps. Jack looked. He could see nothing. Tight-strung with suspense, he lay and listened and looked, and he could feel the light of day stretch across and begin to reach down into deep holes in the pass till they filled up with it and all the stones and plants were to be seen. Everything was to be seen, gray and clear; and far across space to the west, Dragoon Summit was purple, with a line of gold shining along it.

Did he see something move, down there fifty yards, had something sunk down between those two rocks? He dared not ask; he hoped that his body would not take to trembling. He held out one hand to see. He tested each spread finger watching for any quiver in it. Each one was steady; a smile crossed his face, and he turned one dedicating look at his Captain. His Captain must succeed; and he —well, he'd be glad to die for it.

Again his eyes strained to catch sight of some-thing in the open, down below. Only rocks were there, and the spear clumps of cactus and the huge space and silence of Arizona. Was it possible that they had come while he was thinking about the dawn? At grips with his excitement, he sank his forehead against the stones and closed his eyes. A second touch like a feather gave him no second electric start of surprise; one finger of the Captain was pointing.

There they came, as noiseless as a cloud of mist, but clear cut in the dry stillness. He thought of pyramids and of Egypt, which he had never seen save in pictures, of desert and Arabs and ancient strange figures carved on slabs of ruin. Was this actual? Was he here looking at living shapes, dark, painted, slim, that he could almost hit with a stone, and that were going to leap upon dead white bodies unless he killed them first?

All this while, he was rapidly counting them. He could not finish because now they were moving among themselves; like a cloud of mist they were gone, floating down among the rocks and growth a little way up the hill, each side of the road; and here was he close above them, still stretched along the ground, still waiting.

The Captain had to succeed. Jack found that he had been carefully examining his gun when he was almost sure he heard something. He looked quickly across to the opposite hill; not a sign of anything was visible there; and yet, these rocks and cactus were full of men with their hands on their guns.

Memories and thoughts swept through him. How could this place look so natural? Could he have made Toney feel like telling him, if he had only begun after that talk with the Captain? Yes, he could. Toney surpassed any of his experiences so far. What would the next one be? Where? Experiences waited in the world everywhere for such a man as he knew himself to be. Or else—to die here, quick and sharp, helping the Captain win. That would be all right.

Was that the noise again? Not imagination? No, there it was. He had really heard it. Nearer now. On the road. Coming. Pretty slow. A clank; another; a creak. The stage. Absolutely. Anybody inside? Or had they stayed at Lordsburg? It was coming very slowly. Up that grade just there. Was he close enough down on the ground? He tried to flatten himself more, but it wasn't to be done. It had got up the grade. That was the crack of a whip. It was coming down now. Faster. That was a wheel knocking a rock.

He looked at the Captain, and once again ice and fire shot through the whole length of his body; moving toward the Captain was a snake. Sliding slowly out of the cactus into the warming sun, ten feet away, a rattlesnake was headed toward the Captain's face, and the Captain didn't see it. What would it do if it got to him? It must be turned.

Turned now, at once, or killed. But the Indians would hear you. You mustn't move, you mustn't speak. That would spring the trap too soon. That would ruin all, and the Captain must win. Jack seized a little stone. No. Not that. Desperately, he touched James Monk who turned a fierce, heavy frown upon him, but seeing his glare, looked.

Instantly the Captain picked up a pebble like a boy's marble and like a boy's marble flicked it sharp and true. It hit the snake which coiled in a flash a foot from James Monk's face; and as it coiled he blew at it out of his mouth a huge wet quid of tobacco!

It struck the rattler's nose straight. Its soft sloppy mass spattered over his eyes and jaws and head; the juice blinded him—it stuck all over his front. Its taste was awfully new to him. It must have been horrible. He forgot to rattle. In disgust, in sheer outrage and amaze, he uncoiled in a dazed manner and slid away somewhere to wipe off the unprecedented insult.

The clank of the stage is close. One shot cracks. The Captain is up. One horse lies on the road, beating his legs.

Again a shot rings, and there's a shout from the Captain, and more shots. Jack finds himself kneeling, his gun cold and hard against his cheek, sighting, firing, and dropping the wild figures that now leap into sight below. He doesn't remember when he began.

More Indians now; more figures leaping to view all over the hill; smoke and shots from the stage, smoke everywhere, the sharp smell of it; shots high and low and echoing din among the rocks; the stretched arms of soldiers, aiming and shooting; the flung puffs from their rifles. How it smells! How thick the smoke is!

Silence. Down on the road, a stage driver, wiping blood from his neck, with the remark, "Just creased me"; passengers getting out and shaking hands with him; cavalry soldiers moving warily on the hillside; a shot occasionally from one of these; prone figures, dark, painted, slim, stretched quiet, faces down, arms flung flat out; faces up, arms twisted; dark bodies curved backward across rocks, full in view; dark bodies fallen half out of sight, half sticking out of cactus clumps; here and there a dark body still moving, crawling in a tilted falling motion for shelter; one last shot, the tilted body drops.

Silence once more after a time; stage road empty, everybody gone, and no arrests at all; merely a condensed funeral, and the Butterfield stage line safe hereafter in Apache Pass, till the completion of the Southern Pacific shall do away with it.

Captain Monk and his Lieutenant rode back together over the hills in the hot morning.

"Tobacco can be useful at a pinch, Captain," said the Lieutenant. He got one nod for answer, and saw gather slowly over Monk's face that dusky red which Dr. Stoff had seen. It held for several miles and faded slowly. Then Jack ventured a word.

"Have one of your own cigars—now?"

"I don't mind if I do—now."

The Captain and his Lieutenant were within a mile of the post; during that last mile nothing was said until just as they dismounted, when the Captain spoke again with a curiously cutting voice.

"Those cigars are yours, Jack. I'm going to send to San Francisco for a fresh lot."

News had preceded them, and the officers and ladies were gathered outside to see their arrival. The sharp eye of James Junior was the first to notice his father as he walked into sight; and the boy burst out loudly:

"Daddy's smoking!"

Major Brewster stared a full half minute.

"Godo'mitey!" said he.

Once Round the Clock

IT was one of those moments in Flanagan
County, near O'Neil City, Texas, when the
peace in the air, the quiet of the wide land and
the drowsy smell of blossoms are stirred together
in the cup of spring. The few high slender clouds
floated like long skeins of crimson drawn slowly
across the vast afternoon, yellow was the filmy mesquite in its bloom, and flower-stars of apricot em-
broidered the thick tapestry of the cactus. But
upon these trivialities of nature the hardy evangel-
ists of democracy could not squander their attention. Some were thinking about their property;
many about that of their neighbors; and several
leading empire builders were already in session at
the Dos Bocas saloon, O'Neil City, Flanagan
County, Texas, with whisky at their elbows, chips
in front of them and cards in their hands. The all-
night game had begun.

Out of town, the light of the sun was leaving the
day as softly and slowly as a mother on tiptoe when
her child is asleep, and the two white-nosed horses
coming along with Professor Salamanca and the
beautiful young Antonito seemed to be snatching

forty winks as they moved sluggishly, with heads hanging low. As to the state of the object at which the Professor now pointed a contemptuous finger, there could be no doubt; it had long passed the forty winks' mark; no one needed to go on tiptoe for that passive shape over by the ranch well. Against the universal stillness and the noiseless puffs of dust from the horses' steps, the Professor's voice grated acutely, though in a low register.

"As usual." And the pointing finger dropped.

Antonito's smile was dubious. "It may be as you think."

"You think not? Well, you have good chances to hear about the *porco's* habits."

Antonito's face betrayed no response to the thrust in these words. "He often also sleeps when he is sober," he explained, in his soft tenor. His mother was known to be Mexican; little else was known about him.

Two silent riders came by. With apprehensive eyes fixed on the Professor, they lifted their hats and passed on. The Professor took no notice of them, and they took none of Antonito.

Antonito was the Professor's assistant. The pair had drawn rein, and stood in contemplation of the thick, somnolent figure. Half down in the comfortable dust and half up against a windlass, it reposed, face tilted, head bare, mouth open, uttering bulky snores. Its stubby fingers spread upon its stomach, its shirt bulged over its belt, its honey-colored hair was as dense as a door-mat, and its name was Fluke Dade. The family came from the State of Georgia.

"He always sleeps with noise," the assistant now added.

"And Maria Sanchez—does she tell you how she enjoys that?"

At this second thrust, the Professor's watchful eye saw flash out in the seraphic countenance of Antonito, and instantly vanish, a glare which would have given the gravest distress to any God-fearing Christian; but no such person was at hand.

Clink! went something somewhere and they turned their heads sharply, but saw nothing, while they kept their hold upon the weapons at their hips. At that time in Flanagan County, Texas, the six-shooter was the seat of life. The snores of Fluke Dade continued to exhale violently in the stillness, and the riders remained alert; many of the surrounding live-oaks were of sufficient girth to screen a human figure, and if a noise boded no harm, why did its cause not step out into the open?

Clink! it came again; and the beautiful Antonito was the first to understand it. He let his reins dangle loose.

"The Yankee doctor is not sleeping," he remarked in his smooth tenor; "he is not one that sleeps." With this return thrust, he watched his chief's face, and saw there with gratification what a God-fearing Christian would have deplored to see. The Professor looked around for the doctor, but could not find him.

"He is down in the new well," pursued Antonito gently. "He digs it to pay Mr. Dade for his lodging." With eyes still watching for the effect of his words, he proceeded. "The Yankee doctor has been very poor, and Mr. Dade likes so very much to repose. So he sleeps, and now the water will soon be reached in his well. It must be nearly finished. The doctor digs no more the earth, you see, he makes ready for the dynamite. Perhaps he will set it off today, who knows? But I do not think he will work with his hands for Mr. Dade any more. Until lately the few who went to him have not been swift to pay their indebtedness. Now it begins to be different." And Antonito paused in his skilful words.

"So that is what the quack is doing in the swine's well!" observed the Professor, upon whose temper the skill had acted.

"In the Yankee's office I have seen his medical diploma. It is from a place called Harvard," murmured the diabolic Antonito. "He received it but two years ago."

"He is a quack. What took you to his door? I tell you he is a quack."

The beautiful boy raised his eyebrows. "It was your letter to him which you bade me carry——" He paused again, and spreading his hands wide with a gesture of respect and candor, completed his thrust. "How otherwise should I have been willing to approach your upstart rival?"

At the word rival, expressions concerning the Harvard diploma and its possessor burst from the lips of Professor Salamanca. These bore little relation to the healing art.

The respectful Antonito could have listened to them a long while without satiety, but a new sound cut them short; a voice behind them said, "Good evening," and again both Professor and assistant promptly made the gesture of self-preservation habitual at moments of uncertainty in Flanagan County. But it was a friend they saw, and they relaxed, and dropped the seat of life back into their holsters.

"Good evening," he repeated. "Ah, Professor, I'm acquainted with no lady as quick on the trigger as you, ma'am; but if I had harbored designs, your gesture would have been posthumous."

It was Colonel Steptoe McDee, formerly of Alabama, who had ridden thus close upon them, unsuspected through the muffling dust and under cover of the plentiful live-oaks. The set of his old neat coat was punctilious.

" 'Pon my honor, Professor," he pursued, "each day you live makes you ten years younger!" And the wiry, delicate little gentleman swept his hat chivalrously down to his boot. He was first in the hearts of all Flanagan County. Cheerfulness bubbled from him, but it did not dwell in his eyes. These had seen better days of which he never spoke.

The Professor sat unmoved by the compliment, although her large face grew red. Stolid she sat, every inch the personage to whom during twenty years Flanagan County had repaired in times of sickness: a healer supreme; deeply versed in the occult; master of nature's mysteries; in whose impressive consulting rooms amid maps of the zodiac, globes of crystal, specimen horoscopes, and other standard medical supplies, hung a stuffed alligator from the ceiling; while upon the walls glittered blue and gold testimonials from several monarchs of remote empires in the Orient. These sovereigns declared, over their attested signatures, that by the Professor's art they had been cured of ills with names so formidable that such citizens of Flanagan County as could read, when they came to these words, abandoned any further attempt at perusal of the documents.

There sat Professor Salamanca—wide-faced,

heavy-browed, not chilled at all by her forty-five years, her upper lip darkened with down, and her feelings plainly to be read in her countenance. She could veil her emotions when she chose, but seldom took the trouble to do so. Quite different was the youthful Antonito; he usually allowed nothing that went on behind the flawless mask of his beauty to show through.

The Colonel knew why the Professor's face remained so red, but he cared not at all. Revisited by an old trouble, he had changed his medical adviser; he had recently called in the rival! Of course she knew this. What that went on in the county ever escaped her? She was a power in the county; her stuffed alligator haunted the brains of many who had no objection to committing murder, but still dreaded the dark. She was their dark; absent, she loomed in their thoughts; present, their eyes swerved from her as their hats came off. But the Colonel was their light, their sunshine, and every gray hair of his head was safe from her. A snore from the well inspired his next remark.

"That was an extra loud report, Professor. Notwithstanding his uncomfortable position, our friend sleeps powerfully. Don't you opine Mr. Dade can become unconscious at almost any angle?"

Professor Salamanca said nothing, and the Colonel gamboled on.

"Rest is Mr. Dade's chief activity, I do believe. They tell me that back in Georgia the Dades from father to son have handed rest down as a sacred fam'ly heirloom. And they're an old fam'ly." He expected no response, and continued: "I wonder what our friend dreams about? Have you studied the dreams of the lower animals, Professor? Those of the oyster must be well-nigh as disturbing as Mr. Dade's."

"Let us go, Antonito," said Professor Salamanca.

Something at the well turned all heads in that direction. The chain which hung down into it from the windlass was clanking, and shouts from below had restored Mr. Dade to consciousness.

On discovering the Professor, he muttered an uneasy greeting, and began to turn the windlass busily.

"It is the Yankee now coming up," said Antonito.

"Heavy work," commented Colonel Steptoe McDee, observant of how Mr. Dade's strong muscles were straining. "The doctor evidently is bringing truth with him."

"All quacks are liars," stated Professor Salamanca.

"He is a big young man," explained Antonito. "He weighs much."

The little Colonel did not explain. He never explained.

"He will have lighted the fuse," pursued Antonito. "Will you not wait for the end of the work?" he asked his chief. "It will make a grand noïse."

"I will wait," the chief replied; and while the slow clanking of the chain continued, she addressed Colonel Steptoe McDee. "It is some time since we have met."

The Colonel laid a hand upon his heart. "My loss, Professor."

"You do not look very well. How are your spirits on rising?"

"Better than Adam's before he ate the apple. My little old liver goes as gay as a three-year-old."

The Professor raised her voice. "I can read another story on your skin, Colonel Steptoe McDee. You are threatened with—but let others tell you."

"I hope it's something I can pronounce," said the little man.

"Let the Professor tell you what you're threatened with, Colonel."

They had forgotten the well and the windlass, where the chain had ceased rattling. The rival had been hauled out into upper air, and he stood now at the brink of the hole.

"It would help if the Professor told you," he

repeated. "I can't find a thing the matter with you."

Doc Leonard was stripped to the waist; a wet gleam shone over his skin and his hair was matted.

"Quittin' work already?" inquired Fluke Dade.

The young practitioner rested his eye quietly for a moment upon the man whom he was paying handsomely for his board. "For today," he then responded, and addressed the Colonel with more cordiality. "I've tamped that fuse three solid feet in clay. You'd think I was a professional blaster."

"It's early to quit workin'," insisted Dade.

Doc Leonard looked away from his unlovely host and up at the sky, whence the crimson was fading. "I'm through for today," he repeated.

"Say, you've brung your tools up along with you," said Fluke heavily.

"That won't do them any harm," said the New Englander.

"In Texas we leave tools lay where they're wanted," Fluke grumbled, "and don't make folks haul them up where they're not needed."

The doctor now had his shirt over his head, and spoke through it cheerily. "Throw them in again."

To this Mr. Dade's intellect could muster no retort. He stroked his thick yellow mustache, and it was Antonito who spoke now, in tones of disappointment.

"But the explosion, has it gone off already?"

"That's for the first thing tomorrow," answered Doc Leonard, and he added, "and it's my last work on this ranch." His shirt was buttoned, he threw his coat on and gathered the pickax and other implements.

"Well, I guess I'll eat in town at the Pickwick," said Fluke Dade; and thus took his simple leave of the company.

Since the doctor's appearance Professor Salamanca had neither spoken nor seemed to attend to the words of the others. Disdaining to bestow so much as a glance upon her rival, she had sat upon her horse, withdrawn into her private meditations; and now she rode up to the well and looked into it. The rival stood within six feet of her, but her disregard of his presence was complete.

"Come, Antonito," she commanded; "the fireworks are put off till the morning."

The obedient assistant followed his chief, whose face would have given a God-fearing Christian renewed distress.

Colonel Steptoe McDee and the young New Englander were left alone, and the Colonel made his little joke again.

"Well, Doctor, and so you have postponed finding truth till tomorrow."

Leonard laughed a little. "Truth's apt to be

dry. It's wetness I'm after—and release! And no more bargains with brutes like that!''

His eye followed somberly for a moment the thick figure of Mr. Dade in the distance, bestriding his horse on the road to the Pickwick Hotel, O'Neil City, Flanagan County, Texas.

Colonel Steptoe McDee was thoughtfully watching Professor Salamanca and the beautiful Antonito, as they appeared and disappeared among the live-oaks on their way to the home of the stuffed alligator and the crystal globes.

''There goes an edifying couple,'' remarked the doctor.

The Colonel's nod was emphatic. ''Your term 'couple,' sir, is happily selected, since no ceremony has made them one.''

''I know,'' said Leonard, too scornful to laugh. ''I know. And that half-breed's young enough to be her son.''

''It's his bread and butter, Doctor! He never got that from Miss Maria Sanchez—and in these days she is taking a deep interest in our friend Mr. Dade.''

''Sweet-scented bunch, the lot of them!'' The young man from Cape Cod ruminated a moment. ''Can't old Salamanca make that smooth little lizard marry her?''

''She can make him do anything, sir. But mark

you, if she tied Antonito by the nuptial knot Miss Sanchez would vigorously renew her lovely favors to him. And the law in the United States does not allow any man to make two honest women at once!''

To this pleasantry the Colonel won no response. Disgust left scant room for anything else in Leonard's serious young mind for the moment. He pondered again. ''I have been a medical student,'' he then observed, ''but it seems there are some things left I've got to get used to.''

Colonel Steptoe McDee postponed an impulse to moralize. He kept up the jocularity which he had made his refuge when circumstances had first settled him in Flanagan County, and which was now more incessant than his natural bent.

''The Professor is a wonderful woman, sir,'' he began. ''Widely versatile, yet never misses the point. It may be an infant she has to treat for scroll ear or harelip, it may be a horse with bots, or it may be one of her major operations, like when she seeks information from the stars for some anxious husband who has consulted her as to the paternity of his latest unexpected offspring—she goes to the point right away. And that's what you don't, Doctor. You can learn from Professor Salamanca, sir.''

''Can't you teach me instead, Colonel? I doubt if she is sincerely attached to me.''

"There I fear you are quite correct, sir."

"And how well does she love you?"

"Professor Salamanca's affection for me has, I may say without fear of contradiction, its limits. But I don't have to take any steps about that. What she could teach you is method. It's your method, sir, that's a mistake in this community, if you'll let me be so free."

"Be as free as you like, Colonel."

"Well, sir, when I decided, on your arrival in this country, to change medical advisers and come to you about my little old liver that served me so true in my care-free youth—I experienced two shocks, sir. Your office was just a plain room. A couple of chairs, a table or so, a desk—might have been anybody's room. Might have been a dummy room in a furniture-store window. Just that college diploma on your wall. Not a crocodile in sight. No respect for the feelings of this community, sir. Flanagan County demands crocodiles in a doctor's office, and other proofs in plenty of the practitioner's scientific attainment—and you fail to conform to our standards. Next. Did you take care to see the color of my money before you saw the color of my tongue? No, sir, you did not! I got my pulse felt, and my heart listened to, and a thermometer stuck in my mouth and all sorts of things, without paying you a single cent in advance. The

Professor wouldn't treat her oldest friend like that.''

"Colonel McDee," said the young New Englander, "I wish I could ever be sure when you're joking and when you're not."

"I'm not always sure of that myself—any more. But you're the first Yankee I have ever liked, young man. I know I mean that!"

"Have you met many of us, Colonel?"

"Quite a few, sir, between 'sixty-one and 'sixty-five."

"Oh—I forgot. Well, if you went to Boston now——"

"Boston! I'm a Southerner, sir. My roof-tree was burned while I was fighting."

Leonard preserved a moment's silence before he spoke gently. "I was not born then, Colonel. Colonel, a good supper is waiting at Mr. Dade's, and I'll be alone. Will you keep me company?"

"Why, yes, sir, with pleasure."

And as they went along together toward the ranch, Colonel Steptoe McDee looked up at the sky once more. A serene dusk was there, with the high slender clouds barely visible, and in the deepening gray of the light Texas seemed to be expanding its immensity to the edges of the world. Beneath its influence the two men came in silence to the light of the lamp where the table was ready laid; and after a brief salute to each other over whisky and water they sat down to their repast, which Dade's Mexican quietly served. Moths flew in and their fluttering was the chief sound to be heard. At length the guest made an inquiry.

"When he mentioned the Pickwick Hotel, Doctor, don't you think he meant the Dos Bocas saloon?"

"Colonel, I am grateful to whichever institution is depriving me of Mr. Dade's society."

In response to this, a point of light danced for a moment in the Colonel's tragic eyes.

Leonard filled out his remark. "He has gone there every night this week."

Steptoe McDee sat motionless yet alert like an old family portrait; neat, lean, delicate, dried into his philosophy by changeless mental solitude. Presently he still further filled out Leonard's remark.

"Miss Maria Sanchez—but you'll have met Miss Sanchez?"

"She made my acquaintance and dropped in the same day—the day I came to O'Neil City. I disappointed her expectations."

"Then I perceive that you have thoroughly met the lady—without causing anxiety to either of her gentleman friends!"

The young New Englander flushed. His morals were strict. "No anxiety, Colonel. None to Mr. Dade or Antonito—or anybody anywhere."

For a while the moths fluttered on before the guest spoke.

"Doctor, I notice you don't pack a six-shooter along with you on your goings and comings hereabouts."

"Not one of my habits, Colonel."

"Better acquire it, sir. To travel unheeled in Flanagan County is to be conspicuous."

"I don't know that I object to being conspicuous in so harmless a way."

"To free-born Americans, sir, *any* way is objectionable. This community is cast in Liberty's giant mold."

"Why, Colonel, you're always conspicuously well-dressed yourself!"

Not at all displeased by this personality, the guest waved a hand. "That may be, sir, that may be! But I'm an old-timer and you're a newcomer."

This made the young New Englander silent. He thought it over. "Yes. I believe I do feel new pretty often here."

"Don't you ever feel—incautious, Doctor?"

Leonard looked perplexed. "Well, not to speak of."

"Take our recent little party at the well," suggested the Colonel. "You did not go very far out of your way to please Professor Salamanca."

"That's an exertion I'm unlikely to make!" exclaimed the youth hotly. "I didn't notice that you went far in that direction yourself!"

The Colonel's dark little eyes remained steadily thoughtful, fixed on the lamp.

"Well, Doctor," he presently remarked, "I have never classified the varieties of jealousy any more than I have classified the varieties of hornet, but I'd rather stir none of them up. Professor Salamanca is no laughing matter. I can jest with that lady, sir—it's my private joy in an existence where joy is scarce; but she jests with none, let me assure you. I cannot impress upon you too earnestly, sir, that Professor Salamanca is a most remarkable woman."

"Let's smoke out on the porch where it's cool," said Leonard, rising.

As they sat with their chairs tilted back against the wall and their boot heels caught on the rungs, the stars were softly clear and the warm sweet odors of the day still pervaded the night.

"When I came here first," said Leonard musingly, "it used to make me think of home all the time."

"Your home? Massachusetts?" There was surprise in the tones of the Colonel.

"Many typical parts of New England. You see, before they get their leaves, the mesquite might be peach-trees; and the live-oaks sometimes stand like apple-trees in an old orchard. When I rode through them I kept expecting a stone wall and a white church over the next rise. But of course it never was there. Nothing ever was there, except more of the same.''

"More of the same," echoed Steptoe McDee, very quietly.

"So I've got used to that at last," pursued Leonard, after smoking for a while. "But I wonder how long it will be before my education is finished and I am used to everything.''

"A long while, young man; a long, long while.''

"Well, I'll try not to neglect my opportunities.''

"Don't miss a single one, young man!''

"I count your company as one, Colonel. I ventured to tell you so the first day we met at Beehive Bluff.''

"If I can make it so, sir, if I can make it so! You're the first Yank—however, enough of these sentiments. Now when I came to this country I had some prejudices. All are gone but a few pet ones.''

"I'm thick with them," declared Leonard.

"Root them up, sir. Burn them. Scatter their ashes to the free air of Flanagan County.''

Leonard laughed out in the dark. "Won't you let me spare one or two pet ones?''

"Unhealthy policy! Alien to the principles of a liberty-loving community!''

"Well, now, here's one, for instance, you would hardly advise my parting with, Colonel. What do you suppose Professor Salamanca did last week?"

The red of the Colonel's cigar turned sharply toward where the young doctor sat tilted against the wall.

"She sent her Antonito," Leonard pursued, "with a letter to me. In that letter she proposed that she and I should go into partnership. Professional partnership." And again he laughed out in the dark.

But the guest did not laugh. His cigar turned slowly away again.

"From my observations at the well," said he, "I fear that your reply may not have been tactful."

"I tore up the letter and told Antonito that was my answer."

"Good Lord, Doctor!" Steptoe McDee smoked in silence for some time. "A letter may be unimportant," he finally began in a discursive tone. "Ace Brown got one. It gave him ten days' notice to leave the country."

It was Leonard's glowing cigar that now turned toward the speaker as he proceeded.

"Now notices like that had been coming to a number of citizens in Flanagan County. They were citizens who had been considered as eating too much beef without owning any cattle in the country. Some of them failed to give their letters due attention. Well, sir, in eighteen months, thirty-four recipients were buried in consequence. It was clearly not suicide in a single case. So that when Two-bit Stacey received his notice giving him ten days, he made a very sensible remark. 'Ten days!' he said. 'Well, I'll let them have nine days back.' Two-bit always had good judgment and he left that day. He has never revisited this vicinity. I understand he is still enjoying good health somewhere up North.''

"Well, well," said Leonard.

"Now Ace Brown suspected that his notice was not genuine. He decided to stay just as usual. Didn't want to change any plans he had. Of course he took precautions. Wherever he went he packed his six-shooter and a Winchester along with him; rode on high places; avoided thickets; did not go through gates—took fences down instead. Just a panel, you understand. Nippers will do it if you can't lay the posts down. He's here yet. Ace knew it was just somebody's joke. Oh, I got one or two before I had made myself clear to this community. The Professor never got but one. She hadn't been here long, and a fool patient sent it to her, just to have her consult him. She was treating him for dysentery, but she didn't consult him. Nobody in Flanagan County ever believed that he died of dysentery. It was on that occasion,'' the Colonel concluded thoughtfully, "that I informed Professor Salamanca—through the customary channels—that my death—from any apparent cause whatsoever—would be followed by hers inside twenty-four hours, and that no amount of heavenly bodies and dried alligators would help her."

Leonard tossed away the butt of his cigar. Its spark lay visible a moment in the soft dust. Beyond was the dim presence of the live-oaks. He rose abruptly.

"Come inside, Colonel. I'd like your judgment."

The guest followed the host in where the moths were fluttering. His gray head came but little above Leonard's shoulder. Beside his host's brawny, un-wrinkled innocence he was like the weather-beaten sheath of a rapier.

"Your pardon, Doctor," he said, "but since you wish my judgment, never place yourself in a lighted window. That's a habit it costs little to acquire, while failure to acquire it in Flanagan County has cost acquaintances of mine a high price."

"Here, Colonel," said Leonard.

Colonel Steptoe McDee took the paper which his host had produced from an inner pocket. After the glance which sufficed him to take in its purport, his eyes remained upon it while his fingers flattened its creases.

"When did this come, Doctor?"

"It was a week yesterday."

"Then your ten days are nearly up."

"They're nearly up."

"How did it come?"

"It was lying on my office floor."

"Door locked?"

"Oh, yes. Always locked when I'm out. And window fastened."

The guest resumed his flattening of the creases. He turned the paper over and back again, as if in study of it.

"I don't know," said he slowly, "what Ace Brown would do." Then he looked up straight in Leonard's eyes. "Doctor, in my opinion this is genuine." And he handed the paper back to the young man.

"Well?" demanded Leonard with a sudden fierceness. "Well, then?"

Steptoe McDee scratched his head.

"Are you going to advise me to quit?" the youth asked in a lowered voice.

The Colonel's clean-shaven lips seemed about to smile, but they did not.

"Doctor, don't crowd me. This requires a right smart of thinking."

Leonard stood, still holding the paper exactly as he had received it, and still speaking very quietly.

"Because I want no man's judgment when it comes to quitting. Business or no business—and I owe you all I have—I can decide that point for myself." His face was much redder than when he had flushed virginally on the subject of Maria Sanchez.

"What steps have you contemplated taking?" asked the Colonel.

"There's where I wanted your advice—since it's not a joke."

"I wish I could think it was a joke, sir. I imagine you have made no mention of it except to me?"

"None."

The Colonel stretched out a hand. "Will you entrust that paper to me, sir? I think I can take some steps about it."

"I don't want——"

"No, sir. I know you don't. But will you permit me? Unless I am exceptionally mistaken, I am partly the cause of that paper coming to you—and then I can sometimes exert an influence in this community that others might find—— Will you permit me?"

The thread of their discourse was dropped at this point and resumed the next morning. At the sound of a horse galloping, Colonel Steptoe McDee stepped promptly out on the porch—so promptly that he almost pushed Leonard aside as he brushed in front of him.

"Mr. Dade is not at home," he announced in a clear voice as the rider came up. "You will probably find him at the Dos Bocas saloon."

"You've struck it right, first go off, Colonel. I just seen him shot there. It ain't fatal, I'm afraid."

"Oh, it's you, Randy. Glad to see you. Who shot him?"

"Antonito. But Antonito was going to apologize to Fluke just as soon as Fluke came to."

"And he'll come to?"

"I reckon. Bullet just kind o' parted Fluke's hair. Antonito felt he'd been hasty. Antonito said I was to tell you to come right in, Doc."

"Me?" said Leonard. "Haven't they sent for Professor Salamanca?"

"Seems like you've gained a new patient tonight, Doc."

"To be sure," mused Leonard, "she lives two miles beyond me. Well, I'll go, of course." And he hurried away to the corral.

Randy sat on his horse, and spoke mysteriously. "Two miles ain't Antonito's reason, Colonel. It's to spite *her*."

"Isn't a man imprudent to spite his bread and butter, Randy?"

"A man!" exclaimed the other with scorn. "Huh!" He looked over his shoulder, drew close, leaned over and whispered: "Colonel, do you believe she can do all of those things they claim she can do? Them queer things?"

"Randy, I thought you had more sense. If she was as harmless as her stuffed reptiles, Flanagan County could laugh in her face—how did the shooting come up?"

"Well, Colonel, you know when Antonito quit Maria Sanchez for the Professor, Maria she got interested in Fluke. Well, that seemed to worry Antonito some. Made him restless. Shouldn't wonder if Maria took Antonito away from the Professor. Well, tonight at the game Fluke he cashed in early, like he's been doing pretty regular lately, and somebody at the table says, 'Give her my love, Fluke,' and up jumps Antonito, and down goes Fluke. Antonito felt he had kind o' lost his head, so he was waiting to apologize when I come away for the Doc. Well, I guess I'll be getting home, Colonel. Colonel, I'm awfully glad to hear what you say about them reptyles."

The messenger galloped away, and the Colonel stood on the porch alone, mildly whistling a quaint little melody and shaking his head now and then. Presently Leonard passed the porch on his horse.

"You'll excuse my haste," he said.

"Duty calls you, sir. Many a good man has to waste his time on a useless one in this preposterous world."

Doc Leonard's time was wasted. A fast ride into O'Neil City, a very brief visit to the Dos Bocas saloon, and a slow ride back, brought him to his bed and his sleep in the small hours before the first light. Peace and poker had reigned in the Dos Bocas saloon. The card-players turned their heads to see who was entering, and quietly continued their bets. They were henchmen of Professor Salamanca, true believers in the alligator; to them, Leonard with his Harvard diploma and his poorly furnished office, his alien accent, and his Eastern clothes, were objects of suspicious aversion. He stood by the door for a moment, and then inquired for the wounded man.

"I'll have two cards," said a player to the dealer.

Leonard repeated his question.

"Didn't you meet Fluke on the road?" answered a player, without turning his head. "Raise you five."

"And five," said another. "Fluke came to. Came to right after Randy started. Otherwise we should have attended to Antonito."

"Him and Antonito made it up. Balked us," put in a third. "So you didn't meet him on the road?"

"Raise you ten," said the first player. "Fluke will not need any comb for quite a while. Got a big part in his hair. And ten more. But they made it up like gentlemen. Shouldn't wonder if Fluke was paying that visit Antonito delayed some. Call you.''

So Leonard returned to his bed; and after he had blown out the lamp, he spoke some words aloud in the quiet darkness: ''But they made it up like gentlemen. Gosh!''

He awoke feeling his shoulders shaken, and aware of the bright new day. Fluke Dade was standing over him, and he wore his hat.

''You're late,'' said Fluke.

Presently they sat at breakfast, where Mr. Dade still wore his hat and where Leonard still preserved the silence which he had more and more preferred should exist between them, ever since the well-digging had doomed him to so much of Dade's society. His taciturnity disappointed Fluke. Fluke had been sure that the hat would elicit a question, and for this he had ready his answer. This was to be, first, that such things were a man's own business, followed gradually by a condescending indulgence to human curiosity. He had planned to remove the hat, display the part in his hair, and remark: ''That would have killed most men.'' This would have led to everything, the whole tale of the night, with himself the hero in it.

But no opening was given. Leonard drank his coffee and ate his bacon as if there wasn't such a thing as a hat in the room. The hero was deprived of outlet, his recital of glory dammed up in his breast; Antonito's deadly assault, his own large-hearted allowance for a rival's passions, his triumph over the supplanted rival—all choked through Leonard's unnatural conduct; and suddenly it burst forth in words entirely unpremeditated.

"I suppose you think you understand women!"

"To that," said Leonard, after sipping his coffee, "I have never given my consideration."

Fluke sat baffled, feeling the obscure presence of an insult.

"I suppose," he said, "you think you can lick me."

"To that also I have never given my consideration." And finishing his bacon, Leonard rose. It was the last morning of his bondage, and he looked at the seated, sullen Fluke, who reminded him of some mongrel bull. Fluke longed to take off his hat, but he decided that this man was not worthy to see the part in his hair.

"The well's waiting for us," he said.

The happy pair went to the well through the sweet odors and the early light. The crimson had not yet quite left the long, high, slender clouds, which shone with the same hues that yesterday's sunset had given them. The chain rattled in the silence as Leonard slowly descended with his tools; and presently from the bottom the clink of his perfecting strokes ascended into the silence. Zest animated his supple body, again his coat and shirt were off and his skin was glistening. He performed his skilful surgery of the rocks with special pride. He tamped the fuse deeper and firmer than was needed, and was sorry no one would know how neat and pretty a job he had done.

At length the whole crevice was packed smooth and tight. It was waist high; and satisfaction filled him as he leaned back lazily, and looked round upon his completed task like a prisoner who has served his term and is about to leave his cell. He struck a match; and as the long snaky coil of the protruding fuse began to hiss, he gave his signal, and the clanking chain responded, resounding in the hollow depths as it lifted him and his tools upward. What was that? Suddenly he crashed down to the bottom. Had the chain broken? No. He shook it, and looked upward. Had he heard something just before he fell? Waist high, the fuse hissed. To his startled spirit it seemed like something animate, mocking and malign.

He called, and shook the chain, and called louder; but no voice answered and no face looked down. Bewilderment flooded through him. Was this intentional? Could Fluke actually mean——? The sparks of the fuse struck his arm. He shouted wildly and shook the chain with all his force. It hung slack, and he looked at the fuse. It hissed and dwindled in the fierce silence of the narrow prison it shared with him. He took it, pulled, jerked; tilting back, he dragged. It neither broke nor budged. Too few minutes remained to undo the work of his zeal.

His hand dived into his pocket, but his knife was at the house. He seized the pickax and struck at the fuse vainly; its position and the jutting stones foiled him. He snatched his coat and shirt, and wrapped them round the shortened remnant, but the fire merely burned through them. One foot more and it would reach the crevice. With inspiration he jammed the coil between his teeth and ground them savagely; and the burning stump fell into the dust and hissed itself out.

Leonard sat down with his arms across his knees and his head on his arms. He felt such sudden, overwhelming exhaustion that he did not move and took no notice of his thoughts. After a time the sensation of cold stirred him, and he put on his charred clothes and in a sort of trance fingered the protruding shred of the fuse. Then he looked up. There hung the motionless chain, and there was the sky. It was a long way to climb.

"If he did mean it—or if he didn't—why doesn't he investigate?" he said aloud, and he stood leaning against the stones and staring up. At length he sat down. There was no hurry, and resting was delicious, and he was getting warm. He dozed off. He

started awake at the rattling of the chain, and
stared up. A head was showing—the head of Colonel Steptoe McDee.

"Doctor! Doctor! Are you all right?"

"Most decidedly."

"You're not hurt?"

"Not a bit."

"I'll haul you up, sir, if you're in a condition to
come."

"Never was in better shape."

The chain rattled and Leonard was ready in a
flash, tools and all, as if it might go up without him.

"What's the matter with Fluke?" he called.

"Mr. Dade, sir," said the voice, "will never have
anything the matter with him again."

As Leonard very slowly ascended, for the Colonel,
though wiry, was light, he knew well enough what
he should find.

Against the windlass, in a crumpled fashion,
much as yesterday, lay Fluke; but today he was not
snoring. The Colonel's diagnosis was accurate.
Leonard looked up at the Colonel.

"He was stone-cold, sir. You must have been
down there quite a while."

The young New Englander nodded.

"You didn't hear the shot? Well, Doctor, I
thought I did, but I went on clipping my horse
after listening. Then after a while I thought I
heard parties riding over yonder." He pointed

through the live-oaks. "That did start me thinking —and I thought I'd pay you a morning call. I have reached a conclusion, Doctor. Have you formed any theory?"

Leonard shook his head. Utterance came hard.

"You were in the well. And then what?"

"I'd finished. He was hauling me up."

"I see, sir. You had lighted the fuse and the chain was making a noise. Well, sir, that strengthens my conclusion. The party—or parties—had gone, as I say. There are too many who pass here for the dust to reveal much. But yonder live-oaks are very convenient. I believe I have mentioned to you that Professor Salamanca is a remarkable woman?"

Leonard was silent.

"Last night," said the Colonel, "I asked you to permit me to take steps about that paper you found on the floor of your office. I can still take some. It was a near thing."

"Very close, indeed," said Leonard.

"The moment for firing that shot was well planned, sir. But those riders yonder—that was later. I don't see—well, Doctor, let us get him into the house first."

They had to get the Mexican to help them. In time the owner of the ranch was decently laid in his bed.

"Doctor Leonard," said the Colonel, "would you mind making a call on Professor Salamanca in my company?"

"Whatever you advise, Colonel."

They set forth through the live-oaks. About a mile along their way, they saw somebody suspended from a tree. He proved to be Antonito, and upon him a notice was pinned which condemned all persons who apologized and behaved inconsistently.

The Colonel spoke musingly. "So she let her inconstant lover do the killin' of his rival, and then her friends attended to him. *Three* birds with one stone! But she missed the third. By your leave, Doctor, I'll make my call without you."

"Your conclusion, Colonel, is that I am unlikely to succeed in Flanagan County?"

"Doctor, it's not your own health I ask you to consider. The health of any new patients of yours might grow precarious."

"I see, Colonel."

"I wish I could do better for you, Doctor. I wish I could with all my heart. Don't heed the ten days. I am not entirely defeated. Your departure shall be dignified. But this free-born community, sir, would allow no material restraint to be put upon the ideas of a citizen so influential as Professor Salamanca. I wonder who she will find to console her for her sad loss?"

The Right Honorable the Strawberries

AS I look back at his adventure among us, I can count on the fingers of one hand the occasions when his path crossed mine; between whiles, long stretches of it go out of sight—into what windings of darkness not one of the old lot at Drybone has ever known to a certainty. Some of those cow-punchers were with me that first morning when he appeared out of the void. I was new to the country, still a butt for their freaks, still credulous and amazed and curious; and that morning they were showing me the graveyard. Thirty years of frontier history could be read there at a glance, and no green leaf or flower or blade of grass grew in the place.

"May my tomb be near something cheerful!" I exclaimed.

"They don't mind," said Chalkeye.

"Their mothers would," said I.

"Not the kind of mothers most of 'em probably had."

I walked off among the hollows and mounds of

sand, over the sage-brush shorn by the wind. On that lone hill were headboards upright, and rotted headboards fallen on their faces. Drybone, the living town, itself already half skeleton, lay off a little way, down on the river bank. The bright sun was heating the undulated miles, which melted in more undulations to the verge of sight, and the slow warm air was strong with the spice of the sage-brush. The river below flowed soundlessly through the silence of the land.

They rode with me as I walked and paused to copy here and there some epitaph of a soldier when Drybone had been Fort Drybone, or of a civilian of the later day when the fort had been abandoned. Killed, most of them; few women there; one quite recent, buried at the end of a dance, where she had swallowed laudanum—so they were telling me, when they stopped to look off, down the river.

Somebody on a horse.

"Give me your glasses," said Chalkeye.

Everybody took a turn through them, while the object approached.

Chalkeye passed my glasses back to me, remarking, "He'll make you look like an old-timer."

I took my turn, and knew what he was at once.

"He's English," I told them.

He now noticed us, and began to trot.

"Hold him on, somebody!" cried Chalkeye.

"No need," said I. "That's not the first horse he has ridden."

"He's bouncing like you done at first," said Post Hole Jack.

They mentioned derisively his boots, his coat, his breeches, his hat. A shotgun gleamed across his saddle, from which some sage-chickens dangled. He had now turned off the stage road and was coming up the hill. He looked as tired as his horse. He was shaven clean and began to smile as we watched him nearing in silence.

"Made in Eton and Oxford—recently," I decided.

I saw that the sun had burned him unsparingly, that his eyes were blue and merry, his hair a sunny yellow; his smile was confiding and direct, and boyhood shone in his face—but boyhood that already knew its way about in life.

"I beg your pardon," he inquired in the light intonations of Mayfair. "I was looking for a place called Drybone. I was rather expecting to put up there. A place called Drybone."

"You've found it," said Chalkeye.

He turned to the cow-puncher with lifted brows. "I beg your pardon?"

"I said you'd found it," responded Chalkeye. "Drybone's right here."

"Oh, really? Oh, thanks!" He glanced at the

graves inquiringly, and hesitated. "Oh. Really."
He leaned to read the headboard I had been copying.
" 'Sacred to the memory of'—but there's more of
the place than this, I hope?"

"A little more," said Chalkeye.

"Because they told me I could put up there"—
again he glanced at the graves—"and one isn't quite
ready."

"Ready?" repeated Chalkeye.

"To meet one's Maker and all that."

At these words, all in the light intonation of Mayfair, a unified, fascinated silence settled on the cow-
punchers, and out of this spoke one hoarse whisper:

"What'd he say?"

"Because," the Englishman resumed with his
confiding smile, "they do tell one things here. And
the things are frightfully absorbing, but they're not
always wholly accurate. So one can absolutely put
up here without recourse to Abraham's bosom?"

"There's a hotel," I said. "I'm at it. Not ten
minutes off."

At my voice he turned quickly. "Only ten minutes? How very jolly! I say, when did you
arrive?"

The audience grinned; in spite of my sombrero
and spurs and chaps, it was plain to him that I had
arrived lately.

"This summer," I admitted with annoyance.

"But you're not English?"

"I'm from Philadelphia."

"I saw the place. Liberty Bell. I say, I could do with a bath. Five mornings now—by Jove, it's six!—with tin basins that were no better than they should be. And every jolly old towel had been trailed in ignominy. And I'm starving for a dreamless sleep. What do you do about the bugs? Well, thanks so very much."

He took the road, but not alone; escorting him trotted a hypnotized company, hanging speechless on his words.

"These," he said to me, touching the sage-chickens. "They vaguely suggest grouse. Edible? Hallo, there go some more running along!"

He was down, the reins flung over his horse's head, his gun ready.

Two birds rose and fell right and left, and he raced gleefully to pick them up. The cow-punchers looked at each other and again fixed their eyes on him.

"I say!" he cried, swinging into the saddle, "what lots of game! Do you produce dogs? I must manage to have a dog. Are these birds edible?"

"Those young ones," said Chalkeye. "That old one would taste strong. Better draw them now."

"Draw? Now what's that?"

"I'll show you."

"Now is this going to be one of the things they tell you?"

Chalkeye laughed joyously.

"Lying is sweeter than sin to me," he declared, "but Tuesdays I swear off." He slit the birds open and cleaned them.

"Oh, I say!" exclaimed the Englishman. "You do a neat job."

"You'll do it next time," said Chalkeye, visibly flattered. "Your stirrups are too short, but you take your saddle-horn correct. Who learned you about dropping the reins?"

"That? Oh, the consequences of not. They had warned me, but I didn't think. And so there one was."

"Where was one?"

At this note of satire, the youth's eye gave a responsive flicker. "Well, in point of fact, not anywhere at all. There's such a lot of your extraordinary country that's not anywhere at all. And so I walked, and walked, and the horse led one on and on, just out of reach, and the sun was setting, and I felt like such a silly ass. Finally some admirable people appeared above the horizon, and one was tremendously obliged to them. Of course one hasn't mastered your language yet." And the eye flickered again.

"Can you rope?" asked Chalkeye.

"Not yet. Ah, that's quite a game, isn't it!"

"I'll learn you."

"Will you really? Oh, thanks. You'll find I'm a dismal duffer at it. There's been so little chance. Only last week I was in the Pullman. That's a ghastly vehicle. A mere curtain between the world and one's true self. No country but a singularly chaste one—I'm told yours is exorbitantly chaste—would tolerate adjacent dishabille like that among the sexes. They told me Drybone would be a likely spot for seein' a bit of everything. I mean to say, of everything characteristic. I intend to believe faithfully all the things they tell me. It encourages them to tell more—and that is so very apt to be characteristic. Look how the sun has cooked my absurd countenance! I must absolutely procure a hat at once—a sensible hat like yours, I mean. Does Drybone contain hats?"

Chatting along as it came into his head, he was unaware of the town till he was in it, noticed it suddenly, and stopped.

"I say!" And he stared eagerly.

"Is it characteristic enough for you?" I inquired.

He eyed the mangy parade-ground; he took in the silent barracks, the desertion, the desolation, the naked flag pole, the broken windows. New life had adopted many of the old shells. Outlaws of both

sexes were snugly housed here to welcome cus-
tomers. He listened while Chalkeye pointed out the
principal objects of interest—the store, the hotel,
the post- and stage-office, the several dens of the
assorted industries. He listened, and his blue eyes
shone like a child's at a fairy-tale.

"Simply rippin'," he murmured.

From the undulated miles that engirt us, a warm
slow wind brought the fragrance of the sage-brush,
wild and clean among the shells of Drybone.

He sniffed it. "Good smell, that! Bucks one up."
For a moment more he contemplated the town,
stark in the sunlight, and dumb in its noontide torpor. The twinkle waked again in his eye. "From
your engaging statistics," he said to Chalkeye, "I
gather that among the articles of household furni-
ture here, one mustn't count on meeting the cradle
in any abundance?"

The eye of the cow-puncher sparkled an instant
in response; then he replied dispassionately: "They
claim there used to be a few. But the population
always kept even, because whenever a child was
born, some man left town."

The Englishman stared in perplexity.

"Now what's that?" And he thought hard over
it. "Oh!" he cried, "I take you. Yes. A sweeping
denunciation of the local morals!"

On our way across to the hotel, he was sunk in

meditation, but twice muttered to himself, "Simply imperishable." He dismounted absent-mindedly, absent-mindedly wrote his name in the greasy and inky hotel book, and absent-mindedly followed up the stairs the gambler who kept the establishment. From his room door he called down, "Remember, you're going to teach me how to rope."

"You bet I will!" Chalkeye called up to him. With that was sown the seed of their fateful relation.

The punchers' heads were bending over the hotel book, studying his name.

"Give me a whole day," said one, "and I couldn't learn it by heart."

"It's good for a job at the Hat Six," said the Doughgy.

"Why the Hat Six?" I inquired.

"Not a man there goes by his real name this summer."

Chalkeye ran his finger slowly beneath the new arrival's writing.

"Measure that," he ordered.

"Measure it?"

"Did you figure," demanded Chalkeye witheringly, "that any human—don't care if he is an English lord—would invent half a foot of name for daily use? It was his folks. They done that to him at baptism when he was too young to state his objections."

But the Doughgy stuck to his doubts. "If he's a lord, why does he quit his baronial castle?"

"Maybe its roof's leakin'," said Post Hole Jack.

"Maybe he's lost it at cards," suggested Hard Winter Hance. "Lords do that."

"And maybe he's just having a look at life like the rest of us," said Chalkeye contemptuously. "What are his reasons to me?"

"He's got 'em all right," the Doughgy insisted. "You bet. Well, the Hat Six will go without letters till next mail day—I can't wait for that stage any longer." His spurs scraped jingling across the porch, he swung on his horse and was gone. They followed.

The sound of their galloping died away, their dust paled and vanished in the distance, and I loitered in the noon sun and the torpor, waiting dinner and aware of the pervading sage-brush. Who was right? I had never seen Chalkeye take to a stranger so quickly. The Doughgy could hardly know that the startling freedom of speech in Englishmen— freedom where the American is silent—freedom as to their incomes, their families, their gaieties—can go with a fathomless reticence, deep beyond our unversed technique. The American with something behind his scenes generally lets it show through his cracks; a consummate product like this blossom of aristocracy can seem wide open yet be tight shut.

Still, he was young, he must be very young; surely too young to have something behind the scenes already! But a beautiful, consummate product, a thousand years in the making.

"Say."

The voice came from the hotel porch; it was the landlord-gambler.

"Dinner?" I responded.

"Madden's looking after that, I guess."

His hotel was little to him, save to house and detain the traveler who passed—and stopped to play cards. Here often sat the big cattlemen until their thousands were gone, while lesser citizens dropped their hundreds, and the cow-puncher what his pocket still held after he had paid his visits to the women.

"Say," the landlord repeated. "That friend of yours ain't the love's young dream he looks."

Could the Doughgy be right? "Has he dealt you a hand already?" I laughed.

"No," said the landlord reflectively. "No, he didn't deal me any hand. At the rate he was goin' to bed, I guess he's asleep by now." Further meditation led to further remarks. "He mentioned he was expectin' his baggage by the stage. I said in that case I'd like a cash deposit. 'How much?' he said. 'Twenty-five dollars,' I said. 'Right oh!' was the words he used, and out comes his money. He's got plenty. He knowed it was a week's board and he asked for a receipt. Well, he got it off me, I was that amazed. There's no correspondence at all between his kiss-me-good-night-mother face and his adult actions.

"Hot water's what he wanted next, and clean sheets. He's between them sheets now. First time I ever done such a thing. Must have been his language. Kind of stunned me. 'Double or quits,' says he when I come back with the hot water and found him half naked already. You'd ought to see his fancy underwear. 'Ain't you eatin' dinner?' I said, and he says, 'I'll eat it the day after tomorrow. Don't let them break my dreamless sleep!' Who's your friend?"

"I've not made his acquaintance yet."

"H'm. D'you figure he's wanted where he's known?"

"More likely he's *not* wanted where he's known."

"H'm. D'you figure it's some other feller's wife?"

"They'd draw the line at her, not at him."

"Don't they draw the line for lords anywheres?"

"Oh, yes!"

While the landlord was hearing my account of where they did draw the line, a shrill Mongolian voice cried from somewhere indoors:

"Dinnes leddy!"

It was Madden, sole servant of the hotel, cook, waiter, room sweeper, bed maker, who after the day's work lost his wages regularly and incurably at every game he tried in the den.

Still the landlord stood on his porch thinking. "Say. That kid's folks raised him wrong. If they'd exposed him to the weather some, he might have been a credit to them."

"You've not mentioned what came of double or quits," I remarked.

"Ain't I? Oh, well—I don't grudge it to him. He's got his twenty-five back, and twenty-five of mine, and my receipt for a week's board."

"God bless my soul!"

"Oh, it won't be let stay with him long. When we started in to match, I said I'd take a look at his coin. He looked at me. 'Certainly,' he says, with six inches of ice on his voice; and his face got redder than his sunburn. Nothin' was wrong with the coin. 'And now,' he says, takin' another look at me, 'I'll not ask to see yours.' Funny how he made those harmless words sound, but say, how can you hit a person that's only got his underwear on? He's an adult, all right. Oh, it'll be won back off him. I guess he'll not require to be called. The cockroaches will look him up this evenin'."

I wondered a little at his way of putting it— "It'll be won." Why not say right out, "I'll win it"? If you're a professional gambler, why be sensitive?

"Dinnes leddy!" again shrieked the odd Mongolian voice.

"All right, Madden," called the landlord. "But if your friend stays among us, this lonesome country will not miss the circus to speak of."

Madden on certain nights scattered in his kitchen a powder which drove up into the bedroom above it swarms of those rushing insects that haunt sinks. When this occurred, nobody could remain long in a dreamless sleep. We should have our first circus in a few hours. To think of this cheered me throughout dinner in spite of my sullen neighbor, whose very silence was disagreeable. He was a gambler from Powder River, and he too used to win the poor Chinaman's wages. Madden's hand shook as he served him.

Yes, it was my turn to see, instead of to be, the circus. Entertainment for this lonesome country would now be furnished by another—unless he should modify himself, which Englishmen seldom do; they merely wonder why you don't. Why was he here, remote from the feudal centuries which had produced him so flawless, with his confiding smile, his wary wits, his merry blue eye, his poise, his flaxen hair, his leap at the sight of a bird to shoot, that flash of skill with a gun which there and then had won the heart of Chalkeye in spite of any outlandish fashion in speech or dress? Flawless? Or was there a flaw at which they had drawn the line? I hoped that the Doughgy was wrong—and I looked forward to the circus.

After supper, when the night's gambling had begun, my suspense increased. I played poker for a while, as usual a loser, and the man from Powder River did not grow more agreeable over the cards. I had a sense of something in the wind outside my understanding. I left the game and sat in the office by the big table, idly reading the stale newspapers strewn upon it, waiting for the cockroaches.

At length a very marked disturbance was set up above, and to my delight I heard a voice say clearly: "Why, damn it, look at that! Oh, I *say*, just look at that!"

The Englishman came down-stairs. He was barefoot, clad scantily in a garment or two, with the bedquilt clutched round him. He came without haste, candid, cheerful, self-possessed beneath his rumpled tangle of yellow hair.

"Oh, there you are! No ladies present, I hope? One couldn't stop up there, you know. Myriads of active creatures streaking and twinkling. A creature got in my ear and banished sleep, and I felt others hastening over me; so I lighted a lamp, and saw them rushing. Walls—pillow—myriads—they ran out of my trousers and into my boots. One positively can't stop up there.''

''I couldn't,'' I told him; at which his blue eyes fixed me with sudden attention. ''I didn't,'' I pursued. ''I slept on this table.''

''Oh. Really. Oh. Yes. One of those characteristic things! Well, it's a peerless success. But I hope that whatever others are in store will be more subtle. Where's the landlord? Would he mind if I slept on the table?'' He went to the open door of the saloon. ''Landlord, it's a peerless success. Would you mind if I slept on the table?''

''Sleep where it suits you, kid. But now you're awake, what's the matter with a little poker?''

''Oh, thanks so very much, no, I'm too much of a kid, if you don't mind. I'll just coil up on the table.''

The special vibrations in his utterance of ''kid'' went home to the ears of the gamblers, a light sound of laughter at the landlord's expense rose and died.

In his quilt, the barefoot boy stood motionless, watching the dingy, dangerous group at their game. His hair and his slim, erect form were touched by the light of a lamp near him; a high lamp in the saloon shone down upon the players and their cards. Other lamps struck gleams from the thick glasses along the bar, gleams from the bottles stacked above it, and the pictures of pink women and prizefighters flanking the bottles made patches of light on the wall. Big hats hung on nails, and their owners sat at various tables in boots and spurs and flannel shirts and leather chaps, their heads unbrushed, their necks dark and seamed, their hands knotted, scarred, their pistols visible.

He hung so long upon the scene that I thought he might be going to change his mind and join them in the name of the characteristic, but in time he turned away. Was it some trick of light and shadow? His face seemed to look as it might when he should be fifty; not because of any wrinkles, but from whatever spiritual demolition it is that age sometimes wreaks on the human countenance. It must have been a trick of the lamp; as he came forward, he was merely the serene boy that had stalked down from the cockroaches fifteen minutes ago; and with his words, his confiding smile shone out again.

"I say! Simply rippin'! John Sargent ought to paint your friends. It would make a pair with his Spanish den of melody and sudden death one saw in Paris. But that Chinaman should keep out of it. What chance has he got in there?"

John Sargent was not yet even a name to me, and I asked no questions as the boy went on.

"Well, now for your landlord's ample hospitality

on this jolly old table. I could do with a little more bedding.''

He glanced alertly about the office; dragged a saddle from a corner, threw over it the saddle-blanket, stiff and odorous with sweat, and so contrived himself a pillow; he mashed and shaped the stale newspapers into a wad between his bones and the table, got up on it, and was curling himself with his back to the light when a crash in the next room, and voices of violence, and shots, brought him up sitting.

"Get down!" I said to him; and I ran out of range and crouched.

He sat on his table, gazing with an interested expression at the saloon.

"Get down! You'll be killed!" I shouted from my shelter.

He did not turn his head.

The crashes and the scuffling of boots had ceased, and only the shots rang. The duel came through the door into the office: first, the sullen man who had been at dinner, backing, aiming, firing, and so step by step to the front door. Standing a moment there, he shot, his arm swung wild and limp, he slanted backward, grabbing at the jamb, lurched and fell outward, and lay so, his boots with his spurs and long heels sticking stiffly into the room.

Gripping a peg by the door of the saloon, the landlord leaned for support, fired twice more, coughed horribly and pitched forward flat on his face as his pistol bumped a few feet across the floor. Smoke floated thick in the room, its smell bit my throat like a file, and through it I saw the boy, seated on his table still. Faces from various sides began cautiously to peep and peer. The boy moved, got down slowly, and slowly walked to the saloon door, and slowly stooped down.

"He's dead," I heard him say, almost under his breath; and I found that I was still crouching in my corner. I rose, and he noticed me. "So they meant it," he said quietly.

The peeping faces had now made sure that this affair was over, and the emptied premises were crowded for a while with neighbors who had left whatever they were doing to gather details of the incident. So it was those two! Then what was behind it? A split between partners? Or had it come up over the landlord's woman? Well, others were ready to fill the vacant situation. Maybe she'd take Jack Saunders now. Well, neither party would be missed.

And amid such dispassionate comment, both parties were lifted and carried somewhere, while Madden appeared with a bucket, and after splashing water on the floor, went on his knees to scrub it with true Chinese diligence. Before he was done, all neighbors had gone back to their own business, and there were the boy and I alone in the office. Neither of us had spoken while the crowd was talking, and none had spoken to us, or noticed us particularly.

"Do they always take this sort of thing as a matter of course?" he now inquired.

"I suppose so. It's my first experience."

"I say. When you told me to hook it, you know, I believed everybody was ragging for my special edification."

I smiled, and he smiled a little, too.

"I say. What would be your idea as to a good big drink?"

"So be it. On me."

"No, no. One isn't destitute. Come up-stairs." There I shared his whisky, and he shared my room, safe from cockroaches. Destitute! An odd word.

Next day the two parties went to inhabit the graveyard, and their places in Drybone were filled by the living. Sundry horsemen ambled casually into town through this forenoon on various pretexts. Every one of them was to be seen at some time or other stooping over the hotel register, and I wondered if the boy noticed that each, before ambling out, somehow had a word or two with him.

Tom King, foreman of the V R outfit, returned to

Deer Creek, disappointed not to have identified the Englishman he had once seen at O'Neil City, Texas, dealing faro; through that day and the next, others who had met here and there similar nomads of disgrace, ambled in: the lonesome country entertained itself with no circus but with many guesses behind his back. The word he dropped out of silence the second afternoon as he smoked his pipe perhaps gave a clue to his thoughts.

"Can they always find so much spare time?"

His tone may have been a trifle lighter than common, perhaps something like a shadow was present in his eyes; I couldn't be sure, as he smoked on for a while. Destitute?

"Will Chalkeye be coming along again?" he presently asked.

"Probably for the mail, and certainly as soon as he has money to spend."

"I like Chalkeye."

He did not like the hotel, or its new proprietor-gambler, Jack Saunders. This personage had exacted and promptly received a cash deposit, when the boy took steps to find a habitation of his own. He chose what remained of the old adjutant's office, out of which one good room could still be made.

"Aiming to take out naturalization papers?" Saunders inquired.

"Now there's an idea!" retorted the boy pleasantly. "To become your fellow subject one almost would."

"Citizens live here."

"Quite! I beg their eighty million pardons."

With narrowed eyes, Saunders stood for a moment, then went about his business, and the boy made some purchases for housekeeping.

"How do you swallow the filth they give you for coffee?" he asked me. "One could learn to cook as well as to rope. If ever my things do come, you'll see my room won't be half bad."

They came the following week, and his first mail came, many letters, forwarded to Cheyenne first and thence here, with a black-edged one among them. Passengers were in the office, bound north, and punchers had gathered for their mail. These watched him tear open the black-edged letter first, and after a glance, forget his surroundings. He seemed to read it twice, and stood then, holding it absently, and spoke, not to us, but to space.

"Well, I shall miss old John."

In the silence, some boot scraped on the floor. Perhaps they were hoping for a circus. He read the bad news again. "Only a week. And then—gone."

Among the forgotten audience, the fact of Chalkeye penetrated his trance.

"John was such a jolly old sot," he confided to Chalkeye, as if the two were alone.

"There's some here," said the puncher awkwardly, "that could fill his place that way for you."

The boy did not seem to hear him.

"Of course, one wasn't going to see John again very soon, but—well, of course that's one life less between me and the strawberry leaves," he finished in a tone abruptly matter-of-fact.

Stupefaction deepened the noiselessness.

"Us Americans," said Jack Saunders, intentionally ungrammatical, "ain't never studied your foreign fruits. Was John climbin' the tree for them strawberries when he fell?"

A dark flush instantly spread over Chalkeye's face, while the boy looked somewhat long, but very amiably, at Saunders before he answered.

"Oh," he said in his lightest tone, and as if from a distance, "John was my brother, you see."

If this was a circus, it was not he that furnished it. The stage was ready, its passengers left for the north, most of the cow-punchers rode away, and anyone who had come in now to join the few of us that remained, could not have read in the boy's recovered aspect anything of the shock which had been for a brief space too much for him. Chalkeye failed to suppress his customary thirst for information.

"About the strawberry leaves. Would you object to telling some more? Don't, if you do."

"Very glad to. One forgets. If you Americans

only spoke a language entirely your own, it wouldn't
be so baffling. You're so absurdly like us at odd
moments, and so inconceivably not at others—you've
not, for instance, inherited certain ancient—suppose
we say habits? Such as the eldest son. Call it a bad
habit if you like, but there it is!—and you were a
bit slow in getting rid of your own bad habit of
slavery, weren't you? Now I'm rather fond of our
ancient habits, and yet I've always been a younger
son."

"But you're not now that—that—he's gone?"

"John? Oh, yes, I am." Here he turned to me
and forgot the cow-punchers, speaking to me as if
we were alone. "John was next above me, and such
a dear fellow. We hunted pleasure in couples
through the London night. Happy times! The
Criterion after the theaters, and all that, you know.
I couldn't carry my wine like John, but I shouldn't
even in my most careless moments ever have brought
a poll to our house in Portman Square. I never saw
the pater so waxy. That simply isn't done, you
know. Granville's next above John. Bowls, and not
bad at the wicket. Chandos is next above Granville.
He got a blue. He's secretary to Lord Lyons, at our
embassy in Paris. Wymford's rather political—
makes speeches and all that. Of course, Wymford
isn't his own father. What's the matter?" he asked,
for Chalkeye had raised a pleading hand.

"We're beginners," said the puncher. "You'll have to make the strawberries easier."

"Oh. Wymford is the eldest son's title in our family. He'll drop it when he succeeds. One's parents," he continued to me, again leaving the rest out, "were absurdly prolific. If he had met us, Wordsworth would never have stopped his poem at seven, because I'm the eleventh and last, and he could have so readily changed the meter. Wymford —his name is Charles—was the first-born. His title came into the family—but I'll skip that—he'll have the strawberry leaves when he succeeds the pater. If he were to die, my brother Ronald, the next son, would have them. I don't want to bore you," he said to the others.

"You don't. Go on, Prince."

"Not even baronet! Well. How to simplify? How to sketch? Well, it's like this."

They attended closely to his brief account of titles, coronets, emblems, the general scheme of the British peerage.

"I suppose it all sounds awfully odd to you. But it's rather natural to us."

"Is it nine," asked Post Hole Jack, "nine that's ahead of you still? Those strawberries will be ripe."

"Nine? Nine lives? But, my dear sir, one has sisters."

"Don't the girls get any?"

"Dear me, no! Fancy women in the Lords!"

"Then," pursued Post Hole Jack, "you're nothing at all?"

"Nothing but just that." And he displayed to us in turn his name on his letters. As the Doughgy looked at it, the boy looked at him with his confiding smile and said, "I fancy you may have noticed it already in the hotel register."

Triumph gleamed in the glance that Chalkeye gave the embarrassed Doughgy, who slowly mumbled the name aloud.

The boy laughed out again. "The family would never suspect you meant me if you said it like that," and he pronounced it correctly. "Of course we don't spell it so."

"What's the point?" asked Jack Saunders; and at his tone Chalkeye looked sharply at him.

"Oh," replied the boy with his voice light and distant, "no point. It's merely the right way."

"In America," said Saunders, "we tell how to say a word by its spelling."

"But do you so invariably? One's train on a Thursday morning was in a place they called O-h-i-o, and by Friday afternoon they were calling it I-o-wah. Now what have I said?" he asked me.

The general explosion which burst out immediately upon his words drowned the explanation I attempted.

"Well," he said, looking on at our mirth, "it's very pleasant to excite all this cheer. At home one never aroused so much."

The wild joy of living now seized the cow-punchers suddenly. They swung on their horses and galloped through Drybone with shouts and pistol-shots. At this disturbance, a few faces looked out to see if anything unusual was the matter, found nothing, and disappeared. Saunders walked back to his hotel, and it seemed as if a cloud had gone with him.

"An extraordinary country," said the boy to me as we watched the rushing medley of horsemen. "I like them. I like them very much. Will they come back today?"

They came back in a few minutes, soothed and quiet, and meanwhile I had explained Ohio to him.

"Gentlemen," he said, "have one on Ohio. Is that good American?"

We were soon standing along the nearest bar.

"How!" said Post Hole Jack, and "How!" said they all.

"Here's to the Right Honorable Alphabet Strawberries."

"The fall round-up is pretty near due," said Chalkeye, "and I'll be too busy to call him all that every time I want to speak to him. Here's to Strawberries."

"Now you can get a job at the Hat Six," said the Doughgy.

Well, that is the first circus he provided for the lonesome country, and that is how he got his name. Through the weeks following, it fastened upon him, and through the succeeding years he went by no other. He took no job at the Hat Six, or anywhere; at not infrequent intervals, money came to him, always spent soon, often unwisely, seldom on others; like his kind he was close with his cash, and he did not modify this or any other of his native habits. He borrowed readily, paid back casually, yet his pleasant and fearless readiness covered his shortcomings. By his extravagance he kept himself habitually behind, which did not weigh upon him heavily.

Civilized comforts and objects gradually filled his room, where hung hunting-crops, sporting trophies, with the photographs of his past; handsome folk, all with the look of his race, urbane and arrogant, men young and old, and two or three beautiful women, with their names written across the pictures in firm round English hands. When need of money pressed him hard, he would raffle a pipe, or a scarf, or one of the civilized objects admired by Drybone and its vicinity. The lonesome country accepted him, liked him; and one there had become his sponsor and wished to be his mentor.

"Are you acquainted with many of those English aristocrats?" Chalkeye asked one day.

"With very few."

We were gathering stock through the high draws of Casper Mountain, not long before I was to go home. The leaves of the quaking aspens glorified the slopes and splashed the ridges with gold. Among them down below, the boy came for a moment into sight, looking for a white-tailed deer.

"They claim families like his were families before America was discovered," pursued Chalkeye.

"Quite a number were."

"So those dukes and lords have been seeing life for hundreds of years."

"They certainly have."

Chalkeye communed with his thoughts for a while. "He never touches a card," he presently said.

"What's your point?"

"Nothing much. Only with his other goings on, you'd think he'd enjoy that too."

"Too?"

The puncher laughed a little. "He told me lately that he was not my business."

"Said it?—just like that?"

"Said it without words. I don't want him to get into trouble with Jack Saunders."

Then I saw it in a flash; I had been quite blind to it.

"Yes," said Chalkeye, "it's her that got widowed by that last shooting at the hotel. She prefers to console herself with Strawberries. Well, in her place so would I. Jack is fifty, and washes Saturday nights, which for him is insufficient.—D'you figure his folks back in England are really paying him to keep away?"

"Looks like it."

"Poor kid!" Chalkeye fell silent, ruminating. "A better bluff I've never seen."

A small bunch of cattle occupied us before he resumed.

"But now and then—well, now and then he forgets to keep it up, and a man can see he has been through something." The puncher ruminated again. "I made a little talk to Jack. I guess there's talks he has liked better, but I guess maybe he'll bear it in mind."

How deeply the gambler bore it in mind was not made clear that day, or for many days.

A shot far down below startled us unreasonably.

"Hark!" said Chalkeye.

We reined in and listened; no further sound broke upon the great stillness of the mountains.

"He has got his deer!" I declared confidently.

"He has got his deer!" repeated Chalkeye cheerfully; and we rode down to see, driving the cattle before us through the silence which our unspoken thoughts rendered needlessly ominous.

Strawberries had got his white-tailed deer with one bullet, well-placed just behind the shoulder; we had been right; it was merely this; yet that shot has left a mark in my memory, as many a trivial event will do when it is embedded among somber recollections.

As we came near with our cattle, Strawberries was kneeling to skin and dress his game, and he glanced up at Chalkeye. In his eye I caught it then, caught what I should have missed but for that recent word of the cow-puncher's, the sort of look which an enterprising child will turn upon a restraining nurse. "He told me lately that he was none of my business." Chalkeye had expressed it perfectly.

On the trail to camp, a rain came thick and sudden upon us out of a canyon, and this furnished our cattle an excellent pretext to break and scatter. Strawberries was after them instantly.

"Let him do it by himself!" Chalkeye commanded me. "See him get his slicker on! Ain't he learning quick? I'll make a dandy puncher of him!" He watched his apt and active pupil crit-

ically. "He'd ought to have gone round them willows the other side. Well, what'd you know about
that! Did you notice the way he headed that Goose
Egg heifer off at the creek?"

Certainly it was all neatly and swiftly done; a
better job than any of my attempts, in spite of my
three months' start; and the remark of the late
landlord's came to me as he stood on his porch that
first morning and reflected on the boy's parents.
"If they'd exposed him to the weather some," said
he, "he might have been a credit to them."

That had been merely one instance of how this
flaxen-haired aristocrat could disarm the cattle
country's rooted distrust of his kind without lifting
a finger, without even noticing it; and without the
visible lift of a finger he had beckoned to him the
late landlord's woman. So much better to have
done without her, to have let Jack Saunders have
her.

He was now in front of us, driving the collected
cattle along the wet trail. The cloud of storm and
thunder had gone prowling along the farther hills,
the sage-brush gave forth its sharpened pungency
to the sky, and the boy, as he passed an Indian
paint-brush flaming by the trail, swung down and
snapped its blossom off in his hand.

"He might be one of us," said Chalkeye.

"Never," I said to myself. How should Chalkeye, or any of them, discern the line which Strawberries drew between himself and their equality? Or understand that the true aristocrat always is the best democrat, because he is at his ease with everybody, and makes them so with him?

"Only maybe," continued the puncher, to my surprise, "he can't forget his raising."

Perhaps Strawberries seemed more nearly to forget his raising one early morning soon after this than at any other time I can recall. It was at breakfast in the next camp to which we moved, while he was in the act of learning from the cook how to toss flapjacks. Watching the performance sat various cow-punchers in a circle, and Chalkeye as he passed by stopped and gave vent to a prolonged, joyous and vibrating shout.

Strawberries paused with his ladle in midair. "Now why exactly do you do that?" he inquired.

"Can't seem to help it," responded the cowpuncher. "It's just my feelings. When I look at that"—he swept his arm toward the splendid plains and the hills glowing in the sun—"well, I want to swallow it, and I want to jump on a horse and dive into it." He drew in a huge breath and became lyric. "It makes a man feel like he could live the whole of himself at wunst. I'd like to have ten fights, and ten girls, and ten drinks, and I'd come pretty near enjoying sudden death."

"So would I!" exclaimed the boy; and he sprang to his feet. "Let's all howl together! Now!" and he waved his ladle. "One, two, three!"

All of us had jumped up, and in unison we gave forth the full power of our lungs in that crystal air that was like creation's first light. Three hawks sailed out of some pines above, several cattle stampeded below in the sage-brush, the team tried to run away with the wagon, and two or three punchers who were throwing the herd off the bed-ground came galloping in.

And yet Strawberries, when bored or displeased, could withdraw his voice to a great distance. He withdrew it after we had reached Drybone, and with a chill that made the shrewdness of Chalkeye's doubt as to his being able to forget his raising very marked indeed. As we rode to the post-office, all the dark causes of what was to happen in its due season were present and visible: lust of the flesh, a bully's vindictiveness, human frailty, and protecting friendship.

The widow was standing at a door, and she exchanged a glance of understanding with her preferred lover, who had been absent for many days; Saunders was coming along with a saddled horse at which I noticed Chalkeye was staring. Here were all the causes, needing only the right chance to get them in motion. It took its time to arrive, and on this particular occasion, the lonesome country was merely provided with another circus.

The horse was for sale. Strawberries had owned two horses for some time, but he had been looking for a third, with a view to training him to jump. He thought that the neighborhood afforded opportunities for arranging a steeplechase course with but small effort. Steeplechasing would be a desirable addition to the country's pleasures. Here, in the opinion of Saunders, was just the animal for Strawberries, and a bargain.

"Then he can jump?" the boy inquired.

"He can jump, all right," drawled the gambler, which set a bystander laughing.

Neither Strawberries nor I had been long enough in the country to interpret this laughter. And yet —something was in the air, at least, so it seems in the strange afterglow of retrospect.

Strawberries looked the horse over with a practised eye.

"I'll get on him."

"Don't get on him," said a peremptory voice.

At this, everybody stared. It was Chalkeye who had spoken out thus, unwarrantably. He got a very ugly look from Saunders, but from Strawberries he received the perfection of disdain.

"I beg your pardon. Did you speak?" That was when his voice came from extreme remoteness.

"I said not to get on that horse."

If Strawberries had been fully determined not to get on, naturally this would have been more than enough to make him change his mind. He dismounted from his own horse with careful deliberation and walked to the bony animal that Saunders held, a roan with a Roman nose and a watching eye.

"Take your medicine, then," muttered Chalkeye gruffly.

Then I guessed what the matter was, and knew that this was the horse that went by the name of Calamity.

It was quite admirable to see how the boy sat the bucking beast after Saunders had let him go. I should have been flung off in a moment. The struggle began amid expectant silence, the ancient instinct with which Rome watched the gladiator; but when the boy's pluck and skill had held out longer than their expectation, voices broke out here and there calling instructions to him.

The horse went through his list of contortions. Arching his back like a cat, he jumped in the air, landed like lead and shook himself as a dog coming out of the water, reared gigantically, stood on his front legs and kicked his hind ones, sprang forward with a dozen jolting spasms, whirled aside, reared again—until the boy was shot off into the dust, from which he did not rise.

Chalkeye carried him to his room of luxury among the photographs and soft skins and rugs, and put him on his bed, and got his clothes off; while the widow stood by, useless, lamenting, in the way, crying out that if the boy died she would kill Jack Saunders, she would.

"That'll be my job," said Chalkeye quietly. "Get some water and shut your mouth."

She carried out the first part of this direction; the rest was quite beyond her powers. She was a pretty girl, and still young, with an aspect which told plainly what sort of widow she was—quite the ordinary specimen of her kind. She meant no mischief, but she loved to burst on people with explosive news; and so on her errand for the water her tongue was free, and all Drybone learned of Chalkeye's intention. Except that she sowed a few more seeds for the future harvest, I don't think she did any harm. Saunders wished no trouble with Chalkeye; the cow-puncher had too many friends; and no steps had to be taken unless Strawberries died.

Strawberries did not die. After lying unconscious for two days, he opened his eyes and quietly remarked:

"Leon-i-das
On a one-eyed ass."

This was a quotation. He did not go on with it;
he shut his eyes and seemed to fall away from life
again. I suppose that poem must have been the last
thing in his mind before his concussion. Some hours
later, Chalkeye came in from the round-up for news.
At the opening of the door, Strawberries waked and
surveyed us, and after a time asked languidly:

"Am I a one-eyed ass?"

Chalkeye looked at me in alarm. "Good God!"
he whispered.

In the face in the bed appeared a flicker of the
confiding smile.

"Am I in the hands of God? Is it as bad as
that?"

"You'll get well," stated Chalkeye, instantly re-
assured. "And you be quick about it. When the
round-up's over, the boys want you to go on an elk
hunt with them."

So that circus ended happily, and the lonesome
country liked Strawberries better than ever. And
before the boys went on their elk hunt, he received
an unusual honor.

It was remembered that he was interested in the
characteristic. Now a stranger had come through
the country some weeks ago, and after displaying
very marked and exceptional ability by selling the

same stolen horses to a succession of different pur-
chasers, had thoughtfully sought another neighborhood. But here it seemed that his skill had fallen
short. A conversation stopped abruptly upon my
entrance to the cabin of luxury one afternoon. Some
ranch owners whom I knew slightly sat there and
looked at me and said the weather was fine.

If Strawberries was aware that they did not wish
me to know what they had been saying to him, he
chose to disregard it.

"Then you mean," said he, "that you're bringing
me an invitation?"

"You're the only outsider that's in the party,"
said one visitor.

"There'd be no outsider," added another, "only
he has went too far, and deserves no consideration."

"Of course you'll not speak of this," said a third,
to me.

"But you say you haven't caught him yet," said
Strawberries.

"We have him located."

"He might give you the slip, you know."

"I guess you can leave that to us."

"And am I to start at the post and be in at the
finish?"

"That was our idea."

Strawberries shook his head in silence.

They rose.

"You understand," said one, "it's the rule of the game. He knows the rules, he took the chances. That man is too tough for this country. We've got it to do. You understand?"

"Oh, quite, quite! Don't apologize."

"We're not apologizing to anybody."

"I do!" exclaimed Strawberries quickly. "I shouldn't have said that. It was rotten. And thanks so very much. And in your place, possibly, you know, I—but it's not quite the same thing, is it? So you won't mind?"

If Strawberries ever adopted the custom of the country enough to take part in a lynching, it was not in Wyoming. What he may have done elsewhere lies beyond my knowledge in the many regions where his wanderings took him. That visit, when the ranchmen sat in his cabin and showed him this peculiar mark of their esteem, was my last sight of him at this stage of his career, the last, that is, of any consequence.

I was gone when the elk hunt came off, and no tidings of Strawberries reached me in the East for several months, when friends in Cheyenne wrote asking me what I knew about him. There it was again, the Doughgy's doubt on the first day, forgotten as we grew accustomed to Strawberries!

Well, at Cheyenne and at the various ranches of my friends to whom he now paid long visits, it became forgotten in the same way.

The next thing was a newspaper clipping. "Popular Peer Pushes Polo," was its skilful caption. It was mailed me by a ranch friend on the Chugwater. The same friend gave me news of the popular peer when we met at Harvard on Commencement Day. At the Cheyenne Club, on the Chugwater, at Bordeaux, wherever Strawberries went, and he seemed to have gone everywhere in Wyoming, he first raised doubts and then won hearts; and the doubts were forgotten.

The college graduates who had ranches in the country encouraged his long visits, even though they knew he made them to save expense, and even though at the Cheyenne Club on the rare occasions when he ordered a drink, it was seldom for anyone but himself; I have said that he modified nothing. Nobody minded this in an Englishman; they were glad to pay for his drinks, they owed him so much.

His energy didn't stop with the polo he organized—at that time a complete novelty; in the following years he carried out his plan for a steeplechase, and another newspaper cutting came to me in the East. "Swell Snugly Sits Saddle." He sat it in several places, for on my next visit to Drybone, three summers later, he was staying with the cavalry officers at Fort McKinney, and had started them steeplechasing on Clear Creek.

"But none of us can make him touch a card," said my friend of the Cheyenne Club on Commencement Day.

"He never does at Drybone," said I.

He never did anywhere. I saw him often during those years, but there's nothing to tell of our meetings; he had become an institution. Drybone remained his headquarters, but sometimes I found him at Cheyenne, where he would lie in bed at the club for two days at a time, remarking that if I would tell him something to get up for, he would do it. Then his energy would come uppermost, and it would be polo, or steeplechasing, or a journey to Montana for greyhounds to course antelope with (this was a failure), or an extended hunt for elk in the fall or for bear in the spring.

Yes, he was an institution; the sight of him had grown so familiar to the country that it was only now and then that the mystery of his unexplained coming was remembered. His money continued to arrive regularly, and a sporting paper he called the Pink Un; and almost every mail brought him letters that bore English stamps; and these he seemed always to answer within a day or two, giving a long morning to it among his photographs and souvenirs. If I came in at these times, he would look up from his writing, and I knew that he wished to be alone by the very civility of his "Oh, it's you! Come in." And as I went out, his apology followed—"If you don't mind."

That's one picture of him I retain: the latest Pink Un lying near him, his elbows spread flat out, his head near the blue blotting paper, his flaxen hair rumpled in the effort of composition; and on the walls around him, those faces of handsome, arrogant men and women, distant and impassive. What was in those letters? Questions about sisters, horses, dogs, home? Messages to old companions? Was he gazing through bars at sunlight while he bent over the blotting paper?

"D'you figure he's got a life sentence?" said the Doughgy to Chalkeye one day. "D'you figure they'll commute for good conduct? Or will they let him back on parole?"

"I ain't figuring at all," said Chalkeye. "It's his present I'm vouching for, not his past or his future. And I've given all men notice to that effect."

"Humph!" laughed the Doughgy. "You needn't get so hot about it." And he protracted his teasing. "I expect," said he in a tone of judicial thought, "lords and barons and high-ups like that don't condescend to take notice of what low-downs like you and me think of their morals."

"Since when have you been practising morals?"

"Oh, I don't practise 'em or preach 'em, any more than you. But we haven't had his advantages."

A light broke on me, and I addressed the Doughgy. "Do you mean to say that Drybone blames Strawberries for doing just what it does itself?"

"I don't mean to say anything," laughed the Doughgy. "But would he do it at home?"

In that word lay the pith of the matter. The widow, whenever Strawberries went away, had always moved from the hotel into his cabin by way of taking care of it during his absence, and moved out upon his return, but when he had returned this spring, she had remained. Now, although Drybone hadn't a moral to its back, this indifference to appearances in a visitor who would respect them in his own country—weren't the free-born citizens of Drybone the equals of any English subject?

"I see your point," I said gravely to the Doughgy, "though I never met this particular assertion of democratic faith before. But after all, there's a proverb that when you're in Rome, you do as Rome does."

"It don't apply," retorted the Doughgy. "Oh, well," he added, "this country would forgive him a lot more than that." And he dropped his mischievous banter, which had been entirely to reach

Chalkeye through one of the few joints in his armor.

In this it was quite successful and it left Chalkeye moody; and a prolonged silence on his part ended in his remarking when the Doughgy had gone: "He says he doesn't expect to stay here for ever."

"Strawberries says?"

"Yes. It was the other day when I told him he'd ought to send his woman back to the hotel. I wish she had taken Jack Saunders."

"Then the Doughgy was right!"

"Damn the Doughgy. I guess Strawberries is figuring that it has lasted—his stay, I mean—a pretty long while now, and maybe back in his home they'll agree some day that it has been long enough. Especially if they're told by reliable parties that he never——" Chalkeye stopped abruptly and reverted to the widow. "Of course there's never any use me telling him to do or to quit doing a thing," he finished, moody again. "But," he asserted presently, "he'll work through. That boy'll hold on."

A chance word will sometimes wake us up to unsuspected thoughts. When he said that the boy would work through, he said it to help himself to believe it, and it disclosed to me that a question had been buried alive in my mind ever since Strawberries had taken to lying in bed all day at the Cheyenne Club. Was Strawberries, anchored no longer to his home restraints, drifting toward the rocks? There had been more than playfulness in the Doughgy's banter; Drybone might forgive the boy this and that, but we began to hear that the wives of some of the cattlemen had requested their husbands not to bring him to their ranches any more. I don't know whether he ever got word of this or not; but in looking back on it all today, it is easy to see that this point is where the sky of Strawberries and of Chalkeye, his loyal sponsor, who was vouching for his present, began to grow overcast.

The Doughgy was reading the latest Cheyenne paper at the hotel. "Hello," said he, "here's another swell Englishman coming our way."

"One of 'em's already more'n I have use for," remarked Jack Saunders, who was dealing cards to himself because there was no one else to deal them to.

The Doughgy grinned at the gambler. "I wouldn't be anxious. This new one ain't likely to wreck your new home."

"What's his name?" asked Saunders with indifference as he continued to deal.

"Let's see, what was it?" said the Doughgy. "His name's Deepmere."

Saunders grunted, and the Doughgy read more items until he had read them all. "Wonder if Strawberries knows him," he remarked.

To this there was not even a grunt in response,

and the Doughgy lounged out of the hotel. He met Strawberries in a few minutes and told him the news.

"Deepmere coming!"

And so Strawberries did know him; after that exclamation, he went straight to the hotel. He borrowed the paper and pored over the brief paragraph. He might have been learning the words by heart; but when he looked up, his eyes seemed to be staring at a host of memories, and he sat motionless for a long time, keeping his unconscious hand over the paper where he had laid it on the broad table.

From that same table he had watched the shooting on the night of his arrival; today, with many another experience between, through years of unspoken endurance that the recording angel would surely take into acccount when his sins should come to be weighed, the experience of a great emotion was breaking like waves against his spirit. I went out of the office, for although he had himself so well in hand that no stranger would have been arrested by his aspect, for me it seemed like peeping through the keyhole to be near him during that inward storm.

Afterward, just as after his trance in the post-office when he had held the black-edged letter in his hand, he grew loquacious and animated. Even his appearance became more like the boy he had been, and less like the visibly coarsened man he had become.

"That's Deepmere," he said to me the next day in his cabin.

I had often looked at the photograph; a youth in his early twenties, of much the same age as Strawberries had been when he appeared to us in the graveyard that sunny morning in the distant past, while the sage-brush smell was flowing in from the warm, undulated miles. I looked very closely at the face of Deepmere now; handsome, arrogant, impassive; it did not answer the question I was asking; no more did any of those faces on his walls, all handsome, arrogant, impassive.

"We were both at the House," said Strawberries. "Went up together."

So they had been collegemates at Oxford; and I told this to Doughgy.

The Doughgy asked the same question which I had asked of the impassive photographs.

"D'you figure Deepmere's looking forward to meetin' his old friend?"

Some other one of the cow-punchers present rounded this out. "And is the old friend impatient to wring Deepmere's hand?"

Different voices spoke various surmises, until Chalkeye said:

"I guess this country don't need any foreigner to tell it what it thinks on any subject."

They united on that. Drybone was not interested in British opinion of Strawberries.

"But," said the Doughgy, "how about it if Strawberries happens to be interested in British opinion?"

Their curiosity was not idle, but it was less keen than mine; and not even to me was the matter of such crucial moment as it was to Chalkeye: the sponsor's concern for the welfare of his pupil had become a part of his life. I don't know what he might not have done if he had witnessed the meeting which too many of us did see, and which gave the answer to our question. Had nobody been present, or if Strawberries had only avoided the meeting—but why speculate? The exile craved an answer too hungrily, suspense had gone beyond further endurance; that must come to an end; and I am pretty sure that he had grown to believe what he desired to believe, and had persuaded himself that after three years it was all right, it would end well. Chalkeye missed the worst.

Until I reflected that of course Deepmere, having stopped at Cheyenne, was prepared, would not be taken by surprise at coming face to face with Strawberries in this far corner of the earth, I marveled at a performance so perfect. A group lounged in the office waiting for mail; the rattle of the stage brought them as usual to the door to watch its arrival. The stage drove up, the brake scraped against the tire, the mail-sack was flung down, and as the single passenger stepped to the ground, Strawberries appeared out of the office and spoke lightly and casually:

"What are you doing here?" The casualness was well managed; not a hint of anything out of the common; they might have dined together last night.

The passenger looked at Strawberries blank and straight with an empty eye, as if he was not there.

"Does one get dinner here?" he inquired of everybody in general.

"Dinnes leddy!" screamed Madden from the hotel porch.

"Somewhere to wash, I suppose?" said the passenger, again most impersonally; and walked off.

That was all. A few seconds did the whole of it; not much longer than it needs to whip out a weapon and kill a man. Unbroken silence continued as Deepmere departed, followed by many eyes that could not look at Strawberries. By the sound of his steps, and next by the distant slam of a door, it was known that he had betaken himself to his cabin.

In there, the photographs awaited him, those handsome, arrogant faces, looking at him out of his past. He knew now what they thought of him;

their message had been clearly delivered by his old
college friend. When the witnesses of that meeting
had shuffled awkwardly into the post-office, while
the mail was being distributed, they began to mutter
their opinions of the old college friend, whom the
stage presently took across the bridge to Buffalo;
but I doubt if their indignation or their sympathy
would have brought much comfort to Strawberries
in this hour of his blasting disillusion: the only
backing that he craved had been denied him forever.

What could have been in those long letters that
he sent home? Had he actually written himself into
a belief that the hour was on the way when the ban
would be lifted? Nobody will ever know. And what
was in the letters that came to him? These went
on coming, but never again was Strawberries seen
to answer them.

How could he bring himself to remain at the
scene and with the witnesses of his repudiation?
Why did he not leave Drybone and go—anywhere
—so long as it was among strangers? Perhaps
Chalkeye hit the truth when he said that Strawberries had found out where his real friends were.

For a week he kept wholly to himself; and this
seclusion was respected by those same witnesses
whose eyes had looked away from him at the post-
office. No word of his ever gave a hint of what was

in his mind during this time. Was it a spiritual wrestling match, and did his better self make a stand, even though the door of hope had been shut in his face?

At any rate, at the end of those seven days of isolation, he strolled casually into the hotel one evening, spoke to those he met as if nothing had happened, lounged in the office a while reading the latest papers, and then strolled on into the gambling saloon, bought some chips and sat down to the game.

I have never seen a cat when, after long patience at a mouse-hole, the mouse appears; but that is what Jack Saunders made me think of as he watched Strawberries enter the door of his den. His eye changed, a sudden light seemed to fill it, and then his usual look of indifference returned. The momentary flare was nothing that the ordinary onlooker would notice, any more than he would see significance in the step Strawberries had taken.

One or two were there who remarked that they had always thought cards were against his principles, but that they must have been mistaken, for he was evidently at home in drawing and betting; with faro likewise he proved familiar; later, he acquired what Drybone could teach him, and taught Drybone some games of chance not in vogue there.

It was Chalkeye, whom I met one night over at Point of Rocks on my way to the railroad and the

East, who read deeper. He had been for a "whirl" in Cheyenne, as he expressed it; and after hearing from me the latest news of the country, he began to talk slowly, with many pauses; and it was curious how he began.

"I could have made a dandy cattleman out of him," he said, "if he was going to stay in the country." He did not name Strawberries. It was the way you refer to the dead sometimes, soon after their death.

"Perhaps you will do it yet," said I.

"No." There was a long pause. "Does he win or lose?"

"Both."

"Does he play every night?"

"He's at it whenever I drop in."

"What does he do all day?"

"Lies in bed. Gets up at card time."

"Wins, you say?"

"Off and on."

"Saunders will get everything he has." There was another long pause. "You'd think he'd tear those photographs up. They've got no use for him. What use has he got for them any more?"

"Well," said I, "they're likely to be all he will ever see of home."

After an interval, Chalkeye said: "I expect you and I don't need to guess what the trouble was."

This was the plainest word about it he had ever spoken. Silence was my answer to it, and in further silence we sat for a while; I grieved for Chalkeye— he was cut to the depths.

"What is your idea?" he presently asked.

"Why, just that."

"I mean, was it a first offense? Would they come down so hard on just one slip?"

"How should I know?"

"D'you figure that fellow Deepmere represents general opinion?"

"How can I know that, either?"

"D'you figure it has broken his nerve?"

"Why did he begin again?"

"I wonder if he has spotted what kind of game he's buckin'."

We asked each other more questions, like these, which neither of us could answer; it was a way of thinking aloud together. Then Chalkeye drew out a folded handkerchief and showed me a letter it held.

"I was going to get you to put your name to that."

I read:

"To all whom this may concern:

"We the undersigned desire to state that during the several years we have been acquainted with the bearer, we have never seen him take part in any gambling game, or known of his doing so. His strict abstention from all such pursuits has been conspicuous in a community where card games are a general practice. We have found the gentleman uniformly companionable, manly and upstanding.''

To this document many signatures were appended —the names of all the leading men in the country were there.

''They shaped that up for me at the Cheyenne Club,'' Chalkeye explained. ''I got them to do it after that Deepmere fellow had acted that way to him. They claimed it wouldn't do any good. But I thought that if he wanted to go home it might help him some.''

He took the letter from my hand and was going to tear it up.

''Oh, no!'' said I. ''It may come in yet, some-how.''

He shook his head, but put the paper back in its handkerchief.

''Most folks,'' he pursued, ''can drink safely. Now and then you meet some poor fellow that can't. One glass of anything starts him off, and the day comes when stopping has got beyond him, and the only way for him is never to touch it. Cards are the same with some. Strawberries knew that, you see. And I was betting on him. But his old friend Deepmere happened along. How could you foresee . . ." The cow-puncher's voice failed him, and he paused a moment. "Well," he resumed with regained control, "I could have made a dandy cattleman out of him. Well, guess I'll hit the hay."

That was the last that I saw of Chalkeye for six months.

I came up the river in the stage, and there waiting for me was what I missed in cities every day—the air, the light, the mountains, the open world, the welcome of the sage-brush smell; even a look at the graveyard would have pleased me, but we passed the turnout to it, and I was actually glad to see the horrible hotel. Nothing was changed in Drybone—save the luck of Strawberries.

It was the Doughgy who greeted me with the odd news that Strawberries had suddenly begun to win more than he lost. During the winter he had descended through ups and downs to the bottom of pennilessness; he had parted with one possession after another; he had sold everything that anyone would buy; he had pledged his remittances in advance; he had raffled his three horses; he was afoot. To be sure, the Doughgy continued, this made small matter to a man in bed all day and at cards all night.

The boys were sorry for him. His woman stuck

to him. She was just as crazy about him as the first day. She paid the bills when his credit was gone. How she got the money, several could explain. He was still in deep, but last week Jack Saunders had come back from a visit to Laramie and found Strawberries was winning. Not every night. Madden won off him, but he won more off Madden.

It was ups and downs again, but the ups had it.

"Sounds like a fever chart," said I.

"Fever, all right!" the Doughgy laughed. "Severe case. Madden makes a man think some."

"Another severe case," said I; at which the Doughgy gave me a singular stare.

I saw Strawberries once in this hour of his luck, before going to a ranch for a couple of days. His face had become the blighted countenance which had turned toward me like an apparition on that night of his arrival, after he had been staring in at the gambling den. The fever had burned his youth, and more than his youth, away; if you did not look twice, you would hardly see that he had been a gentleman.

A sudden turn of luck, and at this late day? Two and two can readily be put together, if you have the key. I thought of Saunders and the cat and the mouse. Nothing seemed to fit; yet Strawberries winning seemed of darker portent than Strawberries losing. And then, when I was again in Drybone, Chalkeye unlocked the mystery. I was writing letters up in my room at the hotel, and he walked in without knocking and sat on the edge of my bed.

"I am getting Strawberries out of the country tonight," said he, very quietly, keeping his eye on his boots. That put the two and two together: a new offense, and caught in it here, as at home.

"But," I said, "didn't he know that Jack Saunders was certain to see through it?"

"He knew. But he didn't know about Madden?"

"Madden!" I exclaimed. "Madden?"

"Not so loud. Have you supposed the Chink keeps losing his wages for nothing?"

The pen fell from my hand, and I listened to him, dazed.

"Four or five are in it. Do you remember that man from Powder River, and the shooting? He had been dissatisfied with the division of spoils. None of that gang is slicker than the Chink. They got tired waiting, so they greased the slide."

"Cat and mouse," I murmured.

"Sure. And his girl was the mouse. She had known the old ways of the establishment. They figured she would be fool enough to think no changes had been made. Jack went to Laramie, Madden played being busy over his wash—well, she found the cards where they wanted her to find them." Chalkeye sighed. "I'll give you all the particulars tomorrow—the time is short."

"You mean," said I, beginning to see through it, "Strawberries fixed those cards and she put them back?"

Chalkeye nodded. "Jack can pay up old scores now. When Strawberries comes to the game tonight, Jack is going to kill him. It's safe because"—here Chalkeye's voice was very quiet—"Strawberries has been winning from some of the boys who trusted him." After a pause, in which he seemed to sum up and select what more he would say, he added in a voice that was strangely toneless: "I don't want Strawberries killed. We are going to where I have told him a woman was buried with her jewels. I've said it would be death if they caught us. He'll dig. He'd never have stooped so low, once. Then I've fixed up a fake alarm. He'll go. He'll stay gone, I guess. I guess," Chalkeye concluded, "Strawberries would have held on if Deepmere hadn't happened along."

"None of this appeals to me very much," I said. "Why invent——"

"Do you think it appeals to me?" he interrupted, flaming into sudden violence. "Find a better way."

"Let him have the truth."

The puncher's eyes fell, and by that I read his heart.

"Not easy for you," I pursued, touching his knee, "but surely better for him?"

Still he held his eyes averted. He was bent over with trouble. "I couldn't be sure——" he began; he left it unsaid, and again I read his heart. To let the man he had loved and vouched for have the truth was a bitterness beyond his courage, and worse still, he feared there was not enough man left in Strawberries to stand up to it and kill, or be killed. By his fantastic scheme of the jewels, he had provided a way out. But what a way!

"I'd let it alone," said I.

"No, you wouldn't."

He walked out without another word, and I listened to the slow and heavy tread of his boots down the stairs.

I sat with my pen in hand, writing nothing and forgetting time, while the day faded; until Madden called loudly from below that I would soon be too late for supper.

The day grew wholly dark, the lamps burned in the saloon, shining on the stacks of bottles and the pictures of pink women; and the usual group, with a few stray players, gathered at the tables. The sound of chips and of the voices betting was very distinct in the quiet house. The breath of the sage-brush, the breath of the wilderness, the eternal, impassive witness of our deeds and lives, came through the open door.

I saw Jack Saunders look up and then continue his game. Some time elapsed, and he looked up again, watching the door; this time he whispered some impatient word to his neighbor, and the playing went on. It was a good hour later that something far off made one listen, and I saw the head of Saunders jerk up quickly. There were shots very distant; that was all; and once again the gambler muttered to his neighbor.

This time he did not resume playing, but sat scowling at the door. The figure he watched for did not come.

A sort of dreariness dulled me, thinking it all over; it was all degraded and dreary; and I got up to go to bed. As I crossed the office the girl entered and went straight to the saloon door. By her theatrical pose it was plain that the lust for telling sensational news was on her—but Saunders spoke first.

"To hell with *you*," said he. "Where's the tame pet you're keeping?"

Then she had her triumph and her climax; and her voice rose to the level of it.

"Gone where you'll never get him, Jack Saunders! Chalkeye has got you fooled!"

The gambler sprang up and listened to nothing more. While she continued ranting to her heart's content, he dragged on his chaps, snatched his quirt, buckled his holster, and would have been out to get his horse, but Chalkeye stood in the office. Saunders shot so quickly that I did not see him fire; and almost as quickly the puncher shot back. I think both missed; but neither stopped.

They passed me and went out of the house. I heard them as they moved through the dark, firing, and I heard myself counting the shots mechanically; they seemed to cut a trail in the night, they went on and on; and when they ceased, I had forgotten how many I had counted. I was standing in the office where I had been when it began; I had not moved a step.

No one else was in the house, and now I remembered that I had seen them running by. I remained quite still, and next saw the Doughgy at the door.

"Chalkeye is dead," said he. "Both are dead. Maybe you would like to come up and help fix Chalkeye."

"Come up?"

"Saunders ran from him when he found he was hit. Chalkeye followed him up-stairs to his woman's room. He shot Chalkeye from the floor."

The puncher lay across the threshold, a wound through his breast, the only one. Somewhere in the back of the room people were attending to Saunders —I didn't notice. The Doughgy and I did not touch

Chalkeye at once; we stood and looked at his quiet face. There was no violence in it; he lay in a sort of dignity, and there was a grace in the repose of his long arms.

It may have been minutes that we stood looking at the face.

"He thinks it is just as well," said the Doughgy. "He had changed a heap. Dying would not have suited him a little bit, once. He loved living up to the hilt. Better company I never traveled with. Gosh, how he could ride. Yes, these last years had changed him. It must be tough to see the apple of your eye go rotten."

Something in the dead man's pocket caught my sight, and I stooped and pulled out a handkerchief and unfolded a letter and handed it to the Doughgy. It was not too stained to be read, and the Doughgy began aloud, "To all whom this may concern," and then read silently; but when he had gone a few lines he turned his head away, and I took the sheet from his hand as he walked to the window and stood with his back to me looking out into the darkness.

So these two also went to the hill of upright and fallen headboards. At the end of the burying, the Doughgy and I lingered in the sun and the silence, looking off at the undulating miles.

"Do you remember the morning when Strawberries came up the river and Chalkeye borrowed your glasses?"

"Oh, yes. I remember."

"They say the Elkhorn Railroad will get as far as this next year," said the Doughgy. "Good-by, Old West. I shouldn't wonder if I pulled my freight for a new country one of these days."

He did; and from him in California, I had two of the three glimpses of Strawberries I still have to tell after his path wound away from mine. Once from Redlands the Doughgy wrote me that he had seen Strawberries clerking in the What Cheer House, in that town. Strawberries had not seen him; and soon after had lost this job. Again the Doughgy wrote during the days when the Western Pacific was being constructed across Nevada.

"I was getting good pay as foreman of a bridge gang," he said; "and one night I went to the honk-atonk to spend some and make a night of it. Strawberries was pounding a piano as professional player for a roomful of drunken girls with their men. I didn't spend my money. I went out."

My last news was in 1910, when I ran up the river from Cheyenne in a flivver. Two railroads had come. There was a new town called Casper. Drybone had long been wholly abandoned. There were oil claims. Along the river where the sage-brush had grown and the cattle had been rounded

up were fields and fruit and fences: not everywhere: but it was gone, the true, real thing was
gone. The scenery was there, but the play was over.

Just a touch, a whiff of the past met me as we
crossed La Parelle Creek. We came to some high
sage-brush along a bottom, and I smelled it, and one
of those sudden cravings for days bygone rushed
over me—to hunt, to camp, to revel in young joys;
I longed to speak some magic word and evoke the
golden years—no others—and live them again, and
then pass on, or pass out, or whatever follows this.
We came to the turnout for the graveyard. It was
visible still, but I did not wish to look at that. Then
we reached what had been Drybone.

"I'll get out here," I said to the young, green
chauffeur.

"There's nothing here."

"I know. There used to be. Wait here."

I walked through weeds, and splinters of sheds,
and rusted objects. Three boards of the hotel were
standing. Part of the post-office was there. The
cabin of luxury was fairly whole, and all around
it gleamed empty tin cans. There was a door; and
when I saw that, I walked up and opened it.

He was lying in bed, reading a paper.

"Oh, there you are!" he said.

So he had come back, actually summoned by that
same Past which we had shared for a while, the Past

where his real friends had been! I liked this remnant of the man better than ever I had liked the man.

"Thank God somebody has come to lunch," said he. "Now I'll have to get up and cook something."

This he did; and for an hour we talked about anything to keep off the one thing in our minds. The photographs were there. I suppose the widow had sent things after him. And now he lay in bed and ate tinned food, unless company happened by.

The young, green chauffeur came to see what had become of me, and as I was walking away, Strawberries stood in his door.

"It all used to be very jolly," he said.

I nodded and walked on.

"I say," he called.

I turned. There he stood, and into his face came a something that recalled the old smile like a pressed flower.

"Chalkeye was a good fellow, you know."

"Yes."

"I liked Chalkeye."

"Yes."

"I suppose you're thinking he was a better fellow than me?"

"Yes."

"Right."

Lone Fountain

"MARJORIE," said the General to his married granddaughter, "bring me that wrinkled volume in red morocco which stands next my published works."

Fruit of his cavalry life on our frontier, these essays had marked him an authority upon several Indian wars, as well as upon myths and languages among certain tribes of the Shastan, Salishan and Shoshonean stocks.

While Marjorie crossed the great library to fetch the book, we assembled our chairs round the fireplace.

Each night one of us had taken a turn to relate something we had personally witnessed, or had heard from a witness.

"While you held the floor last night," said the General to me, "I wondered if your story was to be like mine. But the parallel ceases with the traditional dread of the Yellowstone Park and its geysers which the Indians used to feel. The history of the Park is curious," he continued, addressing us all. "How many of the thousands who now go there every summer know that Colter, the first white man who ever saw it, was considered merely a liar? National attention did not wake to these marvels we possessed until after the Civil War, when various men had beheld and reported them and thus set afoot more official explorations.

"I went on some of those," pursued the General. "I saw it when the Park was completely wild, soon after Congress had set it aside from settlement and declared it a pleasure-ground."

The General put on his spectacles and sat silent, turning slowly back and forth the leaves of the weather-beaten book which Marjorie had brought. We waited in the warmth, listening to the hollow reverberations of the wind and the hissing gusts of sleet.

"Is it to be a personal experience, sir?" I asked.

Our host held his book up to us, open, and we admired the manuscript, close and beautiful, crossing its pages as straight as if the lines had been ruled.

"My hand was firmer then," said he, "but my pen was lazy. What I saw in those old frontier days would fill two diaries like this. I was a captain when I wrote down what I shall read you after I have told you somewhat at random what I remember about Scott while I was still a lieutenant. A strange being."

He took off his spectacles, and, keeping a finger in the diary on his knee, spoke from his memories.

"I was stationed at Bellingham Bay. Soon after

my arrival there I was talking to Elena Grover outside the stockade about the original characters which
the frontier seemed to collect, when she looked off
and stopped me. I saw a youth approaching from
the trees. He came with long, quiet steps. He wore
Siwash moccasins. His bearing made me watch him.

"As he drew near, he took off his hat to Mrs.
Grover, and she greeted him with some cordiality.
He stood speaking to her easily, with his hat in his
hand. His rich voice had ancestors in it, his utterance was civilized, his thick hair curled low, half-
way to his brows, and fell to the collar of his flannel
shirt; but he had brushed it carefully and was fresh-
shaven. I wondered if one so young could be like so
many there, a fugitive from justice.

"Mrs. Grover took a book from his hand. He was
returning it to the Quartermaster, and she asked
his opinion of it as she gave it back.

" 'Why,' said he, 'how should a Yankee compre-
hend Italians? Let him keep to Salem.' With that
he bowed and went his way to the Quartermaster
with 'The Marble Faun.'

" 'He is nineteen,' said Elena Grover. 'Why
should a man have that chestnut hair? Why should-
n't I? Did you notice his gray eyes? When he is
excited he keeps as cool as when he is not, but his
eyes turn black.' She rolled her own, and humor
gleamed in them. 'I am unlikely ever to give the

Major cause for anxiety; but if I were not just as much in love with him as on the day we married . . .' She lowered her voice, although no one was in sight, and added, 'That boy, Kenneth Scott, that unconscious charmer, is somebody's natural son.'

" 'He will not be unconscious long if all the ladies at this post look at him as you did. How do you come to know his origin?'

" 'Kenneth showed Captain Forsythe what Shakespeare says about bastards. That was his own view, he said; he liked his birth.'

" 'Shakespeare! Hawthorne!'

" 'Oh, it doesn't stop there! In the logging-camp where he has been employed this summer, Scott sometimes read Latin poetry in spare moments; but the suspicions as to his manhood which this naturally aroused were set at rest by his killing a gambler who had cheated him. And not an enlisted man here can beat him in the foot-races. I wonder if he will ever find out that he is tragic.'

"As an officer I could not well seek Scott out with no better pretext than curiosity for his acquaintance. He was not a fugitive from justice, I learned from the Quartermaster. At sixteen, he had left whatever home he had in San Francisco, and joined a surveying party in Oregon. Since that, he had hired himself to various outfits, trapped, hunted, traded, survived. He had cast civilization behind him, but not books.

"Whoever had taught him his books, said the Quartermaster, had done a thorough job; all sorts of remarkable men came across the world to live and thrive in San Francisco, bringing with them the better education and the looser morals of the Old World; one could readily imagine the wild gentleman who begot the boy, said the Quartermaster.

"Before I had another sight of Scott, he had drifted out of Bellingham Bay as he had drifted in, independent, indifferent, unaccounted for, not secretly at all, but without relation to anyone or anything. I felt a brief disappointment, and then forgot the boy's existence, until, in the following year at Vancouver Barracks, I heard an unusual voice, and strange to say knew at once whose it was.

"Yes; whatever his blood, Scott's voice had ancestors in it, and in his eyes was a quality more often to be noticed in the Old World; full, luminous, concentrated, not the mere vivacious emptiness so common in the American.

"Books brought us into familiarity at Vancouver Barracks; he was carpentering on the new stables, and I would find him on my porch with some volume to return, or desirous to borrow another; only, he wanted very few that I possessed. Once or twice when I went to Portland I brought him works he had asked for—Ovid, I remember, in the original, and the Bible on another occasion.

"Against my will he read me some of the Bible stories, which he greatly admired, and said he should learn by heart; he seemed able to carry his will against mine not infrequently. He read some passionate lines from Leander's epistle to Hero in Ovid, and translated them, for my Latin was gone already. Leander recalls the nights he spent with Hero in her tower; and both our faces flushed to think of it.

"But Scott declared that no woman was likely to make him swim so far.

" 'Suppose you loved her,' I suggested.

" 'Have you ever been in love?' he asked.

" 'I told him that certainly I had.

" 'I never have,' said he. 'I suppose there must be such a thing. Who would you rather be that you've read of?'

" 'Until I am thirty, Don Juan,' I confessed.

" 'Yes; but by the time he was thirty, a man would be nothing else. No; Don Juan was too much with women. He didn't live enough out-of-doors on the land and the sea with men.'

" 'Who would you like to be?' I asked.

" 'For first choice, myself!' he exclaimed. 'Myself always. For second—well . . .' He fell to thinking about that.

"Yes; at Vancouver Barracks we grew intimate. Scott swore seldom, and his tongue was never rank, although he spoke of all things with a directness I had never heard before. I fell ill; and what did the boy do but drop his work and nurse me through pneumonia! There again he had his will, against all military procedure. His charm overcame the Post surgeon.

" 'A good dinner will help,' said he, when I was convalescent. 'It shall happen in Portland, where you can have wild ducks and French wine. My belly is only one of my gods.'

"We dined; bowing to his will, I was his guest. I made him accept a horse on a later occasion.

" 'I think I would rather be Ulysses for second choice,' he said at the dinner. 'He traveled splendidly, and his brain and body knew all experience possible to man. Achilles let his passions ride him.'

" 'Have you fallen in love yet?' I inquired.

" 'It's not in me,' he replied.

" 'I'll tell you,' said I. 'It's your passions you're afraid of.'

"His gray eyes grew black, and it was some time before he spoke. 'Do you know,' said he, 'I came rather near hating you just then.'

"A strange creature. Pagan from the womb; holding Christianity impossible, conceding it certain merits, by no means in revolt against it, as I was, owing to early overdoses of Sunday. Calf atheism is often as violent and unimportant as calf-love.

"He drifted off from Vancouver Barracks as he had from Bellingham Bay, without reference to people or things; in spite of his kindness and his devoted care, incapable apparently of feeling a tie.

"I missed him, and I was angry. How could anyone so full of blood be cold-blooded? But anger was powerless in his presence; at my next sight of him I merely rejoiced. And in the end, without understanding him, I accepted him for what he was, unaccountable, electric, a natural force in a human body; quite as ready, I think, to die for you at any pinch as to forget you at any moment. He was very wide between the eyes.

"Trappers and packers brought news of him from time to time before our next meeting at Walla Walla. He was among the Nez Percés for a while, adopted by those Indians with tribal ceremonies because of his fleetness. But the tribe on the Des Chutes River with whom the Nez Percés held periodic contests would not allow him to enter the races; therefore, at the command of Chief Joseph, Scott left a number of sons behind him, reared to be athletes by the young mothers selected by the Chief in the hope that the offspring of these unions would inherit their father's gift of speed, and bring honor to the Nez Percés in their future contests with the tribe on the Des Chutes. I have never heard that they did; but I am told that to this day their descendants can be recognized by their ruddy hair.

"Scott turned up at Walla Walla in that way of his, as if a few hours, instead of a couple of years, had intervened since Vancouver Barracks. I made him some compliments on his experiences with the Nez Percés. He told me of his races without boasting, and of his honeymoons as plainly as if he spoke of fighting or eating. Contrary to his expectations, he had found the women as passionate as any in his experience. He showed me a superb suit of buckskin, tanned and beaded for him by the squaws at Chief Joseph's order. This he wore upon festal occasions, very rarely.

"At Walla Walla we grew into deeper intimacy than ever; it was here that I gave him a fine three-year-old mare, and also made him free of a spare-room I had in my quarters, whenever he should wish to sleep indoors instead of in his tent.

"There I found him one morning, splashed heavily with blood, sitting in a sort of trance, and in front of him a bottle of whisky, its cork undrawn. At a place just outside the reservation, he had again killed a man. For the first time, I heard in his voice the note of human pain.

" 'I would never have done it,' he said; 'I would

never have done it. He was a good fellow. But we got drunk together.'

"He relapsed into silence. Then, quite suddenly, he smashed the bottle to splinters.

"At that time in our Northwest, a man's standing with men outweighed every process of the scanty law; and as it appeared from all witnesses that the victim had precipitated his own death upon him, Scott was not even brought to trial. He passed a long sentence on himself, forswearing totally both cards and drink until he should be thirty years old; and wrote out this pledge, and gave it into my keeping, and, so far as ever I knew, stuck to it rigidly.

"And one day he was gone again, without any good-by, and my next sight of him was after my troop had been stationed for two years at the Mammoth Hot Springs, and was about to be transferred to Arizona.

"The Park was still unknown to the summer mob, and only adventurous travelers found their way to it with pack-horses over the trails.

"No! Civilization paid us but few visits; it was science that paid us visits in advance of the holiday tourist. The reports of our own geologists brought investigators from Europe, some of whom made agreeable breaks in our isolation from the world— some, not all.

"Heavy steps came across my porch one afternoon, and in my doorway stood a square-shaped individual in spectacles, extending a card in my direction. I rose and read it: Herr Doctor Professor Schmidt, he was, from Berlin, with titles copiously printed. He had come to study the geysers, the hot springs, the mineral formation, all the geologic incidents of the 3500 square miles covered by the Park. Now the Park was then no place in which to lose one's way; and as a preliminary I unfolded my map of it.

" 'I do not need instructions,' said he. 'I have in Germany this volcanic area studied.' His voice was dry as a blackboard, a high tenor, issuing from a body which one expected would sing bass.

" 'What do you need?'

" 'Permission to supply my camp from your commissary, und also another man. In Cook City I engaged one, but the fool has left me.'

"My impulse was to remark that the man would have been a fool not to. 'Are you alone, then?' I asked.

" 'I have an Indian.'

" 'An Indian! We know of only five that are willing to venture in your volcanic area.'

" 'Evidently he is one of these.'

" 'What is his name?'

" 'I have not asked. It is not important.'

" 'Two persons are insufficient in such a camp,'
I said. I could easily have detailed an enlisted man
to guide him, but his manner had not appealed to
me. 'I don't know of any man,' I said. 'If I hear
of one, I will tell you. Buy anything you need at
any time. We will try to forward mail. How long
shall you stay here?'

" 'Naturally until I have another man.'

" 'Where are you camped?'

" 'On the Gardner River, perhaps a mile.'

"Before he took his leave I learned that Oxford
had given him a degree at the instance of his friend
Max Müller, that his subterranean studies in Sicily, published at Leipsic, had been translated into
French and Italian, because they proved some error
which I have forgotten about a spring called Arethusa : his fame seemed to rest on putting other geologists in the wrong. Did I know of earthquakes
here? Had the geyser water any taste? He would
report its chemical analysis to the world.

"I did hear of a man who had left some mines
near the Park's north line, and I rode down to
Schmidt's camp. I am not likely to forget that. No.
Not very likely.

"A Sibley tent was by the bank, white against
the dark rocks across the stream; some yards away
was a rough *wickiup;* beyond, some horses grazed,
and an Indian squatted near these, plaiting strings

of buckskin. Schmidt I did not see; but near the
small quiet smoke of the cooking fire a woman sat;
black-haired, full-bosomed, quiet as the fire, looking
down in thought as she stirred something. Grace
flowed in her dark, bare arm, and beneath her light
shirt the curves flowed in harmony with the free
sweep of her stirring. Perhaps she was twenty-five.

"Some paces from the fire, on a tree stump,
motionless, unaware of my approach, gazing at the
woman, sat Kenneth Scott. Scott must have been
twenty-four then. He was wearing his buckskin, his
hat lay on the ground, and his hair shone as I had
first seen it at Bellingham Bay. Neither of them
noticed me as I rode nearer, while the river made
its sounds, the smoke rose and the Indian sat always
plaiting his buckskin. Did her blood know, I asked
myself, that Scott's blood was speaking to it? And
presently I was to receive the answer.

"At my voice, she raised her eyes, but did not
cease her leisurely stirring. Her eyes were deep and
seemed dark as her hair, until one saw they were
blue—and their long, curled lashes set off the white
which encircled the iris. I took off my hat, and her
grave glance waked and flashed a greeting. Had I
at that time seen the Mediterranean peoples, I
should have known she was one, and that the old
centuries of Greece and Rome had molded her with
subtleties and violences, deep beyond the compre-

hension of Northern minds; and that she had her blue eyes from the Normans.

"My speaking had jarred Scott out of his trance; he got up and spoke to me as if we had seen each other an hour before.

"'Surely this is the camp of Professor Schmidt?' I repeated.

"'Hans!' called the woman. 'Hans!' Song and the basking South lurked in her tones.

"There was no answer, and again I saw her beautiful teeth as she smiled, speaking with an accent, and carefully.

"'When my husband is being scientific, I must call him never less than three times before he will hear me. Hans!'

"The Professor emerged from the tent, turned his spectacles vaguely about, and upon seeing me, bowed. 'Ah, Lieutenant, it is you. Good afternoon. I was coming later to see you.'

"'I have heard of a man who has just left the mines,' said I.

"'I am the man,' said Scott.

"'I have engaged this young person,' said the Professor. 'You know him then, already? He assures me that he understands camp work und has been twice through this volcanic area.'

"'That's since Walla Walla,' explained Scott to me.

" 'He certainly understands camp work,' said I. 'And I never have known him to misrepresent himself in any way.'

" 'That is most satisfactory,' said the Professor.

" 'And since it is so well that you have known him,' said the woman, her eyes alive, and with the careful enunciation of a language not her own, 'I am sure you will tell me that you know him to be a good boy, who always is mindful of his place. Is it not true?' And she smiled at him as a mother might.

"Scott's face went instantly scarlet at the indulgent—almost caressing—domination conveyed in her voice. That was the answer to what I had asked myself; the old Mediterranean centuries had spoken.

" 'Professor,' said I, 'did you not give me to understand that only an Indian was with you? I don't remember your mentioning any lady. This Park is very rough and lonely.'

" 'Ach, it is only Nina, my wife! She goes everywhere with me. I married her in Sicily, in Acireale; she is quite used to volcanic areas. Is it not so, Nina? Nina, this gentleman kindly permits that we buy provisions und necessaries.'

"Thus introduced, she rose and came forward, and again I took off my hat. Except for the dusky thicket of her hair, she might have been a bronze Aphrodite, come to life after her long burial be-

neath Mediterranean earth. I dismounted, while
Scott's eyes under his slanted woodland brows followed her.

" 'Nina,' said the Professor, 'is useful in the
kitchen; und very intelligent when she copies my
notes. Und in high altitudes when I am wakeful, she
reads und I go to sleep so. You will excuse me now,
Lieutenant, as I have yet, before we start tomorrow,
some notes to finish. I find interesting that specimen
at your Mammoth Springs which you have so
quaintly baptized Jupiter Terrace.' And with another of his formal bows, he trod his way back to
the tent, and disappeared.

" 'That is a very wrong name you give,' said
Nina seriously; 'Jupiter would never come to this
place here.'

" 'If only all the Greek gods would,' said I, laughing, 'think what a drawing attraction it would be
for the American public!'

"But the spirit of my chaff seemed to displease
her.

" 'This should be the home of many gods,' she
said. 'See that you do not offend them.'

" 'Are you not of the true Church?' I asked, still
laughing; for an image of the Virgin hung from her
neck.

" 'Certainly.' And she crossed herself. 'But
those others have power in Sicily still.'

" 'Do you really believe such things?' asked Kenneth Scott.

" 'At Acireale,' she answered him, 'I could show you in the sea the rocks which a giant once threw.'

" 'Polyphemus!' exclaimed Scott. 'Ulysses!'

" 'Ah, you know! I thought Americans did not know. Then why do you ask if I believe?' She pointed to the distant, unconcerned Indian near the horses; aloof; inhabitant of his own impenetrable world; always plaiting his buckskin thongs. 'It is his gods who must live here. See that you do not offend them.'

"It is a long way even now from Mammoth Hot Springs to San Carlos, where my troop went in a few days, and where, as a mitigation for the evils of that post, I found the Grovers stationed. Elena and I often wondered what were the experiences of that party in the wilderness, and our guesses disagreed. 'She will teach him that he is tragic,' Elena insisted.

"We referred to it until the revolt of the Cibicu scouts concerned us and our lives more nearly. And it was ten years before I saw the Park again, on a furlough. I wanted some fishing and hunting, Grover was now a colonel and commandant of the Park, and I went there, this time in a train; the Park branch of the Northern Pacific had reached Cinnabar. Three hotels had come, two very primitive, and still the tourists were few—only eight or ten were in the train to Cinnabar.

"As we were getting out of the train, two of these noticed a striking figure out of the window, and exclaimed that there was an old-timer if ever there was one.

"I saw the figure on the platform among the railroad employees, and agreed he was a true type. Then I received a great shock; as I looked at him, I recognized Kenneth Scott. His hair was perfectly white.

"I have now reached what I recorded afterwards in my diary."

The General paused, but no one spoke. As he put on his spectacles and opened the book, the thunderous blasts of the storm swept the chimney. He began to read what follows.

When I stepped down at Cinnabar, Scott wrung my hand without words. "They told me you were coming," he said at last.

This was a changed Kenneth; he was not only capable of affection, but even of betraying it.

"Have you been here ever since?" I asked.

He shook his head. "I have traveled. Mexico. Japan. Sicily. But I always come back—so far." In his speech and his look there was that which now checked the question I had been about to ask him concerning the party with whom he had gone as guide. "They said you wanted to fish and hunt," said he.

"And to see what has been done to the Park."

"May I go with you?" In the old days he would not have asked if he might come, he would have said he was coming.

At this point I was told that Colonel Grover had sent an ambulance for me, and my baggage was aboard.

"I'll come for my answer tonight," he said; and I drove off.

Presently, as the mules were galloping along beside the Gardner River, the enlisted man who was driving said: "I saw the Captain talking to Lone Fountain."

"Is that what you call him?"

"Everybody. He's a good guide. About the best. Makes his dudes put their fires out and keep all the Park regulations. Oh, Lone Fountain is harmless. But——" The soldier tapped his forehead significantly.

The Grovers confirmed all this.

"Why Lone Fountain?" I inquired.

"Because he always shows any of his parties that will go off the beaten trail a geyser in which they can see no interest. It is near the trail to some good fishing down in the canyon. He declares it is not extinct. But there's nothing in the idea. Oh, he's harmless." This was the Colonel.

"You should see him," said Elena, "cross a stream by leaping his way on the wet ledges of protruding rocks. His body is still as young as ever. And I would trust him with any horse I ever owned. But I cannot make him talk to me. Perhaps you will admit at last that he is tragic."

When Scott came in, he was dressed in the buckskins, which had withstood the years better than he.

"Remember them?" he said. "Remember this?" And he showed me a battered Ovid.

With some difficulty I overcame his refusal to take money for his horses and his time on the camping trip I decided to make with him. In other days he would have prevailed; but something was gone out of him, and instead of the old fascination, he was wistful. The luminous concentration had died out of his eyes, and the strange interest of his voice was rather gentle than vital, as it used to be.

In all the three weeks of our fishing and hunting north of the Park on Hell-roaring Creek, I never saw a sign to account for the soldier's tapping of his forehead. We talked, we were silent, we slept, we waked, we smoked; and no one unacquainted with Scott's former self would have taken him for anything but a quiet, serene man, surprisingly well informed, and experienced in all woodcraft. Sometimes I had a feeling that he was going to reveal what had changed him so, but in those three weeks he did not. He lived deeply withdrawn into himself, unlike the Kenneth Scott of other days.

Then, suddenly, it came. We were on the trail from Yancey's by Tower Creek to the Falls, and had crossed an open, edged by large pine-trees, into which I was following the trail, when my horse stopped, held his ears forward and backed a few steps, snorting. Scott was fifty yards behind me with the packs, which had paused to drink at a little stream the trail crossed. It might be a bear, I thought, but I saw none, and horses have their whims; so I urged the animal farther into the pines. He went nervously, as I reasoned with him.

Then a little wind from the wood blew in my face and I knew what the matter was: on the wind came that unmistakable volcanic odor which floats from so many steaming pools and chasms in the Park. It is a common thing for horses to shy at the smell if they are unaccustomed to it, or come upon it unexpectedly. In a few moments my voice had quieted the horse.

As Scott came along with the packs, he spoke. "I thought I heard you talking to somebody."

"The horse. I thought he saw a wild animal. But it was just a hot spring that must be in the wood."

"How do you know he saw nothing?"

"I can't be sure; but I didn't see it. The smell would explain his behavior."

"How do we know what they see?"

At this I turned round to look at him, and his face gave me a strange impression.

"I don't think I understand you, Kenneth."

All the horses were now standing still, except one pack that wandered toward the creek.

"If you remember your Bible," said he, "you remember Balaam. 'And when the ass saw the angel of the Lord, she thrust herself unto the wall, and crushed Balaam's foot against the wall: and he smote her again.'"

I looked at the shoulder of Mount Washburn, to which the sun in the west was drawing near; and the pines, and the open, and the rocks rising beyond toward the mountain, all seemed to unite in a presence that watched us. I tried to shake off this idea, of which I felt ashamed.

"Balaam was a great while ago," said I, lightly; "changes have come in the world."

"The eternal does not change," said Scott.

At a splashing sound behind us, I started, and was ashamed of myself again. Scott was galloping to the creek, but he arrived too late; the pack-animal had rolled in the water, and what it carried went under a number of times before Scott made the horse stand up. The load had to be spread to dry in what of the sunshine remained.

Scott looked at the sun and shook his head. "It will be dusk before we make our camping place."

"Why make it, then? Haste is not in our program."

At this he turned to me rather quickly. "You would camp here?" he asked, after a moment.

"It's a good place," I replied.

He hesitated. "Well, why not?" he then murmured.

Without delaying to search for poles, we stretched the tent between two slender pines at the edge of the wood; and while Scott set about the fire, I strolled in among the trees to pick up dry sticks for pegging the guy-ropes.

A breath of sulphur met me as I reached the point where my horse had first shown fright, and in a few steps more through the intense stillness of the pines I heard the sound of the unseen geyser—that soft heavy beat of exhalation from the bowels of the earth.

I stopped to listen for the next beat, which followed after a space of silence. The heavily muffled and suppressed cough suggested to my somewhat disturbed imagination the choking of a deep laugh.

It was humiliating to be jarred as I was by the sudden harsh cry of a Clarke's crow overhead. I watched the bird's gray shape take flight and disappear. One thing and another had brought me to so little creditable state of uneasiness, that my wish was to get away from the trees into the open. And now the final traces of sunlight vanished from the wood, leaving it somber and sinister. To give the lie to my own senseless apprehension, I resolved not to go out of the wood but—just as a child in the name of fearlessness will walk into a dark room sorely against his inclination—to go deeper into the wood and come face to face with the object from which the sulphurous breath was borne on the air.

I went over the rise where the trail led, and there below me in a hollow was the sight; piled and tumbled shapes of stone, gray in hue, flung together once by the convulsions of the planet; and mingled with their castellated mass, the petrified and distorted precipitate from ancient boiling floods. The eruptions must have been furious once, a mighty volume, shaking the earth while its gush poured vapors and gleaming pillars of water toward the sky. Nothing of this was left today, save the embattled accretions heaved up ages ago through that vast gaping slit of darkness. While I looked at it, the breath and the sound rose from the exhausted giant at their rhythmic intervals.

Not cured of my uneasiness, as I strolled on again for pegs among the trees at the rim of the rocky arena, my foot pushed something, and I kicked it free from the dried ground—the rusted remnant of a hunting-knife. Signs of an old camp were faintly visible. My pegs collected, I found the knife again and picked it up, and from the top of the rise surveyed the tumbled rocks and formation, the tomb of a natural force once so fiercely alive. I regained the open country with relief.

Scott let the knife lie across his open palm, considering it. "I had forgotten it," said he.

"Yours?"

"Ten years ago."

"Why did you camp in such a place as that?"

"It was no choice of mine."

"Has that thing in there a name?"

"That thing! Do you think it should have a name?"

"I do."

"It is on their latest map without any. Too many like it here are on the beaten track, alive and tame, willing to perform for tourists to look at. This one would never do that. It's wild."

"Scott, what's the matter with you?"

He answered with a smile of desolation, "She gave it a name."

"I should not wish to camp there," I pursued; "there is something about the whole place . . ."

"If you had been a horse you would have shied

yourself?" he suggested. "You would have been right."

"Kenneth, what on earth is the matter with you?"

"Oh, you needn't waste any fright on me!"

Either he was being deliberately perverse, or the impulse to say more was hampered by his will to say nothing; we finished our supper and arranged the bedding before I made another attempt to unlock his reserve.

"And so you all camped in there?"

He nodded in the firelight. "In there. But not all of us came away." And he set about washing the dishes.

"They were an odd husband and wife," said I. "Had they any children?"

"Lord, no!" he burst out violently.

This was a flash of the Scott of old; and after it he would not say a word; and presently I got into my blankets.

Before sleep came to me I felt him getting into his own; sleep prevented my being aware that at some later hour he rose. I waked in the depth of the night, and his blankets were empty. The moon, though past the full, gave much light. He had left the tent flaps open, and there in front glowed a few last embers of our fire. In the frozen air I jumped up and threw on my warmest clothes, and hastened along the trail beneath the moon and the cold shining of the stars. From the rise above the rocky arena I saw him in it below, sitting beside a fire, his gauntlets clasped over one knee, staring at the geyser. If he knew of my presence, he made no sign of it, or any movement while I was descending to him.

I sat down by him without any word and laid my hand on his shoulder; and with a long-drawn breath he passed a hand over his eyes.

"Anxious in spite of me?" he said, still looking at the geyser. "Could you be at the Mammoth Springs without hearing from somebody that I was harmless?" He stopped, and turned to me with his smile of desolation, which seemed to come from beyond pain. "Harmless. That has been true for ten years. People did not say that once." He looked again at the geyser. "Would you mind listening? I think I can tell you the whole thing here. I think I should like to—now, tonight."

I nodded; and it was some moments before he resumed, while the breath of the geyser sounded recurrently in the silence. I dragged a fallen log to the fire.

"She loved me long before the end," said Scott. "She loved me the first day. Looking back, I knew it. It was in her hands she kept from touching mine; and once or twice her eyes said so; but she was often afraid to let me see her eyes towards the end. She

would look away, or keep her lids over them. Do you
remember her lids, how heavy they were? Do you
remember the blue of her eyes? And she knew my
love of her was a revelation to myself, an amazement, a delirium of discovery and joy.

"That she was the first who had ever waked me
to this would have given us our happiness; if it had
not been for him." Scott pointed to the geyser.
"His power was over her before the love I made to
her began to win her. I was winning, we were on
the threshold of our happiness—had she not that
very day accepted my lips? And then, why so often
could she hold me off and call me a boy? It was the
power he had over her. What man has ever con-
tended with them and come off first?"

The chill of the night was penetrating even
through my thick woolens, and I rose and stood near
the fire while he continued.

"The Professor would camp here instead of out in
the open. He was studying geysers, and it saved him
a walk. He wrote long notes on every geyser and
spring, even when he said they were the same kind.
I suppose he thought it was quantity that made a
man famous. I saw it all—how she came to marry
him.

"Her people were not poor, she had convent education, but there was nothing at Acireale. Nothing,
unless—unless"—Scott glanced at the geyser—"un-

less she got a fright. I have been there. Then he came along with his talk and his microscopes, and she thought she would like a change, and travel in great cities, and be the wife of a great man, and meet other great men.

"But she must have found him out soon. Her ideas of him had changed long before ever they came to America. She never said a word of it to me, she was what you call loyal, I suppose; she helped him every way she could, she was the brains. I saw it all. I used to watch her writing for him, reading to him . . . I don't believe he had ever really seen her in his life—not on their wedding-day, not on their bridal night . . . Oh, how soon she must have found him out!

"When he would lecture in that voice about the mechanical theory of heat, I used to want to take him by the beard and drag him over the rocks. But it is an awful thing to kill a man, unless it is the only thing to be done.

"I suppose it was her convent education that taught her to be dutiful like that, helped her to act up to her responsibilities—but then, how could she believe in pagan gods at the same time?

"For the first weeks of our camping, I never took what she used to say now and then about gods as being something that she meant. After a while she got over her surprise that I knew anything that is to be found in books, and she began to talk to me about her own country. She loved to do that. Sometimes when I brought wood for her cook fire, or when we were riding along, or when the Professor was in the tent and I helped her to wash the dishes, or put camp in order, she would describe her home.

"She told me of orange-trees, and how their smell would fill a valley, and blow seaward to the decks of ships. She told of how the flowers grew. And of wild mountains where the descendants of Greeks lived still, with looks and costumes unlike their neighbors. And of theaters, where puppets played the stories of old kings. And she would come back to flowers often. And in the middle of such talk she would tell me of the Lake Pergusa that filled the hole where the god Pluto carried Proserpine to live with him in his kingdom below. Once she was going to tell me something, and stopped, and would not go on.

"When she found that I knew some of those stories, she often told me others. You see, she was very homesick; she had not seen anyone for a long time who wanted to listen. Do you remember her voice?

"After a while I knew I had loved her from the first minute. Don't you think that she must have known? I had never been afraid before to make a beginning with any woman. After I had made a beginning, she stopped calling me by my name, and called me Child.

" 'It's a long time since any man or any woman has found me a child!' I said.

" 'That is because no one in your country is grown up. You are a nation of children.'

" 'You can't do without me,' said I. 'I mean you. You know it. You're feeling it now.' She had been looking at me, but now she looked away. 'Tell the Professor,' I said. 'Tell him about me.'

"She made a very weak answer. 'I don't want to trouble my husband with anything that is not dangerous.'

"I suppose it was not a weak answer, because it made me angry. I went off and rode my horse all that morning. She is fighting me, I said to myself. But she has to fight. That's something. It's her religion that makes her fight. I'm not much afraid of any religion. I thought that, and more like it, all the hours I rode.

"When I got back to camp, the Professor was late and we had dinner, she and I and the Indian. When he was gone away to fish, she took it up where we had left off, although I did not realize this at first. She began to sew and while she stitched she told me a new story. In Sicily, she said, a nymph named Arethusa had been fleeing from her lover, and he was near overtaking her, when Artemis the goddess of chastity descended and stepped in between them, and changed the nymph into a flowing spring.

" 'You may see it still flowing today at Siracusa,' she said. 'I have seen it often.'

"It is sometimes a good move to make a woman angry. 'If your nymph's safety depended on any goddess,' I said, 'I pity her.'

"But she laughed with joy. 'My safety needs no goddess at any rate, so long as I am pursued only by a child.'

"I could have killed her; I was wild with love; but I said, 'A child too old to believe in a child's tale of goddesses.'

" 'What faith you have in your unbelief!' she remarked quietly; and resumed her mending.

" 'If I could speak Italian,' I said, 'I could make you listen.'

" 'I will teach it to you with pleasure. You are a clever boy.'

"It was then that I kissed her for the first time. I sprang before she could move, and she did not move then; but when I stopped, she had a stiletto in her hand, and her eyes glittered as I had never seen them. Nevertheless, she spoke as calmly as ever—no, not calmly, but quietly.

" 'Do not force me to use this.'

" 'Use it! Use it!' I said. 'I'm ready.' And I tore my shirt open. I was neither quiet nor calm.

"Nothing I had said or done before, not even my kisses, had affected her like this. The stiletto slid from her hand, her eyes changed, and she stood looking at me without a word. Mechanically I stooped and picked up the weapon and handed it to her. She took it mechanically.

" 'You are a beautiful child,' she said; 'there is no doubt of that. And some day it may be that you will grow up.'

" 'That day will be on this trip,' I replied.

"But in some way she had regained herself, again had the upper hand of me. That was a new thing in my experience; no man, or woman either, had ever got the upper hand of me before. But I wanted more than love with her now, I wanted life with her. And I would have won it. Won it in spite of the fight she had put up. She was not always able to stand me off . . . And she grew less and less able. And then . . ."

Scott went no further for a while.

"How could I, how could you, or any man," he resumed with less emotion, "get into his head that she believed those things were true—nymphs, gods, and the giant beneath Mount Etna? In an Indian you expect such superstitions; but she had been educated, had lived in Berlin, Paris, London. I asked her if other Sicilians had such ideas.

" 'They are not ideas,' was her reply. 'All Sicilians know it.'

"She actually began to teach me Italian. Knowing what I did of Latin was a great help. I made a progress that she had not expected. Between his specimens and his note-books, the Professor noticed it and approved of it. Think of that! I suppose it was unimaginable to him that any property of his, woman or dog, would fail to place him first. But it was long since she had belonged to him—if ever she had. She belonged to her church. I am sure that was the rock which held her.

" 'You will some day speak Italian very well,' she said. And then, answering what she saw in my eyes, 'And you think I am playing with fire. If you were fire, I would have you sent away.'

"I could not find any reply. It was one of the days when she was the stronger. It is true that her age, though the same as mine, was beyond mine, far beyond, centuries—but I would make her for that very reason love what I was—my body's strength, my spiritual April, my innocence of her spiritual autumn, which ancient Sicily with its Greek ruins and its tales of gods and bloody massacres had given her when she was born. Do you remember her when she walked? Do you remember her voice?

"A certain experience on a definite day let into my mind the first glimmer that the stories she told me were not mere mental playthings but some mysterious part of her, deep down and through and through.

"There was one of those little bubbling geysers, a little round shallow thing, hardly the size of a plate. The water came up through a small hole in the middle of it and trickled across the formation, down into the Firehole River. Once in about ten minutes it would rise into a diminutive activity, and sink. The Professor saw it, and said that now he would show us something which demonstrated the mechanical theory of heat very neatly. He called us to watch.

"We did not know what he expected to do with the thick solution of soap that he was making in a basin of hot water. As he began to pour this into the little geyser which had just sunk down, the Indian made a movement and gave a sharp grunt. We wondered at him. Almost at once the geyser foamed again, violently, rose much higher than its normal eruption.

"'You would not have believed that!' exclaimed the Professor in triumph. 'You will be my witnesses. I shall be the first to announce this.'

"'Not good,' said the Indian. 'Not good. I go if you do that.'

"She was standing near me. 'His gods live here, and are offended.'

"'It need not be done again,' said the Professor. 'It is a complete demonstration.'

"After that day the Indian was different. After

that day she was different. I was further from her. Something had come between us that was not there before. Her power increased over mine. But I was not to be stopped by that. I felt power in me which I would make prevail at the right time.''

Scott rose to drag a log to the fire, and I threw on another; and for a while we watched the spray of the sparks, and heard the beats of the geyser beyond them, heavy, rhythmic, unceasing.

''It may have been a couple of weeks after that experiment that we camped here, when the nights were growing cold. The Professor would not hurry, though I told him snow came early. He wished to omit nothing.

''When he saw this one, he said it might be important, that the formation was of interest; and so we had to camp here, farther from water, and where the Indian and I could not watch the horses so well. The first day, the Professor said that this was dying. He made calculations.

'' 'Must it die all alone?' she murmured as she stood in contemplation of it.

(''She stood there,'' said Scott, pointing. ''There, by that rock. Do you see?'')

''That was the first day. The sun still kept the days warm, and there was nothing but sun, never a cloud. She sat on that rock, watching it.

''It was the third morning that she came into

camp with some flowers, climbed to the brink of the chasm, threw the flowers into it and said: 'They are for you, Lone Fountain.'

One instant after she had spoken those words her face was stricken with terror; she gave a cry, and then the terror changed to rapture. We all saw that. And I saw the Indian nod as if he approved.

" 'Ach, Nina,' said the Professor, 'have you then not left those silly notions in Sicily? You will make yourself ridiculous to this intelligent young man.'

" 'Suppose,' said she, 'Etna should come to Yellowstone?' And she smiled at me.

" 'Nina, you are incorrigible. Well, I must go to see those hot springs in the canyon,' and he rode out of camp.

"She came down from the rim of the geyser, and I saddled her horse and mine; for I was to show her Tower Falls that day. While I was tightening the cinches, the Indian spoke to her. I knew very well that it was about what she had done; and after we had left him to guard camp and were half-way to Tower Creek, she told me that he was glad of her offering of flowers; it would atone for the experiment which her husband had made.

" 'He did not say it in that way,' she continued, 'but he made me understand him.' And then she spoke a few words in Italian. 'Do you understand that?' she asked.

" 'I know the meaning of your words. It is you I cannot understand.'

" 'Kenneth, you are like my husband!'

" 'Not at all like your husband.' And I looked at her as I had not been able to look for many days. And she was not able to meet it. 'My turn!' I thought. And I felt the resurgence of my power.

"She had said in Italian: 'Lone Fountain is not dying. They do not die.' And that word about her husband had escaped her. Never before by word or look had she given me the slightest glimpse of her mind as to him. Everything he demanded of her, to read aloud, to take dictation, to copy notes, she did loyally, as if she asked nothing more than these chances to be of use.

"But today was mine, I knew it; it must not be lost; and as we were choosing the place for our nooning above Tower Falls, I said again: 'Not at all like your husband.'

" '*Sicuro!*' she said, and laughed in that joyous way she had sometimes. 'Not like him. And when you have ceased to be a child, and become a man, you will not be like him. Now run away, Boy, and catch some trout to fry. And I will make the fire and boil the pot for our coffee, and get all things ready.'

"It always stung, that word child. But the sting was a challenge today, and I liked it. As I climbed down to the pool in the creek just before it meets the **river**, I remember stretching my arms out and feeling my returned power. And I caught enough trout at once, and then because down there it was very hot in the noon sun, I stripped and plunged into the pool.

"While I swam round where the water was deep, I looked up and there, on some rocks above, she stood. It took away my breath, and I felt the blood come to my face.

"She walked down a little nearer, because of the noise of the water, and then she called, laughing:

" 'You need not look so bashful. I have been but a moment here. Everything is ready, except your fish. Now you must not hide any longer in that cold water. I will go away, and you can dress and recover from your blushes.'

"But when I came in with the trout, I could find nothing to say, no answer to the natural talk she made. I sat in stupid silence, eating the lunch she had prepared; until at last she exclaimed:

" 'What is the matter with you? Have I not said that I was not a spy? And suppose I had seen you! Do you also suffer from the false and ridiculous American shame of the body?'

"I gave her no time, I took her before she knew: and she did not fight this meeting of our lips; and she closed her eyes.

"But to my whisper she answered by opening

them quietly and looking at me from far away, divided from me once more by her greater power. Her beauty wrung my heart—and her sadness. I saw into the depths of her sadness, unveiled by any of that gaiety and laughter which she could wear so well.

"'I love you so much,' I said to her, 'that dying for you would be a much more easy thing than living as you keep me living. But against your decree I will never revolt, I will only implore.'

"And I fell on my knees, which I had never done, and had despised; and I wept, which I suppose I must have done as a child. But it wasn't for myself! It wasn't for myself!

"She touched my hair, and it was like a sword of bliss killing me. 'If you have always been a boy,' she said, 'you are a man today. I know I have given you much reason to think me nothing better than a very cruel woman.'

"I shook my head as her hand lay on it; I could not speak then.

"'Yes, cruel. But I have not meant it. I have not understood you. I have been very cruel, and I do not forgive myself.'

"'Not cruel, not cruel,' I said under my breath; and I kissed her dress.

"'Now let us go home,' she said. 'And perhaps you would forgive me if—if—perhaps it is not a

decree . . . And yet—to risk my soul . . .' She left
her thought unspoken.

"At that, joy swept me in a flood, and I looked at
her; but the power was in her eyes, and it quelled
mine.

"My joy grew with me as we rode along slowly
on our way to camp. Plans half shaped themselves,
plans for the future with her, what I should do; I
knew very well that I could take care of her. And
she believed at last that I was a man! My plans
stopped when that thought surged up in them; it
unsteadied my mind.

"Then, coming towards us on the trail, I saw the
Indian, and supposed that our pack-horses had
strayed.

" 'How,' said the Indian. Their faces never show
anything.

" 'Hunting the pack-horses?' I asked.

" 'I go,' said he.

" 'You leave? You go away?'

" 'I go. She made bad medicine.'

"Stunned, bewildered, I watched the Indian grow
distant on the trail. Bad medicine? Bad medicine?
The words reiterated themselves. He was going
away because he was frightened; and a sort of fear
began in me.

"She had not understood those words 'bad medicine,' and I was finding it not perfectly simple to

convey their superstitious import, when her mind
leaped ahead and suddenly comprehended what I
did not, and could not.

"All in a moment her face had changed; it expressed both triumph and terror. 'Then he has
thanked me for my flowers!' The words were just
audible.

" 'He?' I repeated dully. 'For your flowers?'

" 'Oh, let us hurry!' she exclaimed.

"Arrived in camp, she sprang from her horse, and
ran to the geyser, and climbed to the rim.

"The Professor came out of their tent, looked
about through his spectacles, and spoke to me. 'I
thought we should go tomorrow. But we must stay
until I have made further observations here. I have
been mistaken in the nature of this geyser. It is not
often that I mistake.'

" 'Do you know what caused the Indian to leave
us?'

" 'Ach, is he gone? He did not inform me.'

"But if the Professor could not explain it, explanation was given. From the geyser came a sound
which I had not heard before.

"The Professor called my attention to this. 'Yes,
I must make further investigation. It is an interesting case.'

"She had come down from the crater, so deep in
her silent thoughts that only I, who had begun to

know her, discerned the agitation which she concealed. Sometimes I saw her looking at me with something like appeal. Once during the evening, I thought that the ground trembled; and it was then that again for an instant her eyes fixed me with a piercing search, as if for shelter, for refuge.

"'Tell me what I can do,' I muttered to her. But she made no answer.

"Presently the Professor requested her to read aloud to him. As she followed him to their tent, she said to me:

"'I will come.'

"I lay in my blankets, roofed by the canvas covers flung over some cross poles. I lay in a tumult, watching the light in their tent, listening to her voice reading and reading. The late moon came out, and still she read; and I must have fallen asleep. You cannot have such emotions as that day had brought me, one after the other, without exhaustion.

"Suddenly I found myself sitting up in my blankets, wide awake, grasping the cold barrel of my rifle. She stood at my feet, shining in the moon, ready. I stretched my arms, I saw her stretch hers, and I saw her smile.

"Then to the moonlight some other light was added, for no moon ever shone like that. All the trees, all the rocks, all things grew visible as day. And awful. Her smile changed to terror, and she stood as if stricken, while I sat numb, as if stricken too.

"Something crossed. Passed across. High. I mean, tall, but over the ground. It moved along over the ground, floating. It was steam, and I could look through it in the blinding light. Its top was—I don't know where it reached—but up, over the trees. It was a cloud of steam, but I could see right through it, right through it; it was nothing else; only it moved over the ground, floating across to her, and melted somewhere beyond. After it a second came. Just like the first. Floating to her and going. But no wind. Not one breath. The whole sky was still. A third came moving across. Not slowly. Faster than a man walks. And not one breath of wind.

"That is how they all begin. First the steam, with the small spurts of water that fall and are followed by more, coming on and on, until the true column bursts upward, mighty, and thunder-like.

"But as I watched her, powerless, her eyes opened wide and wild, and I saw her call my name. Then I was able to leap out of my bed, answering her as I rushed to her. But I did not hear my own voice, any more than I had heard hers. Horror reeled in my brain, because there was no noise anywhere. They make a roaring, yet there was none; and still the pouring vapors rose as if they were breaking from a long prison.

"We clung together in the frightful clearness, greater than day, that came from no moon or sun, and we stared at that thing.

"As each new cloud shot from the vent, it left the piled rock and formation, and glided across to her, one herald following another, a train of messengers. They came and came, and thicker and closer, till they moved in a file unbroken; pillars, messengers, wrapping her and me in thick folds, and passing on, and vanishing beyond, leaving us an instant in the terrible light that filled the wood, and wrapping us again, as we clung together.

"We spoke to each other, we knew what it was we said, but we could not hear it; the appalling spell of muteness lay on everything, while those vapors spouted higher and higher that should have thundered, yet were noiseless as a dream.

"She knew that I would die with her if this was to be death instead of love; her eyes answered mine steadfastly, till fear swerved them, and I looked where they were gazing, distended.

"It had begun, it was coming now. In the midst of the steam clouds, down low, just above the crater's rim, the true column showed. It paused there, it gathered strength and rose, it was twenty feet above the crater, it extended and soared, and I lifted my eyes to follow its upward mounting, sparkling in that light, gleaming, flashing, magnificent, towering far above the tree tops into the sky.

"And then, all in a moment, without beginning, he stood there inside the crystal pillar of water, shining out from its midst like a statue of white fire. The stream poured upward, enclosing him; it rushed over his body; he was at its center, in its heart; yet not a line of him was blurred, he stood a chiseled shape, motionless as stone, living as flame or molten ore, a figure symmetric that could have cloven the air as the lightning crosses the sky.

"A glow radiated from his young form, fierce through the streaming might of the flood, turning to fiery flashes every drop flung above the trees into space, tingling through my own senses as though they were being steeped in the elixir of life. All winds and streams and elements and forces vibrated in that terrific apparition.

"Had he come from Etna, summoned by the evocation of her flowers? Had he watched her there from the secret chambers of the mountain as she wandered in the savage valleys above Acireale? Had he desired her then, but in some way been thwarted, and had she known this? Was her offering of the flowers made in the spirit of a game, not quite believed in, such as children play and frighten themselves with? Or had she wittingly played with fire? My gasping brain seemed like to turn over and crash to demolition, as these maniac fancies pursued each other through it, and I strained her closer and closer to me.

"He had been motionless, standing august, yet stealthy, as if on the alert to guard against her escaping him here—if she had once escaped him on the sides of Etna. And through the whirl of my thoughts came this: 'He cannot step outside the circle of that water. When it sinks down, he will go with it.' And with all my might I resolved to stand where we were and hold her fast.

"His arms still hung relaxed against his sides, but with his head he made a barely perceptible sign. I could not hear the shout of defiance that I gave at feeling her body tremble at that command; whatever influence was diffusing that terrible light, still totally deadened every sound.

"She passed out of my arms, I could no more hold her than if she had been a spirit or a mist, and her eyes no longer sought me, they were on him. Slowly, step by step, she left me and drew near him, while I called desperately her name—phantom cries! I leaped for my rifle, and poured into him all the shells in its magazine—phantom shots! But he was aware of it. He turned one glance from his eyes upon me, and I fell, and could not move; I was bound fast in every nerve and muscle. But my sight was not stricken. I lay and saw it.

"Slowly, step by step, like a sleep-walker, never stopping, never struggling, she moved on, and he waited. His face changed as she came . . . became human . . . a lover's face . . . wicked with all the wickedness of the immortal gods. She reached the rocks, she began to mount them, she was close to that crystal torrent, when his arms lifted and opened to receive her. I did not see him take her. I could not look any more . . .

"I saw the dawn, and the sunrise, and knew that their light was of this world; a Clarke's crow came flying and calling through the wood; sound had returned, the place was once more natural. But my muscles still seemed rigid, my strength hopeless. So I lay, battered in body and mind almost to inanition. I saw the Professor come out of their tent, trace her foot-steps to the rocks. Then he came running and seized me, and lifted me up, and it broke my impotence, and I spoke.

"In his ravings that day I was of little help to him, he passed into incoherence. The next day he seemed to have recovered some balance, but it was only a seeming. Our horses were gone. There were signs that my picketed animal had violently dragged his rope loose. After two days' search, I told the Professor that we must walk out. He would not. To save his life, I had to leave him. In two days more, I met some soldiers and sent them to find him. Snow had come. They found him at last. He had been eating berries and twigs, and was crawling on his knees. He recovered his mind in the hospital at the Post.

"But she? Where is she now who would have

clothed her body and soul with mine and lived in happiness? Is she with him? Or has he, like Zeus and Dionysus and those others, cast off the mortal woman when once his lust was slaked? Shall I ever find her again?

"I can understand her belief now; I can believe, as she did, in many gods. But if her Christian God is all-powerful . . . why does He . . . how can He . . ." Scott's question faded into silence, and he sat looking at me with his smile of desolation.

The General laid the diary upon his knee, and no one spoke. The storm had died down; only the quiet falling of embers was to be heard, until our host resumed.

"That journey was my last meeting with Kenneth Scott; once again I had news of him.

"Before I left the Park, dim rumors were the only answers to the questions I asked. Some men of the first cavalry had found a crazy German, wandering lost between the Upper Falls and the lake; at least, people had once said so; but the people were gone, the soldiers were gone. It was clear that Scott's own tale had never been told, except to me. At that time in that region, ten years made forgotten history.

"Yes; I never saw him again—but here is a part of a letter that Elena Grover wrote me from Taormina, while her husband some years later was our military attaché at Rome.''

The General reopened the wrinkled morocco volume at another place, and read:

'' 'The natives here speak of a man with long white hair, who is dressed oddly in soft leather, and frequents the crevices of Mount Etna. They tap their foreheads and say, ''*È Pazzo.*'' I tried my best to find him. We had to go. I wish I could have done something for him.'

''There is the whole of it,'' said the General. ''Kenneth Scott—ah, well, every man who lives a long while survives many with whom he once talked and laughed—and never thinks of most of them. But he keeps a few—still sees the look in their eyes, can still recall their voices. I shall miss Kenneth to the end. The closest friendships, even the longest loves, are but islands in the vast and uncharted solitude of the human soul.''

Absalom
and Moulting Pelican

DOC LEONARD with his valise stood on the platform. No other objects were there. The name on the station was Soto de Rey. Inside was an agent fanning himself. Doc Leonard watched the train leaving him here, nowhere at all, a speck in space. The train moved south toward Mexico, with cautious reluctance. Suddenly its wheels were gone. The cars floated apparently on a shining sea of quicksilver, dead calm. Now the cars dissolved in the tricky dazzle of light. Up in the air the wide top of the smoke-stack without visible means of support puffed brown clots straight up at the sky. Then its black shape trembled, blurred, and melted away. The last lingering sign of the train's reality was a receding column of smoke that rose from nothing and slowly grew distant, leaving a diffused taint of thin darkness which hung like a veil, staining the glassy infinity.

"Beats Texas," muttered Doc Leonard.

Off a little way across the cactus and stones, he saw buildings in a ragged clump, patching the gray desert, a dishevelled spot quivering in the noon.

Northward across the naked floor of Arizona, stretched the railroad track straight to the horizon whence he had come.

"Worse than Texas," he repeated. "Am I going to be sorry I came?"

Inside the station, the agent's continuous fan was the only thing in sight which moved. In the stillness, the temperature of the platform burned through the soles of Doc Leonard's shoes. He walked to the open ticket window, and saw a thermometer within.

"Is that thermometer right?"

"Nothing wrong with it that I know of." The agent looked neither at the instrument nor at Leonard.

"I don't see my trunk."

"Trunks generally come along after a while."

"I'm expected at Fort Chiricahua. I'm the new army surgeon."

"Not much surgery needed since Indian excitements are over. Folks don't get sick in this country."

"I suppose they'll send for me?"

"Can't say."

The agent never stopped his fan, his feet were on his desk, and Doc Leonard would have liked to kill him.

"Is it generally as hot as this?"

"Hotter."

Doc Leonard turned his back and left the fan going. He stood six feet in his socks, his chest measured 42, he was 27, weighed 175 stripped, and he regretted that his principles forbade murder.

Two horsemen were approaching. These wouldn't be coming for him? No. They crossed the track and headed for the clot of buildings. One was an Indian. Old. Looked feeble. Sat his horse like nature. Why did the white man wear his hair so long? Away down his spring chicken neck. Did he think he was Buffalo Bill? He couldn't ride much. Talking. Odd bird. Didn't look like the West. When he bounced to the horse's trot it jolted his hair. If his shooting was like his riding he was no twin of Buffalo Bill's. The Indian was listening to him, hard. What could it be? Queer pair. Fort Chiricahua was twenty miles off somewhere near those mountains. A dust was coming across the desert. For him? Then he wouldn't have to carry his valise to that awful town and sleep there. He knew those towns. Texas was lousy with them. Yes, it was for him. The driver was urging his horses.

A buggy swung up to the platform, a blond young giant sprang out, tall as Doc Leonard. Not a soldier. He dragged off his gauntlet and extended a strong hand in greeting.

"My name is Hugh Lloyd. I am sorry to have

kept you waiting. I am always late. My birth was
behind time. M' fawther has reasoned with me in
vain.''

He stopped. His deep voice rang with a welcome
which would have disarmed Leonard had he been
waiting for hours.

''Jump right in. Let me have your valise.''

He caught it and swung it behind the seat. A
quiet and enchanting smile shone for a moment in
his serious face.

''Major Wyckling asked me to meet you. He
presents his compliments and apologizes for not
sending the ambulance. The only ambulance broke
down up the canyon yesterday; and the lone blacksmith monkeyed with a Gila monster on Tuesday.''

''Was the bite fatal?''

''Entirely so for the monster, and the blacksmith
nearly perished with fright. His health is returning.''

Leonard looked at Lloyd's unmoved countenance.
The blue eye seemed in constant diversion at the
solemnity of the rest of the face.

''Is one blacksmith enough?''

''Major Wyckling says that one of anything is
considered very extravagant by the War Department since the final collapse of the Indians. I must
buy some ketchup. Do you like ketchup? We can
make my ranch by supper time, and I'll drive you

into the Post in the morning. Do you want anything in town?"

Leonard wanted a shave. On the way, he learned that Fort Chiricahua was now a two-troop Post, with four commissioned officers, three married, and a contract Chaplain, also married, who seldom preached less than forty minutes, and had strange notions about the ten lost tribes of Israel. These he was apt to spring upon his congregation when he ran dry of other subjects. He had got hold of an unfortunate Indian—

"Why I saw them!" Leonard interrupted. "Is that funny thing on horseback a parson?"

"So he's in town today. Well, you are going to see him every day of your life."

"What's he want to look like that for?"

"I have been tempted to get intoxicated and ask him. Temptations often assail my weak nature."

"Why does his wife let him?"

"She's the mother of his continual offspring."

"Poor woman."

"He's only thirty. The ladies at the Post know she is forty. Her husband is surely faithful. Why pity her?"

"Well, I'll skip church."

"You'll go. All go. Major Wyckling prefers it. Soon it will be like an event to you. We starve for events. The defeat and destruction of the Apaches last October was an event. The sand storm on the 3rd of April was the next event. Nothing between. In this glorious territory, sir,'' Hugh Lloyd continued—and the oratorical turn his voice and language had suddenly taken caused Leonard to look at him again—''in this glorious territory, Mother Nature is not quite herself.'' Lloyd shook his head gravely. ''If it may be said without irreverence, she is a freak.'' Again he shook his head. ''But she is a grand one, and powerful. Beneath her influence I have become a freak with all the rest of the population. In due time, so will you.'' His voice sank to a deep bass note of prophecy.

Into whose charge have I fallen? wondered Leonard. Freak? But another look at Lloyd's eyes reassured him. Deep in it, the spark of diversion burned brighter, though otherwise the gravity was unchanged. Had the sonorous voice trembled and steadied again? No brain I have met, thought the young surgeon, has taken these wild flights straight out of the matter-of-fact into the fantastic.

''Can I persuade you that the Indians are the ten lost tribes of Israel?'' Lloyd now inquired.

''Our American Indians? Jews? You cannot.''

''I cannot persuade myself. Do you know why? If they were, we'd be confined to the reservations, and they'd go to Harvard and have offices in Wall

Street and spend their summers in Paris." He pointed up the street as they reached Soto de Rey. It was the old Indian. "That is Moulting Pelican. He's waiting for Absalom, who is having his inexcusable hair trimmed."

"Why doesn't his wife do it for him?"

"She is no Delilah, though he's her Samson."

"Isn't it time you told me his real name?"

"The Rev. Xanthus Merrifew, to whom you will listen for forty minutes next Sunday. Here we are. Get your shave, and I'll be back for you.—You have known better days, have you not, Moulting Pelican?"

"How," returned the savage meekly. His eyes in his wrinkled face had a look of resigned confusion, which warmed and brightened when he saw Hugh Lloyd.

"Do you feel Abraham and Isaac and Jacob boiling in your veins this bright beautiful morning, O Pelican?"

"It is a fine day," pronounced the savage, and he actually smiled at Hugh.

"As you see, he has not yet recovered his ancestral memory. Go in and get shaved." Hugh Lloyd now spoke a pleasant word or two in the Apache's own tongue, and drove down the street. The old man looked after him as a dog turns to his master whom he must not follow, and then settled into his saddle with a long breath, and the look of resigned confusion back in his eyes.

Inside the shop, the barber was engaged with the clergyman behind the privacy of a curtain; and as his young assistant began with brush and razor upon Leonard's face, the unemployed of Soto de Rey gathered at the window to stare earnestly at the operation. I wonder how long this weather will last, thought Leonard. Freaks? Well, there were a good many in Texas. This barber is rough. Curious how you miss a life that is over, which you hated while it was going on. I hope I'll see a good deal of Lloyd. I suppose they'll transfer me to another Post some time. This barber is getting more awkward. Then the razor cut him.

"Excuse me, sir." The assistant stropped his razor nervously.

"You've done it again!"

"I'm sorry, sir, I'll take care." But the stropping was still nervous.

"Now look here. Are you doing this on purpose?" And Leonard sat up.

"Honest to Pete I'm doing my best, sir," wailed the assistant, now stropping his razor with a quaking hand. "I don't think it'll happen again."

"It will not." Leonard leaped out of the chair, and saw himself in the glass; and the assistant trembled beneath his oaths. "Bring me a sponge.

Do you think I'll pay for this?" Noise outside turned his attention to the window. "What are those fools laughing at?"

"I won't charge you nothing, sir. You're my first job. The boss is my uncle and I only come here yesterday for my lungs. I black boots in Los Angeles."

"What's he kicking about, Charlie?" It was a hoarse, dangerous voice behind the curtain—the sort of voice that goes with thrust-out jaws and short hair down the back of the neck. "We want no kickers here."

"You come out," said Leonard, "and I'll kick a goal from the field with you."

The unemployed of Soto de Rey had fallen silent, and as many noses as could reach the window were flattened against it. They had been hoping for such an incident as this. Charlie's uncle came out. Physically he was one with his voice; even his stunt mustache bristled with danger. He looked silently at Leonard, and war faded from his eye.

"Don't hurry," said Leonard.

"Say," said the uncle, "I don't want trouble with you."

Charlie ventured out of the corner, and the unemployed took their noses off the window, and began dejectedly to disperse.

"Bring me a sponge," said Leonard.

"Charlie, get him a sponge. Say, the joke's on us. Will you take five dollars?"

"Dear me!" said an amiable voice. It was the Rev. Xanthus Merrifew with his hair smooth and glossy from treatment. "If I had my pharmaceutical kit I could stop that bleeding."

"I can stop it," said the uncle, "if he'll just leave me do it." He approached with a box of white powder.

"Give me that," said Leonard.

"Oh, all right. Suit yourself." And the uncle appealed to his recent patron. "I offered him five dollars."

"Yes, but it shouldn't have happened. I wish I could be of use, sir. I feel guilty. But you seem skilful. Am I addressing Dr. Leonard? Ah, we are all expecting you. My wife will be very glad to see you. I trust those gashes will be soon healed. Well, I mustn't keep David waiting any longer. I shall expect to tell you much about poor David."

"David? Oh, that Indian! I thought his name—"

"Ah, has Hugh begun with his jokes already? There's no real evil in that joyous nature—but the boy is always having his fun. You see, David is the last one of his band. The soldiers brought him in alive. His native name was unpronounceable, and when they translated it—well, no gentleman, let alone a lady, could possibly make use of it. He was at first most reluctant to receive baptism, but our religion is already making him tractable and gentle, and David seemed a fitting name, since he is descended direct from Abraham. I shall have much to tell you of this. The Papagos have just sent me a stone. There is Hugh, ready for you. Ah, Hugh! always poking your fun. Good-bye, doctor.''

Hugh watched the clergyman spring actively into his saddle and amble away with the hapless Moulting Pelican. Then he turned and caught sight of Leonard. "For the love of Mike!'' he said.

"Yes, my face is a beauty spot.''

"I offered him five dollars,'' said Charlie's uncle.

"It's not worth two bits,'' said Lloyd; and Leonard gazed with silent rancor at the looking-glass, while the boss explained that his nephew had to make a beginning like everybody else. Hugh extended his strong hand to the boy. "Cheer up, Charlie. You'll go far. If it had been my face you'd have gone through the window already. Give the glad hand to life. Do you know why? It expands the chest. Your lungs will soon be playing around like maltese kittens.—The grocer's thermometer registers 115 in the shade.''

"It was that at the railroad,'' said Leonard.

"Doctor, would you mind packing a couple of the ketchup in your pockets? The road is rough.''

It needed care to distribute the bottles between

various folds of blankets, some in front, some behind. There were a dozen.

"Three cents cheaper each bottle that way," Lloyd explained. "M' fawther wants me to learn economy. Why don't you take off your coat and sling it—no, I forgot the ketchup—lay it over the valise! Now we're off." And he took the reins.

"That man at the railroad," said Leonard, "told me it could be hotter."

"It can. But a case of sunstroke has never been heard of at the Post—and that's been here since the Territory was organized."

"Humidity always low, I suppose?"

"Dryness was created here. It's all that usually happens."

"Well, I feel as if a good deal had happened already."

Hugh looked at Leonard's raw scars. "Any man would. But that will never happen again, and you're going to miss it."

The long-tailed horses took them swiftly out of town to a road that wound among the cactus and the stony mounds of the desert.

"Do you know French?" said Hugh. "Do you know the meaning of *ennui?*"

"I know the feel of it."

"You do not. Excuse my contradicting you on such short acquaintance."

Far away on many sides, sharp mountains jotted up like icebergs, pale blue above the quivering flood of heat.

"I should think it might be a hundred-and-any-thing here," said Leonard.

Two dots grew visible ahead; two horsemen. One bobbed visibly.

"If that parson is a bore," said Leonard, "why don't they get rid of him?"

"They can't until his contract expires. This was a big Post when he came."

"Well, it's a small one now. Why isn't he moved to where he'll have a bigger congregation?"

"In the opinion of the Secretary of War," responded Hugh gravely, "the fewer persons that hear his sermons, the larger will be the attendance of our army at divine service."

They drove on in silence for a while.

"He's got three children," Hugh next observed. "Their names are Alpha, Epsilon, and Iota. The one they are expecting is to be Eta. It was his wife's idea, because they became engaged while she was studying Xenophon."

"What's he going to do when they've used up all the Greek vowels?"

"They have anticipated that, and they will then begin on the diphthongs. You see, a Greek vowel suits a boy or a girl equally well."

For the third time Leonard turned for a look at his new acquaintance, whose face, however, wore merely its accustomed seriousness. How much am I to believe of all this? wondered the young army surgeon. But I shall meet those children. Perhaps freaks grow bigger here than in Texas.

They were drawing nearer to the preacher and his passive victim.

"Absalom is hard at it," said Hugh.

"At what?"

"Restoring Moulting Pelican's ancestral memory."

"Ancestral memory? What can he know about that?"

"Cast your eye on the books he buys. He met the Higher Education when his brain was still in short pants. If you give a baby lobster salad and whisky, what will the baby do? Absalom struck the very latest psychology when hymns and Longfellow's poems were his mental limit. So he goes and mixes ancestral memory and latent personality and the Lord knows what else with the Indians and the ten lost tribes, and along comes Moulting Pelican for him to try it on."

"Well," said Leonard, "it's quite harmless compared with Free Silver or Free Love, or some of the other experiments they want to try."

They were now close to the riders, who separated

for the buggy to pass; and the Rev. Xanthus Merrifew hailed them in triumph.

"David will tell you what he has mastered to-day." And he addressed a few words in Indian to the old Apache.

Obediently, like a mechanism, Moulting Pelican croaked some English words. "Take ye the sum of all the congregation of the children of Israel."

"The text of my next sermon. First Numbers, part of the second verse. I always reward David when he does so well." And from his saddle bag the Rev. Xanthus Merrifew drew a yellow banana, which Moulting Pelican accepted, and began to peel without enthusiasm. The buggy drove on and the riders fell behind.

"More cranks per square mile in the U. S. A. than anywhere on earth," mused Leonard.

"Because more American brains jump into long pants before they should quit diapers," said Hugh. "But in time you will envy Absalom."

"Do you believe that the climate will affect me as far as that?"

"You will. I do. You'll wish you had some absorbing hobby to fill this vacuum." Hugh swept his arm toward Arizona in general.

"But why does the Indian stand it? Why doesn't he run away? What keeps him?"

"He has nobody and nowhere to run to. Last

October most of his friends and relations met with sudden death when he was captured alive as being too harmless to shoot. All he wants now is to be sure of his three meals a day and his I. C. tent and his bed at night. He doesn't want to be sent to Florida with the squaws and children and those who surrendered. He'll do anything anybody says to escape that. He's quite tame, though he's still wonderfully supple and active for his years. Oh, yes, Moulting Pelican realizes there is nowhere for him to run to any more.''

"The story is not entirely gay.''

"Do you know many stories that are entirely gay if you choose the right angle to watch from? My gracious, but I'm glad you've come!'' Once more the enchanting smile stole out, shone a moment, and stole in again.

"You know,'' said Leonard presently, "to hear those English words escaping from that throat— well, he quacked them in the parson's own voice, just like this phonograph jigger they've invented lately. Uncanny. But the parson's all off in baptizing him.''

"Oh, no.''

"Yes he is. When Moulting Pelican discovers he's a Jew, he'll be furious at having been subjected to Gentile baptism. He might scalp the parson.''

"I earnestly beg you will say that to Absalom."

"Say it yourself. I present you with it. And here's another thing. Why teach him English? If he's to recover his ancestral memory, he should start on his ancestral language—what's the matter now?"

Hugh Lloyd had uttered one sudden enormous laugh: his first.

"I'll tell you later. Dawn. There's dawn in me. I, too, may try an experiment. It needs meditation. I believe you have presented me with something. But how unfortunate that m' fawther removed me from the Higher Education!" One more irrepressible laugh burst from Hugh, followed instantly by seriousness. "Let us try to fill the vacuum that lies between here and my ranch. In 1862 I was born in San Francisco."

"I was born in Hyannis in 1859."

"You do not realize that I have begun to tell you the story of my life in order to fill a vacuum. If any vacuum is left, you shall tell me yours, but bear in mind that I am easily shocked. I am the son of wealthy but religious parents. A simple calculation will apprize you that I am now twenty-three. One of my indelible memories is m' fawther saying grace in front of our big silver soup tureen. Another is breakfast on the morning I was eight, when m' fawther said, 'Hugh, I have a birthday present that

I know you will prize. From now on, you are to be allowed to say grace.'

"At the age of thirteen I entered the 3rd form at St. Paul's School where I made the acquaintance of Caesar's *De Bello Gallico* and failed in all my examinations. By the time I reached Virgil's *Aeneid* in the 4th form, I had attained puberty and was ready for Cicero's Orations in the 5th. I entered Harvard College from the 6th with a little Latin, less Greek, and much careful instruction in the Holy Scriptures. I also held the school record for the 220-yard dash. Yes, sir, the Higher Education and I have met. Did you go in for athletics?"

"Half-back at Harvard for three years. Got my letter sophomore year."

"Your games with Yale shall fill some of our vacuum. So I was in Cambridge while m' fawther was busy in San Francisco running his big enterprises. He paid my bills the first month. When he got them the second month—he came East. I ate my Thanksgiving Dinner with my parents in San Francisco, and it was the first time since the Summer vacation that I had said grace.

"M' fawther put me to work in the office of his lumber mill and tannery. He said my character needed building.—Did you hear something just then?"

"I don't think so."

"Well, one night at the tannery, I was busy building my character in charge of the superintendent, when he laid down three aces and stared at me strangely. There seemed to be a rumbling.

" 'I have heard that before' said the superintendent, and jumped out of the window three stories up.

"I followed him fearlessly. We both landed on a soft pile of bark, and watched the tannery rise into the air and come down in distant places.

"The superintendent explained that a boiler always gave you warning if you knew how to listen to it; but in my place, would you have felt anxious to become a tanner?

"But m' fawther said my character needed a great deal of building and I passed a month at his mines at Las Yedras before he transferred me to his ranch here. There was a timely vacancy ready for me. The superintendent had shot himself. I hope you don't mind my talking so much. The cattle have kept me at the ranch, and it is eight days since I have seen a soul except Mexicans. Have you ever wished you were a cow? At times I envy the cow. She does not depend on conversation for her happiness.—Are you sure you didn't hear something?"

"Are you sure that tannery didn't get on your nerves?"

"I never used to be nervous. My character must have begun to build. I've more to tell you, but if you will talk for the next four miles, I shall feel very grateful, and less ashamed."

"Can I get a drink of water on the road?"

"In four miles we shall reach my well at the ranch."

"I should think it might boil in this weather. I was born at Hyannis in 1859. My aunts educated me. They were going to leave me their cranberry bog—"

"That's what it is!" shouted Hugh. "The ketch-up. Look at your coat."

Both of them now heard it; a third bottle had gone; and as Leonard saw a thick red ooze coming out of one of his coat pockets, the other pocket was shaken by an explosion; at the same moment he felt a sensation of wetness in his ankles, and stooped hastily.

"Look out for broken glass," said Hugh, lashing the amazed horses. "On, you bastards!"

"In spite of everything you say," said Leonard, "I feel as if we had no need to fill a vacuum."

"On, you bastards!" repeated Hugh, while Leonard clutched the seat. "If we can save one or two we'll cool them in the well. M' fawther wants me to practise economy. Can you count the living?"

"If I let go I'll be among the dead," said

Leonard. "Didn't you say sunstroke never occurred here?"

They lowered three surviving bottles into the well, and after a quiet evening with soap and sponge, they sought slumber, which Leonard found little of.

"Did you study Hebrew at Harvard?" inquired Hugh at breakfast.

Leonard snarled bitterly. "Yes, I know my face looks like a dead language."

Hugh sighed. "Well, something will occur to me I feel sure.—With that sunburn of yours, I couldn't have shaved or put plaster on. It must hurt."

"It'll be all right in a day or so," said Leonard, lightly.

As they neared Fort Chiricahua, the thin call of a trumpet sounded "Stables" across the empty air, betokening routine in the lifeless Post; and soon they met a lady slowly walking. She was Mrs. Wyckling, wife of the Commanding Officer, and she greeted the new doctor warmly. He was grateful for her tact in taking no notice of his appearance, and offering no condolence.

"And we are hoping," she said, "that you may possibly understand ice machines, because ours has just gone through the roof of the shed, and we are expecting a visit from the Secretary of War."

"I suppose it is the ammonia. But I'm afraid I don't understand them at all."

"That Secretary," said Hugh, "has been expected since last Fall."

"But when he does come," said the lady, "we mustn't be without ice."

"I hope he comes tomorrow, and all his butter runs, and all his water is tepid, and his milk sour, and his meat smelling; then he'll get a taste of what his two-cent policy is making you people put up with."

"Thank you for your fierceness, Hugh. But we must entertain him properly." And laughing, the lady went on, just as another came up.

"Welcome to our desert home, Doctah," said she. "Ah, I see you have been making a night of it with our Hugh. Hugh is ever gay."

"I—"

"No apologies, Doctah!—We Southern ladies just wouldn't think anything of a gentleman if he wasn't spirited. Captain Jonter, my husband, will call at once." She departed in trills of girlish laughter.

Fury was in Leonard's eyes. "So that's what they'll all believe!"

"Absalom saw you and Charlie," Hugh reminded him.

"I suppose that cat's husband is spirited."

"Old Jonter's vacuum is filled by ten every morning."

"If that cat gets sick, I'll give her poison."

But he gave nobody anything for a while. This was settled by his face. The first day it rebelled against its treatment by Charlie's razor and the sun of Arizona. Dressings of ichthyol brought Leonard through alive, and Hugh found him in front of his mirror one morning.

"I'll report you as out of danger," said Hugh. "First time you've showed any interest in your personal beauty." And he helped him back to bed.

"I know I was dotty," said the patient. "How long did it last?"

"You have filled a lot of vacuum for both of us," replied Hugh. "And you escaped last Sunday's sermon. You can have an egg today."

"What is today?"

"Wednesday."

"Why you must be living here!" Leonard exclaimed suddenly.

"Right across the hall. By next week you'll be looking after yourself—but for me the vacuum has no more terrors at present."

Leonard was too languid to ask or to care what that meant. "A nice way for a doctor to begin his new job," he muttered feebly. But after the particular fever which had devastated Leonard, even such a celebrated half-back as he does not generally spring to full strength in the twinkling of an eye; and day after day, as he felt his energy trickling back into his body drop by drop, he perceived also the invading vacuum.

"What's today?" he would ask Hugh each morning, even if he knew. And Hugh would tell him.

"Anything happened?"

"Nothing."

"Anything going to?"

"Nothing."

"News of any ice machine?"

"No."

"Any Secretary?"

"No."

"What's the thermometer?"

"A hundred and twenty."

Into their silence would fall the thin note of the trumpet, sounding some call of routine. Sometimes the questions and answers varied slightly.

"What's today?"

"Monday."

"Did he preach about ten lost tribes?"

"Ran 'em in for twenty minutes."

"Enjoy a nice nap?"

"Yes."

"And the ice machine?"

"Promised early next month."

"And the Secretary?"

"No news."

"And the thermometer?"

"A hundred and twenty-two."

"Anything else?"

"Potted ham blown up."

"Who did that?"

"Thermometer at Commissary store. Other canned goods followed ham. Olives reported as holding on. Do you feel strong enough to resume the story of your life where the ketchup broke it off at your aunts?"

"I'll skip them."

"Don't skip a single aunt, waste nothing. I'll listen to you if you listen to me, and we'll fill the vacuum."

Visitors filled it, too, when Leonard began to sit up. The Post called. Captain Jonter came in a spirited condition and suggested cards. His wife gossiped to the patient about people of whom he had never heard. There was some dear Lilly just engaged to some dear Harry at some other Post; a wife ten years older than he was just what he needed to keep him straight. Harry was so spirited; and Lilly was so sweet; and gentlefolk were so uncommon now in the Army; wasn't it a real tragedy that dear Lilly's legs were so crooked she almost walked on her ankles? I will certainly poison her, thought Leonard on his sofa. The Rev. Xanthus Merrifew brought books on psychology and about the lost tribes, and a Spanish grammar, because Padre Garcia's work was in that language. Honora, his wife, brought Alpha and Epsilon to cheer the patient. Iota was too young. So Hugh, thought Leonard, is not a total liar. Leonard had often heard the children's voices out of his window, generally in obvious disagreement. Both could talk fluently, but both sat dumb now, and Alpha glared at Epsilon, whose hair Honora stroked while she entertained Leonard with a stream of talk which a man in his full strength could hardly have stemmed. Suddenly Alpha broke out: "Mother, *can* a lady lay an egg?" "*Can't* she, mother?" screamed Epsilon. "Hush, darlings, never interrupt mother. As I was saying, Doctor, Xanthus is making wonderful progress with poor David. It is all so wonderful. Xanthus says that by Thanksgiving David will be able to stand up before us all and tell the wonderful story in good English. How his Hebrew forefathers got up into China, and how at last after many centuries they wandered across the Aleutian isthmus to America, long before it was discovered by Columbus. Run down stairs, darlings, and play with pussy." Poor little cat, thought Leonard. "As I was saying, Doctor, Xanthus would have brought you the Papago stone this morning, but he went to the barber's."

Wails of controversy out on the parade ground took this mother away.

Freaks? thought Leonard. "It is all so wonderful," he said aloud, as he sat by his window. He was saying it again, imitating the lady's sing-song, as Hugh entered, followed by Moulting Pelican.

"Why, you're alone!" said Hugh. "Were you not talking?"

"Freaks," replied Leonard. And Hugh took the Indian across the hall.

Leonard was out in time for the next sermon. This was about the Papago stone. It was held out for all to see. "Another proof of the mosaic tradition," the preacher was saying, as Leonard came out of a doze. "What does its rude carving tell us? You see it is a feathered serpent. What is that? Quetzalcoatl. And what is Quetzalcoatl but the serpent which Moses lifted up?" At this point, Leonard swooned to sleep again. A rustling restored him to consciousness. All heads were turned where Absalom was pointing to a corner at the back. "Lo, the poor Indian. The time is not far distant when our Old Chief will tell us the wonderful story of his Hebrew ancestors." And there sat Moulting Pelican in his corner, blinking like the faithful hound when we rebuke him.

"I've got used to you," said Leonard to Hugh. "Why sleep at your ranch?"

"As often as I can," said Hugh, "we'll fill the vacuum together."

So he kept some clothes in the room across the hall; and Absalom preached about the Pittsfield Strap, and the Newark Slab, and Padre Garcia's book, while they dozed in their seats, and Moulting Pelican blinked in his back corner, Sunday after Sunday.

The confidential pair did not abandon their ritual of greeting, they merely modified it variously, as, for example:

"What's today?"

"Any day you say."

"What is our Old Chief saying?"

"It is all so wonderful."

Over such exchanges the pair betrayed no smile. The new ice machine came; the thermometer began to go down; the potted ham ceased to blow up; the flag rose on its pole each morning and was lowered each evening; and across the successive hours, the thin calls of the trumpet sang the repetitions of routine.

Some mysterious routine had been keeping Hugh busy with Moulting Pelican for several weeks. When Hugh rode out to his ranch the Indian often went with him, unless he was with Absalom.

"Wish you were back in civil life?" asked Hugh, as they sat together one evening.

"Not any longer," Leonard answered, staring at Hugh.

"Going to stick to the army?"

"I am."

"Got any more Texas experiences to tell?"

Leonard shook his head.

"If you keep on looking at me like that," said Hugh, "I shall cry."

"What outrage are you at across the hall, anyhow?" demanded Leonard.

Hugh rose. His solemnity deepened, so did the blue of his eye, so did his bass voice.

"Hombre, it was you that sowed the seed," he said.

"Don't you think that wretched Indian has enough trouble without you?"

"I have felt obliged to step in," said Hugh. "And he prefers me to Absalom."

"Well, step in when I've stepped out and can't hear your abominable noises."

Hugh's eyes gleamed, and he tossed the yellow hair back from his forehead. "David is happy," said he, in the Chaplain's innocent and eager voice, "and I am happy, for I, too, have now a hobby. Do you object to gambling?"

Leonard sat looking at him.

"I should love to trust you," continued Hugh, with earnest sorrow. "But m' fawther always says not to tell your secrets even to your dearest friend. Don't put your money on Absalom. Bet on me.

When the time comes for our Old Chief to tell us
the wonderful story of his Hebrew ancestors—''
the bass voice trembled here, and then one of
Hugh's great laughs prevailed over his gravity for
a moment; he recovered and continued, "I have
assumed a daring hypothesis, and it is now time to
go to bed.''

It was not many nights later that Leonard having fallen asleep early, was wakened. Hugh was
sitting on the edge of the bed. Leonard was very
cross.

"It is only nine o'clock,'' said Hugh. "I cannot
share my secret with you, but this I can.''

He struck a match and lighted the lamp.

"What's that thing?'' asked Leonard, still very
cross.

"We will now fill some vacuum together.'' And
Hugh began to peel the tin foil off what he was
holding.

"What is it?'' repeated Leonard.

"Cannabis indica.''

"Hashish? How did you get it?''

"I wrote a friend to procure it in DuPont Street,
San Francisco.''

"Then you've taken it before?''

"Never. The idea just came to me in a flash.
Variety! Don't you crave it?''

Leonard sat up. "For the fluid extract the dose

is fifteen minims, one for the essence, and a half
a grain for the extract. But how strong is this
gum?''

"You chew it," said Hugh. "It causes delicious
visions in Chinatown."

"Orientals are different. I believe it's never
fatal. Its effect varies with individuals. Sometimes a preparation does not act at all."

"Will you begin?" said Hugh.

Leonard felt it. "Why not?" said he. "Variety,
after all." And he nibbled a very little. "Sweet.
Sort of paste. They must have mixed fruit with
it." And he handed it to Hugh.

"Yes," said Hugh. "Sort of sweet. It must
take a lot of this to make a grain."

"Look out," said Leonard. "We don't know.
But I'll take care of you."

Together they sat on the edge of the bed, waiting.

"Feel anything?"

"No. You?"

"No. Wonder how long it takes?"

Again they sat awhile.

"Do you suppose they eat a whole package?" inquired Hugh.

"I'm not going to eat half a one," said Leonard.
And they waited.

"Have another nibble?" said Hugh.

Each took one; and they sat.

"This is very slow," said Hugh. And he took a larger nibble.

"Better go easy," said Leonard. He took a small one. And they waited.

After a silence, Hugh rose and walked about.

"No visions yet," said he; and bit off a little more.

"If you try that again," said Leonard, starting up,—"please don't, Hugh."

"All right, Doc." And they waited.

"I guess it's old," said Hugh. "I guess it's stale. Let's go to bed." And they went, leaving their doors open. Hugh looked at his watch: 9.30.

Hugh lay awake. He waited. Nothing happened. Would anything now? He waited. Hours passed. Wide awake still. Must be midnight. Better read. He got up and lighted the lamp. Must be nearly one. He looked at his watch: 9.40. Queer. He held it to his ear. It was ticking about once a minute. He looked at the second hand. It did move slightly, if you kept watching. At that rate it would be three days behind time by morning. Must have it fixed. Loud sobbing. Leonard. Hugh went to see. It took him an hour. "Oh, how wicked I've been!" sobbed Leonard.—"No, no, old man. Listen. It's in the Bible. 'And Absalom weighed the hair of his head at two hundred shekels after the King's weight.' Second Samuel, fourteenth chapter, twenty-sixth verse." "Oh, how wicked I've been!" sobbed Leonard. "No, no, old man; no. Not wicked. Sick. Listen." And Hugh sat down on the bed.

"Take him off me!" said Leonard. And he dived under his bed and came up on the other side.

"Inexcusable hair," said Hugh. "And the Old Chief says he was Pharaoh's pawnbroker. Don't be a squirrel, old man. Listen."

"Take him off me!"

"Don't say that."

"Oh, how wicked I have been!" said Leonard; and he went round his bed again. Hugh immediately started after him. They pursued each other round and round.

Into this activity a sane moment would drop, when they would stop and wring each other's hands, saying, "Too bad, old man!" and resume circling round the bed. Or was it a vision, and did they in reality only go round once? Nobody knows. If I can get to the bath-room for a drink of water, thought Hugh. He looked and saw the bath-room, infinitely distant.

"Why do you sleep in a telescope?" he said to Leonard, who now sat quietly, looking on.

"It didn't use to be," said Leonard mournfully. "Don't let him scalp him."

Hugh shook his head. "Harmless. Merely pawnbroker's ancestral memory. Why do you speak so slow?"

"That's what you're doing," said Leonard. "Oh, how wicked I have been."

"I'll never get to the bath-room," said Hugh. "I don't see why you like a telescope."

"Do you think you could get as far as the mantel-piece?" suggested Leonard. And he watched Hugh reach the mantelpiece. "Don't be so slow at it," he said. "There. Now you're part way to the bath-room."

"But it has taken me fifty years," Hugh said. "I'll not live long enough to make the bath-room, and I'm so thirsty."

"But it is wicked not to excuse his hair," said Leonard anxiously.

"The Old Chief says, 'Nize gentleman, mind your beezniss'; that's what the Old Chief says. I am dreadfully thirsty."

He took a bottle from the mantelpiece and began swallowing it, and instantly foamed at the mouth. They both saw the foam pouring out in ribbons.

"I'm a conjuror!" cried Hugh, and lay down on the floor, and the ribbons ran over it.

This sight acted as an antidote to Leonard's dose of cannabis indica; he came out of his visions.

"That's ipecac!" he exclaimed, returning to full

responsibility; and he rushed to his medicines; and not knowing any too well what to do, he did a thing that did no harm, though it was painful. He gave Hugh a twenty minim injection of brandy.

"Do you remember what we did?" said Hugh the next day. "And what we said?"

"Perfectly. I don't know why I thought I was wicked. I am rather good, compared to you."

"Yes. But if the bath-room looked 300 miles off to me, think what your New England conscience must have been doing!"

"Now and then," said Leonard, "you show dawning powers of reason."

"Now and then," said Hugh, "I believe that you were young once. And Mrs. Jonter will tell the Post that we have been making another night of it."

"She would be quite right—but I shall not mention the incident."

"Don't mention anything I happened to say, either. And don't put your money on Absalom."

"What are you at, anyway?"

"I have set our Thanksgiving entertainment," Hugh answered, again resorting to his oratorical bass, "as the moment for announcing my discovery to the scientific world. On that night the Secretary of War is to pay us his long expected visit; and as the program of song and recitation seemed to me a little frivolous to offer a member of the President's cabinet, I shall introduce a note of seriousness directly following the story of the ten lost tribes, with which Absalom is to conclude the formal exercises."

"Keep your damned secret!" growled Leonard.

"We suspect what you and Hugh are plotting," said Mrs. Wyckling to him, a day or so later.

"Then I wish you'd tell me," said the surgeon. "He won't."

"Oh, Dr. Leonard! How discreet your profession is!"

"But I mean it!"

"Well, never mind the curiosity of a poor frontier Post with only gossip to fill its time."

"David has become so devoted to Hugh," said the Rev. Xanthus Merrifew to Major Wyckling. "He is more contented than ever."

"What does a lively boy like that," said the Major, "find in an old scarecrow like that?"

"I trust," said Mrs. Jonter earnestly to Leonard, "that you will not allow Hugh to teach David the use of drugs."

So the cat knows about the hashish, thought Leonard.

But their minds were turned to hospitality by the approach of the Secretary of War. For him they would do their best, and he would do his best for them when he was back in Washington—a second ambulance—a repaired water supply—something, surely. Out of their slender purses they bought delicacies for him to eat; for his drink they brought good bottles from San Francisco.

When he arrived from Soto de Rey with his escort the first night, they could not serenade him according to military etiquette, because two trumpets, one fife and a drum will execute but little music fit for a Secretary. He expressed relief. He had listened to a string of serenades in this tour of inspection of our Military Posts in the Southwest. He praised the mountains, praised the desert as the grandest he had seen, praised the drill, the hospital, the general discipline, and also the bed in the Wycklings' spare room. No food anywhere had equalled what Chiricahua gave him.

"He'll give us anything we ask for," said Mrs. Wyckling to the Major.

Moulting Pelican had a busy Thankgiving Day.

"David is inclined to be nervous this morning," said the Chaplain on meeting Leonard on the parade ground. "And how natural that is! But I know that he will acquit himself well before the Secretary tonight." And the Chaplain retired with Charlie's uncle, the barber, who had brought his implements to the Post because at such a crisis the Chaplain could not go to Soto de Rey for the usual treatment.

Leonard, sitting alone that afternoon in his quarters, heard the gentle, unmistakeable step, and the well-known gentle knock across his hall. He opened his door on Moulting Pelican.

"How," said the Indian. He was stately, in his tribal dress, a fillet binding his Apache hair, in gala for the occasion.

"Hugh will come soon," said Leonard. "Here is a chair for you."

The Indian took it. He could have sat so, untroubled all day; but the silence embarrassed the white man.

"Hugh is your good friend," said the white man.

The Apache's eyes grew warm. "Good friend," he repeated.

"My good friend, too," said Leonard, pointing to himself.

The Indian rose and shook Leonard's hand. "I know," he said.

"Mr. Merrifew heap good man," suggested Leonard.

Moulting Pelican's eyes searched him; was it a twinkle he saw deep in them? At any rate, he saw a deep, long, Indian smile upon the old face.

"A heap good man," Leonard insisted.

"Heap good man," assented Moulting Pelican, as Hugh came in.

"Spying?" said he. "You'll get no tales out of school."

"Don't I know it!" exclaimed Leonard, laughing.

All the while, Moulting Pelican stood looking from one friend to the other.

"Don't you bet on Absalom," said Hugh. "That's all."

And the door across the hall closed upon them and their secret. After their dress rehearsal was over, the Apache went out, and Hugh stood on Leonard's threshold.

"The Old Chief wanted to beg off, at first," said he, "like any young lady at a seminary. He feels better now. He knows I'll be there to prompt him." The shy smile came, shone out, and went. "He thinks," continued Hugh, "that I have become his father and his mother and all his nearest relations."

The Secretary of War applauded Honora, who played the melodeon at the entertainment, and sang *Sweet and Low, Clochette,* and *Nancy Lee.* He applauded Mrs. Jonter, who recited an unpublished poem by a Southern lady from Atlanta. He applauded the minstrel show given by some enlisted men.

"You will have to put up with what is coming now," Mrs. Wyckling whispered to him, as the Rev. Xanthus Merrifew mounted upon the stage with

Moulting Pelican. "But Hugh Lloyd is preparing something for the end, and his mind is very ingenious."

It was not hard to put up with, this next number on the program, because nobody had ever seen anything like it in the whole course of their experience. They had heard of the theory of the ten lost tribes of Israel here and there, but none had witnessed a demonstration of it offered in this manner. They stared at the rapt expression of the Chaplain, at his flowing locks, as he proclaimed his fixed idea; they stared with amazed eyes, as Moulting Pelican, in obedience to his motion, opened his mouth and began. Forgetting all laughter, they listened in a hushed concentration to the painfully memorized sentences pronounced to them. They heard Spanish, texts from the Bible, scraps from the Apocrypha, sentences from lay historians; and then in conclusion, they heard that the speaker's name was David, because he was descended from Abraham.

When it was done, still their hush held, and there was Hugh beside Moulting Pelican.

"Mr. Secretary," said he, and Leonard had never seen him more solemn, or heard his voice so deep, "and ladies and gentlemen: The Old Chief has told you in his simple and affecting way, how he has recovered his ancestral memory by the help of the recent discoveries in psychology. But he has

told you only in part. What remains is the out-
come of a daring hypothesis that he traces his line-
age back to the days of the captivity in Egypt. His
forefathers in those times were wont to accommo-
date the needy sons of the Pharaohs with trifling
sums, on the deposit of sufficient collateral, such as
royal trinkets, and other valuables, redeemable by
tickets upon repayment of the loan. This ancient
practice of his people will now be illustrated by the
Old Chief.''

''Hugh is always poking his fun,'' interjected
the Rev. Xanthus Merrifew.

And then, with the characteristic gesture, accent,
and idiom of many recent New York citizens of that
day, Moulting Pelican addressed Absalom in these
words:

''Nize gentleman, what you want for that nize
hair? I gif you ten dollars.''

He took hold of the hair, and stroked it, and was
going on with his speech, when Absalom in alarm
most inexpediently jerked away.

Screams rose from the ladies, other sounds from
the men. Absalom stood before them, bald as an
egg, and an aboriginal yell of terror rent the air and
shattered the hearing. Moulting Pelican stood by
Absalom, petrified, glaring at what he held. It
dropped from his hand.

''It ain't his natural hair!'' roared Charlie's

uncle, rising from his seat. "I can fix it right away."

At this offer of first aid to the scalped, the company sank into hysterics. When they next remembered anything, the stage was empty. Moulting Pelican had vanished. Out of a side door were seen departing the backs of Honora and Absalom, over whose skull the over excited uncle of Charlie was trying to spread the desecrated wig like an umbrella. A very sober Hugh was descending the steps from the stage.

"So that was your daring hypothesis," said Leonard to Hugh, when the Secretary had wrung Hugh's hand and implored him to come and stay with him in Washington; and everybody had chattered their say, and supped their fill; and the two were undressing for bed.

"No," said Hugh quietly, "I didn't mean that. I never suspected that."

Standing on one leg, he slowly pulled off a sock; then he slowly pulled off the other in the same way. "I never dreamed of such a thing," he repeated.

"Moulting Pelican didn't dream of it either," said Leonard.

"I didn't think of his leaving," muttered Hugh. "I didn't see him go."

"Well, he has nowhere to run to any more."

"Yes. That is what I am thinking about now."

"Oh, he'll turn up," said Leonard easily. "Let's get some sleep."

But ease was not in the mind of Hugh, that night or in the morning. Dressed and dusty, he entered the room while Leonard was still asleep, and waked the sleeper.

"I should have followed him last night," he said. "He is not in his tent. He didn't go there. Nobody has seen him."

"I wouldn't take it so hard," said Leonard.

"He is a very old man," said Hugh.

"Oh, he'll find out about it. It's all over the country by now. He'll come back when he hears what it was."

"How did I ever happen not to guess what it was?" demanded Hugh. "Have you often met a man of thirty without a hair on his head?"

It sent Leonard into the giggles between his sheets. In his mind's eye he saw the whole catastrophe, vivid. But the self-accusing anxiety of Hugh did not brighten. "Well, get up," he said, "and we'll have breakfast."

"I'll help you look for him, if you say so," said Leonard at breakfast.

"Come along," said Hugh.

The pair started on their horses.

"If you don't find the poor old relic today," said Major Wyckling, "I'll turn out the Post on his trail tomorrow."

But there was no trail on that hard ground. The mountains with their rocks and canyons offered countless chances of concealment; and the hours went by, and the November sun moved low in the Southwest. They came upon a little pool of ice, where a tiny mountain trickle of water spread to stillness.

"He would be afraid to make a fire," said Hugh.

"Would one ever have expected," said Mrs. Jonter, down at the Post, "that Hugh would take any thought about it?"

Mrs. Wyckling looked at her a moment before she said:

"Hugh doesn't show that side to everybody."

"Good fello'," said Captain Jonter. "Hope they find him."

"I hope he'll visit me in Washington," said the Secretary of War. "Tell him so. He's a boon in a sad world." And the official with his escort departed to resume his tour of the Southwest. In the same train with him departed the Rev. Xanthus Merrifew, with Honora, Alpha, Epsilon, and Iota.

"Well!" said Mrs. Jonter, "I hope Hugh will be satisfied with his joke! To drive that mother away in her delicate state!"

"I'm satisfied," declared Major Wyckling. "I guess—what's the next one's name?—Eta will be born at El Paso."

After dark, two dusty horsemen rode into the Post and reported failure to the Commanding Officer.

"I don't see how he had strength to go further than we have been," said Hugh.

"I'll send E Troop out tomorrow," said Major Wyckling.

"Could he possibly have taken to the open?" said Hugh next day to Leonard—"We'll try it."

The two rode out into the desert. After many hours, silent and hungry, they turned for supper towards Hugh's ranch, as the sun was low in the southwest.

"But after all," said Leonard, "who is going to feel that you are to blame?"

"I don't care what they feel," said Hugh moodily. His eyes were always watching the ground for possible foot prints. And in time the ranch lay before them.

"Who is that sitting on your porch?" said Leonard.

Hugh looked up from the ground. In a moment he was galloping forward. Leonard contented himself with following at a brisk trot. He saw the figure of Moulting Pelican rise at Hugh's approach, and stand with arms spread in a gesture of surrender and appeal. He saw Hugh spring to the ground and grasp both hands of the lonely Apache.

As he came up to the porch, a conversation in the Indian's language was ending.

"The Old Chief says," began Hugh, and stopped, for his voice had trembled—but not with mirth— "he says he had nowhere to run to but me."

"How," said Moulting Pelican to Leonard, timidly.

"And so that," said Hugh, regaining his customary tones, "is what you get for trying to serve the cause of science."

"Well, you got Absalom out of his job," said Leonard.

At this Hugh gave one of his enormous laughs.

"And you got an invitation from the Secretary of War."

"I hope m' fawther will let me accept," said Hugh.

When the Secretary of War in Washington received the petition for a second ambulance and other improvements, he was greatly astonished, and refused it promptly. "Never at any frontier Post that I have inspected," said he, "have I been so well entertained. They've nothing to complain of."

But when the thermometer had risen high again, the order came to abandon Fort Chiricahua. Its usefulness was over.

The officers were starting for their new station in

Montana in advance of the troops by a few days.
Two sergeants, with the men, were left to superin-
tend the dismantling of the old frontier Post. Hugh
and Moulting Pelican were on the sultry platform
to see the last of their friends.

"Well," said Hugh to Leonard, "be good to yourself."

"When I'm gone," said Leonard, "try to be more
like me."

"M' fawther 'd object to that. He wants me to
build my character."

"Then keep away from the hashish."

"Never was tempted that way till I met you."

"All aboard!" said the conductor.

Leonard jumped on the rear platform, and stood
there. Hugh with Moulting Pelican stood by the
steps. The wheels turned.

"Next time you want a shave," said Hugh, walking beside the steps, "don't hire a boot-black."

The wheels began to purr, Hugh fell behind, and
stood.

"Watch the thermometer," called Leonard, "before you buy ketchup."

"Send for me," called Hugh, "if you need a
strong trained nurse."

The train quickened.

"What does the Old Chief say?" shouted Leonard.

"It's all so wonderful," yelled Hugh.

But now the train was moving away. The two smiled at each other, silent. Leonard waved his hat.

"He heap good man," said Moulting Pelican.

"Heap good man," Hugh assented.

They watched the receding figure waving the hat. The stretch of straight track was lengthening. Suddenly the cars floated on quicksilver; then dissolved; a waving motion without form lingered; vanished; the wide smoke-stack blurred; vanished. Hugh watched a column of smoke creep away toward the horizon, staining the glassy infinity.

"Let's go home, Pelican. There's nobody now but you and me to fill the vacuum."

They jumped on their horses and rode slowly into the desert.

Inside the station of Soto de Rey, the fan of the agent moved ceaselessly back and forth.

Skip to My Loo

"WHEEL me nearer the window," said Doc Leonard.

"You're better this morning," said Hugh. "But you will find the condition of the landscape unchanged."

"Is it Thursday, or Friday, or what?" inquired the convalescent.

"Some days ago, I think somebody said it was Tuesday. But I'm not sure when it was. It's your turn to continue the story of your life, and mine to listen."

"How shall we fill the vacuum when we have told each other all that we are willing to disclose?"

"By then, you will be attending to your duties as contract surgeon of this Post."

Doc Leonard sighed among his pillows. Out of the window he looked at southern Arizona, extending hot and vacant beyond the roofs of Fort Chiricahua. Hugh stretched himself on the sofa.

"I must have been very sick," said Leonard.

"You have repeated that truth every morning since you came out of your delirium."

"How many mornings is that?"

"I have lost count."

"Did you say this was Tuesday?"

"When are you going to continue the story of your life?"

"Oh, well.—College and football: That's done. Harvard Medical School: that's done. Why I came to strike out and try my luck in Texas: that's done. Well, I got to Texas. This experience happened at once, the second day in Texas. First day was all train, and nothing new but the Jim Crow cars, which some of my Massachusetts relations were trying to have abolished by law. Directly I saw them, I saw the sense in them. If any part of the United States understood or cared about any other part, don't you think the country would get on better?"

"Are you asking me to be serious so soon after breakfast?" inquired Hugh from the sofa.

"Oh, well. The second day, the railroad part of my journey came to an end at Beehive Bluff. A branch of the Gulf Colorado and Santa Fé had its terminus there. It was a town—small—but a town, not just one of those wide places in the track. Wide streets, dust, board sidewalks, a few brick buildings they called your attention to—you know. Houses mostly one story with new little trees in the front yard. On the platform a nigger seemed to be waiting for strangers. He must have been six foot four, and he must have weighed four hundred pounds. He

was looking at me, and somehow I took a dislike to
him. Couldn't have said why, then. But I asked him
if there was a hotel. His manner remained a little
odd. He stared at me with a sort of over-familiar
knowingness. I didn't understand it. Then he replied by asking if I intended to stay in town for the
night. I was not sure about the rest of my journey
to O'Neil City, and I wished to secure a room. Was
I sure I wished to sleep in the hotel? he inquired,
always with his curious impudence; and I suppose
that I got angry. His interest in me dropped suddenly, as if he had made a mistake, and he approached another passenger, a salesman, whose anec-
dotes in the Pullman smoking compartment had
been typical. They spoke together briefly, and left
the station, laughing with a glance at me.

"Before I had decided what to do next, four
cream-colored ponies came round the corner; a
pleasant sight; driven in a two-seated buggy by an
upright, slender man with gray moustache and a
pointed, gray beard; also a pleasant sight. He tooled
his four-in-hand up to the platform with much
style; then took off his rakishly tilted sombrero so
ceremoniously that I removed my own hat; on which
he addressed me gravely, in an agreeable Southern
accent.

"That was how the only true friendship I formed
in Texas began.

"His first words were an apology for not being
at hand on the train's arrival. He introduced himself as Colonel Steptoe McDee, and he was to be my
neighbor, as neighborhood was measured in Flanagan County. He had heard of my venture, and
could assure me that there was an opening for an
educated young doctor of determination and phys-
ical vigor; my practice would cover a large territory, and he trusted that I was accustomed to horseback. O'Neil City lay fifty miles to the south of
Beehive Bluff, and as the stage had gone there this
morning, and would not go again for two days, he
would be very glad if I allowed him to drive me
over the next day.

"On our way to the hotel, we passed the negro
with the salesman, and it seemed to me that my new
acquaintance eyed the pair with contempt. I asked
him if he knew the negro. He replied that he did
not, in a manner which forbade my going further
with it.

"When I had registered and come down from
seeing my room, Colonel McDee suggested a drive
in the interval before supper, and that I should eat
this meal at a ranch which he was about to visit on
business. I was only too glad to have company, and
to see things I had never seen. We started; and he,
with his cream-colored ponies, was evidently a
figure of mark in the town. Citizens saluted him

with that shade of ostentation which people of no
importance are apt to display when seen speaking
with influential or prominent persons. Their greet-
ings were returned punctiliously by Colonel McDee.

"The aspect of its streets as we drove through
Beehive Bluff corresponded but little to the faces
of its inhabitants. The streets were surprisingly
trim. There was no litter to be seen, no skins of
oranges, not a newspaper blowing about. On the
other hand, I had never seen so many countenances
that were precisely the opposite of neat. It was
not that the men were unshaven, or that the hair
of the women was neglected; these showed the ordinary decency. The slovenliness was—it's not easy
to describe—the slovenliness—it was in the whole
put-together of their features, the way their noses
were, and the absence of point in their eyes, and the
want of accent in their mouths and chins. A total
slackness. As if they were wax that had been too
near the fire and had run slightly, and it had melted
the meaning out of whatever mouths and noses they
had started with. Any good dog or horse has a
neater, more personal expression. Or any good
rooster, for that matter.

"I suppose Colonel Steptoe McDee may have
been watching me.

"'And what's your first impression, sir, if I
may ask it, of Beehive Bluff?' said he.

" 'I have never seen a town in better order,' I answered.

" 'Ah! That is their point, sir. Or perhaps I should more correctly say, a part of their point.'

"I noticed that he said 'their' and not 'our' point.

"At the edge of the town, he pulled up to speak to a man of circumstantial and pious appearance, who walked as if about to enter a church, and turned upon us an eye on the alert to rebuke sin. I did not catch his name when the colonel introduced me to this personage; and after the personage had accorded me a somewhat elaborate welcome to the great state of Texas, I hardly saw what we had stopped for; since what the two had to say to each other amounted to nothing.

" 'And what,' said Colonel McDee as we drove into the open country, 'should you say was that gentleman's walk in life?'

" 'I should imagine,' I replied somewhat unguardedly, 'that he might be a preacher of one of those churches who rescue brands from the burning by fireworks in the pulpit and mob hysterics in the congregation.'

"I don't know why I burst out like that. It was very young and fresh.

"The old gentleman attended to his ponies in silence for at least a mile, and more than once I glanced at him uneasily, and was on the brink of some sort of apology. But when he spoke at last, it was not in displeasure.

" 'In Beehive Bluff,' said he, 'you may read a regulation posted in sundry conspicuous spots, forbidding any one to throw paper or refuse in the streets or alleys, except in the barrels or boxes placed for the purpose. I may add, sir, that women of professional immorality have been run out of Beehive Bluff. There is no red-light district in the town. As to cards—there is an ordinance against gaming. An elder of the dominating church, having his reasons to be suspicious, climbed on a roof here one night, and looked down through a window. There in a private room he saw the saloon-keeper, and a professor of the high-school, and other prominent citizens playing poker. When they were indicted at his instance, he was rendered highly indignant by the professor inquiring of him very bluntly how he came to be aware it was poker they were playing.'

"I laughed. But Colonel McDee had a way of not permitting himself to laugh very often, or very much. I believe that he considered too audible laughter as unworthy of a man's dignity. However, he excused it in me.

" 'Human nature can be revengeful, sir,' he now continued. 'Those people were sore at being spied on, but they kept quiet until they caught that church elder playin' progressive euchre for prizes. So now he is also under indictment. I thought it might interest you to meet him, and therefore I introduced you to him back there.'

" 'Is Texas your native state, sir?' I inquired presently.

" 'By no means, sir. We are an Alabama fam'ly. I removed to this state at the end of the War for Southern Independence.'

"It was not by this name that my teachers on Cape Cod had taught me to call the Civil War; but I had sense enough to hold my peace; and I was beginning to like the colonel extremely. This I was impelled to convey to him.

" 'I feel very fortunate,' said I, 'in the privilege of having you as a neighbor.'

"He acknowledged this with a formal bow. 'You have the appearance of being accustomed to manly exercises. Am I correct?'

"I mentioned football.

" 'And shootin', sir? You have brought firearms?'

" 'Yes. But I haven't carried a pistol since I used to go with the hospital ambulance.'

"As we approached the ranch, I learned that here its owner ran his cattle; that he was away attending to his sheep in a distant part of the state; that Colonel McDee had grown tired of waiting

week after week for his return, and would transact
his business with the foreman; and that I lost nothing in not meeting the owner. A herd of children
was gathered by the door to stare at us, and was
temporarily scattered by a scrubbing brush hurled
out of a door at it. This was followed by shrill ex-
pletives, more commonly used by men, and entirely
unheeded by the children, who had at once re-
assembled to stare at us. The head of a woman was
thrust out of the door. At the sight of us, her stream
of language ceased in the middle of a word, she
transformed her fury into smiles of overdone welcome, which covered the recent unpleasantness like
a flowered quilt flung hastily over an unmade bed.
I was presented to Mrs. Maxson, the absent ranchman's wife. Like her children, she could stare, too.
Her eye-lids were thick. Her good looks made you
think of bill-posters. Her manner was rather got-up.

" 'Too bad Wyatt ain't come home yet from his
sheep,' she said; 'I'm expecting word any day.'

" 'I knew he was away, ma'am,' said the colonel.
'But Macomb and I can fix it up.'

" 'Eat supper with us,' said she. 'It's about
ready.'

"At supper she waited on a long table of men,
carrying in the dishes from an adjacent kitchen,
and coming and going. My new friend had been
placed opposite me, and we seemed to fall under

the contagion of the restraint which governed the rest of the company. After the first, his conversation ceased, and I followed suit, attending to my plate, until a phrase spoken by one of the cowboys raised my curiosity. There had been some fragmentary discussion which concerned horses that were at pasture; and I heard one of them say what sounded like *caviard horse*. I repeated this to Colonel McDee, and asked what it meant. An odd expression crossed his face; he replied that he would explain that later.

"Presently an incident occurred which left me perfectly bewildered.

"One of the cowboys had needed a monkey-wrench and found none after looking everywhere.

" 'It's in the boar's nest,' another informed him.

"Instantly at this, Mrs. Maxson, who had been setting a dish on the table, whirled round as if she had been stung, and literally stamped out of the room. Her exit was followed by a series of choked school-boy giggles, and big hands were placed over mouths, while the cowboys glanced roguishly at each other.

"This was so extraordinary that I asked no questions.

"All enlightenment was postponed by the woman's asking for a lift, if we were returning to town. While the colonel transacted his business with the

foreman, and I strolled about, she busied herself
with her dishes and preparations. Her children
idled and stared.

"'Eudora!' screamed the mother, and a girl of
sixteen appeared. 'Eudora, you can lock up at nine.
I'm staying the night with Aunt Mary.'

"'I'll take you there, ma'am,' said the colonel,
'it's on our way.'

"'I— Mrs. Bodock is giving a party,' said Mrs.
Maxson hastily. 'I don't want to be any trouble.'

"'No trouble at all!' exclaimed the colonel.
'Doctor, here's a chance for you to see a local entertainment. If you're willing, we'll all pay our re-
spects to Mrs. Bodock.'

"Mrs. Maxson was silent at this, and looked
sulky. She seemed to lose her manners easily.

"'I'd like to go,' said I. 'But Mrs. Maxson
will find me an awkward partner, if there is
dancing.'

"She drew herself up rather grandly, and told me
in an offended voice that she would not do such a
thing; that the church forbade it as a vicious indulgence, leading to worse, and that if decent
people had their way, there would soon be a
law against it. If I wished to dance, she supposed
that I could find companions at some other kind of
party.

"While she was talking, I noticed that Colonel

Steptoe McDee had his eye on me with the same enigmatical expression which I had noticed during supper. I tried to mollify the offended lady by assuring her that I danced so badly it didn't count; but this joke was coldly received; she remained offended.

"The party was called a Play Party. Some girls and young men arranged themselves alternately in a line and stood opposite another line similarly arranged. A parlor organ furnished the music. A girl at the end began to sing some words to a hymn-like tune. They went something like this:

'Lost my sweetheart
Skip to my Loo
Lost my sweetheart
Skip to my Loo
Lost my sweetheart
Skip to my Loo
Skip to my Loo, my darling.'

These words made the running accompaniment of corresponding action. Stepping in time to them, each girl left her partner and crossed over to the opposite row, swung the young man facing her away from his girl.

Being deserted, he lifted his voice and skipped to his Loo on the other side. Each deserted one set up the song in turn, 'Lost my sweetheart,' and after

a line or two, crossed to another couple on some new
words:

> 'I'll get another one
>   Skip to my Loo,
>   Prettier'n t'other one'

and so forth, all the way down both lines, until
every one was swinging actively, and the action
grew gayer and more energetic, and not so very unlike a Virginia reel—only, it was not dancing; the
singing saved it from being this forbidden fruit.
Other verses there were, serving as the means to
declare personal feeling all the way from sentiment
to passion; and as I was wondering how many of
these partners sincerely believed that their singing
made it all right, and that if they stopped it would
be all wrong, I caught sight of Mrs. Maxson slipping
away.

"Presently I had seen enough of the Play Party,
and we left the house.

"'Well, sir,' said the colonel, 'and what's your
opinion of that entertainment?'

"'I have traveled very little,' I answered. 'It's
new to me. But I'm glad they manage to enjoy
themselves in spite of their preposterous church.'

"'So would I be, sir!' he exclaimed with heat,
'but they grow up under the fetid curse of
hypocrisy.'

" 'Won't you explain now,' I asked, 'those incidents at supper? What is a *caviard horse,* if I got the word right?'

" 'It's a corruption from the Mexican word caballado, which may be translated a herd, or better, a stud. There are many in familiar use here. You're likely to hear mention of a *lover wolf.* Lover is just the Mexican lobo, which means wolf. *Caviard horse* means stud horse, stallion.'

" 'I don't see why it's not easier and shorter just to say stallion.'

" 'I saw that you observed, sir, how our hostess left the room.'

" 'Yes. That's the other thing I didn't understand. And they all laughed.'

" 'She was insulted, sir, because one of the boys alluded to the *boar's nest.*'

" 'Does that mean something unmentionable?'

" 'Not at all, sir, it's just their name for the bunk-house, where the cowboys sleep. But in the presence of a lady he should not have employed the word *boar,* he should have said *male pig.*'

" 'Oh, *no!*' I shouted right out.

" 'And I must warn you to go around all such words, if you want to be accepted in this community. You must take care to say *male cow, male hen,* when a lady is present.'

" 'My brain for a fantastic moment suggested to

me that I was being made game of; that the colonel, with all the rest of them, was playing a well concerted and traditional hoax upon the traditional tenderfoot, instead of shooting at my heels. But I saw that this could hardly be.

" 'Why, Colonel,' I exclaimed, 'think of the language she used to her own children!'

" 'Oh yes, sir; but how could the pore lady know we were within hearin'?' "

Hugh raised himself and sat straight up on his sofa.

"How much of this are you making up?" he demanded.

"None of it. Who could make up such things?" And Leonard resumed this chapter of his experience.

"After the ponies had been left at the livery stable opposite the station, we parted; the colonel went to bed, for which I was not ready, and I loitered and strolled: Beehive Bluff and its people were like nothing I had ever met, or could possibly have imagined; and I gave thanks for the colonel's existence, and prayed that there might be at least one or two others like him where I was going.

"With other idlers at the station, I watched a train arrive. The big negro was waiting there too. He ran his eye over the passengers as they stepped out, and selected one of them just as he had selected me. This man did not become irritated as I had been, he stood listening, and then plainly assented to some offer. But he did not walk uptown in the negro's company as the salesman had done, the negro fell behind, as if by an understanding between them, and lingered across the street from the hotel, while the traveler went inside with his bag.

"When I sauntered in a few minutes later, he was lounging over the desk, chatting with the clerk.

"'I guess sheep will go big this year,' said the clerk. 'Congratulate you on the deal.'

"'Put it through quicker than I'd hoped.'

"'In your place I'd be in a hurry to get out home,' said the clerk.

"'I was,' said the man, 'but—' and he whispered something.

"The clerk grinned. 'Sure!' said he. And he pushed the hotel book round, and while the man registered, the clerk continued: 'Us married men must stand together. I've found alibis useful myself. I'll swear you slept here.'

"Then the man went out.

"A bundle of mail was presently carried in, and the clerk offered me the morning paper from Fort Worth, and discussed the weather and other topics with me in the again deserted office.

"While we chatted, and I began to think I would go to bed, he turned sharply, and listened.

" 'Didn't you hear something?' he asked.

"I had not.

" 'Sounded like a shot,' said the clerk. 'Well, maybe it wasn't anything.'

"Then one of the travelers ran into the door and asked if a doctor was not registered. 'Folks in trouble up the street,' he said. 'Man down, trying to get away.'

"He hurried me to a house with its door open. In a room by the entrance, I found the negro lying on the floor. Mrs. Maxson was sunk in a chair, her eyes closed; standing beside her was the traveler of the alibi. Before I could reach her to see what was the matter, she opened her eyes, and screamed, and clutched the man. I am not sure now that she had ever fainted; there was nothing the matter with her. If it was her Aunt Mary's house, where was her Aunt Mary?

" 'What are you doing here?' demanded the man suddenly, scowling at me. 'How many more are butting in on this?'

" 'I was told that a doctor was wanted,' I answered, looking round. But my informant had disappeared.

" 'Well, you're not,' said the man. 'Clear out.'

"I jumped and caught his hand and wrenched his pistol from him, and gave him a little tap on the head with the barrel, not too heavy. He went down, and I examined the negro. He had never had time to need a doctor. All the while, the woman sat staring at me, evidently frozen with alarm lest she should be my next victim.

" 'Why, madam,' I said, laughing, 'you needn't worry. Your friend will come to in a minute.'

" 'If you have murdered him—' she began in a shrill voice, and stopped; for the man took hold of the arm of her chair with a shaking hand, and helped himself to sit up.

" 'I'm in the way, it appears,' I said. 'Before I go, would you object to telling me who killed that negro?'

" 'I did,' said the man. 'And suppose you mind your business and quit annoying peaceful folks.'

" 'Oh, don't talk that way,' I said, laughing again. 'Do you want another tap?'

"At this the woman gave another scream, and flung her arms round him.

" 'The negro is unarmed,' I continued. 'You prefer them unarmed, don't you?'

" 'Say,' said the alibi, and his various emotions raised his voice to a sort of wailing falsetto, 'where you come from, don't a man protect his own home?'

" 'A pleasant night to you both,' I answered; and I dropped his pistol in my pocket. 'Your friend the hotel clerk will give you this to complete your alibi.'

"He slammed the door, and locked it. This moved

me to add through the door: 'You ought to let Aunt Mary know her niece is safe.'

"The clerk was in his chair behind the counter, on which I laid the pistol.

"'Your friend will call for this, but probably not till morning. He has just shot that big negro with it.'

"'You don't say!' said the clerk in his chair, as if I had mentioned it had come on to rain. 'Well, niggers don't count in this section.'

"'I realize that dancing's worse than murder in this section,' said I. 'I suppose the nigger must have somehow frightened Mrs. Maxson.'

"Then the clerk jumped up. 'Did you say Mrs. Maxson?'

"'Oh, she's all right. Her lover was in time. I left them together.'

"'Her?' stammered the clerk, 'and—him?' He pointed to the pistol.

"'She came in town to meet him. I wouldn't disturb them just now, if I were you.'

"'But she—but she—but she didn't—but he didn't—but the nigger—did he say he shot him?'

"'He said so. He didn't look as if he was lying just then.'

"The clerk gave a long whistle. Then he took the pistol thoughtfully, and looked at it, and put it in a drawer, and shut the drawer slowly, and sat down.

'Well,' he said, 'in that nigger's business, a man ought to make sure who the parties are that he's bringing together.' Then he whistled again.

"I went to bed, entirely at sea. I suppose I was slow. I couldn't get it.

"Next day, the man had called early and got his pistol and left. When Colonel McDee came for me with his ponies, I was all set to impart my adventure. He was obviously unaware of anything. Instead, I made no mention of it at all, because he began at once by asking if I would mind a little delay; he had said nothing to the foreman at the ranch about delivering some horses he had agreed to purchase. So I put off my story, I don't know why. And I was so silent as we drove out of town, that the colonel expressed the hope I had not slept badly. I suppose I was excited to know if I should see Mrs. Maxson, and if so, what then?

"I did see her. She was in front of the house, throwing feed to chickens. She also saw us coming. One look, and she ran away round the corner, and did not reappear.

" 'Why,' exclaimed the colonel, 'it surely can't be that she hasn't forgiven you yet!'

" 'Well, Colonel, I think it can!'

"He had no time for more than a look to see if I was joking, for we arrived at the door, where the children were already gathered to stare. Out of the door behind them came the man who had shot the nigger, and he stopped short.

" 'Why good morning to you, Mr. Maxson!' said the colonel, 'Mrs. Maxson must have been surprised to see you ahead of her expectation!'

" 'Yes,' mumbled Mr. Maxson. 'Put my business through earlier 'n I'd figured on.'

" 'Let me introduce Dr. Leonard—Mr. Maxson,' said the colonel.

" 'Glad to know you,' mumbled Maxson, with averted eyes.

"That was when I got it,'' said Leonard.

Hugh said nothing for quite a little while. He had got it.

Little Old Scaffold

COLONEL STEPTOE McDEE, sometime officer in the Army of the Mississippi, respected ranchman since 1865, dwelling in the neighborhood of O'Neil City, Flanagan County, Texas, sat at his table with some cigars by his empty plate. He was waiting for a young cowboy who sat opposite and plied his knife and fork vigorously, yet with diffidence. The old gentleman's light meal was finished; he smiled inwardly at his guest's haste and embarrassment over a third helping.

"Don't bolt your food, Randy," said he. "It's a pleasure to see a good appetite."

The boy looked up gratefully, and tried his best not to hurry. His host was fragile, sparing of meat and drink, his fine hair was gray and thin, and the past seemed always to be looking out of his dark eyes. The present with all its vigor filled the boy, and he felt somehow guilty about his appetite. He had never been asked to break bread in this house before; it surprised him, puzzled him, made him proud and awkward, but had not prevented the third helping. This was soon all gone, for he had hurried, after all; and the host bestowed a cigar upon his shy and taciturn guest.

"Randy, I have my reasons for bothering you this evening."

"It ain't no bother, sir," mumbled the guest, letting fall his lighted match, and recovering it in confusion.

" 'What can that old fello' want with me?' you'll have been wondering."

"Oh, no, sir!" protested Randy, untruthfully, "I wisht I got such grub—food, I mean—every day!"

"It was Crip King you rode for when you started, if I remember?"

"Yes, sir."

"An early start. Were you fifteen?"

"Not quite, sir."

"And now you're working for my partner, Judge McCoy. The judge speaks highly of you. You've been about a year with him?"

"Fifteen months."

"Well; the judge is aware that I may have use for a lusty young fello' who can keep his mouth shut. Can you keep your mouth shut?"

"Always have, Colonel."

"Well. Well. That's good. I reckon you have. The judge and I agree that the present state of this community is—not what it ought to be."

"You bet it ain't!" declared Randy, quite forgetting to be shy. He had participated recently in the hanging of a cattle thief.

"The judge," continued the old gentleman, "will let me borrow you now and then, if you're willing— let me finish, please—but it would be well that as few persons as possible should notice that you are— occasionally—on detached duty."

"Yes, sir." Randy's eyes were intent and excited.

"The judge, also, has nothing but good to say of your work and faithfulness."

Randy looked down, and scraped a foot. They smoked a while. In their silence the distance between them seemed to grow less. In time, the colonel began:

"We don't think—and others share our opinion— that Flanagan County stands in need of any novel industry such as we fear there are signs of. Are you acquainted with the towns of Ultima Thule or Dripping Lick?"

"I've ridden in the races at both of 'em."

"It does not look," said the colonel, "as if some folks here were profiting by the experience of those towns with the railroad."

"Railroad! Why las' time I seen 'em, there wasn't no railroad near 'em."

"And never will be. That's what Flanagan should bear in mind. The railroad intended to go to Ultima Thule. Planned to make a division point there. Had

you known that? Well, the citizens over there don't
brag much about the affair. When representatives of
the railroad arrived to discuss the purchase of property, every citizen valued his real estate at just
about worth its weight in gold. Now a railroad likes
fair treatment, just like anybody else. The Gulf
Colorado and Santa Fé skipped Ultima Thule by
eighteen miles. Same thing at Dripping Lick. They
surveyed around it, twenty-five miles away. The
citizens of those towns would almost beg your ac-
ceptance of their real estate as a gift to-day.''

"Colonel, will that spur touch O'Neil City?"

"Not a chance of it. But what route has been
decided upon, nobody knows—or whether any decision has been reached. Expectations are busy, and
whispers and hopes are plentiful—you must have
heard some?''

Randy had. Didn't bother much over such things.
All one to him where the railroad went. The colonel
continued:

''Now the novel industry—in a rough and ready
community like ours, Randy, have you anything
against requesting an undesirable citizen to leave
the country in ten days?''

"Why, what else can you do, sir—as a start, I
mean?''

''In short—you would deem it merely a humane

and considerate way of producing his absence without resorting to—harsher methods?''

"Why yes, sir, sure!" assented Randy, and
thought, What's he driving at anyway?

Colonel Steptoe McDee now approached the heart
of the matter:

"Randy, I reckon one of these days I'll be asking
you to be courageous."

"Ask me any day you want, Colonel. Fifteen seconds of asking is all you'll need." Randy was only
nineteen, and often spoke like it.

"I'll maybe want you to hide out near Professor
Salamanca's house and tell me who goes there after
dark."

The boy's face changed; he was silent.

"Randy, I wouldn't have thought it of you. The
judge wouldn't have thought it of you." He led
the way out of his dining-room to where it was
cooler.

"But, Colonel," remonstrated the boy, following
in his wake and talking to his back, "it's known for
a fact. She has a circle drawn around that house.
Human eyes can't see it; but once you step inside it,
you don't step out until she's willing. And she
knows your errand, and she's arranged accordingly.
We warned Aleck Brush not to go there alone. We
picked him up ten miles off without a mark on him,

and his eyeballs staring at whatever last sight it was he saw. Quick as Aleck crossed the circle, she knowed he knowed it was her spells had cast the fever on his cattle. So she was ready for him when she said, 'Come in' to his knocking.''

"We'll say no more about it for the present, Randy. If it becomes important, I'll do the watching myself.'' And nothing that the old gentleman could have said would have made the boy's cheeks burn so hotly.

The colonel touched the heart of the matter from another angle. "Happen to see Crip King before he went?''

"I hadn't heard he'd went anywheres.''

"To Memphis, I believe, where he has friends of influence to get him a position.''

At this remark, which the colonel made in an easy voice, as if it was without importance, Randy's expressive eyebrows curved low, and set as he stared. "Not—ten days? Not *him?*''

Steptoe McDee nodded.

"He's gone for good? And Mrs. King and Amanda and Johnnie—gone, run out?''

Steptoe McDee nodded again.

"Crip's quitting that ranch of his on Honey Creek for *good?* Why, what has anybody ever had against *him?*''

"Nothing that I can guess—unless it is the desirable location of his ranch. It would interest me to hear of any offer to purchase that vacated property, and to be sure of the source from which such offer came. And in the case of a purchaser disclosing himself, I should become very much interested indeed.''

The boy's thoughts roved, apparently. ''I shouldn't wonder if Ace Brown was making a wrong guess this time.''

Steptoe was quick. ''This time?''

''Didn't you hear? He has had ten days served on him again. Of course the one last year was a joke just to scare Ace, and he didn't scare. But, Colonel, Ace's standing in this community to-day ain't like Crip King's was—not since Ace's law suit it ain't. Crip, he'll be a loss.''

''And you don't think Ace would?''

''Well, Colonel, I'd not have said it a year ago. And Ace has his friends. But there's those that would like it explained how their chief witness against him happened to come up suddenly dead in the Dos Bocas saloon the night before the trial.''

''That was just a card game!''

''Sure it was *in* a card game!— but there's those who don't call it *just* a card game now. I think Ace is guessing wrong.''

It was the colonel's thoughts which now apparently roved. "Randy, if anybody should buy Crip's ranch on Honey, don't you think they might be disappointed?"

The young fellow fixed his eyes upon the old one, but comprehension did not awake in them.

Steptoe drove it home. "I have explained to you that the disappointments over in Ultima Thule and Dripping Lick have been very severe."

It knocked Randy breathless. He sat taking in by degrees its full import.

"When you have traveled as long and far from your mother's teaching as I have, Randy, the world and its doings will surprise you less."

"Why, Colonel, haven't they told you about me? I've never knowed who I was; but I've quit caring, for I've noticed I enjoy life quite a heap more than some that has regular mothers and fathers. There's times when I wisht I knowed reading and writing. *Well!* So that's it! Ten days for Crip King and away he goes, and ten days for Ace Brown and here he is!"

"Undoubtedly," said the colonel, "one survey is along Honey Creek—but there are others. A well managed company like the Gulf Colorado and Santa Fé calculates probable costs and possible returns and compares routes before making its mind up. There's no need for hurry here, you see, for no competitor is in the field."

"So that's it," repeated Randy. "Now I know— why, all kinds of things are explained!"

"You and I will wait for some more to be, Randy. If Crip King is the only honest man that gets a notice—well, in that case we'll have to drop our present theory and hunt for another." He rose. "Let's see what the weather says." The two had been sitting on the colonel's ranch porch, and the boy remained in his chair. His host turned to him. "Randy, I am over sixty and you are under twenty. Among George Washington's rules for a man's behavior that he wrote in a copy-book when he was younger than you are, there was one about standing up when anybody on their feet was speaking to you."

Randy got up instantly. "Thank you, sir. If you'll just keep telling me such things, I'll be obliged."

Steptoe McDee laid his hand on the boy's shoulder. He had to reach a little to do it. "The stars are clear, Randy. A quiet night. Not a breath of wind. Very quiet. Very clear. It's late, boy. Go home. Go to bed—better make it your own bed oftener than some are saying you do in these days."

He could not see Randy flush, but he knew it; it was not so dark on the porch as to hide the slight movement of the youth's head.

"I've done nothing a man need be ashamed of," muttered Randy. "He's no friend of mine."

"Your code is not a new one, boy. Many husbands in Flanagan County make free with their neighbor's homes, but they mostly defend their own. If you were to come up dead suddenly, I should miss you."

Randy stepped down from the porch and jumped on his horse, and Steptoe McDee envied his young strength and the spring in him.

"You're not riding the buckskin. Didn't you buy him?"

"Me? Never!" There was something odd in the boy's tone.

"Well, good night."

"Good night, sir. What you ask ain't so easy. I'll not promise you nothing—not now. But I'll not forget."

"The weather seems settled, Randy. But short of the Unforeseen, which dogs us all, I shouldn't wonder if you and I lived to see a cloud-burst one of these days."

The old gentleman stood on his porch listening to the hoof-beats grow distant through the live oaks that spread in plenty over the land where the boy was riding. Then he sighed, and went to his door and shut it.   * * *

There were honest men in Flanagan County who were sure that "things would have gone different if Crip King had acted different." Perhaps. Yet when their turn came, their haste was equal to Crip's; one after the other they left their homes well within the ten days given them, and the cases of this new industry broke out "like it was small-pox," as Randy remarked to the colonel in one of the little talks they held from time to time. It led the colonel to reply that they might see the day when vaccination would be made compulsory by the local health board. And following hard upon the small-pox, a further inconvenience had now appeared—a split in the party. There was no danger of the other party's getting in, because in Flanagan County there was no other party—but what had Uncle Cayce Hartle ever done to dissatisfy the people? Yet the upstart candidate, Jinks Fleming, was winning a support that nobody could despise, not even Colonel Steptoe McDee. Office was a thing he never sought or accepted, but nobody else had ever sought it without consulting him first—until now. He lived in no dread of a ten day notice; his leadership rested firm upon too wide a respect and affection; but he was aware of the presence of another leadership in this region, founded upon fear. Jinks Fleming had developed a knack for public speaking; he was making headway; foolish women with fool husbands liked him.

They were sitting crouched—Steptoe McDee and the boy who had meanwhile become twenty, but not otherwise any older—they were sitting out in the open, and it was a lonely spot. Hither they had ridden several miles for the sake of a good view, which they had now watched together for some while in silence. Beneath them yawned the vast deceiving plain, impersonal as eternity, candid as the day to the eye, teeming with human secrecy.

"Randy," said the old gentleman, "what are your principles?"

"Why, Colonel, you know I said I couldn't promise."

"Psha! I said your principles. I know your morals."

The boy looked down. "I didn't mention it that night. It should never be mentioned, I reckon. But —well—it's different when a woman tells you no, because that's just a disappointment. But turn it the other way around, and—well, sir, a man—a man don't want her to laugh at him. No, sir!" And Randy looked up firmly.

The colonel would have liked to smile. Instead, he went on, "Since recent events have changed your delicate situation, don't court any others of that nature. No act is wrong that does no harm to man or woman. That he was no friend of yours is a miserable excuse—don't ever tell me such a flimsy thing again. They have been driven from the country by a cowardly notice. Let their unmerited misfortune be at least some help to you. And now, boy, let's drop this for good. It's just between you and me, and what we're here for concerns a heap more folks than that."

"Please, Colonel, I'd like to say one thing more. I didn't forget. You'd never say I was doing harm now."

"That cloud-burst is coming, Randy," said the colonel, as he stared over the edge of Flanagan Mountain at the serene and stupendous beauty of the plain. Into the crystal light were filtering the faint hues of a day that was drawing slowly and dreamily to its end. Nothing of disturbance was visible, nothing of portent. McDee put up his field glasses and swept them from one point to another. Close in near the foot of the mountain, he saw the red roof of a sheep shed, made out the branches of the trees that grew not thickly near it, the scattered cabins, quiet with their shut doors and nobody visible there, nothing moving at all anywhere, except the slight motions of distant sheep, and the white dots of some poultry at the nearest ranch. Beyond all this, the floor of the plain stretched away to the pale blue line of the Santa Anna ridge, and a softly colored radiance ennobled the whole prospect. Presently he handed the glasses to the boy. Both remained in their cautious attitude on the ground in a slight depression of the soil, too slight to screen them from any careful observer out in the plain, should they stand up, but sufficient to conceal them and yet permit them to watch anything which might go on down there, provided they took care not to be outlined against the sky. They had left their horses a good distance behind them, well away from the sight of anyone below. The colonel took the glasses and again fixed them on a particular cabin. Then he spoke with some doubt in his voice.

"Word of a meeting at Mesh Tyler's came pretty straight."

"It's a smart little old scheme, if your guess is right, Colonel."

"Between '62 and '65 I had to do a heap of guessing, Randy. Maybe I have forgotten how. Take a look at these." He handed the boy two letters, but the boy glanced at him and shook his head, smiling.

"You'll have to tell me what they say, sir."

"Excuse me, boy, I forgot. Look at them all the same. Does the writing seem alike to you?"

Randy studied them with a frown, and again shook his head. "I'd be afraid to judge, sir."

"Both were written lately from Flanagan County, this one to Honoré Devereux at Shreveport."

"An offer?"

McDee nodded. "Honoré Devereux, you'll remember, got a ten day notice soon after Crip King got his. And this other letter was sent to Crip at Memphis. Each enclosed his letter to me at San Saba, because they distrust the postmaster at O'Neil City. They didn't want to take any chances of his noticing the post marks. They think that I might be able to trace the source from which these offers came. The signature means nothing. The address is a post office box. And these are not the first I have been shown. The spelling is good and the style is better than good, it is trained. Somebody advised the wording.—I'm just thinking it out aloud, Randy, how it might be, just figuring the probabilities, filling my scanty facts with guesses. Here is the way Honoré's goes . . . 'Supposing you have no further use for your domicile on Little Brady Creek I am writing to inquire for a party I represent if you would consider selling said property . . .' Crip's letter goes just about like that . . . 'an authorized representative could meet you with credentials to discuss the value . . .' well, they're very much alike. No trouble taken to vary the language. Trouble taken about the handwriting, I think. But don't forget I'm guessing at it, Randy. The handwriting is bad—illiterate. Why should that be, since the expression is good? The two are not quite alike. Were they dictated? Or copied? Did the same hand write both, but fail to make them entirely dissimilar? Anyway, it's not a perfectly executed job.''

Randy did look at them now. ''It's the same paper,'' said he.

''Yes. But you find that paper anywhere. It's in general use. Maybe you and I will never know exactly all about this—but maybe we'll know all we need to.—You misunderstood me when I asked what your principles were. That young Yankee doctor last year—when I think of his being run out—and I had to sit down under it! The thought is distasteful still.''

''You couldn't body-guard him night and day, Colonel. Everybody knowed who sent him his ten days.''

''You touch it, you touch the point! I could have made it a personal matter with a man. The first Yankee I ever liked. I esteemed him, sir. No quack remedies, no consulting the stars. A sane influence, and winning his way. Cured me, sir, without dealing any cards. Put me on rations. Old Salamanca got uneasy about her prestige. I had to advise that capable young man to leave the country. It was bitter, sir, bitter! But if—but if—'' the old gentleman pointed a finger to mark his words—''my Southern chivalry has its limits, Randy. If I find she is behind all this''—he shook the letters—''if I discover this disreputable Jinks Fleming to be her contemptible dummy—would your Southern principles forbid you to retaliate? I have begun to suspect that my position is being assailed, the influence my character has commanded in Flanagan County undermined and challenged by deliberate and despicable means. Did you know it was hinted to Crip and Honoré that I was behind their notices, because I had private knowledge of where the railroad was going? Both warned me of this before they went."

"It's mostly your personal friends who have been run out," said Randy. "I never thought of that before."

"Yes, it happens to be, and very convenient too for the instigator, if my suspicions are correct. But, Randy, it is the lay of the land that's back of this. The railroad may not go through all those vacated ranches, but it has got to go through some of them. Anybody who buys up all cheap, is bound to have profit far exceeding their loss. She is equal to an idea like that, and her following is still numerous. If ever I become sure, Randy, my friends will be seen back here in spite of their notices; and that day I may feel obliged to take steps."

In his vehemence, the hot old gentleman had attended to his thoughts only, and was now surprised by the boy's position. Randy was flat down, tense, looking over into the great valley. "There!" he whispered. He was not listening to the colonel's harangue. McDee's humorous lips parted instantly in amusement. He put up his field glasses. Down below, far off, was a horseman. He handed the glasses to Randy. "What do you make of him?"

"I ain't sure," breathed Randy. "I'll be sure in a minute."

The colonel's laugh now became audible. "Why Randy, my gracious, he's three miles off!"

"Yes, sir, sure he is."

"Well, then, you young sinnah, what are you whisperin' for?" In his jocular moments, the colonel's hereditary accent always flavored perceptibly his excellent, easy use of words.

The youth turned round. "Was I?"

"Randy, when you're just an old sinnah like me, you will reserve your whisperin' for occasions when folks might hear you if you didn't."

"Well, Colonel, I reckon you have called the turn on me. Maybe I *am* what you might consider excited in these days. What a man knows excites him, and what he don't know excites him worse. And before I looked through your glasses, I got a new astonishment."

"You young sinnah! Don't you dare to tell me you recognized him with your naked young eye!"

"It was the pony. I'd have sworn to him before I would to his rider."

"Your property?"

"No, sir, never! I'd not accept him as a gift. It's that buckskin."

"Afraid of a horse!"

"Not the way you're thinking, Colonel." Randy looked through the glasses at the distant horseman. "But if I was Ace Brown," he continued, "I'd sooner walk to where I was going, I'd sooner not go at all, than ride that buckskin."

"Don't add to the mysteries that surround us, Randy!"

"I'm not, Colonel. But you never do nothing but laugh at me when I mention it."

"Go on. I'll do my best."

"You was in N'Yawlans time o' the races, or you'd never need any telling about it. Jim Turner brought that buckskin into the country, and he raced him against her blue roan she used to win everywheres with. And that buckskin beat her roan. And she dropped more money than she liked. And she walked up to Jim—I was right there—and she didn't say what was on her tongue—I saw her change her mind—she asks Jim what will he take for his pony, and Jim he tells her there's better money in keeping him than selling him. And she gives the buckskin a long look, and she don't say nothing, she walks off."

"Well?"

The boy lowered his voice. "That's when she done it. I seen it."

"What?"

"She put her evil on the buckskin," muttered Randy, staring at the colonel with eyes of fear.

The colonel had given his promise; he did not laugh; nor did he lose his temper. Ranchmen of Flanagan old enough to be fathers—even grandfathers—of this twenty-year-old boy were quite shy of ill words about Professor Salamanca; looked apprehensive when they heard them, lowered their voices when they spoke them. In such a community as this, the waif had drifted to his adolescence; Steptoe McDee did not scold him.

"Randy," he began, "I have sometimes believed that you held me in respect."

"Why, Colonel, you *know* it!"

"Randy, suppose I furnished my parlor with a stuffed alligatah hangin' from the ceilin', and had other objectionable reptyles crouchin' in corners, and a great big crystal ball for squintin' into when I wanted to throw prophetic fits; and suppose I took to squattin' under a black canopy spangled with gilt bats and lobsters and stars when you dropped in to ask if I had anything good for the belly-ache, or if I could tell you when it was goin' to rain—then of course you would be sure that I could just cast my eye on your little old pony and put an evil on him, as you call it?"

It ended as a question needing an answer, and the colonel waited; but poor Randy stared at his mentor, and not a word came from him. McDee apostrophized him for the third time.

"Randy, somewhere inside of you is a gentleman, with some in-born but highly neglected right feeling, and a good healthy brain waitin' to be used. And I expect to live to see you use it."

"But, Colonel" (the boy stretched out his arms) "you was away in N'Yawlans, I keep a telling you. Others seen her give that look to the buckskin—they knowed the look—they'd saw it given more than once when consequences followed—and it wasn't three weeks before consequences followed this time. Jim started out on the buckskin one day, aimin' to race him at the San Saba meeting; but he never got there; and her roan won; and the buckskin trotted into the livery corral he was used to at O'Neil City, with an empty saddle and blood on it. They found Jim on Still Creek. Jim had been shot in the back." Randy whispered those last words, nodding ominously over each one.

The colonel met this with a pause, and a solemn inquiry: "Did the alligator do it?"

Randy looked reproachful. The colonel labored the point.

"Aside from his impudence in racin' against white folks, I'll bid you recall the fact that Jim Turner was an undesirable nigger *anyway*. I'll bid you recall that last March you helped Bruce Maxey into the next world with a decent rope and the approval of all upstanding citizens, and no assistance from stuffed reptiles. Let alone the crowd she employs to deal with her enemies, don't you know that old Salamanca can shoot quick and straight herself? Why, it's scarcely a year since she ran out the Yankee doctor and had her faithless lover attended to right after he'd attended to his rival in the favors of Miss Sanchez; and you talked good sense to me about crocodiles that self-same night."

But still the boy looked merely unhappy, and so the colonel dropped his expostulations: better to let it alone; time corrects a multitude of errors.

"Well, well," he said; and his hand waved crocodiles aside. "Power is a treacherous drug, Randy. Maybe the Professor has had an over-dose of it, and thinks she's goin' to ascend the throne in Flanagan County. I came here for peace. . . ."

The old Southerner put up his field glasses. "It's sure enough Ace Brown on your little old buckskin. Why, he's heading for Mesh Tyler's ranch! Now will you tell me what *that* means?" He laid the glasses in his lap, and looked at Randy. Randy's eyebrows curved down in perplexity, but for the moment he had no ideas to offer, and the colonel continued:

"If that blemishless skunk has gone over to the enemy . . ."

Again he looked through the glasses—but the glasses had no ideas to offer.

"Ace told me—he gave me his word—he was on our side. . . ." he pursued, as he surveyed the valley. "Not another person in sight." He let the glasses fall and looked at his watch.

"Why did Ace have to give you his word," inquired Randy, "if it was the truth?"

McDee laughed. He bent a quizzical eye upon the boy. "Randy, sometimes your brain displays a maturity greatly in advance of your years, you young sinnah!—Well" (he shut the glasses and put them in their case, slung from his shoulder) "there's nothing to wait here for. You and I will go home to supper. I don't make out why we saw nobody except Ace Brown. Either that meeting was called off, or we came too late. We'll go round by Mesh Tyler's and make a friendly call on our political opponents."

"Would you do that, Colonel?"

"Randy, don't you know there's nothin' like being sociable with the foe?"

The boy gave a quick little nod of assent. It was not at all for his own safety that he had spoken.

The two crept with caution away from the edge of the mountain, and presently were following the trail which led down into the great valley. The quiet and the beauty of the day's long decline imposed its spell upon them; it was some time before Colonel Steptoe McDee broke the silence.

"I came here for peace," he said once more, musingly; and he looked at the wide country beneath its veil of sunset hues. "My roof-tree was burned in 1865," he continued, always musingly. "I had fought a war for Southern Independence. We lost. I left my old plantation and my home where I was born, and my fathers were born. I wonder if there is a God of battles? Surely we were not in the wrong? I left everything that I had loved, and came to this new country. And I came for peace."

As the boy was hearing these words, he looked away from the old man, and down at the ground. When the words ceased, he stole one glance at the colonel, who did not see how tender the wild young eyes had grown. His roving thoughts took a swerve and came back to present things, and his voice, that had sounded as if far away, came with them.

"Do you believe he ever served under arms in the Civil War?"

Randy followed this train of association perfectly. "Him she's backing? Jinks Fleming? Ain't he old enough to?"

"Plenty. Also good and plenty old enough to be a liar."

"I expect he began early, Colonel. I know I did."

McDee shook his head impatiently. "I'm trying to guess this thing out, Randy. We're in quite a tangle. He's speaking at O'Neil City last time before election. The way he is winning support has been a surprise to me. We have very little time."

"I wouldn't be too anxious, sir. I'm not."

The colonel smiled. "Aren't you afraid the crocodiles will vote?"

For a moment Randy again looked reproachful. "I'm doing some guessing of my own about the tangle," he said.

"Well?" inquired McDee.

"I'll tell you when I'm ready."

The old gentleman wondered what he could have done to ruffle the boy like that. Perhaps the jest concerning crocodiles would not have been made if he had noticed the boy's face after the words about the burned roof-tree.

"Now this Jinks Fleming," he went on as if nothing was the matter, "I've only listened to the fello' once—once was enough for me—talks a heap o' trash about operations round Corinth and Shiloh in '62."

"He does," said Randy, still rather short.

"He had a lot of trash about how it rained on the night of April 5th."

"I've heard it," said Randy.

"Now I fought at Shiloh. It *did* rain that night—

and other nights too. I belonged to the Army of the Mississippi. Started 2nd lieutenant in the 25th Alabama. But that Jinks fello' seems to know so much more about the whole thing than I ever did—he's so glib with his bivouacs here, and his capture of General Prentiss there, and how he had his men say their prayers in the rude log chapel at Shiloh—he spouted a lot of pathos about the rude log chapel—that when he was through, I didn't feel sure I hadn't been in Europe during the whole war.''

"Did he tell about his feet?''

"Held 'em out to show us, the boots he had to wear in consequence of his wounds at Owl Creek. I suppose it's all that stuff that sways 'em.''

"No,'' said Randy. "That isn't what sways 'em.''

"What does then?''

"I'll tell you when I'm ready.'' But this time the boy grinned; and the colonel knew that whatever the matter had been, he had got over it—or almost over it.

"Of course,'' he said, "you can read about the battle of Shiloh in books. But the fello' doesn't look like much of a student.''

Randy made a suggestion. "Nothing to stop her reading the books and telling him.''

Again the colonel was obliged to remark that the boy at times displayed reasoning powers which were surprisingly mature.

"But that's not it, Colonel," declared Randy with eagerness, "that's not the half or the quarter of it!" He had become suddenly warmed up, and was now burning to disclose what he had been making a mystery of a few minutes before. "It's Smith that works the trick."

"Dirty-Face Smith!" cried McDee, sharply.

"Not him. He's all right. It's Sweet Potato Smith."

"I never heard of the fello'."

"Oh yes, sir! You must have seen him more than wunst, I reckon. Last trip the Professor made to San Antone, she brung Sweet Potato back with her to be her new—well, she calls the good-lookin' young men she hires her *assistants*, y'know. Antonito that quit her for Miss Maria Sanchez was her last assistant. I suppose she was tired of single life, having been used to the other kind so often,—well, this is it, Colonel. Miss Sanchez feels sore yet about the Professor and her getting her friends to lynch Antonito. She ain't going to forget the Professor a little bit. Miss Sanchez knows how to wait—and it won't be in her last will and testament that she remembers the Professor."

"She knows how to play the cornet very well," said the colonel irrelevantly.

"Beautiful, sir!" said Randy. "Best I've ever heard. She was playing *Niccolas* just yesterday. I've learned it on the concertina with her."

McDee looked at the boy. "Randy, single life
would be more desirable than to let Miss Sanchez
make an honest man of you."

"No, sir! none of 'em shall do that to me," exclaimed Randy with determination. "So Miss Sanchez asked me early in the campaign, when Jinks
Fleming was making his first speeches, if I had
noticed how well acquainted he seemed to be with
everybody's troubles, and everybody's good luck,
and how many children everybody had, and everything like that. Well, I *had* wondered about that
when he spoke over at Dripping Lick. And I'd
noticed how quick this made friends for him. So
Miss Sanchez told me that if I followed the trail of
Sweet Potato Smith, she thought I might get a line
on their tactics. Well, so I made friends with Sweet
Potato. He's a harmless boy. So—"

"What's that?" interrupted Colonel Steptoe Mc-
Dee.

He pointed along the road ahead. They were now
down in the valley, and were nearing the ranch of
Mesh Tyler. The colors had gone from the sky, and
the long twilight was dissolving into dusk. No rain
had fallen for many weeks, and the trodden soil
was light. They both watched a dust cloud moving
gently towards them in the middle of the wide road
between the wire fences. It concealed no company
of riders, it was too small, it could be only one horse-

man; yet still, from pure habit of self-preservation, the two made ready for trouble, in case it should not prove a friend. Moving with the slight breeze, that blew no faster than the horseman was going, the cloud accompanied him, enveloped him so thickly, that in the dusk, even at no further than fifty yards away, who this might be was not possible to tell. They watched the cloud come on steadily, evenly. Then, when it was but twenty paces from them, they were suddenly able to see into it, and they saw that it was no one. No figure of man or of woman sat in the saddle; it was empty; and the buckskin pony trotted quietly by them. Randy's body from head to foot went cold, but he said nothing. He looked at Steptoe McDee, whose face was set straight ahead; and so in silence the two rode on at a walk, with their hands always ready to shoot. As they passed by Mesh Tyler's house, it stood so quiet in the dusk that its windows, out of which no face peered, seemed to young Randy to be watching them with their blank glass eyes; he half drew his pistol, and the next moment let it slide back, in shame at his inward perturbation, and hoping that the colonel had not observed the unworthy gesture. It grew plain to both of them, that if any meeting had been held in the house, it was empty now: no horses were waiting for their riders; whoever had been here was gone;—and next, by the hoof prints clear in the deep dust, it was plain that a number must recently have been here;—but where was Ace Brown, whom they had watched from the distant edge of the mountain as he headed for this hushed and darkening grove of live oaks on the buckskin pony? They knew where he must be, almost as surely as if they were seeing him; and in this climax of their suspense, their walk quickened to a trot, and the trot to a gallop, and so they rounded a turn in the road among the trees, and there, over the middle of it, in the air, was Ace Brown.

Their ponies slid, almost sat, as they pulled them up short. Neither said a word. Neither had spoken since McDee had stopped Randy's talk on the appearance of the moving cloud. They sat there motionless, looking at Ace Brown, while the dust from their violent halt slowly settled. Away off beyond the body, a star had come into the sky, where the last of the faint daylight made a background; against this the figure swung to the edge of the star, and back about three inches. The limb of the oak stretched out not far above the dead man's head. Ace Brown must have sat on the buckskin while the rope was arranged, and then the pony had been driven from under him. A dim white spot was visible on the suspended shape.

"They've left a notice," said Randy in a low voice.

McDee nodded.

The boy rode toward the corpse, stood in his stirrups, reached up, paused, and spoke.

"He's warm."

"Bring that thing with you," said McDee.

Randy came with the paper, and the colonel bent close to read it.

"Shall I strike a match?"

"Let's get away from here, boy. We'll study this in better light. Put it in your pocket."

During the five miles which they covered then to the colonel's ranch, he spoke once:

"*There's* one I shall not need to distrust any more."

That was all the words they had. And so when they swung off their ponies at the colonel's porch, he preceded the boy up the steps, and into the room where a lamp was burning, and stretched out his hand for the paper. Then he saw that Randy's hand was shaking.

"You sit down," said he.

"I don't know what's the matter with me, Colonel."

"Sit down."

"Colonel, I don't know what's the matter with me."

"Sit down, I tell you."

The old gentleman went off somewhere, and in a minute returned with a bottle and a glass.

"Here's what will fix you up in the shake of a lamb's tail."

"Colonel, you'd ought to kick me."

"Bosh. Here, more than that. D'you want water? No? Fill it higher boy, don't be bashful." He went out again, and came with a second glass. "I'll join you, sonny. That little old buckskin gave me quite a jolt too." They emptied their glasses together. "Have another? No? Had enough to make supper taste good?" He carried away the bottle and glasses, and said as he re-entered, "And now I suppose you'll be expecting me to believe in crocodiles! Well:—they'll have supper for us inside of ten minutes. Let us see what kind of obituary Ace's friends posted on him." He read the sentence aloud:

" 'He is gone to a trial where he cannot head off any witnesses.'—Well, there's no gainsaying that." And the colonel ruminated.

"Is that all it says?" Randy was looking at it.

"What more would you have?"

"That may not be all it says."

"What trash are you talking now?"

"Mighty funny how all this paper kind o' matches."

"Psha. I have often had paper like that." But the colonel pulled out those letters which they had discussed on the edge of the mountain. "Psha," he repeated; and they were called to supper. The sheets were spread on the table. The colonel re-asserted that this style of cheap, lined paper was a standard article anywhere in Texas.

"It's not the only brand there is, though," said young Randy. He was coming to. Time, food, and the comfort in the colonel's bottle had pushed the crocodiles to a safe distance in his thoughts. "I say it's mighty funny that all these mystery communications are on the same paper."

"Co-incidences are often startling, Randy, very startling, as you and I have seen this afternoon—but what do they prove?"

"I think enough of them prove things."

"Then I'll need some more.—Well, here is certainly one point about Ace's obituary: I've seen these eulogies pinned on departed acquaintances before, and usually they are scrawled on the spot in haste. This writing is very neat, and it's in ink. And that highly interesting fact has been staring you and me in the face, and we've been too busy to notice it! Randy boy, let us smoke over all this a while, and see what we've got."

They smoked, and they summed it up: Ace Brown had been intending to double-cross the colonel in politics, but had been conspicuously double-crossed himself. Why? and who did it? Was the motive in

the obituary perhaps a blind? Unimportant. Good
people were being warned to leave the country.
Why? To buy up their ranches cheap. Were several brains behind this, or only one? Important.
Old Cayce Hartle had been re-elected to office so
regularly, that you'd vote for him in your sleep.
Was one brain behind this present menace of revolt?
It looked that way. Motive—the railroad? Doubtful. What influence had Jinks Fleming with the
railroad? The colonel suspected the upstart candidate to be just a dummy set up to challenge his own
power in the district. Who else in the district had
following enough to challenge? Only one other.
Crocodiles!

"Randy, does that fello' look as if he'd fought
at Shiloh?"

"Looks like he'd sold female millinery."

"Do you believe he had his feet shot?"

"Naw! He stuck his head in a haystack and slep'
with 'em out, and they froze on him."

"Well, Randy, guesses are the best we've got so
far, guesses and co-incidences."

"I've had all the co-incidences I want."

"I know that. And I'm not going to ask you to
watch the crocodiles by night. I think I'll pay them
a little call by day. And I'll not ask for your company on that visit."

The colonel looked at Randy, but Randy looked
away; and the colonel smiled.

"But I was telling you," said the boy briskly, "back there, y'know, about me and Sweet Potato. That's no guessing. None whatever. I was sayin' how I'd noticed Jinks Fleming talk to the mothers. 'Why, is this Mrs. Daly?' he'd say. 'Well now, Mrs. Daly, I certainly *am* glad to shake yore hand. And how is yore good husband? Do tell me if yore little Gertrude has got well of her measles? Ah, our little ones! What a blessin'! What a care! Gertrude is yore eldest? No? To be sure! Your second. Now isn't that good news! Dear little Gertrude! She loves candy. Take her this choc'late from me.' "

Randy had shot off all this suddenly, in the candidate's voice, and actually managed to look something like him; and Colonel McDee was delighted.

"Go on, boy, go on! Why didn't you ever do it before? Joe Jefferson is nothin' to you!"

"Oh yes," said the boy, now wound up entirely, and elated by his success. "Then Mrs. Daly she smiles like—like strawberries and cream, and she says, '*Mister* Fleming, meet my sister, Mrs. McGuffey.' '*And* is Mrs. McGuffey yore sister, Mrs. Daly! Well now, I'd have knowed it, ma'am, if we'd met up in Noo Yawk.' Squawk!" interpolated Randy, in a croak of scorn; and the colonel beat his knee and guffawed. "Oh yes," continued Randy. " 'And how are Mr. McGuffey's bald-faced cattle doing? Herefords is what I always say. Ah yes, indeed. Herefords. Does yore boy Horace still

ride the black pony to school? He'll soon be able to
lick his old daddy.' Squawk!'' Randy dropped his
impersonation. ''That's the way it goes, every town
he speaks in; and it goes big with the women, and
the women go big with the votin' men of their
fam'ly—because y'know, sir, a woman can easy
make it hell in the home for a man before he
goes away mornings, and after he comes back
nights.''

Randy announced this pithy generalization as if
he had been subjected to matrimony for a decade;
and it surprised him that the colonel should be
shouting more heartily than ever. He stared at him
gravely, and waited.

''Well?'' said McDee, at length.

''Well, sir, it's all Sweet Potato. Just him. He's
pleasant-like, as I believe I mentioned—and not
overly smart. That's why I said you needn't be
much scared about the election. Mrs. Daly and Mrs.
McGuffey—do they think to inquire how this Jinks
knows about their little Gertrude and their bald-
faced cattle? But I sort o' mouzed around after
Miss Sanchez dropped me the word about Sweet
Potato. The day Jinks spoke at Liberty City I
picks up a little slip of paper where he'd been surrounded by ladies hanging on his words. Maria—
Miss Sanchez—she read it to me next time I saw
her. Names it was, sir, names and facts. Notes about

the Gertrudes and the bald-faces in that locality. Y'see, Sweet Potato he travels ahead of Jinks— kind o' turns up with business of his own some- wheres a few days before Jinks is due to speak, and makes himself pleasant, and hears this and that, and goes to Jinks with it. So Jinks he has it salted down on a little slip of paper.''

"Did you tell me Sweet Potato wasn't smart, Randy?''

"That ain't smart, Colonel. I could do that my- self. If Sweet Potato was *really* smart, d'you think he'd be lettin' me get confidential with him, playin' cards and everything? So when he comes around O'Neil City a few days before Jinks is due to speak there—I've promised to introduce him to Miss San- chez. She's more than willing.''

"I should think that you would be less willing.''

"Oh, no, sir, she's not interested in him that way, though she may let him hope she is. To her, Sweet Potato looks like the best chance she's had to get even with Professor Salamanca.''

"Randy, I feel greatly encouraged about your brains.''

"It's nothing," said the boy, lightly. "It's just that me and her may be able to fix up a little sur- prise for Jinks.''

"Am I to be kept in the dark?''

"I'd just as lief wait, Colonel, if you don't mind,

till we strike the point. We've only got the general scheme so far.''

''Very well, boy; your business isn't mine, till you make it so. It's late. We always seem to talk late, don't we? Will you stop here to-night?''

''Thank you, sir, I reckon I'd better get home. Thank you, just the same.''

He went down the steps, and was in his saddle, and had started away, when he turned and rode back to the colonel, still lingering by his open door, a lonely figure.

''Colonel,'' began Randy, ''Colonel.''

''Yes?''

''You—you'll not really go to see her?''

''Our friend the Professor? Oh yes, I'll go to see her.''

''To-morro'?''

''I'm not certain when. And I'm not asking you to go with me.''

''No. Good night, sir.''

''Good night.''

Many live oaks covered the country between Colonel McDee's place and the home of Professor Salamanca, where young Randy believed unearthly doings to be lying in wait for any one to whom she wished ill. The trees stood seldom close together, but never very far apart; when among them, there

was no seeing to any distance. It was a landscape
different from that open valley where the boy
and his adopted mentor had watched Ace Brown
on the buckskin jog confidentially along to meet
some old acquaintances who waited for him with
a rope.

Colonel Steptoe McDee, silver-haired and slender
and small, sat alert, eyes and ears wary, hand convenient to gun, as he rode alone through the live
oaks in the morning sun. A year ago, he would not
have dreamed of being so careful; times were changing, he thought; not for the better, he thought;
well, he had his day; it was the turn of the young
folks to run the world. But old Salamanca shouldn't
run it! He would put a stop to her, somehow, if it
was the last thing he ever did. Which of the two
was it, going to pay a call on the other this morning,
Mahomet, or the mountain? That should be tried
out. It would have to be tried out. What is the
sense in expecting you'll find peace anywhere you
go in this world? Got to wait for the next.

The old gentleman passed by the ranch which had
been Fluke Dade's. He looked at the well by whose
brink sudden death had caught the heavy, sensual
Fluke when it just missed the Yankee doctor down
at the bottom. Not long after, the colonel passed
the live oak where he and the Yankee doctor on
their way to visit the Professor, had come upon

the beautiful young Antonito hanging by the neck, with a notice pinned on him, unfavorable to his character. Who was it in history never got tired of having lovers? Catherine of Russia. An able woman. The Professor was an able woman. Perhaps a multitude of lovers was a concomitant of ability. I wish I was a boy back home. Back home in old times. Just running around and hating bed time. No I don't. Go through all the meanness of the years again? Not for all the gold in the world. That Yankee doctor was homesick too. Said these live oaks made him think of apple trees where he'd been raised. Said these mesquites might be peach trees. Said he kept catching himself looking for a white church steeple. Nothing here is like my home. Nothing. Then the colonel whipped out his pistol, and his thoughts stopped their wandering. He swerved to the side of the road between two live oaks, ready for whoever it was that galloped so hard through the trees. But it was only Randy.

"Well, I caught you," said Randy.

"Boy, you 'most had me scared. What you doin' here?" The colonel's old plantation vernacular came out strong; his feelings were moved.

"I guess you know what I'm doing here." When Randy's feelings were moved, he was apt to sound sulky.

"You young sinnah! Do you presume to insult

me by insinuatin' I'm too feeble to go around by myself any more?''

The boy sat easy and lounging in his saddle, looking at his mentor with a steady eye and a dogged smile. That was all he had to say.

The colonel glanced about him. They were off the road, between two live oaks. There was silence as far as you could listen and no living creature as far as you could spy. To anyone approaching along the road, they were not visible, but they were quite exposed, should such a person pass; the colonel led the way farther from the road, until the many intervening live oaks cut off any view from it.

''Randy,'' he began, ''aren't you just the precious young gander to come tracking me down with a noise that would wake the dead!''

The boy grinned obstinately.

''And I see you're proposing to go along with me to hold me on my horse and walk right into the spider's parlor with me during her office hours. Do you want to give notice to all the world that you and I are workin' together? Have you forgotten so soon what I told you about keeping it secret? And only last night I felt encouraged about your brains!''

The eye and grin were keeping firm with an effort.

''Man to man, Randy, here it is. Changes have

come in Flanagan County, but"—the old gentleman's finger was pointed in the direction where lay the ranch of Professor Salamanca, five miles away through the live oaks, and his voice rang as he spoke —"yon great big quack, greedy shameless astrological strumpet isn't boss in Flanagan County yet. Don't you be anxious about me. I'm as safe under her roof as I am here with you, my dear boy, right now. She has known this long while that any unexplained scratch on my old hide will lead to her bein' immediately flayed alive. And she knows that not one of her stuffed reptyles can help her if that day comes. Go home, boy; and maybe I'll have news for you this evening. And some day, maybe, you and I will be riding up to her front door and nailing a ten days' notice on it."

The boy slowly wheeled his horse round in the direction whence he had come so fast. "All right," he muttered.

Steptoe McDee watched his dejected back moving off at a walk, and he called after him:

"God bless you all the same for bein' a young gander!"

The boy made no audible response, nor did he turn round; but he raised his right arm above his head, and waved his hand.

"Oh yes," said the colonel aloud, addressing the live oaks; "some Southern gentleman is responsible for him. I wish I could claim him!"

He wound his way back to the road; and as the miles between him and Professor Salamanca grew less, the thoughts of the little colonel grew livelier, because he was going to be sociable with the foe— as he had expressed it to Randy. Will they let me in? Why, it's office hours. If they didn't, what idjits they'd be. Some of 'em are. I hope that Sweet Potato fello' is. Jinks Fleming must be pretty near one to try conclusions with Uncle Cayce Hartle— and me. You set down 80 per cent of any community as idjits, and you'll not be very wide of the mark. But she can furnish brains for a good many idjits. Well, I suppose if everybody was smart, the world would be an awful place. Hullo. What have we here?

His hand went to his gun; but nothing could be less threatening that the two horsemen who were approaching. One was the rival candidate, elderly, ample, benevolent; his countenance glazed with that I-am-glad-to-be-in-your-beautiful-city expression which American politicians, even some American presidents, feel obliged to wear. But who was the young man with him on the buckskin pony? The buckskin? Oh, well, it couldn't be that one. If Randy had been here—

"Good morning to you, Colonel McDee!" cried the hearty candidate.

"Good morning, sir." The colonel was absolutely polite.

"A fine morning, surely, Colonel McDee. And weather that plainly agrees with you, if I may put it so."

"Put it any way you please, sir: I'm pretty well for an old man, I thank you.—It's Tuesday week you're speaking in O'Neil City?"

"Tuesday week. My wind-up speech before election. I cannot venture to hope, Colonel, that you will come to hear a political adversary—but only political, Colonel. Only political!"

"Why yes, sir, I think I'll be there. My friend Mr. Hartle is speakin' that morning, you know. And I'll wait over to hear you that evening.—Goin' to tell us all about the railroad?"

"Ha, ha, Colonel. Ha, ha, ha! If you don't know about the railroad, who does?"

"I've not the slightest idea, sir, who does. If I did, I'd—but I'll not trouble you with what I'd do. I'm on my way to tell Professor Salamanca what I'd do."

Did the old gentleman feel some quiver in the air, responsive to this little shot he had fired at random? At any rate, he detected no exchange of glance between the two: both were looking at him intently, and neither seemed ready with any remark to fill the slight silence which had fallen. He went on, chattily:

"I'm an old patient of the Professor's, you know.

She used to prescribe for my liver. It was an obstinate organ, sir. Stubborn. Refractory. Deaf to every appeal, till that young Yankee doctor talked to it, and made it behave.—Goin' to tell us about that third horse you brought General Braxton Bragg after two had been shot under him at Shiloh?"

"Ha, ha, Colonel. Ha, ha, ha! What a life it was! The bivouac! The charge! Comrades! The music of a bugle thrills my blood to-day. You knew it all, too, I'm informed."

"I did, sir. But it isn't my way to drag it in."

"Well, I expect you could tell more about it than I can, if you only would."

"That's as it may be, sir. I certainly know more about it than I do about where the new railroad is going."

"Pardon me, Colonel. I have forgotten to introduce you to my good friend, Mr. Lycurgus Smith."

"I am very happy to have Mr. Smith presented to me. Is this Mr. Smith from San Antonio?"

"Yes, sir, that's my native town."

"I hope you're finding the practice of medicine lucrative—and unattended with risk?"

"I'm not—I don't—I'm not a doctor."

"But surely — assistant — to Professor Salamanca?"

"Yes, sir."

"I remember!—The Professor's last assistant

was not a doctor. He was most unaccountably hanged. May I express the sincere hope, Mr. Smith, that no such untoward incident will affect the comfort of his successor?'' The colonel made it charming with a smile.

The mouth of Lycurgus gaped; he had already turned a violent pink at the tone in which the colonel had said 'assistant.' The colonel continued:

''On your way to a speech, Mr. Fleming?''

''Waxhaw to-day, Colonel. Topaz Hills to-morrow. A busy life is politics.''

''I shall have the pleasure of hearing you at O'Neil City, Mr. Fleming.''

''To know you're listening will be an inspiration, Colonel. Am I never to hear you?''

''I don't talk much, Mr. Fleming. Not much. Not skilled at oratory.—Well, sir, I'll wish you good morning.''

They separated; and as the little colonel ambled on toward the house of crocodiles, his thoughts turned upon the recent interchange of remarks with the opposition candidate and his somewhat soft looking companion. The man's a fraud. It's in his voice. It's in his face. Anybody can see that. No they can't. Just what they don't see. A little trash about bugles, a little trash about little Gertrude, a little chocolate—and they're fooled. And they vote. And that's government of the people, by the people, for the people. Abraham Lincoln was a good man, I'll admit; but when he said you couldn't fool all of the people all of the time, didn't he forget the supernatural powers of the windbag? No windbag lives forever, but there's always a fresh one ready in the United States. Bugles don't thrill my blood. Not since 1865. She might have picked a smarter tool, I should think. But he can talk all around poor old Cayce Hartle. Well, Randy's up to something. That young Sweet Potato Smith! Well, he had the decency to blush. When she brought him into the country, I expect he didn't know all that was ahead of him. So it's Waxhaw to-day. I expect the advance agent was teaching the candidate all about the little Gertrudes waitin' for chocolate in Waxhaw.

Professor Salamanca opened the door herself for the colonel—and stood there a second, as if to bar his passage; but quickly recovered from whatever her massive countenance was masking. He spoke first, most amicably.

"Surprised to see your old patient back, Professor? It's not my liver to-day."

"What can I do for you?"

"Maybe nothing; but something, I hope. And I just decided I'd consult you."

"A great many are ahead of you. A special appointment—"

"I'll wait my turn, I'll wait my turn! Time's no matter."

He saw her decide that to keep him out would be less wise than to let him in. She pointed to a waiting-room quite filled with men—all of them acquaintances, but none of them, apparently, very glad to see him, judging from the nods they gave and the brief grunts they voiced by way of greeting. I wonder if I've been a fool to come here? he thought—but thought not, at once, and hailed them successively. "How are you, John? How are you, Jake? Why, Ragland, I thought the Professor had you cured up a month ago! Have your boils come back? Good morning, Mesh Tyler. You were out yesterday afternoon when I called. Not a lady here to-day! Wives and daughters all well? Not a baby sick? Professor, I congratulate you on the number of your male patients—and your treatment plainly agrees with them. Never saw a healthier lot of invalids. Why, Mesh, you look as if you could fell an ox!" Mesh undoubtedly did; and so did some of the others. But the colonel was now enjoying himself completely. The bovine natures that confronted him were no match for the tempered steel of his personality, and he held them subdued. Perhaps two or three present were even for the moment sorry that they were no longer of his adherents in Flanagan County. They had no quarrel with him. "Go on having your pulses felt," he continued, "I'll read the paper. No paper here? Then I'll take a book. 'The Voice of the Planets.' That's beyond me. 'With the Army of the Mississippi.' That will do. It wasn't an hour ago that our fellow citizen Mr. Jinks Fleming told me he could hear the bugles of Shiloh yet."

Steptoe McDee seated himself, the only one at his ease amid this company that was dumb, and staring, and so plainly at a loss how to take his unexpected and undesired presence. But Professor Salamanca had now had time to gather her deliberate but formidable wits.

"You shall not wait, Colonel McDee, if these gentlemen will not object."

They did not; and so the visitor passed into the spider's den, where all the crocodiles lived; and the mystic door was closed. The Professor did not seat herself beneath the black canopy, spangled with gilt lobsters; with the colonel there was not the slightest use in such a proceeding; she sat in a very ordinary chair, and McDee sat in another. He didn't quite like the black canopy, because it covered a good deal of the wall, and you couldn't know what was behind it. His eyes took sharp and quick note of all objects visible—books, cards, pens, paper, crystal ball.

"Well, Colonel McDee?" said Professor Salamanca. "What's the point?"

"I'll come to it right off, ma'am. This stationery of yours appeals to me." He saw the dark, watching eyes instantly harden. "The stars don't tell me their secrets. I don't know which survey the Gulf Colorado and Santa Fé will finally adopt. And so I ask myself, why five or six gentlemen through whose property the road may run, have all quit the country and removed their fam'lies? I never saw folks flee from the presence of a railroad till now. Have you any opinion as to that?"

"To an old inhabitant like you, Colonel McDee, sudden departures from Flanagan County can hardly be anything new."

"True, Professor. I have caused several myself; but they were not honorable citizens in good standing."

"And how do you know these others were in good standing? Have you the secrets of everybody?"

The colonel did not like the looks of the black curtain. He rose; and he made a quick invention.

"I will save Judge McCoy, and some other friends on the road here, the trouble of coming all the way. They will feel, as I do, that you have answered our question. One thing more they might like to know." Here the colonel tossed out on the table those three papers which Randy and he had discussed. "I have stationery resembling that—and you, I notice, also use it. It's in very general use. Who can say how many more samples of it you and I may see before

election day?—I see your next patient is waiting."
The colonel looked straight at the black canopy.
"Good day, Professor. I know the way out. Keep
the little samples, I'm through with them."

And away from the house of crocodiles ambled
the little colonel, not caring much what the patients
he had kept waiting would do there when relieved
of his presence. Near home, he found the boy among
the live oaks, on the watch for him.

"Randy, I flustered 'em all.—What are you glar-
in' at me about?"

"Sweet Potato's riding the buckskin."

"Little Old Scaffold! I thought I recognized that
pony. Well, the new assistant will come to no harm
from him now. The Medicine Woman has got the
animal she coveted, and she'll lift that alarming
curse she put on him. Young Sweet Potato is 'most
as pretty a boy as Antonito was. I flustered 'em all,
Randy!"

Randy listened to the tale. "What do you think
was behind the curtain?" he asked.

"A crocodile's ghost, Randy, waitin' to spring."

"My idea," said the boy, concentrating his brows,
"would be, that she had no plan against you. She
wanted a witness—or help in case you tried something on her."

"Let it go. Whoever it was, heard what I said;
and much good may it do him!"

"I don't think you did much good."

"You impertinent young sinnah! There was the war book, there was the stationery, and there they all were havin' a meeting."

"There's things you know without having to *know* them. And, Colonel," the boy's eyes were full of anxiety as he reasoned with his mentor, "those men—Mesh Tyler and the rest—were only her friends before but now they'll be your enemies. And why did you leave those papers?"

The old gentleman's eyes twinkled with pride. His protégé was fulfilling his hopes. "Boy, are you explainin' to me that I'm an old superannuated idjit that has lost his grip? Don't answer me. I'll listen to no apology, for I'm in a hurry. D'you think I haven't got other papers of the same pattern?" He took some from his pocket. "The balance of the bunch. I hadn't mentioned it to you. Crip King has been in communication with his fellow victims of this land raid. And now I'm in a position to write to all of 'em a little invitation. Can you fool all of the people all of the time?"

"You can come awful near it," said the boy.

"Randy, I reckon you must eat a whole apple off the forbidden tree every day. Your twenty-year-old brain is acquiring a knowledge of good and evil that ought to shame you. You go home now, I'd have you eat dinner with me, but—well, from now till Jinks makes his speech at O'Neil City, what use would you be if the enemy caught us talking? Just you continue to be a young cowpuncher who works for Judge McCoy, and frequents the Dos Bocas saloon, and the society of Miss Maria Sanchez, and, being under age, isn't interested in this political campaign.''

''Miss Sanchez is very much interested in the campaign.''

''Give her my compliments when you see her this evening.''

Randy grinned.

''I'll have some letters I'll want you to post—anywhere away from O'Neil City. They'll be in my saddle-bag. I'll hitch my horse in front of the Pickwick Hotel. You might be loafing in the office casually, say nine o'clock. Now you go home. Why do you keep me talking this way?''

The colonel wrote invitations for some time after dinner. Then he went to sleep. Then he rode round his property and gave some directions about this and that. Then he supped with his friend Judge McCoy, and had a long talk with him in private. Then he ambled into O'Neil City and tied his black mare in front of the Pickwick Hotel. Up above, through the street, sounded the music of a cornet, accompanied by a concertina. He was early. A few traveling salesmen sat discussing politics, their glasses beside them, their feet on the table. One had happened to be over at Waxhaw that afternoon. He was talking to Sweet Potato Smith, who of course had also been at Waxhaw.

"And what have you done with Mr. Fleming, Dr. Smith?" inquired the colonel.

"*Mr.* Smith," corrected the assistant, with a worried smile. "Mr. Fleming is resting at Topaz Hills to-night. I'm here to make a few arrangements for Professor Salamanca. Well, Colonel, good night. The Professor will be wanting to know how Mr. Fleming pleased the people."

"He's quite a speaker," said the man who had been at Waxhaw.

"Ah," said Colonel Steptoe McDee, "I wish I could hold an audience like that!" He seated himself among the company, and sipped his whisky in sociable silence, feet on the floor. Pair by pair, the feet on the table came down. The cornet and concertina played *Niccolas* down the street.

"That the town band?" inquired a salesman.

"It's a lady you'd like to know," said another. "Only some young cowboy has the inside track."

"Seems politics are quite lively up here," said a third salesman.

"You bet they are!" said the proprietor of the Pickwick Hotel.

"Mr. Murdock, how is the enemy progressing in your opinion?" said the colonel to the proprietor.

"Well, Colonel, if you don't know, I don't. I wish Uncle Cayce could talk better. What have you done to Mesh Tyler?"

"Mesh? Is he getting anxious about his real estate speculations?—Yes, I'm afraid this Jinks has us beat on talking."

"He was strong on war memories," said the man who had been at Waxhaw. "Fought with the Crescent Regiment. Got lamed at Tanner's Ford near Pittsburg Landing." He was saying this as Randy strolled in.

"Is he sure of that?" inquired the colonel.

Murdock smiled, the salesman looked inquiring, and ready for more, Randy flung himself into a chair. He nodded to a salesman, called for whisky, and looked round without taking notice of Steptoe McDee. The colonel took no notice of him.

"When I heard him talk," he continued, "it was at Owl Creek his foot was shot."

"He has two feet," said Randy, addressing the colonel as if he was a stranger. "Right foot for Owl Creek, left for Tanner's Ford."

"Which way are you voting?" asked the salesman.

"No way," responded Randy. The strains of *Suwanee River* now floated plaintively on the night air, but alone, unassisted by the concertina.

"Well, gentlemen," said the proprietor, "let's be fair. An old Confederate soldier was through here last week''—at this Randy's head turned very slightly, and so did Colonel McDee's—''he'd heard Jinks Fleming at Ultima Thule. He'd known the man at Corinth in '62. Had seen him in hospital after a twelve hours' fight they'd had on a Sunday. Never saw him again till Ultima Thule. I said to him, that seemed a short allowance of war to supply such a plentiful stream of talk. But he said he'd met talkers who could fill four years of battles out of a single desertion.''

The salesmen laughed. Randy and Steptoe thoughtfully sipped their whisky and water. *Suwanee River* had changed to *La Paloma*.

''Know the cow camp Mexican words for that?'' said one salesman to his neighbor, who did not know them. ''Well, they'd make a horse blush.''

Randy finished his whisky, and strolled out, as he had strolled in, casually.

''Who's that young man?'' inquired Steptoe Mc-Dee.

''He rides for Judge McCoy, Colonel,'' said proprietor Murdock. ''They say over there that he's an up and coming boy.''

''He's the lad that has the inside track with the señorita,'' said a salesman.

''Well,'' said another, ''next time I come through, political excitement will be over.'' And he left for his room.

"So Mr. Fleming actually did see military service?" resumed Steptoe McDee to the proprietor.

"Looks that way, Colonel. He plays it for more than it's worth; but he's got the right notion about mothers and children."

"Psha. Cayce Hartle knows every family in the district!"

"But he don't play his knowledge like Jinks does." Concertina and cornet were at it again; "taps" was being expressively sounded.

"That a hint?" commented a salesman.

"Probably a program," another suggested.

"I suppose he talked about bugles singin' in his heart?" said the colonel to the man who had been at Waxhaw.

"I was afraid he was going to sing himself."

"I don't like frauds," said McDee, rising, "I'll take their hint," he added, with a gesture toward the music of "taps." Then he addressed the proprietor. "I don't lay wagers, Mr. Murdock. But if I did, I should back my good old friend Cayce Hartle. Good night, gentlemen." He bowed.

The salesmen had all risen. When the colonel was gone, they reseated themselves.

"Who's that?" asked one.

Proprietor Murdock explained the importance of Colonel Steptoe McDee. "And there's fire in him yet," he finished.

"That kind is getting scarce," said the salesman. "Most of 'em are in church-yards—or hanging among the ancestors on the wall."

No meeting between the colonel and Randy followed that night. After what had passed in the hotel, the colonel half expected to find the boy waiting by the black mare; and finding no one, he felt proud of Randy's blossoming caution. Sweet Potato Smith was in town; he was not "overly smart" as Randy had said; but his friendship with Randy, so carefully worked up, might suffer a rude shock if ever he saw Randy in the society of Professor Salamanca's avowed enemy. The boy had been to the black mare, however. Those invitations which the colonel had written so busily that afternoon were gone from the saddle-bag. He pulled out a sheet of paper. This he shoved in his pocket. By the light of his lamp at home he read:

"Weere going to setel Jinks al rite. You watsh. Dont trubble."

"Why the rascal is learning to write!" said the colonel aloud.

And the last thing he did before he went to sleep was to laugh out in the dark.

Not until the great day came were mentor and protégé seen together in public; and to meet in private had not been necessary. Each was busy in his own way, improving the shining hours. The colonel conferred with Judge McCoy, weighing the situation every evening. Could superstition wedded to greed prevail at election? Could greed and superstition be exposed in the sight of the people? Would the Gulf Colorado and Santa Fé, if urged, send an emissary to Cayce Hartle's meeting and definitely announce its route? What would be the most effective moment to use those sheets of paper in the colonel's possession? Would Professor Salamanca believe, or not, that he had left with her the only specimens he had?

In the middle of these consultations, she returned all three with a message to say that the colonel might have use for them. He reflected: Now is that so smart a move, when you come to think of it? When I threw them on her table, wouldn't she have thrown them at me quick if she'd never seen them before? Now, if she had done that, I'd have called that pretty smart. Faced with a person not impressed by her crocodiles, she is less up to the scratch. When young Randy told me that you know some things you didn't have to *know*, he sized this situation up—and many more I've met in my time.

McDee and Judge McCoy laid the collection of sheets beside each other. They made an interesting exhibit. Good enough for anybody, except a court of law. Fortunately, as Judge McCoy pointed out

to his partner the colonel, no criminal lawyer had
so far inflicted his presence on this community.
And then young Randy, who could see Judge McCoy
without arousing any suspicion about his activities,
since he was in the judge's employment, put his
shrewd finger on a point which had escaped both his
elders: Since the colonel had become active in his
probing for the land raiders, not a ranchman whose
property might be crossed by the railroad had received a ten days' notice. More stationery of the
same make would not be desirable, and a change of
stationery even less so. Very suggestive. It might
have come from an old hand at reasoning, instead
of from a twenty-year-old boy. Young people are
like fine dogs in this: they develop beyond their
apparent limits when their superiors make companions of them. Yet the campaign was doubtful.
Something more would help.

At his end of it, Randy had improved the shining
hours by introducing his friend Sweet Potato Smith
to many families in the neighborhood of O'Neil City.
The earnest and amiable young man became welcome in several homes. His relation to the dreaded
Salamanca gave him importance with some, and was
not much against him with any. He was even recom-
mended quietly not to see quite so much of Miss
Maria Sanchez; Professor Salamanca did not smile
on her assistants' visiting other ladies; there was

Antonito; he had visited Miss Sanchez; of course, it was not known for certain who the parties were who had lynched him; but it was quite certain that ever since that day, Miss Sanchez had hated the Professor like poison, and wouldn't forget it in a hurry. When you have Mexican blood in you, you are pretty sure to have a long memory and a sharp knife.

Sweet Potato, with the constant aid of Randy, gathered any quantity of family facts about little Gertrudes and kindred details for Jinks Fleming to select from and memorize before his visit to O'Neil City. Randy was especially skillful in preventing any suspicion that his new friend was acting as advance press agent for the candidate: Sweet Potato was universally known and respected—or pitied— as the successor to Antonito in Professor Salamanca's establishment: yet he was not perfectly happy. San Antonio is not a city of undiluted innocence; but the young man's yellow hair, had it been less silken, would have often risen to hear the neighbors talk about each other in Flanagan County.

"It's not the kind of job I like," he confided to Randy. "I wish I hadn't left the soda water fountain."

"Well, you can quit when the campaign's through with. Meanwhile the pay's good."

"I've seen very little money yet," said Sweet

Potato. "Couldn't you take me to visit old Jim Craig? I know Mr. Fleming would love to meet an old comrade again."

"I'll take you just as soon as his diphtheria ain't ketching any longer. He's bound he'll come to speech day, whether the doctor says yes or no."

And so the day arrived—the day which it was felt would decide how the election would go, according to the welcome given to the rival candidates. Uncle Cayce Hartle would speak from the balcony of the Pickwick Hotel in the forenoon, Jinks Fleming would tell Flanagan County later in the day all the benefits he was going to bring it—more roads, better roads, new schools, less taxes—the program was as old as the first demagogue and as new as the latest campaign. And then—perhaps this Jinks was closer to the railroad than Uncle Cayce.

The voters of both parties with their families and wagons and lunches and horses and babies were in O'Neil City early, and made camp for the day. The light dust of the region rose at all points of the compass, and moved toward the town, marking the approach of the citizens. It might have been a race day, or the county fair; and flags fluttered from the festive balcony of the Pickwick Hotel. The colonel's people and Judge McCoy's people rode along in a loose cavalcade from the neighboring ranches, and Colonel Steptoe hailed Randy in the crowd.

"Don't you think you owe something to your friend Sweet Potato?"

"He owes me a lot of drinks."

"Have you warned him about the magical powers of the Little Old Scaffold? I've met him on that buckskin more than once."

The boy gave a sheepish grin. Then suddenly he looked startled. "Why, if there isn't Crip King!"

"So he is!" said the colonel quietly. "So he is. Looks as if his recent absence had agreed with him. Wonder what he's back for?"

Partial comprehension came into the boy's face as they jogged on, and were joined by others in the broad road between the wire fences. Sweet Potato appeared in the cavalcade.

"Good morning, Dr. Smith," said the colonel cheerily.

The young man replied with his customary worried smile. "I keep telling you it's Mister," said he.

"Why where's your buckskin to-day? Anybody given you a scare about him?"

"Oh, that!" said Sweet Potato. "I'm going to buy him, if the old witch'll sell him."

"Dear me, Mister Smith! Aren't you afraid the crocodiles will hear you?" But the assistant shook his head scornfully.

Randy crowded up. "Colonel! Honoré Devereux is back too."

"You'll not forget about old Jim Craig?" said Sweet Potato to Randy.

"Not if he comes, I won't."

"Craig?" said the colonel. "Who's that?"

"Didn't you read what I wrote in your saddle-bag?—Colonel, I tell you Devereux is right ahead of us."

The mentor looked at his protégé sharply. "Don't you wish to meet that husband?"

Randy's cheeks flamed. "I'll meet any man that wants to meet me."

The mentor let it drop. "All my absent friends accepted my invitations you posted. All will turn up to-day and enjoy the oration of Jinks Fleming. Short of the Unforeseen."

"I expect you'll have let them in for a disappointment," said Randy.

"What do you mean by that?"

"I said, didn't you read what I put in your saddle-bag?"

"Oh, well, well, go along with your mysteries!"

"Colonel—have the families come back, too?"

Steptoe McDee became stern in an instant. "Am I to understand by that, sir, that your interest . . . that you would attempt to resume . . . he's my friend, sir."

"Him and me was just acquaintances," muttered
the boy. "And I don't think you'd any call to say
that."

"Very well, sir. I don't remember that you gave
me your word. I'll accept it.—I am in hopes that
matters will go well, and I shall welcome back the
wives and children, as I have already welcomed
their husbands.—Short of the Unforeseen, which
dogs us all.—Well, we'll assume you'll settle Jinks,
somehow. There's a worse one than Jinks to settle."

"Miss Sanchez is a good hater, Colonel. She's
only waiting for a chance to be useful to you—this
day, or any other."

"The ladies are mightier than we men both in
love and in hate," said the mentor.

"Sure they are!" said the protégé.

"Has Professor Salamanca let her assistant come
alone in all this crowd?"

"He tells me she'll be in later to hear her candidate."

The boy moved off; and in the eddies of the crowd
in O'Neil City they were apart. Confluences of
opposite factions met everywhere in the little town,
met with nods and gruffness. The railroad and the
Professor had come between many friendships. It
was all a new thing in Flanagan County, this mut-
tering dissension over politics, and the fact that
each side kept asserting throughout the day that

it was sure to win, was the best possible proof that both felt uncertain. The applause that greeted Uncle Cayce Hartle when he appeared on the hotel balcony to address the voters was particularly loud, and the spots of silence in the crowd were particularly silent. He spoke simply, and at no great length. He made no allusions to his rival, or to the railroad. He said that he knew they had trusted him to attend to their interests, or they would never have trusted him for so long: and that if he had now forfeited this confidence in any way, he would gladly see a better man have his place. No, no, murmured many.

"Have you got the railroad in your pocket?" a voice asked.

"I'd like to have it there," replied Uncle Cayce promptly. "I never saw a man's pocket that was big enough—" He paused and surveyed his audience. "Maybe a woman's reticule could hold it," he added; and this sally brought much shouting and laughter—and spots of deeper silence.

"I don't know," continued Uncle Cayce "whether it's humans or whether it's crocodiles that drove so many friends of mine out of the country. I didn't know how far from tide-water a crocodile could flourish." Great silence from everybody.

Bull-faced Mesh Tyler raised his fist angrily, but the fist was hastily pulled down out of sight.

"I'm glad to see many familiar faces among you that I've been missing of late. I hope those faces are going to stay with us, and it's my personal belief that they will." Applause, assent, and spots of silence unchanged.

"It's heading up, Colonel, it's heading up our way," said Dirty Face Smith, who was brushed and cleaned for the occasion.

Steptoe nodded.

"You're going to show 'em the papers when the time comes? And tell about them?"

"That's the plan," said Judge McCoy.

"If the time comes," said the colonel. And as Uncle Cayce concluded, there were calls for the colonel.

He rose a moment on the balcony. "Friends," he said, "all of you know I'm a mighty poor speaker. But if you want to hear from me for a minute at the end of the day, I'll certainly obey your wishes." Much applause and enthusiasm, and then a general dispersing for refreshments.

"Short of the Unforeseen," repeated Randy to himself. "He likes to say that. Well, we're going to give him some Unforeseen."

A hand touched him on the shoulder, and he whirled round.

"Do you know me?" said the man.

"I expect so. I've seen you before."

"My name is Honoré Devereux."

"Yes, that's what I thought."

"You used to—meet—my wife."

"That's news to me." Randy looked the husband placidly in the eye.

"No it isn't. You used to meet her."

"It's news to me. If I were your wife's husband, I wouldn't assault her reputation to a stranger."

"You're a good liar," said Devereux; and for the second time that morning Randy's face went scarlet.

"You can have as much trouble as you want, that way," said he quietly, never taking his eye from Devereux. "But either you don't know me, or you're crazy."

"You'll sure not forget about Jim Craig?" said the anxious voice of Sweet Potato behind them.

"You go straight to hell and stay there!" said Randy furiously.

"Oh, excuse me! I just wanted to remind you." And Sweet Potato faded away.

"When I say you're a liar—"

"Can't you put it off till to-morrow? Don't you know the colonel has me workin' for him every minute?"

"I mean a compliment, in a way."

At this Randy's eyebrows curved down; his impervious expression changed; he noticed the man more narrowly, and saw it was a strong face of settled, complete sadness.

"I am fifty," said the husband. "She is twenty-five. You're twenty. How were you to own up to it?"

"I don't see how you get this idea," persisted the boy.

Devereux gave a smile, bitter, disillusioned, not wholly hostile. "She told me herself," he said quietly; "in excitement: woman's excitement."

Randy bowed, through an instinct that had risen in his blood.

"Will you put it off till to-morro'? I'll give you any satisfaction you want."

"Satisfaction?" said Devereux drearily. "I meant to kill you. If you had owned up I would have killed you—but what's the gain in destroying a good man for a bad woman? I know you're working for the colonel. He has spoken about you. Go on. You're in luck to have won the regard of such a noble gentleman. Keep it—and keep away from me and mine."

Devereux turned on his heel and was gone.

Of the two or three supreme forces that will mature a youth, if the power of growth lie in him, one is experience of woman's nature. Mere experience of woman's sex had not deeply affected the wild and natural Randy: at the beginning of this day in

O'Neil City, he was still a good specimen of twenty; at the end of it— The face of the husband he had been used to laugh at lurked in his memory as he went here and there among the voters and their families, or in and out of the Pickwick Hotel, or now and then ran up the stairs of Miss Maria Sanchez for a word with her. All through his activities, the joyless face of Devereux came back to him. Why didn't he hit me? If he'd only! thought Randy. Curse her to hell!

"What are you looking so solemn for, this lively day?" inquired Dirty Face Smith. "It's all heading up for us, I tell you. Put your trust in the colonel—and smile some!"

Jinks Fleming was among the mothers, according to his custom; and if Randy could not smile, the war veteran was smiling enough for two at least; and the mothers were smiling at his happy remarks. They'll do a lot more smiling, thought Randy, when the time comes; and it looks like the time was 'most here. He'll have to speak his piece before dark, on the balcony. No hall big enough for this crowd. And then I'll touch it off as things happen to go. Where's Sweet Potato? And Randy entered the hotel once more, and found the assistant.

"It's all right," he said. "Craig's come into town. He's resting."

"That's good!" said Sweet Potato. "That's great. Mr. Fleming will thank you." And he hurried off to seek the candidate.

I'm awful afraid, thought Randy, that he'll forget to thank me. And putting his hands in his pockets, he leaned lazily against the side of the door, and watched the crowd slowly mass beneath the balcony, and fill the street. Short of the Unforeseen, he repeated in his mind; and broke into a laugh at last.

"Come upstairs, boy, and sit with the judge and me," said the colonel.

"Thank you, sir. I've got to be ready down here."

"To show the Professor her chair on the balcony when she arrives?"

Randy smiled, and remained leaning against the door. Then he went out at the loud applause. Mr. Jinks Fleming had come out on the balcony and stood at its railing until the noise died down.

"My friends," he began, "before I talk to you about the great present of Flanagan County, and its greater future, I must say a word to you about the past. To-day I have been listening in my heart to the music of the past; the music of my young days; the strains that used to sing in the fields of strife when hearts were high and we leaped upon the foe; and the soothing song that spoke to weary limbs and bid us lay ourselves down to sleep. I have heard great bands, I have heard great operas—but give me the notes of the bugler who fought with me in the days of '62. Jim Craig! His lips blew sounds that none I have since heard have approached. His melodies, his calls, am I to hear them again? I have learned this very hour that he lives among you, weakened by sickness. Is it true that, even now, he is resting in this hotel?"

The orator paused. Heads below him turned inquiringly to each other. Randy had disappeared.

"Friends—if I heard that bugle in a desert wilderness, I would know it. None that listened to Jim Craig could ever forget him."

The heads below looked more inquiring.

"There ain't no such person," spoke an angry voice. "You've been lied to."

But the voice was answered at once by the sound of "taps" from behind, within, somewhere in the hotel, but now at hand.

"It's Jim!" cried Jinks. "My old comrade's bugle bids me welcome! Come out, old Jim, old minstrel, and let them hear the music of old days!"

And out of the window came Miss Maria Sanchez, blowing her cornet; and the stunned audience never moved until she finished "taps."

Then indeed they moved, and surged, and riots of derision rose, roars of mirth, and oaths of rage, high shrill voices of women, a storm of words—but none from the paralyzed Jinks; and the white teeth of the Señorita Sanchez gleamed at him, and she stood beside him and smiled at him with mocking eyes.

As this violent tumult broke like a flood upon O'Neil City, the heads of Judge McCoy and Colonel Steptoe McDee had appeared at a window near the balcony. The two stared in amazement at the scene —the fists shaken, the hats waved, the swaying turmoil down below, and statuesque on the balcony, the dumbfounded Jinks with the señorita posing triumphant at his side, like some swarthy and tropical goddess of Victory. There flashed on the judge a partial comprehension of the frightful trap which had been set by Randy and the señorita, and sprung upon the candidate.

The judge shook his partner's shoulders in glee. "Seize the moment!" he cried. "Hit it while it's hot!" and he pushed the colonel from their room, and in another moment out ran Steptoe McDee upon the balcony, his silver hair ruffled.

Silence swept the street at the sight of their veteran citizen, respected, beloved; a sweep of silence, then cheers, then silence again; for he was lifting up his hand, and the hand held something.

"My old friends," he began, "here's what every mother's son of you will want to have a look at."

He shook the crumpled papers. "I'll read them to you before—"

From somewhere below a shot cracked. Steptoe McDee's hand sank suddenly, he wavered, and fell forward; and a choking gasp came up from the crowd as he was caught by Fleming and Maria Sanchez. Voices began to break out below, and more shrill cries of women; and Randy flung himself out upon the balcony, and put his arms round the colonel.

"Get out," said Randy quietly to Jinks.

"He is so light, so light," said Maria Sanchez sorrowfully, supporting the relaxed form. "Let me help."

"I'll lift him," said Judge McCoy, appearing.

"Can you, without me, then?" she asked. "Then I will help all the same. I will go in a hurry, quick, quick, quick." She was in the street the next moment, and on a horse, talking with wild gestures to men who crowded to hear her.

"You'd better get out," Randy repeated to the dazed Jinks.

"Has she gone for a doctor?" said the candidate. "I'll run for a doctor."

"Run somewhere, or you'll never run anywhere again. Don't you hear them down there?"

"I'll go for a doctor," Jinks said again. "I would like to do anything I can."

The boy, the judge, the wounded man were alone.

He was carried in silence, easily, from the balcony to the hall, where a way through the confusion was made, and so he was laid on a bed. The two said nothing to each other, while they shook their heads at importunate suggestions, motioning people out of the room; and confusion was still noisy up and down the stairs, and in the street outside. Randy sat by the bed, the judge guarded the door. Hush came slowly over the building. Water, brandy, this and that, were brought in by people who stood a moment, looked at the figure on the bed, and went out softly. The hush increased; creaking steps would sound clear on the stairs, would come to the door, inquiries would be made in a word, and answered in a word by the judge, and the steps would depart and go creaking down the stairs.

The colonel opened his eyes.

"Yes, sir?" said Randy.

"Have me taken home."

"Can you, sir?"

"I wish to go home. Get a wagon."

The judge nodded, and stepped from the door, the colonel closed his eyes, and Randy sat. No noise was anywhere, outside or in, and Randy heard the sound of the wagon. The judge came to the door again.

"Ready?" asked Steptoe McDee, without opening his eyes. "Let somebody lift me down."

People were there, a few. He was lifted down,

and placed in the straw and the blankets, which
the judge had arranged. The judge took the reins,
the boy sat in the straw; in case they might be of
use, two more mounted on horses and followed.
The street was empty, the town quiet, strangely
still after so much excitement; neighbors had gone
home to talk the day's doings over. The wagon
drove slowly out of O'Neil City, between the wire
fences, along the road that had been so crowded
in the morning, and where now there was no one
to be seen. At length they passed beyond the wire
fences into the open country, the mesquite, the live
oaks.

Steptoe McDee lay in the straw, with eyes closed,
very quiet; and Randy watched him.

"This will settle the election," said the old colonel in the silence.

The judge looked round at Randy and he looked
back at the judge; and they drove on.

Suddenly one of the men on horseback spoke:

"What's that coming?"

All looked; and a light sound, a mutter without
syllables, brief, came from all, while Steptoe McDee
lay motionless.

A buckskin pony was trotting quietly towards
them, by himself, his saddle on him, and no one in
it. He came as steadily as if he were guided, turned
out to pass them, passed without haste as steadily

as he had come, turned into the middle of the road
again, and pursued his way.

After that first mutter, none of them had made a
comment; and the colonel spoke the first word.

"Little Old Scaffold," he said, looking at Randy;
and the boy nodded.

In their united suspense and their united certainty, they drove on, meeting no one in the gathering dusk among the live oaks; yet in spite of this
certainty an exclamation came from them all when
what they had been expecting was there, confront-
ing them.

Steptoe McDee knew what they were looking at.

"Lift me," he said.

Randy raised him enough for him to see. The
judge stopped the wagon. No one spoke. Distorted,
worse in death than in life, she hung there, Professor Salamanca, she and all her works at an end.

"Amen," said the colonel; and Randy let him
gently down into the straw, and they drove on
through the live oaks with him.

On the way, one of the men riding behind spoke
once:

"Flanagan County will thank Maria Sanchez."

The doctor who reached the ranch not long after
they had got the colonel in bed, had little to say
that they did not already feel sure of. "Perhaps
before morning. Perhaps later. Let him alone. I'll

come early to-morrow. Give him anything he asks for.''

He lay for a long time, not asking for anything. He seemed unconscious. ''Who did it?'' the doctor asked as he was leaving. They shook their heads. They did not know. They never were to know. Suspicions drifted, reprisals were meditated, but abandoned.

At length Steptoe McDee stirred, and spoke Randy's name.

The boy was there, alone with him, the others within call. The colonel asked for some water. When the boy suggested brandy, he shook his head.

Some sort of life stirred in him presently, and his eyes twinkled.

''Randy.''

''Yes, sir.''

''You can't fool all of the people all of the time.''

''But it costs hell to unfool 'em,'' muttered the boy, hardly trusting himself to speak.

''Cheap this time. And I have been tired of it all, this long while.''

The boy did not trust himself to speak.

''That bugle was a great thing, you—young— sinnah,'' whispered McDee. But his eyes twinkled still.

Randy could not help it; he sank down, and

buried his head in the blankets, and his shoulders trembled.

"Tut, tut, boy," said the colonel. "This won't do."

"It was that," said the boy. "If it hadn't been for that, you'd—you'd—"

"Well, if I had never been born, I'd not be dyin'. Tut, tut, boy, I'd have liked to help you grow into a fine man. But you'll do that, anyway. And I was tired of it all. I'm a thing of the past, Randy —the judge will tell you—this ranch—yours—I've no kin—"

"I don't need nothing. I wish you were my father."

"I'd like to have been. Well—between us—Flanagan County—" once more the twinkle flickered in the dark eyes— "a woman—but don't let her make—an honest man—of you—"

Light went out of the eyes, the voice spoke no more, the breathing continued gently.

But in the morning when the doctor returned, there was no more for any doctor to do.

Many came, all the friends, most of the recent enemies, to look their last at the colonel. More than ever, his tranquil face resembled, as the salesman had said, the ancestors who hang on the wall. And it was not surprising, when the community learned of the inheritance which had fallen to Randy, that neighbors should say that the boy would "act no more than decent" to take his benefactor's name, whether or not he had any right to it before; and naturally the legend became established that it was his by rights—or wrongs. The judge did not take the trouble to explode a fallacy so harmless and he told Randy to do exactly according as his feelings should prompt him.

"Nobody seems to want Little Old Scaffold," he remarked one day, "even though the Professor is gone and the railroad has picked its route."

Nobody in Flanagan County did, not even Sweet Potato Smith. But a rich young man came to Texas from the north, in search of polo ponies and consequently for a number of years the buckskin took a brilliant part in the international matches played on Long Island; no deaths resulted, and Englishmen with titles laughed when his owner related the pony's story to them while they sipped cooling drinks in comfortable clubs.

Randy fell in love at last quite earnestly with Amanda, the attractive daughter of his old employer Crip King. He had taken small notice of her when she was twelve and he fifteen, but when she was twenty, she caused his twenty-three-year-old heart to beat in a manner hitherto never experienced by him. His father-in-law deemed his daughter a lucky bride; she deemed herself so—and continued of this opinion after their honeymoon was long over. Tame oats, she knew, were not the only sort that young men sowed in Texas, and she was ready to make allowances for reasonable rotation of crops in a husband, provided that he was a model husband as husbands go; and when this happy pair became parents for the first time, it was the right sex, and they gave him the name of Steptoe McDee.

Maria Sanchez amazed Flanagan County by making an honest man of Sweet Potato Smith; and they stayed married for almost a year.

Jinks Fleming retired from politics, and went to live in Ultima Thule; while Uncle Cayce Hartle continued to guard the interests of Flanagan County, undisputed by witch-doctors or competitors.

At the Sign of the Last Chance

Largo ♩=63

MORE familiar faces than I had hoped to see were there when I came in after leaving my horse at the stable. Would I eat anything? Henry asked. Not until breakfast, I said. I had supped at Lost Soldier. Would I join the game? Not tonight; but would they mind if I sat and watched them till I felt sleepy? It was too early to go to bed. And sitting here again seemed very natural.

"Does it, now?" said Stirling. "You look kind of natural yourself."

"Glad I do. It must be five years since last time."

"Six," said James Work. "But I would have known you anywhere."

"What sort of a meal did he set for you?" Marshal inquired.

"At Lost Soldier? Fried beef, biscuits, coffee, and excellent onions."

"Old onions of course?" said Henry. "Cooked?"

412

"No. Fresh from his garden. Young ones."

"So he's got a garden still!" mused Henry.

"Who's running Lost Soldier these days?" inquired Stirling.

"That oldest half-breed son of Toothpick Kid," said Marshal. "Any folks to supper but you?"

"Why, yes. Six or seven. Bound for the new oilfields on Red Spider."

"Travel is brisk down in that valley," said Work.

"I didn't know the stage had stopped running through here," said I.

"Didn't you? Why, that's a matter of years now. There's no oil up this way. In fact, there's nothing up this way any more."

They had made room for me, they had included me in their company. Only two others were not in the game. One sat in the back of the room, leaning over something that he was reading, never looking up from it. He was the only one I had not seen before, but he was at home here quite evidently. Except when he turned a page, which might have been once every five minutes, he hardly made a movement. He was a rough fellow, wearing the beard of another day; and if reading was a habit with him it was a slow process, and his lips moved in silent pronunciation of each syllable as it came.

Jed Goodland sat off by the kitchen door with his fiddle. Now and then he lightly picked or bowed some fragment of tune, like a man whispering memories to himself.

The others, save one or two that were clean-shaven, also wore the mustaches or the beards of a day that was done.

I had begun to see those beards long before they were gray; when no wire fence mutilated the freedom of the range; when fourteen mess-wagons would be at the spring round-up; when cattle wandered and pastured, dotting the endless wilderness; when roping them brought the college graduate and the boy who had never learned to read into a lusty equality of youth and skill; when songs rose by the camp-fire; and the dim form of the night herder leaned on his saddle horn as under the stars he circled slowly around the recumbent thousands; when two hundred miles stretched between all this and the whistle of the nearest locomotive.

And all this was over. It had begun to end a long while ago. It had ebbed away slowly from these now playing their nightly game as they had once played it at flood-tide. The turn of the tide had come even when the beards were still brown, or red, or golden.

The decline of their day began possibly with the first wire fence; the great ranch life was hastened to its death by the winter snows of 1886; received its mortal stroke in the rustler war of 1892; breathed its last—no, it was still breathing, it had not wholly given up the ghost. Cattlemen and sheep-men, the newcomers, were at deeds of violence with each other. And here in this place, at the poker table, the ghost still clung to the world of the sage-brush, where it had lived its headlong joys.

I watched the graybeards going on with this game that had outlived many a player, had often paused during bloodshed, and resumed as often, no matter who had been carried out. They played without zest, winning or losing little, with now and then a friendly word to me.

They had learned to tolerate me when I had come among them first; not because I ever grew skilled in what they did, either in the saddle or with a gun, but because they knew that I liked them and the life they led, and always had come back to lead it with them, in my tenderfoot way.

Did they often think of their vanished prosper-ity? Or did they try to forget that, and had they succeeded? Something in them seemed quenched— but they were all in their fifties now; they had been in their twenties when I knew them first.

My first sight of James Work was on a night at the Cheyenne Club. He sat at the head of a dinner-table with some twenty men as his guests. They drank champagne and they sang. Work's cattle in those days earned him twenty per cent. Had he not overstayed his market in the fatal years, he could be giving dinners still. As with him, so with the others in that mild poker game.

Fortune, after romping with them, had romped off somewhere else. What filled their hours, what filled their minds, in these days of emptiness?

So I sat and watched them. How many times had I arrived for the night and done so! They drank very little. They spoke very little. They had been so used to each other for so long! I had seen that pile of newspapers and magazines where the man was reading grow and spread and litter the back of the room since I was twenty.

It was a joke that Henry never could bring himself to throw anything away.

"I suppose," I said to him now, as I pointed to the dusty accumulation, "that would be up to the ceiling if you didn't light your stove every winter with some of it."

Henry nodded and chuckled as he picked up his hand.

The man reading at the back of the room lifted his magazine. "This is October, 1885," he said, holding the shabby cover towards us.

"Find any startling news, Gilbert?"

"Why, there's a pretty good thing," said the man. "Did you know sign-boards have been used hundreds and hundreds of years? 'Way back of Columbus."

"I don't think I have ever thought about them," said Henry.

"Come to think about it," said James Work, "sign-boards must have started whenever hotels or saloons started, or whatever they called such places at first."

"It goes away back," said the reader. "It's a good piece."

"Come to think about it," said James Work, "men must have traveled before they had houses; and after they had houses travel must have started public houses, and that would start sign-boards."

"That's so," said Henry.

A third player spoke to the reader. "Travel must have started red-light houses. Does he mention them, Gilbert?"

"He wouldn't do that, Marshal, not in a magazine he wouldn't," said James Work.

"He oughtn't," said Henry. "Such things should not be printed."

"Well, I guess it was cities started them, not travel," surmised Marshal. "I wonder whose idea the red light was."

"They had sign-boards in Ancient Rome," answered the man at the back of the room.

"Think of that!" said Henry.

"Might have been one of them emperors started the red light," said Marshal, "same as gladiators."

The game went on, always listless. Habit was strong, and what else was there to do?

"October, 1885," said Marshal. "That was when Toothpick Kid pulled his gun on Doc Barker and persuaded him to be a dentist."

"Not 1885," said James Work. "That was 1886."

"October, 1885," insisted Marshal. "The railroad came to Douglas the next year."

"He's got it correct, Jim," said Henry.

"Where is Toothpick Kid nowadays?" I inquired.

"Pulled his freight for Alaska. Not heard from since 1905. She's taken up with Duke Gardiner's brother, the Kid's woman has," said Henry.

"The Kid wanted Barker to fix his teeth same as Duke Gardiner had his," said Work.

"I don't think I've seen Duke Gardiner since '91," said I.

"When last heard from," said Henry, "Duke was running a joint in El Paso."

"There's a name for you!" exclaimed the man at the back of the room. "'Goat and Compasses'! They had that on a sign-board in England. Well, and would you ever guess what it started from! 'God encompasseth us'!"

"Think of that!" said Henry.

"Does it say," asked Work, "if they had any double signs like Henry's here?"

"Not so far, it doesn't. If I strike any, I'll tell you."

That double sign of Henry's, hanging outside now in the dark of the silent town, told its own tale of the old life in its brief way. From Montana to Texas, I had seen them. Does anybody know when the first one was imagined and painted?

A great deal of frontier life is told by the four laconic words. They were to be found at the edges of those towns which rose overnight in the midst of nowhere, sang and danced and shot for a while, and then sank into silence. As the rider from his round-up or his mine rode into town with full pockets, he read "First Chance"; in the morning as he rode out with pockets empty, he read "Last Chance." More of the frontier life could hardly be told in four words. They were quite as revealing of the spirit of an age and people as Goat and Compasses.

That is what I thought as I sat there looking on at my old acquaintances over their listless game. It was still too early to go to bed, and what else was there to do? What a lot of old tunes Jed Goodland remembered!

"Why, where's your clock, Henry?" I asked.

Henry scratched his head. "Why," he meditated —"why, I guess it was last January."

"Did she get shot up again?"

Henry slowly shook his head. "This town is not

what it was. I guess you saw the last shooting-up she got. She just quit on me one day. Yes; January. Winding of her up didn't do nothing to her. It was Lee noticed she had quit. So I didn't get a new one. Any more than I have fresh onions. Too much trouble to mend the ditch.''

''Where's your Chink tonight?'' I inquired. Lee was another old acquaintance; he had cooked many meals and made my bed often, season after season, when I had lodged here for the night.

''I let Lee go—let's see—I guess that must have been last April. Business is not what it used to be.''

''Then you do everything yourself, now?''

''Why, yes; when there's anything to do.''

''Boys don't seem as lively as they used to be,'' said Work.

''There are no boys,'' said Henry. ''Just people.''

This is what Henry had to say. It was said by the bullet holes in the wall, landmarks patterning the shape of the clock which had hung there till it stopped going last January. It was said by the empty shelves beneath the clock and behind the bar. It was said by the empty bottles which Henry had not yet thrown out. These occupied half one shelf. Two or three full bottles stood in the middle of the lowest shelf, looking lonely. In one of them the cork had been drawn, and could be pulled out by the fingers again, should anyone call for a drink.

"It was Buck Seabrook shot up your clock last time, wasn't it, Henry?" asked Marshal. "You knew Buck?" he said to me; and I nodded.

"Same night as that young puncher got the letter he'd been asking for every mail day," said Work.

"Opened it in the stage office," continued Marshal, "drew his gun and blew out his brains right there. I guess you heard about him?" he said to me again, and I nodded.

"No," Henry corrected. "Not there." He pointed at the ceiling. "Up-stairs. He was sleeping in number four. He left no directions."

"I liked that kid," said Stirling, who had been silent. "Nice, quiet, well-behaved kid. A good roper."

"Anybody know what was in the letter?" asked Work.

"It was from a girl," said Henry. "I thought maybe there would be something in it demanding action. There was nothing beyond the action he had taken. I put it inside his shirt with him. Nobody saw it but me."

"What would you call that for a name?" said the reader at the back of the room. " 'Goose and Gridiron.' "

"I'd call that good," said Work.

"It would sound good to a hungry traveler," said Stirling.

"Any more of them?" asked Henry.

"Rafts of them. I'll tell you the next good one."

"Yes, tell us. And tell us when and where they all started, if it says."

In the silence of the cards, a door shut somewhere along the dark street.

"That's Old Man Clarke," said Henry.

"First time I ever heard of him in town," said I.

"We made him come in. Old Man Clarke is getting turrible shaky. He wouldn't accept a room. So he sleeps in the old stage office and cooks for himself. If you put him in New York he'd stay a hermit all the same."

"How old is he?"

"Nobody knows. He looked about as old as he does now when I took this hotel. That was 1887. But we don't want him to live alone up that canyon any more. He rides up to his mine now and then. Won't let anybody go along. Says the secret will die with him. Hello, Jed. Let's have the whole of 'Buffalo Girls.'" And Jed Goodland played the old quadrille music through.

"You used to hear that pretty often, I guess," said Henry to me; and I nodded.

Scraping steps shambled slowly by in the sand. We listened.

"He doesn't seem to be coming in," I said.

"He may. He will if he feels like it, and he won't if he feels like not."

"He had to let me help him onto his horse the other day," said Marshal. "But he's more limber some days than others."

Presently the scraping steps came again, passed the door, and grew distant.

"Yes," said Work. "Old Man Clarke is sure getting feeble."

"Did you say it was Buck Seabrook shot your clock the last time?"

"Yes. Buck."

"If I remember correct," pursued Stirling, "it wasn't Buck did it, it was that joker his horse bucked off same afternoon down by the corral."

"That Hat Six wrangler?"

"Yes. Horse bucked him off. He went up so high the fashions had changed when he came down."

"So it was, George." And he chuckled over the memory.

"Where does Old Man Clarke walk to?" I asked; for the steps came scraping along again.

"Just around and around," said Henry. "He always would do things his own way. You can't change him. He has taken to talking to himself this year."

The door opened, and he looked in. "Hello, boys," said he.

"Hello yourself, Uncle Jerry," said Work. "Have a chair. Have a drink."

"Well, maybe I'll think it over." He shut the door, and the steps went shambling away.

"His voice sounds awful old," said Marshal. "Does he know the way his hair and beard look?"

"Buck Seabrook," mused Stirling. "I've not seen him for quite a while. Is he in the country now?"

Henry shook his head. "Buck is in no country any more."

"Well, now, I hadn't heard of it. Well, well."

"Any of you remember Chet Sharston?" asked Marshal.

"Sure," said Stirling. "Did him and Buck have any trouble?"

"No, they never had any trouble," said Henry. "Not they."

"What was that Hat Six wrangler's name?" asked Work.

"He said it was Johnson," replied Henry.

Again the shambling steps approached. This time Old Man Clarke came in, and Henry invited him to join the game.

"No, boys," he said. "Thank you just the same. I'll sit over here for a while." He took a chair. "You boys just go on. Don't mind me." His pale, ancient eyes seemed to notice us less than they did the shifting pictures in his brain.

"Why don't you see the barber, Uncle Jerry?" asked Marshal.

"Nearest barber is in Casper. Maybe I'll think it over."

" 'Swan and Harp,' " said the man at the back of the room. "That's another."

"Not equal to Goat and Compasses," said Work.

"It don't make you expect a good meal like Goose and Gridiron," said Henry. "I'll trim your hair tomorrow, Uncle Jerry, if you say so."

"Boys, none that tasted her flapjacks ever wanted another cook," said Old Man Clarke.

"Well, what do you think of 'Hoop and Grapes'?"

"Nothing at all," said Henry. "Hoop and Grapes makes no appeal to me."

"You boys never knowed my wife," said Old Man Clarke in his corner. "Flapjacks. Biscuits. She was a buck-skinned son-of-a-bitch." His vague eyes swam, but the next moment his inconsequent cheerfulness returned. "Dance night, and all the girls late," he said.

"A sign-board outside a hotel or saloon," said Marshal, "should have something to do with what's done inside."

"That's so," said Henry.

"Take Last Chance and First Chance," Marshal continued. "Has England anything to beat that,

I'd like to know? Did you see any to beat it?" he asked me.

"No, I never did."

"You come for fishing?" asked Old Man Clarke.

"I've brought my rod," I answered.

"No trout in this country any more," said he.

"My creek is fished out. And the elk are gone. I've not jumped a blacktail deer these three years. Where are the antelope?" He frowned; his eyes seemed to be asking questions. "But I'll get ye some meat tomorro', boys," he declared in his threadbare, cheerful voice; and then it trailed off. "All at the bottom of Lake Champlain," he said.

"Have a drink, Uncle Jerry?" said Henry.

"Not now, and thank you just the same. Maybe I'll think it over."

"Buck Seabrook was fine to travel with," said Stirling.

"A fine upstanding cow-puncher," added Work. "Honest clean through. Never knew him to go back on his word or do a crooked action."

"Him and Chet Sharston traveled together pretty much," said Henry.

Stirling chuckled over a memory. "Chet he used to try and beat Buck's flow of conversation. Wanted to converse some himself."

"Well, Chet could."

"Oh, he could some. But never equal to Buck."

"Here's a good one," said the man at the back of the room. " 'Bolt-in-Tun.' "

"How do they spell a thing like that?" demanded Marshal.

It was spelled for him.

"Well, that may make sense to an Englishman," said Henry.

"Doesn't it say where sign-boards started?" asked Work.

"Not yet." And the reader continued to pore over the syllables, which he followed slowly with moving lips.

"Buck was telling Chet," said Stirling, "of a mistake he made one night at the Southern Hotel in San Antone. Buck was going to his room fair late at night, when a man came round the corner on his floor, and quick as he seen Buck, he put his hand back to his hip pocket. Well, Buck never lost any time. So when the man took a whirl and fell in a heap Buck waited to see what he would do next. But the man didn't do anything more.

"So Buck goes to him and turns him over; and it isn't any stranger, it is a prospector Buck had met up with in Nevada; and the prospector had nothing worse than a flask in his pocket. He'd been aiming to offer Buck a drink. Buck sure felt sorry about making such a mistake, he said. And Chet, he waited, for he knowed very well that Buck hoped he would ask him what he did when he discovered the truth.

"After a while Buck couldn't wait; and so in disappointment he says to Chet very solemn, 'I carried out the wishes of the deceased.'

" 'I was lookin' over the transom when you drank his whisky,' says Chet.

" 'Where's your memory? You were the man,' says Buck. Well, well, weren't they a nonsensical pair!''

"I remember," said Henry. "They were sitting right there." And he pointed to a table.

"They were playing cooncan," said Marshal. "I remember that night well. Buck was always Buck. Well, well! Why, didn't Buck learn you cooncan?"

"Yes, he did," said I. "It was that same night."

"Boys," said Old Man Clarke over in the corner, "I'll get ye some fresh meat tomorro'."

"That's you, Uncle Jerry!" said Henry heartily. "You get us a nice elk, or a blacktail, and I'll grub-stake you for the winter."

"She's coming," said Old Man Clarke. "Winter's coming. I'll shoot any of ye a match with my new 45-90 at a hundred yards. Hit the ace of spades five out of five."

"Sure you can, Uncle Jerry."

"Flapjacks. Biscuits. And she could look as pretty as a bride," said Old Man Clarke.

"Wasn't it Chet," said Work, "that told Tooth-pick Kid Doc Barker had fixed up Duke Gardiner's teeth for him?"

"Not Chet. It was Buck told him that."

Henry appealed to me. "What's your remembrance of it?"

"Why, I always thought it was Buck," I answered.

"Buck was always Buck," said Marshal. "Well, well!"

"Who did fix Duke's teeth?"

"It was a traveling dentist. He done a good job, too, on Duke. All gold. Hit Drybone when Duke was in the hospital, but he went North in two or three days on the stage for Buffalo. That's how the play come up."

"Chet could yarn as well as Buck now and then," said Stirling.

"Not often," said Henry. "Not very often."

"Well, but he could. There was that experience Chet claimed he had down in the tornado belt."

"I remember," said Henry. "Down in Texas."

"Chet mentioned it was in Kansas."

"San Saba, Texas," said Henry.

"You're right. San Saba. So it was. Chet worked for a gambler there who wanted to be the owner of a house that you could go upstairs in."

"I didn't know Chet could deal a deck," said Marshal.

"He couldn't. Never could. He hired as a carpenter to the gambler."

"Chet was handy with tools," said Henry.

"A very neat worker. So the house was to be two stories. So Chet he said he'd help. Well, he did better'n help. Said he built the whole thing. Said it took him four months. Said he kep' asking the gambler for some money. The day he could open the front door of his house and walk in and sit down, the gambler told Chet, he'd pay him the total. So they walks out to it the day the job's complete and chairs ready for sitting in, and the gambler he takes hold of the door-knob and whang! a cyclone hits the house.

"The gambler saved the door-knob—didn't let go of it. Chet claimed he had fulfilled his part of the contract, but the gambler said a door-knob was not sufficient evidence that any house had been there. Wouldn't pay Chet a cent."

"They used to be a mean bunch in Texas," said Stirling.

"I was in this country before any of you boys was born," said Old Man Clarke.

"Sure you were, Uncle Jerry," said Henry. "Sure you were."

"I used to be hell and repeat."

"Sure thing, Uncle Jerry."

For a while there was little sound in the Last Chance Saloon save the light notes which Jed Goodland struck on his fiddle from time to time.

"How did that play come up, Henry?" asked Work.

"Which play?"

"Why, Doc Barker and Toothpick Kid."

"Why, wasn't you right there that day?"

"I was, but I don't seem to remember exactly how it started."

"Well," said Henry, "the Kid had to admit that Doc Barker put the kibosh on him after all. You're wrong about Buck. He didn't come into that." Henry's voice seemed to be waking up, his eyes were waking up.

"Sure he put the kibosh on him," Work agreed energetically.

"Wasn't it the day after they'd corralled that fello' up on the Dry Cheyenne?" asked Stirling.

"So it was!" said Marshal. He too was waking up. Life was coming into the talk of all. "That's where the boys corralled him."

"Well," said Stirling, "you couldn't leave a man as slick as he was, foot-loose, to go around and play such a game on the whole country."

"It was at the ranch gate Toothpick Kid saw those new gold teeth of Duke's," said Marshal.

"It wasn't a mile from the gate," said Stirling.

"Not a mile. And Toothpick didn't wait to ask
Duke the facts, or he'd have saved his money. Duke
had happened to trail his rope over the carcasses of
some stock. When he was roping a steer after that,
his hand was caught between a twist of the rope and
his saddle horn. So his hand got burned."

"Didn't Buck tell him he'd ought to get Doc
Barker to put some stuff on it?"

"Buck did warn him, but Duke wouldn't listen.
So Buck had to bring him into the Drybone hospital
with an arm that they had to cut his shirt-sleeve
for."

"I remember," said Henry. "Duke told me that
Buck never said 'I told you so' to him."

"Buck wouldn't. If ever there was a gentleman,
it was Buck Seabrook. Doc Barker slashed his arm
open from shoulder to elbow. He didn't want Duke
either to die or to lose his arm. And in twenty-four
hours the arm wasn't so big. But it was still pretty
big, and looked like nothing at all, and Duke's
brother saw it. They had sent for him. He rode into
town, and when he saw the arm and the way it had
been cut by Doc Barker he figured he'd lay for Doc
and kill him. Doc happened to be out at the C-Y on
a case.

"The boys met him as he came back, and warned
him to keep out of the way till Duke's brother got
sober, so Doc kep' out of the way. No use having

trouble with a drunken man. Doc would have had
to shoot Duke's brother or take the consequences.
Well, next day the brother sobered up, and the boys
persuaded him that Doc had saved Duke's life, and
he was satisfied and changed his mind and there was
no further hard feelings. And he got interested in
the traveling dentist who had come into town to
pick up business from the boys. He did good work.
The brother got a couple of teeth plugged. They
kept the dentist quite busy.''

''I remember,'' said Marshal. ''Chet and Buck
both had work done.''

''Do you remember the grass cook-fire Buck and
Chet claimed they had to cook their supper with?''
asked Work, with animation. Animation was warming each one, more and more. Their faces actually
seemed to be growing younger.

''Out beyond Meteetsee you mean?''

''That was it.''

''What was it?'' asked Marshal.

''Did they never tell you that? Buck went around
telling everybody.''

''Grass cook-fire?'' said Old Man Clarke in his
withered voice. ''Nobody ever cooked with grass.
Grass don't burn half a minute. Rutherford B.
Hayes was President when I came into this country.
But Samuel J. Tilden was elected. Yes, sir.''

''Sure he was, Uncle Jerry,'' said Henry.

"Well, Buck and Chet had to camp one night where they found a water-hole, but no wood. No sage-brush, no buffalo-chips, nothing except the grass, which was long. So Buck he filled the coffee-pot and lighted the grass. The little flames were hot, but they burned out quick and ran on to the next grass. So Buck he ran after them holding his coffee-pot over the flames as they traveled. So he said Chet lighted some more grass and held his frying-pan over those flames and kep' a-following their trail like he was doing with the coffee-pot. He said that his coffee-pot boiled after a while and Chet's meat was fried after a while, but by that time they were ten miles apart. Walked around hunting for each other till sunrise, and ate their supper for breakfast."

"What's that toon you're playing, Jed?" inquired Stirling.

"That's 'Sandy Land,'" replied the fiddler.

"Play it some more, Jed. Sounds plumb natural. Like old times."

"Yes, it does so," said Henry. "Like when the boys used to dance here."

"Dance!" said Old Man Clarke. "None of you never seen me dance."

"Better have a drink, Uncle Jerry."

"Thank you kindly. Just one. Put some water in. None of you never did, I guess."

"I'll bet you shook a fancy heel, Uncle."

"I always started with the earliest and kept going with the latest. I used to call for 'em too. Salute your partners! Opposite the same! Swing your honey! That's the style I used to be. All at the bottom of Lake Champlain. None of you ever knowed her."

"Have another, Uncle Jerry. The nights are getting cold."

"Thank you kindly. I'll have one more. Winter's coming."

"Any of you see that Wolf Dance where Toothpick wore the buckskin pants?" asked Work. "Wasn't any of you to that?"

"Somebody played it on Toothpick, didn't they?" said Stirling.

"Buck did. Buck wasn't dancing. He was just looking on. Toothpick always said Buck was mad because the Indians adopted him into the tribe and wouldn't take Buck. They gave him a squaw, y'know. He lived with her on the reservation till he left for Alaska. He got her allotment of land with her, y'know. I saw him and her and their kids when I was there. I guess there were twelve kids. Probably twenty by the time he went to Alaska. She'd most always have twins."

"Here's a name for you," said the man at the back of the room. "What have you got to say about 'Whistling Oyster'?"

"Whistling Oyster?" said Henry. "Well, if I

had ever the misfortune to think of such a name I'd
not have mentioned it to anybody, and I'd have
tried to forget it.''

''Just like them English,'' said Marshal.

''Did Toothpick have any novelties in the way of
teeth?'' asked Stirling.

''If he did, he concealed them,'' said Work.

''But him and Doc Barker had no hard feelings,''
said Henry. ''They both put the mistake on Duke
Gardiner and Duke said, well, they could leave it
there if that made them feel happier.''

''Doc was happy as he could be already.''

''Well, a man would be after what came so near
happening to him, and what actually did happen.''

''Did you say Buck was dead?'' asked Marshal.

''Dead these fifteen years,'' said Henry. ''Didn't
you hear about it? Some skunk in Texas caught
Buck with his wife. Buck had no time to jump for
his gun.''

''Well, there are worse ways to die. Poor Buck!
D'you remember how he laid right down flat on his
back when they told him about Doc and the Kid's
teeth? The more the Kid said any man in his place
would have acted the same, the flatter Buck laid in
the sage-brush.''

''I remember,'' said Stirling. ''I was cutting
calves by the corral.''

''Duke was able to sit up in the hospital and have

the dentist work on his cavities. And the dentist edged the spaces with gold, and he cleaned all the teeth till you could notice them whenever Duke laughed. So he got well and rode out to camp and praised Doc Barker for a sure good doctor. He meant his arm of course that Doc had slashed open when they expected he was dying and sent for his brother.

"Duke never thought to speak about the dentist that had come into Drybone and gone on to Buffalo, and the Kid naturally thought it was Doc Barker who had done the job on Duke's teeth. And Buck he said nothing. So Kid drops in to the hospital next time he's in town for a spree at the hog ranch, and invites the Doc to put a gold edging on his teeth for him.

" 'Not in my line,' says Doc. 'I'm a surgeon. And I've got no instruments for such a job.'

" 'You had 'em for Duke Gardiner,' says the Kid. 'Why not for me?'

" 'That was a dentist,' says Doc, 'while I was getting Duke's arm into shape.'

"So Toothpick he goes out. He feels offended at a difference being made between him and Duke, and he sits in the hog ranch thinking it over and comforting himself with some whisky. He doesn't believe in any dentist, and about four o'clock in the afternoon he returns to the Doc's office and says he

insists on having the job done. And Doc he gets hot
and says he's not a dentist and he orders Toothpick
out of the office. And Toothpick he goes back to the
hog ranch feeling awful sore at the discrimination
between him and Duke.

"Well, about two o'clock A.M. Doc wakes up with
a jump, and there's Toothpick. Toothpick thumps
a big wad of bills down on the bureau—he'd been
saving his time up for a big spree, and he had the
best part of four or five months' pay in his wad—
and Doc saw right away Toothpick was drunk clear
through. And Toothpick jams his gun against the
Doc's stomach. 'You'll fix my teeth,' he says.
'You'll fix 'em right now. I'm just as good as Duke
Gardiner or any other blankety-blank hobo in this
country, and my money's just as good as Duke's,
and I've just as much of it, and you'll do it now.' "

"I remember, I remember," said Marshal.
"That's what the Kid told Doc." He beat his fist
on the table and shook with enjoyment.

"Well, of course Doc Barker put on his pants at
once. Doc could always make a quick decision. He
takes the Kid out where he keeps his instruments
and he lights his lamp; and he brings another
lamp, and he lights two candles and explains that
daylight would be better, but that he'll do the best
he can. And he begins rummaging among his
knives and scissors which make a jingling, and

Toothpick sits watching him with deeper and deeper interest. And Doc Barker he keeps rummaging, and Toothpick keeps sitting and watching, and Doc he brings out a horrible-looking saw and gives it a sort of a swing in the air.

" 'Are you going to use that thing on me?' inquires Toothpick.

" 'Open your mouth,' says Doc.

"Toothpick opens his mouth but he shuts it again. 'Duke didn't mention it hurt him,' says he.

" 'It didn't, not to speak of,' says Doc. 'How can I know how much it will hurt, if you don't let me see your teeth?' So the Kid's mouth goes open and Doc he takes a little microscope and sticks it in and looks right and looks left and up and down very slow and takes out the microscope. 'My, my, my,' he says, very serious.

" 'Is it going to hurt bad?' inquires Toothpick.

" 'I can do it,' says Doc, 'I can do it. But I'll have to charge for emergency and operating at night.'

" 'Will it take long?' says the Kid.

" 'I must have an hour, or I decline to be responsible,' says the Doc; 'the condition is complicated. Your friend Mr. Gardiner's teeth offered no such difficulties.' And Doc collects every instrument he can lay his hands on that comes anywhere near looking like what dentists have. 'My fee is usually two hundred dollars for emergency night operations,' say he, 'but that is for folks in town.'

"Toothpick brings out his wad and shoves it to Doc, and Doc he counts it and hands back twenty dollars. 'I'll accept a hundred and fifty,' he says, 'and I'll do my best for you.'

"By this time Toothpick's eyes are bulging away out of his head, but he had put up too much of a play to back down from it. 'Duke didn't mention a thing about its hurting him,' he repeats.

"'I think I can manage,' says Doc. 'You tell me right off if the pain is too much for you. Where's my sponge?' So he gets the sponge, and he pours some ether on it and starts sponging the Kid's teeth.

"The Kid he's grabbing the chair till his knuckles are all white. Doc lets the sponge come near the candle, and puff! up it flares and Toothpick gives a jump.

"'It's nothing,' says Doc. 'But a little more, and you and I and this room would have been blown up. That's why I am obliged to charge double for these night emergency operations. It's the gold edging that's the risk.'

"'I'd hate to have you take any risk,' says Toothpick. 'Will it be risky to scrape my teeth, just to give them a little scrape, y'know, like you done for Duke?'

" 'Oh, no,' says Doc, 'that will not be risky.' So Doc Barker he takes an ear cleaner and he scrapes, while Toothpick holds his mouth open and grabs the chair. 'There,' says Doc. 'Come again.' And out flies Toothpick like Indians were after him. Forgets the hog ranch and his night of joy waiting for him there, jumps on his horse and makes camp shortly after sunrise. It was that same morning Buck heard about Toothpick and Doc Barker, and laid flat down in the sage-brush.''

"Buck sure played it on the Kid at that Wolf Dance," said Work. "Toothpick thought the ladies had stayed after the storm."

Again Marshal beat his fist on the table. We had become a lively company.

"On the Crow reservation, wasn't it?" said Henry.

"Right on that flat between the Agency and Fort Custer, along the river. The ladies were all there."

"She always stayed as pretty as a bride," said Old Man Clarke.

"Have another drink, Uncle Jerry."

"No more, no more, thank you just the same. I'm just a-sittin' here for a while."

"The Kid had on his buckskin and admired himself to death. Admired his own dancing. You remember how it started to pour. Of course the Kid's buckskin pants started to shrink on him. They got up to his knees. About that same time the ladies started to go home, not having brought umbrellas, and out runs Buck into the ring. He whispers to Kid: 'Your bare legs are scandalous. Look at the ladies. Go hide yourself. I'll let you know when you can come out.'

"Away runs Kid till he finds a big wet sage bush and crawls into it deep. The sun came out pretty soon. But Toothpick sat in his wet sage bush, waiting to be told the ladies had gone. Us boys stayed till the dance was over and away runs Buck to the sage bush.

" 'My,' says he, 'I'm sure sorry, Kid. The ladies went two hours ago. I'll have to get Doc Barker to fix up my memory.' "

"I used to be hell and repeat," said Old Man Clarke from his chair. "Play that again. Play that quadrille," he ordered peremptorily.

The fiddler smiled and humored him. We listened. There was silence for a while.

" 'Elephant and Castle,' " said the man at the back of the room. "Near London."

"That is senseless, too," said Henry. "We have more sensible signs in this country."

Jed Goodland played the quadrille quietly, like a memory, and as they made their bets, their boots tapped the floor to its rhythm.

"Swing yer duckies," said Old Man Clarke. "Cage the queen. All shake your feet. Doe se doe and a doe doe doe. Sashay back. Git away, girls, git away fast. Gents in the center and four hands around. There you go to your seats."

"Give us 'Sandy Land' again," said Stirling. And Jed played "Sandy Land."

"Doc Barker became Governor of Wyoming," said Work, "about 1890."

"What year did they abandon the stage route?" I asked.

"Later," said Henry. "We had the mail here till the Burlington road got to Sheridan."

"See here," said the man at the back of the room. "Here's something."

"Well, I hope it beats Elephant and Castle," said Henry.

"It's not a sign-board, it's an old custom," said the man.

"Well, let's have your old custom."

The man referred to his magazine. "It says," he continued, "that many a flourishing inn which had been prosperous for two or three hundred years would go down for one reason or another, till no travelers patronized it any more. It says this happened to the old places where the coaches changed horses or stopped for meals going north and south every day, and along other important routes as well. These routes were given up after the railroads began to spread.

"The railroad finally killed the coaches. So unless an inn was in some place that continued to be important, like a town where the railroads brought strangers same as the coaches used to, why, the inn's business would dry up. And that's where the custom comes in. When some inn had outlived its time and it was known that trade had left it for good, they would take down the sign of that inn and bury it. It says that right here." He touched the page.

The quiet music of Jed Goodland ceased. He laid his fiddle in his lap. One by one, each player laid down his cards. Henry from habit turned to see the clock. The bullet holes were there, and the empty shelves. Henry looked at his watch.

"Quittin' so early?" asked Old Man Clarke. "What's your hurry?"

"Five minutes of twelve," said Henry. He went to the door and looked up at the sky.

"Cold," said Old Man Clarke. "Stars small and bright. Winter's a-coming, I tell you."

Standing at the open door, Henry looked out at the night for a while and then turned and faced his friends in their chairs round the table.

"What do you say, boys?"

Without a word they rose. The man at the back

of the room had risen. Jed Goodland was standing. Still in his chair, remote and busy with his own half-dim thoughts, Old Man Clarke sat watching us almost without interest.

"Gilbert," said Henry to the man at the back of the room, "there's a ladder in the corner by the stairs. Jed, you'll find a spade in the shed outside the kitchen door."

"What's your hurry, boys?" asked Old Man Clarke. "Tomorro' I'll get ye a big elk."

But as they all passed him in silence he rose and joined them without curiosity, and followed without understanding.

The ladder was set up, and Henry mounted it and laid his hands upon the sign-board. Presently it came loose, and he handed it down to James Work who stood ready for it. It was a little large for one man to carry without awkwardness, and Marshal stepped forward and took two corners of it while Work held the others.

"You boys go first with it," said Henry. "Over there by the side of the creek. I'll walk next. Stirling, you take the spade."

Their conjured youth had fled from their faces, vanished from their voices.

"I've got the spade, Henry."

"Give it to Stirling, Jed. I'll want your fiddle along."

Moving very quietly, we followed Henry in silence, Old Man Clarke last of us, Work and Marshal leading with the sign-board between them. And presently we reached the banks of Willow Creek.

"About here," said Henry.

They laid the sign-board down, and we stood round it, while Stirling struck his spade into the earth. It did not take long.

"Jed," said Henry, "you might play now. Nothing will be said. Give us 'Sound the dead march as ye bear me along.'"

In the night, the strains of that somber melody rose and fell, always quietly, as if Jed were whispering memories with his bow.

How they must have thanked the darkness that hid their faces from each other! But the darkness could not hide sound. None of us had been prepared for what the music would instantly do to us.

Somewhere near me I heard a man struggling to keep command of himself; then he walked away with his grief alone. A neighbor followed him, shaken with emotions out of control. And so, within a brief time, before the melody had reached its first cadence, none was left by the grave except Stirling with his spade and Jed with his fiddle, each now and again sweeping a hand over his eyes quickly, in furtive shame at himself. Only one of us withstood it. Old Man Clarke, puzzled, went wandering from one neighbor to the next, saying, "Boys, what's up with ye? Who's dead?"

Although it was to the days of their youth, not mine, that they were bidding this farewell, and I had only looked on when the beards were golden and the betting was high, they counted me as one of them tonight. I felt it—and I knew it when Henry moved nearer to me and touched me lightly with his elbow.

So the sign of the Last Chance was laid in its last place, and Stirling covered it and smoothed the earth while we got hold of ourselves, and Jed Goodland played the melody more and more quietly until it sank to the lightest breath and died away.

"That's all, I guess," said Henry. "Thank you, Jed. Thank you, boys. I guess we can go home now."

Yes, now we could go home. The requiem of the golden beards, their romance, their departed West, too good to live for ever, was finished.

As we returned slowly in the stillness of the cold starlight, the voice of Old Man Clarke, shrill and withered, disembodied as an echo, startled me by its sudden outbreak.

"None of you knowed her, boys. She was a buck-skin son-of-a-bitch. All at the bottom of Lake Champlain!"

"Take him, boys," said Henry. "Take Uncle Jerry to bed, please. I guess I'll stroll around for a while out here by myself. Good night, boys."

I found that I could not bid him good night, and the others seemed as little able to speak as I was. Old Man Clarke said nothing more. He followed along with us as he had come, more like some old dog, not aware of our errand nor seeming to care to know, merely contented, his dim understanding remote within himself. He needed no attention when we came to the deserted stage office where he slept. He sat down on the bed and began to pull off his boots cheerfully. As we were shutting his door, he said:

"Boys, tomorro' I'll get ye a fat bull elk."

"Good night, Jed," said Marshal.

"Good night, Gilbert," said Stirling.

"Good night, all." The company dispersed along the silent street.

As we re-entered the saloon—Work and I, who were both sleeping in the hotel—the deserted room seemed to be speaking to us, it halted us on its threshold. The cards lay on the table, the vacant chairs round it. There stood the empty bottles on the shelf. Above them were the bullet holes in the wall where the clock used to be. In the back of the room the magazine lay open on the table with a lamp burning. The other lamp stood on the bar, and one lamp hung over the card-table. Work extinguished this one, the lamp by the magazine he brought to light us to our rooms where we could see to light our bedroom lamps. We left the one on the bar for Henry.

"Jed was always handy with his fiddle," said Work at the top of the stairs. "And his skill stays by him. Well, good night."

A long while afterwards I heard a door closing below and knew that Henry had come in from his stroll.